Men of the Year

Between the Lines Publishing, LLC

Published by Between the Lines Publishing, LLC (USA) as
Willow River Press (imprint)
410 Caribou Trail, Lutsen, Minnesota 55612, USA

www.btwnthelines.com

Cover artist: Jim Tetlow

Men of the Year by Colleen McMillan

Paperback ISBN: 978-1-950502-14-1

Also Available in Ebook format

This book is dedicated to Andra, who loved a good story

Before

The water park was crowded, but she didn't mind. Pete walked from the snack bar with fruit juice and chips, nothing she usually ate, but they were on their anniversary date, so no food was off limits. Pete said she had better things to worry about than her "already awesome" figure, but a girl had to watch what she ate to maintain the body.

Children ran by, chased by frantic mothers wielding sunscreen, and she imagined her friend Alicia racing after her kids: their blond hair glowed in the sun, and Alicia's arms pumped up and down as she ran behind the speedy toddler, her youngest. How exactly did kids get so fast? Maybe it wasn't that they were fast; maybe it was because their parents had to lug diaper bags around.

Pete settled into the folding chair next to her, and she sighed.

"This was a great idea. It's so hot today."

"The water feels pretty good," he said and handed her a juice and Doritos.

"Didn't they have cool ranch?"

"Picky much?" She shoved his arm and he mimed falling out of his chair. "No need for violence. They're just chips."

"But I love cool ranch so," she said in her best Scarlett O'Hara voice.

"My dear," answered Pete as Rhett Butler, "I don't give a damn."

They laughed and spilled some juice while a group of expectant mothers glared. When Pete leaned over and kissed her, the mothers flew into a squawking tizzy, whispering that there were young children about, and such displays made them sick.

"Tough crowd today," she said and giggled. Pete attacked her, tickling and trying to kiss her nose. "Stop! I'll pee!"

"You'll be fine. You only peed that one time."

"Shut up I did not!"

They wrestled in her chair until a lifeguard sauntered by and gave them the "settle down" eyes. Each retreated to his and her chair and lay back. She reached into her tote and pulled the sunscreen away from her spare clothes and *Vogue*.

"Honey can you get my back? I'm going to lie on my stomach."

"Sure."

She lay down on her stomach and tilted her head to the side. Sunglasses askew, she saw half of Pete in shade and half in sunlight.

"Where are we going for dinner?"

"That trick won't work."

"What trick?"

"The one where you ask me so many times that I eventually give in and spill."

"You're no fun."

He knelt beside her chair and looked hard into her eyes. This was his serious face; one she rarely saw. He reserved it for his parents when they drank too much or for her mother, who pried into their relationship like a Maine tourist into a lobster claw. He thought it was none of her business what he and Cassie did.

"I didn't mean it. You're tons of fun," she said.

"There's something I've been meaning to ask you, for a long time."

"What is it?" She started to sweat more from nervousness than the sun. A lotion smear whitened her nose, and Pete reached over and wiped it away gently. "Come on Pete what's wrong? You know I hate surprises."

He grinned and pulled a small black box from his backpack. It fit in his palm. Her heart beat faster than it ever had, even more so than when they'd first made love on a Mexican beach. The memory of this milestone flooded back, and she smelled roasting, powdery sand and the fresh ocean air. Seagulls cried in the distance and a small party blared music down the beach near the market where they drank margaritas each night. She felt his lips and hands and fingers again, all caressing her body. The towel rumpled beneath them, and his hands in her hair. He laughed at her braided cornrows when she got them, but he twined a few strands around his fingers and pulled lightly until she gasped.

"Cassandra McTiernan, will you make me the happiest man in Minnesota and the universe and marry me?"

The crashing Pacific waves disappeared, replaced by splashing children and piped-in oldies music. Her hair lay plastered against her head, and she felt her skin crisping in the sun. This was the moment she had waited for since she first read "Cinderella." Pete wasn't a prince, but he was damn close. No one had ever made her feel more special, even her father. She thought of the necklace he bought her in Mexico that sat in her tote, the puka shells small and adorable. She wanted to clutch it in her hands as she thought about all the reasons to say yes and if there was any reason to say no. When she couldn't think of any, instead of reminding him that he'd taken his sweet time asking, she said,

"Yes. Of course, I'll marry you."

"You know I'm stressed about the flowers, why are you calling me now?"

She walked from the florist, seething. When she called earlier that week, the clerk assured her that her arrangements would be ready in two days, in plenty of time for the ceremony. Now, the store manager informed her that someone sold some of the lilies needed for her bridesmaids' bouquets. He did not divulge the employee's name; fearing brides' wrath was commonplace for him, and he saw no reason to doom his employees in the same fashion.

She texted her mother and explained that she didn't want to talk to anyone for at least an hour, especially about the wedding. She felt like eating another doughnut but tried to think about something else. A doughnut was the last thing she needed.

So, her mother called the instant she sent her text.

"Don't be so catty. I just needed to tell you that your cousin's been in an accident and can't make it to the wedding."

"But she's one of my bridesmaids! The lineup will be screwed!"

Her footsteps echoed off the sidewalk pavement, and other walkers scooted out of her way when they saw her unwavering posture. One man mumbled, "Crazy bitch," as she elbowed past him.

"Cram it d-bag!" she yelled. "Not you Mom."

"I was saying, before you screamed in my ear, that her sister can fill in."

"I hate Jessie. Everyone knows I hate her."

"But they're twins, and Jessie will fit in the dress."

"I told you not to mention dresses." She had needed to let out her dress even more at her last fitting. If she'd known how stressful the wedding would be, Cassie would have subscribed to a food management program before planning started.

"Sorry dear."

"I can't worry about the flowers or Jessie anymore. Tell Aunt Judy it's fine if Jessie agrees to do it, and can you try and talk some sense into the florist? He won't give me a discount even though they sold my flowers to some civilian."

"Anything else?"

"No. I'm meeting Pete for lunch. We still need to get his ring! Can you believe he left it so last minute? I told him to pick it up three weeks ago!"

"Good-bye Cassie." Her mother hung up, and Cassie tried to erase her tone of voice from her eardrums. She sounded shriller as the wedding crept closer, and she hated it. She missed the days when she was calm. Where had those days gone?

She walked the four blocks to the café, figuring any exercise would help, and saw Pete's truck parked outside. Good. He was already there. Maybe they could get all their errands done in a couple hours. At least the gift registry was finished early, because she couldn't get Pete to confirm anything else for the ceremony or reception after they left Target months ago. At first, she didn't mind planning everything, but as more details piled up, she wanted Pete to step in and take on some responsibilities. When he didn't, it fueled her frustration. She yelled at him once. Seeing that it did no good, she brushed him aside and continued the planning solo.

As she neared the café, a gorgeous blond woman passed her and smiled, and Cassie wished she had her body back. If she were her old self, she would have been able to smile back at the model-esque woman. Someday she'd be healthy and fit again. As soon as the wedding was over.

The tiny café smelled divine. She ogled the fresh pastry case but fended off her craving. She needed to fit in her dress, and she pushed away the thought of it being two sizes bigger than her first fitting.

No need to worry about that now. They had two days left before becoming Mr. and Mrs. Horowitz. She knew Pete couldn't wait for the circus to be over. "I can't believe this got so huge," he said after they told their parents.

"I have a big family, and yours isn't small."

"I know. I just wanted it to be quiet, more intimate."

She saw him sitting near the window, staring outside. He wore his usual uniform of long-sleeved t-shirt, jeans, and fancy sneakers. He loved his overly expensive athletic shoes that had nothing to do with sports. His pensive look clouded his face, the one she despised. Lately it signaled a sour, whiny monologue about how things had gotten too big. She had pared the guest list down as far as her mother allowed, but it was still too big for Pete. His sullenness killed whatever good feelings she had. She barely had any left.

"Hey," she said and plopped down across from him, setting her planner on the table. She leaned over to kiss him, but his lips stayed pursed and tight. Great. Something else was bothering him. She couldn't take much more sulking. "What is it now?"

"There's something I need to tell you."

"Did the tux fitting not go well?" In a small way she hoped it had been a disaster, then he would feel how awful she felt for gaining so much weight. She blushed and found a guilty expression crowding her smile away.

"I didn't go."

"What? But the wedding's in two days! That was your final fitting!"

"I called and canceled the appointment."

"Are you nuts? When are you supposed to fit it in now?" She grabbed her planner from the table and looked through it. "There's no way you can do it tomorrow! That's the groom's dinner. Your parents are flying in."

"I called them. They're not coming."

She dropped the planner and gaped at him. What the hell was going on? Did his parents suddenly disapprove of her? They loved her!

"Is something wrong? You're freaking me out."

He wouldn't look at her when he said, "The wedding's off."

Whoever made up the expression "hit like a ton of bricks" must have been a woman dumped by her fiancé two days before her wedding. Cassie's limbs went numb and limp. What did he mean? The wedding's off? The wedding they (she) had been planning for almost nine months? The wedding he had wanted?

"Off?"

"Dammit, you always do this!" He pounded his fists on the table, and she glanced up, startled. "You make me feel terrible when it's not my fault! I should've just called you. This is a nightmare."

"Nightmare? You have no idea what I'm feeling right now."

"I never do! All we ever talk about anymore is the stupid wedding! If I'd known you'd get so obsessed and so…" He looked her up and down.

"Fat. You forgot to finish that last part."

"That's not what I meant."

"Yes, it is!" She threw the planner at him and tears streamed down her cheeks. She hated crying, mainly because she'd been sobbing over her ever-expanding midsection since January. "I'm sorry about the weight! Do you think I like looking this way?"

"I didn't mean—"

"We don't have to call off the wedding for that! I can lose weight, Pete."

"It's not just that." He looked outside again and stopped, petrified.

She followed his gaze and saw the stunning blond she'd passed on the sidewalk strut by the window. She looked inside and saw Cassie glaring back. She dropped her eyes and fled. At least she had the decency to do that.

"You're cheating on me?"

Whatever repentance Pete felt disappeared when she said, "cheating." He sat up straight and looked directly in her eyes, like he had when he proposed.

"It's over. I'm sorry."

He stood up and she grabbed his hand.

"Pete, please." She begged him with her eyes to remember their time together. The five years they were happy. She wanted him to think of their first date, the time they went skinny dipping in the winter, and when they'd had the pregnancy scare and got excited for a second when they thought they might have a baby together.

"You can keep the ring."

As Pete left the café, Cassie realized that whenever she thought of him, she'd smell fresh-baked pastries. Muffins, doughnuts, candy, bagels, cookies. Clotted cream, caramel, chocolate fudge, and white flour. The sugary scent made her retch, and she ran for the bathroom to throw up. She knew she'd never touch one again.

Lots of crying

May

A girl's twenty-ninth birthday should be normal. There's no anxiety or excitement about hitting the big 3-0, no twenty-five Jell-O shots like on your twenty-fifth. Things should go as planned: brunch with Dad who tells agonizingly long stories about his youth, which you secretly love; coffee with Mom, whose flowers are flourishing and who still cannot believe that you don't have a boyfriend; light lunch with a work colleague or two where you discuss the newest addition to the office; and dinner and drinks with your three best friends where you bitch and moan about problems you're having with your Dad, Mom, and work.

Make that three *EX*-best friends.

It started as a normal birthday in May, the most beautiful month in Minnesota. The sun's not too hot, the humidity hasn't started its oppressive regime, and the mosquitoes are hiding in forest puddles. Birds and flowers sing May's praises, and though I'm allergic to pollen, I don't mind the blossoms outside in my apartment window-box. Just keep a box of Kleenex handy and you'll be fine.

I wake up at six, like I do every morning, feed my cat Prospero, brush my teeth, throw my red hair up in a ponytail, grab my t-shirt, shorts, and shoes and head outside for a run. I live on the fifth floor of my building, so I take the stairs. Anything I can do to keep this body from returning to its former state, which will not be discussed right now. The sun has just come up, so the residual evening coolness rests like a dust layer on the sidewalk. As my feet go faster, my ankles tingle from the chill. It won't be that way for long. It doesn't take much to make me overheat. Stupid pale skin.

After three miles around the neighborhood I turn back at Bentley Park Grocery. I live in a pleasant area of the city: tallish old-style brick buildings with awnings and minimal street traffic. Long streets with stylish names and greenery growing in the sidewalk cracks. It could be described as an arty district, but I suppose it's a bit posher than that. Not upper class but not disintegrating like other Twin Cities neighborhoods.

When I run, I see people walking their dogs, jogging like me, or waiting in line at Minnie's Café for the best chai latte in the state. They stand like sleepwalkers next to green cast-iron tables with umbrellas down and chairs are pushed in. Tiny flowerpots rest on each table. Minnie keeps sweet pea, peonies, and Gerber daisies for the table arrangements, and bright yellow daffodils and hardy lilac bushes are planted against the walls. Minnie has an employee whose only job is to take care of her flowers.

When I get home, the sun is out but not too hot. I run up the stairs and list off the day's itinerary in my head. But first I have to call my mom for our daily chat.

When I was thirteen my mom and dad sat me down for a "talk." It was the talk many children dread, but I was ready for it. It had been coming for a long time. Parents never think their kids pick up on all the little spats and negative body language. They think they're so careful and clever, but when it comes to concealment, they're about as useful as Jacques Clouseau on a police investigation. Mom and Dad explained that they were getting a divorce, that it wasn't my fault, that they still loved me blah blah blah. Of course, they still loved me. It was each other they couldn't stand.

I call Mom every morning to give her yesterday's happenings and any juicy gossip I might have heard.

"Hello?" she answers, in a questioning tone, as if she has no idea who's calling. She's at work, slaving away in her office on some sort of financial business. Always in a hurry and very important, that's my Mom.

"Hi Mom. What's going on?"

"Oh, Cassandra, it's you," she sighs, a dramatic edge in her tone. "Just the usual crap they throw at me in the morning. I can't work with these idiots much longer." She says this every morning and has yet to quit her job.

"I know, but things will be better tomorrow."

"Not likely, but where else would I find a job these days?" That's another topic she likes—the economy. "Anything new today? Did you watch *Dancing* last night?" Mom enjoys reality TV shows where ordinary people dance, sing, cook, yell, buy wedding dresses, or try to lose weight, and she feels that I should follow their progress as well.

"Missed it. I had some things to go over from work."

"The people you work with are incompetent. You need a raise."

"I know. Anyway, are we still on for coffee today? I can come by your office this time."

"No sweetie I'll come to you. It's your birthday!"

I can't help but smile when she mentions my birthday. Hopefully she didn't buy me a checkbook cover like she did last year. Leopard print isn't exactly my style. Neither are checkbooks.

"Thought you forgot," I tease.

"Never! How could I forget the day my baby was born? You're less a pain in the butt now."

"Thanks." She laughs and forgets how much she hates her job for a moment. I love it when she laughs. A huge guffaw of a laugh fit for a lumberjack. "I'll meet you at the usual place. Around one thirty. Remember I have brunch with Dad today too."

"Of course." Her laugh disappears.

After my talk with Mom, my birthday went on without much to-do. Brunch pancakes with Dad hit the spot, coffee with Mom entertained (weren't you supposed to be married by now? You were four years old when I was your age.) and my croissant with Justin and Kevin from work satisfied. At least they don't ask for daily updates on my love life. Why is it that parents feel the need to meddle in love lives? Is it because their parents did? Were my great-great grandma's mom and dad harping to marry Kerry O'Donnell from the next village over because he had the most sheep? If only it were as easy as exchanging livestock. These days you've got to date, and that's one thing I certainly don't do.

It's time for dinner and drinks with the girls. Alicia, Keeley, and Lindsey are a lot like me, as you'd expect best friends to be, but they're also bogged down by things I don't worry about.

Alicia is mid height and blond, both frivolous and frugal. She once bought this insane blown-glass crane figurine from China and managed to talk the seller's shipping cost down because she said the price was extravagant. She should have looked at the crane's price tag. Could have bought a new bedroom set with that kind of money. She has three kids, a loving husband, and a cockapoo, all blond like her. Going over to her house is like walking into the Von Trapp house. She moved to the suburbs when her first son Mickey was born, so we rarely see her.

Keeley is more normal than her name implies. She suffers from Idiot-Boyfriend Syndrome, but that can be said for a lot of women in this country. She's tall, buxom (God I'd kill for her boobs) and sweet as chocolate chips. Last week her newest boyfriend dumped her because her thighs are too big. What the hell is wrong with men? She called me at three in the morning and sobbed for two hours about her bad luck and why does she pick guys like that and why can't she just meet someone nice already? She's two years younger than me, so she's still an idealist. Can't afford that on the dating scene. She's easy pickings for the roaming bar hyenas.

Then there's Lindsey. She's like my mother, divorced and quite happy, thank you very much. She's five years older than Alicia and me, and she loves to regal us with war stories from her marriage. Her most memorable catchphrases include: "I should have dated more," "why the fuck would I want to be seen with *that* guy?" and "let's get the fuck out of here, I'm starving." She likes to swear, says her husband never let her. Religious type. She's the source our laughter, because honestly, who can resist a story about trying to get laid at a church retreat in the Boundary Waters? Canoes, God, and sex; what else do you need? Lindsey is rail thin and smokes more than anyone I've ever met.

We meet at Brit's Pub downtown, which is one of my favorite places. I lived in Europe for two years as a student and have yet to find a suitable American alternative to the British pub. Brit's comes very close, but they don't have real English beer on tap; just doesn't taste the same. Alicia and I used to come here during our senior year in college, mainly for her to meet older guys. They were usually impressed with our knowledge of beers both local and imported. She lured more than one guy home by explaining the difference between ales and pilsners.

We sit inside. The patio's open, but I'd rather sit near the bar. It feels more authentic that way. And Lindsey doesn't mind.

"Four pints of something good and keep 'em coming!" she yells as we sit down. Luckily, no one pays attention.

"You don't have to yodel. Someone will come by," says Keeley. Lindsey waves her away and we sit.

"Happy birthday, chica!" she says, slapping me on the back. "Have a good day so far?"

"Of course, she did," says Alicia. "Cassie has the best birthdays."

"Same old, same old isn't good enough for our girl. She needs adventure!"

The bartender sees us and brings over our usual drinks. He's really young so Lindsey watches his ass when he saunters away.

"I have plenty of adventure: just look at the in-tray in my office," I say, sipping the Smithwick's the bartender brings over. He knows my preferences.

We're soon surrounded by beer and pub food, and that's when the conversation really gets started.

"So, Cass, anything new going on in the single life?" asks Alicia who stirs her beer's head with a cocktail straw. She never asks me about guys, so I'm instantly suspicious. Keeley and Lindsey glare at her, and Alicia coughs into her fist. "It's just I haven't seen you in a while."

"Nothing's changed." Which is true. The last male encounter I had was at the New Year's Eve office party when Kevin and I sang a Sonny and Cher song together, both incredibly drunk with tinsel wrapped around our shoulders. And he's enormously gay, so I didn't have much of a shot.

"Boring's what you are," says Lindsey and she downs her beer. "You need to get out more."

"You *could* come dancing with me," adds Keeley. "Work's all you ever talk about."

"It's all I have to talk about. No one's interested in my cat's daily escapades."

"You can't live alone all your life. Look at Brian and me," says Alicia. "We're perfectly happy."

"Nobody who lives in the suburbs is happy," burps Lindsey, and she rises to get another round from the bar. "I hope you're ready for a long night." She pats my shoulder and leaves. "Don't tell her without me."

When she's gone I turn to the other girls. "Tell me what?"

"Nothing, it's nothing," says Keeley who nearly chokes on her drink. "A surprise birthday present."

"You didn't get me one of those weird vibrators again, did you? Try explaining that to my mother."

"You weren't supposed to *show* her," Keeley answers. "They're not for old people."

"Old people like to get off too." Lindsey's back with four frosty mugs and passes them out. "She mention the vibrator incident?"

"She always does."

"You need to get over that, Cass. It's not like your mom knew what it was."

"Yes, she did."

"So what? Your mom knows you have sex. Big freaking deal. My mom had the sex talk with me when I was four."

"And you married a pastor," laughs Alicia.

"Don't remind me. Five years of the missionary position will make a girl buy ten vibrators."

Lindsey mocks her terrible relationship decisions with such eloquence. Her former husband and pastor is a sweet guy, but there's no way he could keep up with Lindsey. Their marriage was a mystery from start to finish. None of us could imagine the pastor with Lindsey's legs wrapped around his head, and apparently, after five years, neither could he.

"Here's to you, you dirty bitch! Happy birthday!" Lindsey cheers, and we clink mugs and drink. I wish I could chug beer like in college. The best I can manage now is about half. I'm grinning when I set my mug down, happy that my birthday has gone so well, all according to plan. But the girls are all looking at me, a hungry gleam in their eyes, like a French chef ogling a rising soufflé.

"What? Is there foam on my lip?" I wipe my upper lip but find nothing. Maybe there's a booger in my nose.

"We have a proposition for you," says Alicia, suddenly in let's-make-a-deal mode. Her tone fits a power suit more than her jeans and sequined top.

"More of a bet, you guys said it was a bet," says Keeley in a much more anxious voice than Alicia. There better not be a male stripper waiting at my apartment building when I get home. Hopefully they didn't shave my cat like last Fourth of July.

"You're such an ass Keel," says Lindsey, in no way helpful. "She won't *win* anything if she does it."

"Oh, she'll do it. She's curious already." Alicia's grinning now too, but I feel my smile fading. It's like I'm in front of a court-marshal hearing.

"What did you do?"

"It's really awesome! I think it's a really good idea! Lindsey and Alicia thought of it."

"Great, so what is it?" The music changes to the Dropkick Murphys' thudding beats, and I notice how many people are in the bar. A public place. Somewhere I can't lose it and scream at them. *"What is it?"*

They all talk at once, cutting each other off.

"Don't be mad—"

"Who cares if she's mad, she's doing it—"

"It was a good idea, right?"

"Enough you guys!" I pound the table with my mug, sloshing beer. It spills on my hand and I reach for some napkins. "Did you get me something stupid like a pony?"

"You wish," says Alicia.

"It's better than a fucking pony."

"It's a boyfriend!" Keeley's exclamation startles me. She covers her lips with her fingers. "Sort of…"

"Not very easy to wrap," I say and cross my arms over my chest. Please not a blow-up doll, please not a blow-up doll, not in front of all these people.

"It's not the sort of thing Macy's gift-wraps for you with a sprig of mint or whatever," says Alicia as she waves her cocktail straw back and forth in a motion that suggests scolding one of her children. "We got you something thoughtful this year. Something you actually need."

"I *need* a new loofa," I mumble. And maybe some nice bath soaps. Is it too much to ask for nice bath soaps? Maybe honeysuckle-scented?

"Stop bitching and listen," says Lindsey. "Alicia, Keeley, and I got together and really thought this through. Step one: you need to stop moping about dating and just get on with it, or 'get *it on* with it' if you will, you're not getting any younger or thinner."

"Thanks a lot."

She ignores me and goes on, "Step two: stop whining about your job and get a better one."

"She means start writing again," whispers Keeley, trying to sound supportive.

"So basically, what you got me is an inspirational rant from a divorcee whose sole purpose in life is to sleep with as many men as she can before her vagina falls off."

"Ha ha. Listen. We signed you up for an online dating service."

"You did what?" I seethe, wishing steam could pour from my mouth and scald them. "You're joking, right?" Shit, please be joking. My friends would never meddle in my love life. Keep repeating that Cassie, and this will all go away. We'll drink a few more beers, grab cabs and go home.

Are my hands shaking? Do I normally blink this much?

Keeley shakes her head and leans closer in excitement. She's been keeping this a secret for a long time, and I can tell, because her skin is shining and she's clenching her fists. I haven't seen her this antsy since she met my favorite of her ex-boyfriends. He turned into an immense ass like the rest.

"No, it's for real! You're going to meet someone I just know it!" She sounds like the heroines in the books I edit. All hope and no brain.

"It's planned out," says Alicia, very self-satisfied. "We're taking care of everything."

"We wrote you a profile and paid for it and found some interesting prospects," Keeley lists, ticking items off on her fingers. "And we'll even pick the dates for you!"

"I don't understand." It's all I can say. I'm sure Alicia and Lindsey will explain it differently than Keeley, but it's going to come out the same way: they're all dirty, trampy, horrible, soon-to-be-ex-best friends.

"Shut up Keel," says Lindsey, taking over. "It's not as terrible as you're thinking, and I know what you're thinking, because your face looks like a knife. We're trying to help—"

"You can help by staying out of my business." Keeley recoils from the table and looks sheepish, but Alicia and Lindsey stare with flinty eyes. I try another tactic. "You know I don't date."

"Not since Pete, we *know*," says Lindsey, but not harshly. She reaches out to touch my hand, but I pull back. I can't believe she mentioned him.

"It's been three years," says Alicia and she smiles sympathetically. "It's about time you tried dating again."

"Give some other guy a go at you," says Lindsey.

"You make her sound like a mechanical bull," says Keeley and scrunches her upper lip toward her nose like she smells rotten onions.

"I heard that's what she's like."

"Thanks, bitch," I say. Lindsey smiles and takes a sip of beer.

"Now we're getting somewhere. If she's swearing at me all's forgiven."

"I'm leaving."

"No, you're not. Can't you just listen to our plan?" asks Alicia.

"This is so not funny. Please tell me you're kidding. It's funny to poke the dragon, but seriously. A dating service?"

"An *online* dating service," corrects Keeley.

"You haven't got a choice," says Alicia, and she pulls a notebook from her purse. It's purple and covered with intricate silver designs, faintly Indian-inspired. Oh shit. It's a planner. Alicia organizes everything important in a notebook. She's got loads of notebooks, ranging from home purchases to grocery lists. If she's got a special notebook for this effed-up experiment I'm screwed. "We thought trying it for a year would be best."

"What? Wait just one—"

"One man per month, no protests. We're not going to line you up with perverts and uggos."

"No assholes, drunks, man-whores, slobs, smokers, teenagers, college students, lawyers, or professional emotionally unavailable fuckwads either."

"You want me to date a different guy every month for a year?"

"That's the gist."

"Are you all insane?" They look at me as if I'm the crazy one, as if this scheme is fricking brilliant, like their design for the Ark would have blown Noah's plan right out of the proverbial and literal water. "I am not doing this. You can't make me." Now I sound like a kid who can't have dessert because she didn't eat her broccoli. "My life is not some stupid romantic comedy."

"We actually got the idea from one of your books," says Keeley, perky once again. "I think it's genius."

"I know what you think," I snap. She's stung, and I feel better. But Keeley's not my main concern. "And you two need to cancel that subscription or whatever and get your money back. I'm not doing it. I'm happy right where I am."

"Honey, if you were, we wouldn't have done this for you," says Lindsey.

What can I say to that? I'm shell-shocked, and I shouldn't have to put up with that from my friends on my birthday. Surprise birthday presents suck. Couldn't they have bought me crotch-less panties instead?

"I'm not doing it." I think my voice sounds firm, but Alicia smirks and says, "Wait until you get to work before you decline our generous offer."

What the hell does that mean?

Still May

Those bitches. They got to my boss.

The morning after my birthday debacle, I'm off for a run then to work. I'm a junior editor at Weston's Publishing Company. We have three offices in the Midwest and deal mostly with local writers, a lot of wannabe Nora Roberts and Robert Ludlums from the Twin Cities, Chicago, and Des Moines. Sometimes we handle textbooks and other large projects, but it's mainly fiction and nonfiction. I feel for the staff down in Des Moines, because they deal with Iowa Writers' Workshop alums. Needier and whinier writers, I have never met. If they want instant approval, they should send their manuscripts to their mothers. Not to mine, though. She's the meanest critic I've ever known.

I'm in charge of new acquisitions after Kelly Riley, my boss, accepts them for publication. Reading other peoples' "masterpieces" is both refreshing and dull. The editor in me wants to start correcting minor grammatical errors immediately, but the writer in me wants to enjoy the story first. If the manuscript has no punctuation problems on the first page, I read through to the end first then start correcting, but the instant I find one comma out of place in the first sentences, the red pen-wielding editor takes the wheel.

I dreamt of writing professionally, but circumstances got in the way. In college I worked as a cocktail server and bartender, so the nights ran late, and I was too tired to write after work. Classes ran all day, so finding time to write during the day was also hard. I read a lot and tried to write a journal in between school and work, but nothing stuck. Now I'm focused on editing other writers' work and have left my unfinished stories and characters by the wayside. What does that even mean, "by the wayside?" It comes from the *Bible*, but who thought of it? That's one reason I love the English language. It's constantly changing and mutating. Writers dream and imagine new words and someday they might join the everyday lexicon.

I get to work at 9:00am every morning and greet Amy the receptionist. Her nails and hair are impeccable, and I wonder how she can afford to get French manicures every week. She's a nice girl and eager to please; she also wants my job. Nothing like a younger, prettier, slimmer version of you to keep a work ethic strong.

My tiny office is near the back, but it fits my needs: desk, computer, bookshelves, filing cabinets, and the dreaded in-tray. Its contents totter like poorly stacked Jenga blocks. I set down my coffee thermos and briefcase and head to Kelly's office for the morning briefing. I almost forget the stack of CDs in my coat pocket and toss them on the desk. I promised Kevin almost two months ago that I'd give him my entire collection once I finished uploading it to my computer. Lots of CDs.

The office décor is edgy but not over the top. Kelly Riley has been senior editor for ten years, so every wall and corner reflects her personality, and things can change overnight if she feels a creative whim. The caramel-colored walls make it seem like we're working in a confectionary. Tall, slim-silhouetted vases stand in the corners with seasonal reeds, flowers, and plants. May means cattails and lilac sprigs, all made from silk. If she could put topiaries in the mailroom she would. The walls carry framed photos of our most illustrious authors and publications: one writer went on to be a best seller, and she sends Kelly blown-up cover art or majestic prints from her globetrotting book tours. My favorite is a twenty by twenty portrait of Hugh Yeardley, my favorite contributor. In the photograph his face is scruffy, eyes bloodshot, and flannel shirt askew. He holds a half-burned cigarette in one hand and a pen in the other. His expression reads: change one syllable of my work and you perish.

The office hums like a well-tuned string orchestra, people bustling about with copy, mail, and odd breakfast bits. Wally from marketing struts by with a huge stack of freshly printed paper, and I wonder what he's doing up here with that. Kevin smiles at me from his cubicle and raises one eyebrow, silently asking for his CDs. I nod and keep walking. I hear a delighted squeal and know he's run to my office to retrieve his prize.

Kelly's office is tidy, just like her. She dresses like a *Vogue* writer could walk into her office at any moment, asking for an interview. She brought me a box of chocolates from her trip to New York Fashion Week, so she knows her clothes. I'm relatively proud of my wardrobe, nothing threadbare or trendy, just classic. I can't pull off her style, like sequins on a weekday afternoon. This morning we're discussing her newest options, a few short novels from two romance writers in Northern Minnesota.

"All right," she says when I walk in and shut the door. The room contains three other junior editors: Carly Witstead, Joe Carlson, and Justin Conroy (my other close colleague). They tip me nods and refocus on Kelly. But she surprises us by saying, "Everyone out but Cassandra. We have an urgent matter to discuss." Her crisp tone hurries the others out and Justin's eyes widen when he leaves. I shrug and start sweating. Am I in trouble for Saffron Thomas's sci-fi thriller? The ending was terribly mundane, so I lost track of things in the final chapter. I don't think I missed any spelling errors or general grammar mishaps. What if I left a comma splice?

I close the door and she motions me to the chair in front of her desk. She types a few lines on her computer before addressing me.

"You have been here for five years, Cassandra?"

"Five years this fall. You hired me around mid-September." I resist biting my lower lip. If it starts to bleed, I'll have to flee. She nods to herself and finally looks at me, her cat-eyed tortoiseshell glasses gleaming.

"I received a very interesting email yesterday regarding your work."

"Oh?" I ask, quavering.

"Yes, intriguing…" she trails off and looks at her computer screen once more. "It seems you are in line for some time off." Huh? "I believe it is time you had a small sabbatical. Nothing permanent. Just a few days to sort some things out."

"I don't have vacation scheduled until Thanksgiving." She's firing me! Her protégé! Her confidant!

"This is not a suggestion." She peers down her nose at me over her glasses. "I will have the others cover your duties for the week and expect you back next Monday."

"I don't understand. Did I do something wrong? Has my performance level dropped?" I'm panicking now; chest heaving, breath shortening, spittle forming in mouth's corners. "I can do better."

"You are the best editor I have seen in many years. It has nothing to do with your work ethic or performance. You are an exemplary employee."

"Then why—"

"I believe this will explain everything." She opens the drawer next to her right elbow and reaches inside. The envelope is creamy and soft with an imprinted paisley design. The angry dragon inside my head roars, and I almost miss Kelly's parting words. "Good luck, Cassandra."

May

To-do List

1. *Kill former friends or hire someone to kill them.*
2. *Cover up murders with clever alibi, possibly utilize mother for said alibi.*
3. *Find new friends who will not ruin life with ridiculous notions of fictional romance.*
4. *Ask Justin if online dating ever worked for him and upon hearing negative answer, make him write treatise as such.*
5. *Find way to get back to work before enforced vacation time is up. Possibly use old mountain climbing equipment for office break-in.*
6. *Remember how to use old mountain climbing equipment.*
7. *Buy more cat food.*

I decide to look at the envelope's contents over a white wine, so I wait until 11:00am before racing to the nearest bar. I should wait until noon before drinking, as an upstanding young woman would, but who the hell cares.

The Two Jacks is close to work and nicely gloomy; the perfect atmosphere for this envelope's malevolence. I don't know how they managed it, but Alicia must be the mastermind. She must have sent the envelope to Kelly, and Kelly loves a good intrigue, especially if she's allowed to play a role. Go join a community theater and let me get back to work! If Carly so much as pokes her little finger into my office, I'll destroy our whole building with homemade explosives. I imagine receptionist Amy waltzing into my office, dumping my stuff in the garbage and putting her feet up.

I breathe deeply and enter the bar.

I'm the only one in the place, and the bartender looks fairly put out when I come in. Don't give me that look, buddy, at least it's not five to close or something. If there's one thing bartenders hate, it's last minute customers. But I'm a first minute customer today, and I need a drink.

"Morning," he drawls. Built like a Minnesota farmer, the bartender's forearms could probably squeeze my head like a zit.

"Hello. A white wine please." I sit on the first barstool close to the windows; it's murky in here.

"Any particular flavor or should I surprise you?"

"Whatever expires today is fine." He's surprised by my answer and I can tell he now respects me more than when I came in. Wasting booze is serious in bars, and wine doesn't last that long. "Chardonnay it is." I hope it's not too bitter.

I don't have to worry, because he pours me a hefty goblet of straw-colored wine. It tastes better than I feel, so that's a start.

He leaves me alone, using that ultimate bartender power of discerning if a customer wants to chat, and walks out from behind the bar and back into what I presume is the kitchen. Thank God. I didn't want any witnesses if my head explodes.

I lay the envelope on the bar and stare at it. Alicia's work for sure, because of the paisley embellishments. Care went into this envelope, into the whole plot. I pick it up and slit it open, careful not to rip the paper. I want to tear it open like an ADD-afflicted four-year old on Christmas morning, but I restrain myself. I'm a grown up.

Inside are three sheets of paper:

The first page is in Alicia's calligraphy-style cursive: "Greetings my dear and welcome to your dating game. It's not really a game, finding love, but then again, what about life isn't about playing games? You pick teams, you keep score. Someone loses, someone wins. It's all the same to the referee who comes out on top, so long as someone plays. And you are going to play. I know you hate us right now, but we're trying to help you back into the real world. It's not all about work. You need to get back into your life, because you checked out about three years ago. Let this experience take you somewhere new. Welcome back, honey, and I hope this time you win."

Keeley's slanted print comes next: "You three underestimate me all the time, calling me a hopeless romantic and thinking I'm naïve. In some ways you're right, but I'm not all paper hearts and candy kisses. Cassie, Alicia hasn't been around enough to notice that you're coming apart. I don't think you notice it, or if you do, you bury it so far in your heart it will never surface. But I see it. I hear it when you try to console me on the phone. You think it's foolish to try and find love, but I think you just need a different option, and you need to lose control. I hope this works because if it doesn't you'll kill me. Love you tons."

I know Lindsey's the closer, the pitcher the manager calls in to clinch the win, and I expect her spiky scrawl to cover the third page, but I'm wrong: "Your first date will be in June, and his name and the location of your date will be sent to you through one of us. Don't worry. We'll give you details about the guy so you're not flying blind. Topics to discuss and whatnot. We also have one other task for you. Keep a journal about every date you go on. We want details. Write about how you're feeling. Even if the first ones are all barbed comments for us, we want them. Just write something. You wanted to be a writer once. Your other friends are in on this and will report any infractions. We have spies everywhere."

The last page is typed on expensive paper, so it came from Alicia. Although I'm fuming, I can't believe Lindsey didn't send a manifesto. Maybe she's on rationality's side.

I swallow the wine and wait for the bartender to come back. Am I actually thinking about doing this?

I reach for my purse and fish out my cell phone. Kevin is speed-dial nine. He's still at the office, but that boy is never without his phone. A gay man without a cell phone is like a Ken doll without an ascot; those are Kevin's own words.

"Ciao bella, spill it? You left in a huff and everybody's talking."

"I've been ambushed by heartless wenches," I can feel tears coming and suck them back. The last thing I need is the burly bartender seeing me cry.

"Oh, you got the envelope," he gasps.

"I thought you knew nothing," I say, trying to whisper ice through the phone and into his ear.

"I may know certain details."

"They got to you too. I hate my life. Is this really my life?"

"Stop being so dramatic. It doesn't suit you."

The bartender returns from the kitchen and puts my tab down next to the empty wine glass. He politely turns away and moves down the bar again.

"I'm not being dramatic, you asshole. Did I ever even *hint* that I wanted help getting a man?"

"Babe, you can get laid if you want. Half the single male population would give their left nut to sleep with you. But that's not what you need."

"I wish they had gotten me a prostitute, then at least the nightmare would be over, and I could go back to a normal life."

"Normal is beige and you're turquoise. Normal doesn't fit you. Kind of like those jeans I keep telling you to throw away."

"I think I might be sick."

"Don't ever yack in a public place. That's one of my top three rules."

"How do you know I'm not at home?"

"If I were you, I'd have *my* head in a wine bottle."

My mother would have been more supportive than him.

WRONG.

I call my mom when I get home, and she answers on the second ring.

"Hello?"

"Did you know about this?"

"Hello Cassie. Nice of you to call your mother while you're at work." I hear her typing through the speaker and realize that I've interrupted something. It dawns on me that it's half past noon. Other people are still at work, where I should be. "Are you on lunch sweetie?"

"No, Mom," I sigh and settle on the couch. "I came home early today. I'm not feeling well."

"Being sick never stopped you from staying at work before," her voice is preoccupied, but she's trying to follow our conversation.

"Kelly sent me home." I feel like a grade school kid complaining about a mean teacher, like I was sent home from school for throwing sand when I did not. "On account of my villainous friends."

"Is today *that* day? Completely escaped me." More typing, faster now. She's on a roll.

"What day?"

"The first day of this escapade the girls planned. I think it's a grand idea."

"YOU KNEW?" I don't mean to shout in her ear but can't hold back. I've been waiting to scream at someone since I left the office. It might as well be Mom. "You knew they were going to do this to me, and you didn't say anything?" Deep down I'm impressed that she kept this a secret. I never tell her anything too important, because she blabs to her sisters, co-workers, street vendors, anyone who will listen. How the hell did she manage not to spill this? "The whole world has gone insane. Is there anyone who *doesn't* know that my life's been hijacked?"

"Possibly your father. I didn't say a peep to anyone." She relays this information triumphantly, and it's hard to stay angry. "I didn't even tell your brother, but he knew about it somehow." Even Joel hates me. My own dear little brother. If he weren't in California I'd go over to his house and stick carrots up his nose like when we were kids.

"You could have warned me." I rub the bridge of my nose in frustration, almost wishing I still wore glasses, so I could take them off and clean the lenses; anything to keep my hands occupied.

"Where's the fun in that? This will be good for you. It's not normal for an attractive girl like you to be single."

"Guys ask me out all the time, Mom! Being single's a choice, not some big scarlet "S" tattooed on my chest."

"It might as well be. Three years since you've had a prospect."

"I don't want to talk about Pete."

"You never do. Maybe if you let someone be there for you, or if you cried at least once you'd be over him." She sounds exasperated, and she stops typing, the signal that she intends to settle in for a long conversation. That's my cue to say goodbye.

"Bye Mom. I'll call you later."
"Dinner tonight? I'm making stuffed zucchini!"

The End of May and My Life as I Knew It

Those few days off work are pure, unadulterated torture. With no manuscripts to look over and no fellow employees to laugh with, I'm at a loss. What do unemployed people even do? I've had a job since I was fifteen. Working in restaurants shortened my life by at least ten years, but the money was worth it. I saved up enough during high school to afford my freshman and sophomore years in college, something none of my friends could boast. Even when I lived overseas, I taught English in Paris and Berlin, if only to afford more expensive beers.

I've always had a job; I've always worked hard for what I have. Not working makes me feel incompetent and lazy. The weekend is for downtime, not Wednesday, Thursday, or Friday, which is the prescribed term of exile. This must be how Napoleon felt on Elba; only he had servants to talk to. Prospero's not the best chatter. He likes toy mice, food, and belly rubs. He is annoyed with me by 8:30am after I come back from running and getting a chai from Minnie's place. She was surprised to see me at the counter so late in the morning but polite enough not to question it.

At 9:00am I call someone who might commiserate with me.

Justin Conroy is my second-best work friend. Kevin and I adopted him when he started at Weston's three years ago, mainly because when he came in on his first day, he dropped his box of possessions and spilled his full thermos of coffee into the box. Kevin and I took pity on the new guy. Instead of staring at him like he was a clumsy alien, we helped him clean his stuff and sort through what papers we could salvage. One bedraggled copy of Yeats had to be thrown, but he assured us it was okay: he had three copies at home. His poetry jones cemented him in our hearts, because how can you not adore a straight guy who owns four books of Irish poetry?

The office is in consensus that Justin and I should be a couple, but neither of us agrees. Even Kevin is against the match, using one of his many euphemisms: "You don't drink from the company well." Kevin has ignored his own advice for years but expects Justin and I to hold firm. Justin *is* attractive, just not what I'm looking for. He's over six feet tall, fairly muscular, with a bright, easy smile. His sandy hair and freckles sprayed across his nose are probably what turn me off; I've never been attracted to someone whose features resemble my own. Justin can tan though, that asshole. Dark hair and olive skin are my main turn-ons when it comes to appearance, which didn't work out so well for me three years ago.

He answers on the first ring. "Hey hot stuff. How's prison?"

"This is a nightmare! You have to tell me what happened yesterday." Like me, Justin lives at the office. If he's not reading something he might wither away like an un-watered fern. "What did Kelly say when I left?"

"You're sounding a little desperate, and that's not attractive."

"Shut up and spill."

"You didn't miss much." What a liar. There were new acquisitions to go over and four new hires in the mailroom to degrade. "Kelly didn't tell us why you left, but Kevin filled me in." He gets bonus points for not laughing. At least someone finds my situation humiliating. "We went over one of the new manuscripts, but she wants to wait for you to get back to divvy up the work. It isn't so bad is it?"

"Are you kidding? What would you do if you were stuck at home with only a cat for company?"

"Can't you go visit someone during the day?"

"Who do I know that doesn't work during the day?"

"Lindsey?" He knows my three jailers pretty well, especially Lindsey, who makes it her mission to hit on him. It's all in good fun for her, but I think she makes Justin a bit nervous. "Doesn't she work nights?"

"She's sleeping right now, and if the phrase 'never wake a sleeping bear' had an origin…"

"I get it," he says, and hums some rock tune. "I'd probably read a lot or workout, I guess. There are a lot of books in my queue right now." Justin is a bibliophile and needs a monthly book-buying intervention. Books he plans to read cover his shelves; including three years of *New York Times* top ten list selections. He still hasn't gotten through the last Harry Potter book and becomes irate if I hint at spoilers.

"I've read all my books and have no desire to be judged by the Barnes and Noble barista."

"It's not like Kelly fired you. You'll be back on Monday. We could meet for lunch today. Kevin will call you when we go."

I'm grateful for the offer and say so, but it will feel weird doing a working lunch and then not working afterward.

"I don't think I can take three days of this."

"You could always go out and buy a journal. Don't the rules call for that?"

"I hate you."

"Have a great day!"

Men of the Year

Things to Do on Weekdays When You're Not at Work

1. *Catch up on news both national and local. I had no idea a massive volcano erupted somewhere over in Europe.*
2. *Re-read old magazines until mind wanders.*
3. *Do the crossword puzzle in the paper and get angry when you only have one answer left and the clue is "Port City in Ecuador."*
4. *Curse self for not knowing South American geography.*
5. *Paint toe and fingernails different shades until settling on Pink Peony.*
6. *Call friends at work and ask them how work is going. (This is not a good option, as said friends won't answer your calls).*

I'm so giddy on Monday morning that I forget to run. For the first time in a year I don't lace up my shoes and fix my earphone's twisted cord. I'm so excited that I upset my own routine. In my mad dash to get out the door and be the first person in the office, I also forget my coffee. Luckily, I remember the briefcase.

When I walk in a few people mill about or listen to music at their desks. These perpetually early people tense at my entrance like a meerkat community sensing a predator. Their ears perk up and they stare, following me with their eyes.

The light is on in Kelly's office, which is unusual. She never ventures into the office this early. Her door is open, so I bypass my office and peer inside. She sits at her desk and watches something on her computer screen, oblivious to the world. Her elfish features are best highlighted when she thinks no one is watching. At five foot one and slender, she makes the perfect fairy, and her crisp, short hair shows off shapely cheekbones and a pointed nose. She taps her manicured fingers on the desk as if bored. She manages to look stunning despite the early hour. A dainty gray cardigan rests on her chair's back, and she chose a pink sheath dress with a huge smoky quartz necklace.

"Hi, Kelly. I'm back."

She turns from the screen and smiles. A steaming mug sits next to her computer, and lavender and chamomile scent the air. I've never known Kelly enjoys tea. The things you notice about people early in the morning are usually the most revealing.

"Welcome back. Have a nice vacation?"

"You know I didn't."

"Absolute torture?"

"I almost slid into sloth and gluttony." I had no idea what to do with my time off. Normally I call my friends on weekends and we get together, but as I'm shunning the integral part of my friendship circle, it made planning difficult.

"It was good for you. There's color in your cheeks today." She notices my cheeks? I would never compare Kelly to my mother, but this is odd. "I can tell you are all business as usual, but we need to chat before the other editors get here for our meeting. Please sit."

I take my place across from her, and she offers the mug. "Tea? I just made this blend last week."

"No thank you. I'll get coffee later. Forgot mine at home."

"Indeed," she says and lifts an eyebrow. "I was under the impression that you forget nothing." Another strange comment. Bosses are supposed to watch and nurture their employees, but this is something new. Kelly has never shown more than a casual interest in my comings and goings, unless it relates to work.

"I'm flustered. I hate feeling idle, and this week has been an exercise in futility."

"Meaning?" She senses my agitation and leans across the desk as if to hear me better. It feels like talking to a psychiatrist.

"The whole situation is frustrating. I can't believe my friends got so many people involved, especially you. It's embarrassing." I shift in the chair and look away. I can't handle her transparent gaze. Nothing makes me feel more uncomfortable than being judged by a superior. It's like tiny glass flecks embedded in my skin. I feel itchy.

"I found the charade amusing. Why do you feel so threatened by change?"

"Excuse me?"

She steeples her fingers together and tilts her head to the side. After a moment she rises and walks to the door. She closes it, turns to her filing cabinet and grabs a file off the top. She leans against the cabinet and opens the file.

"You have been with Weston's for five years and have received a raise each year. You have been promoted twice and make more money per annum than your three counterparts." All true, but I deserve every penny. No one in my department can claim my accomplishments. I'm good at what I do, dammit! Why can't people leave me alone and let me live my life?

"I believe it is time for another promotion. One you have been waiting for since joining this company." Oh! She's hinting at the job right under her, senior editor! We hadn't had one in a long time. Kelly handles a lot. I would be the youngest person to gain that position in company history. Kelly managed to snap up the spot at thirty. I knew she was grooming me!

"There is a catch."

"Do you need me to show you the prep work I've done on those novels we optioned?" What will Mom and Dad say when they hear I've been promoted! Beat that Joel! I'm now the more successful sibling! He can take his online catering service and shove it!

"The proviso is far more interesting." She sets the file down and crosses her arms. She takes a deep breath before saying, "I want you to entertain the notion of going through with your friends' scheme."

"What?" I laugh. She cannot be serious. Next, she'll say she was kidding, and I'll be promoted! New office! My own parking space! Okay, maybe not the parking space.

"I have noticed a decline in you these last few months. I was not aware until someone pointed it out."

"I'm perfectly healthy, Kelly."

"Physically perhaps, but emotionally…" She shakes her head and removes her glasses before going on. "I see the way you sneer at the new romance novels that come in. When you're the chief editor on that particular genre, your work grows cold and detached. You do not let yourself become the characters. You rob them of glamour and frivolity. And so, you inject the work with frigidity."

I might vomit. I'm not sure what she's talking about. I hate the romances, but what single girl doesn't secretly wish those prissy, lovesick heroines a swift death? I never eliminate all the cheese from romance manuscripts, but one can only read about quivering members and lengthy, lovelorn glances for so long.

"You're angry with me, but I don't care. The truth always stings." I realize how much I hate Kelly's voice. She's not in Austen England! And what's with the criticism? She sounds like my college advisor: there's almost no chance of ever becoming a published author, much less one famous enough to make it your sole profession.

"You want me to go along with Alicia and the girls? To go on twelve dates with twelve strangers they pull off the Internet?"

"Yes," she seems pleased that I figure it out so quickly. "Exactly. It's not because of some bet. Because of your attitude toward the romances, which we tend to publish a lot of, I cannot see you in the position. The senior editor must handle all genres. Maybe this little trial will help you reengage with romance in general. Even if the experiences are difficult, you'll get something out of them."

She thinks I can't handle romance novels? I've tackled far more daunting subjects than puppy love and ridiculous sex scenes. Who is she to tell me I can't handle something? Especially something so trivial?

"When they said you were in on it, I had no idea you'd sink this low," I say.

"I'll sink as low as I must to help your career. I may be your boss, but I'm also your friend, and I wish you well." She walks back to her desk and sits. She calls herself my friend, but are these the actions of a friend?

"You think I have no heart." I almost whisper. Is this what everyone thinks? That I can't feel anymore? That I can't love?

"That is *not* what I said. Persons involved in interventions have a tendency toward pity, but I expect more of you. Of course, you have a heart, but it's not open."

"There's a good reason—"

"I do not doubt that, but has it been long since this person broke you?"

I nod and fold my hands in my lap. Have I been a depressing load on everyone I know for three years? I had no idea my friends, colleagues, and family felt this way. Why did no one talk to me before? Did I close myself off?

"It's been three years since I've dated anyone."

"Well," she says and claps her hands, "then it's time to get back out there. I don't expect you to fall for the first man you see, you're too cautious for that, but don't hold the entire male population hostage with your derision."

She turns to her computer, which is my signal to depart. My briefcase feels like I loaded it with weights.

"Meeting at nine as usual," she mentions before I close her office door.

Kelly assigns me *Kiss and Tell,* a new romance novel by Elizabeth Hanks. Justin earns my devotion by voicing sympathy but also mentions a new bookshop where I might find a suitable journal. Jerk.

June

Tony Two-Phone and Rule Number One: You have to go on at least two dates per month with each month's guy…unless he's a huge jackass.

Email: <u>Aliciasweetheart@sojourn.net</u> to <u>Shakespearelover@gmail.com</u>

Date One Information:

Anthony Schwartz, age 32, height 5'11," is a sports enthusiast who enjoys running, cycling, softball, and bowling. He works for an advertising company in the Cities and owns a golden retriever named Stan.

Your destination: Axel's Bonfire on Grand Avenue for cocktails at 7:30pm. I know you can drink but keep it to two of something and don't mix your boozes! Remember Prague?

Love,
Alicia

That's all they give me: a name, some "vital" statistics, and a location. And I can handle my alcohol just fine. Prague was a fluke; a dreadful vomit-drenched fluke.

This is a journal of my dating scene exploits, a kingdom I have not visited in three years. I should count the wasted years with Pete, but since I was technically in a relationship I was off the market. Why does dating make you feel like a fish market display? They catch you, chop off your unnecessary parts and put the tender bits on display at a set price. If no one chooses you it's off to the garbage can.

I'm nervous and fidgety getting ready. What do I wear? Should I curl my hair? Put it up or leave it down? Which lipstick goes with this eye shadow? Oh God, it clashes with my silk top, now there's a wardrobe crisis! Nothing in the closet looks good enough for a date. Why did I buy that ugly sweater? Why did I keep those jeans when I knew I'd never wear them again? Did my *mother* hand those shoes down to me?

I don't remember it being this difficult.

Why is it that when you're preparing to meet someone new you notice all the little things about yourself that you hate, like that permanent zit near your left tear duct or that one stray arm hair that grows the opposite direction? My freckles make me look like some kind of red-haired jungle cat. I'm too fat, too pale, too old, and too short. Every negative shoves its way to the brain's forefront and squabbles for attention.

And I'm sweating. I'm out of napkins and paper towels (makes mental note to go to the store), but I'm sweating so much I put panty-liners in my armpits and leave the apartment.

As I drive out to Grand Avenue, which is a long strip of bars, restaurants, chic boutiques, and cafes, I unravel. What if this guy's ugly or thinks I'm ugly? What if we have nothing in common besides a love of running and pets? If I need to fall back on talking about Prospero's shenanigans, I'll know the date was a bust. I can spend hours talking about him, but Jesus that's boring if you're the other person, or so my brother says.

Speaking of my dear little brother, he has been surprisingly silent about the affair. He knows about it, because Mom mentioned he did, but he hasn't called or emailed to ridicule me. Maybe he's too busy stuffing fancy sausages to bother. I must remember to write him a scathing email berating him for inattention.

Grand is busy on Friday nights, so I have trouble finding a parking spot. After circling the area for ten minutes I settle for the ramp and swallow the bitter parking-fee pill. I almost drop the ticket under my car but snatch it inside, straining my arm and losing the left sweat-coated armpit panty-liner out the window. Lopsided perspiration rings are so attractive.

By the time I park and walk down to street level, it's twenty after seven. Bonfire sits across the street next to my favorite pastry shop and café. I wait at the light and cross with the crowd, most of them dressed for warm weather but not for a super-chilled restaurant environment. They scoff at my sweater, but I'll wind up triumphant and comfortable.

Inside Bonfire I ask the host if Anthony Schwartz is in the bar waiting for someone.

"Yes, he's seated at one of the high-tops. Right this way."

He's early, a good sign. Lateness appalls me. If a guy really wants to meet you, he'll be on time. If he's late, there's a subconscious gnome tripping him up. I'd rather not bother with someone who's not ready to meet me. But I'm not ready for this encounter either. I hope he's easy to talk to, because it will be a short date if he's not. I plan on having one glass of wine then leaving. I have just the excuse ready: when in doubt, blame it on cramps.

The host leads me past the thick oak bar with its many beer taps and infused vodka cauldrons and shows me to Anthony. He sits at the third table in, next to the big bay windows, his back to me, cell phone up to one ear. He gestures smoothly with the other hand, making circular motions with his fingers. As we approach, he spins, sees me, and says, "I'll call you back."

He's not bad looking; taller than me thank God, trim, brown hair and dark eyes. One eyebrow arches higher than the other, but it gives him a confused, endearing appearance. He wears a blue long-sleeve button-down shirt and khakis, the perfect casual uniform. He's either a first-time dater who didn't know what to wear, or he knows exactly what looks good on him.

"Cassandra?" He extends a hand and smiles. The smile puts me more at ease and I reach for his hand.

"Cassie's fine. Anthony?"

"Tony." He seems pleased with my appearance, and then I remember the other horrible thing under my right armpit. When he pulls out the stool for me, I say, "I just have to run to the bathroom for one second. I'll be right back." He smiles and shrugs, as if implying, silly women and their constant bathroom use. I try not to run for the restroom, and I accidentally bump a server typing in someone's order on a computer.

"I'm so sorry," I say, mortified. Head down I race for the bathroom. The mirror shows a reasonably put-together young woman. I'm glad my anxiety hasn't shown. I toss the panty-liner and take a deep breath. Remember yoga: deep inhalation, long, slow exhalation. I almost clasp my hands to my chest and say "Namaste" but go back into the dining room. As I pass the host stand, I hear laughter and think it's about me, though they're probably talking about plans after work. Hosts are young and prone to giggling. Looking at their hip ensembles, my black slacks and silk blouse choice seems misinformed.

Back at the table, Tony is on the cell phone again, but he hangs up when he sees me. Strange, it didn't look like the first phone he had out. Maybe I'm just confused.

When I sit down the server swoops in and takes our order. Tony got two waters for us before I arrived, and he orders a tall Tanqueray and tonic with lime. Not a bad choice if you like pine trees. I order the house chardonnay.

"So, how's your day going?" he asks and sips his water. An un-squeezed lemon floats on top and distracts me. If people order lemon for their water, why don't they squeeze it in? It's not doing any good sitting there. I fish my lemon out with my fingers, shield the glass from over-spray, and squeeze. Acidic juice runs down my hand.

"Fine. I work at a publishing company, and we recently acquired new stock. We have to go through the manuscripts carefully and edit out the author's mistakes."

"So, you're kind of like a copywriter?"

"A little, but my job encompasses more editing than grammar and spellchecks. I'm there to work out the kinks. But you'd be surprised how poor people's grammar is."

"Huh, I thought all writers had good grammar," he chuckles.

I smile. I love talking about writing. I wonder if he's read anything I've edited. "Some do, but writing a novel takes a lot of time, and sometimes the author misses things. I mix up 'bear' and 'bare' all the time." When I say "bear" I make clawing motions with my hands, and he laughs again. "I got in trouble in my college writing workshops for that."

"You don't seem like the type who gets in trouble."

"Not much anymore, but when I was younger…"

"Rebellious?"

"That's putting it lightly. My little brother is the family saint. I get by on redemptive qualities and parental adulation."

"Such as?" I think about my teenage years for a moment, and all I see are curfew violations, heated arguments with my mother, and running away to stay with Dad after they divorced.

"I call my mom every day and have lunch with my dad once a month, whereas Joel lives in California and never talks to them. It's a long, hard road back to 'favorite child.'"

"I wouldn't know. Only child." Great, so he's used to getting his own way and will throw tantrums when enterprises fail. Only children never have to work for their parents' attention. One of my cousins is an only child, and her parents couldn't care less that she's a selfish brat who lives in Indiana, asking for money every month. "But don't think less of me. It's just my dad and me, no suburban dreamscape for this guy." He points a thumb at himself.

Ah, sweet relief, but children coming from single-parent households have their own issues. I thought my life was rough. I'm feeling more normal and at ease knowing Tony is most likely just as damaged. Confidence rising. Becoming more attuned to conversation. Dating isn't so hard after all! Intense dread lifting to be replaced by inner poise and newfound trust in girlfriends' ability to find me an eligible guy. I might not have to date twelve men after all! What if Tony turns out to be perfect?

After two hours discussing our favorite authors (mine are Shakespeare and Stephen King, his are William Faulkner and somebody called Robert B. Parker) and the best running haunts, we say goodnight and agree to meet again for round two. He did not hesitate to ask for the check either, so there was no awkward "are you going to pay, am I going to pay?" moment.

When I get home, I slide through the front door and perform a sort of slinky freestyle dance where I gracefully avoid tripping on the cat, sweep into the kitchen, pour his food, and pirouette onto the couch. The apprehensive feeling slides from my body like old skin. Whoever knew dating could be fun after such a long hiatus?

I like dating quite a lot.

I call Alicia the day after date number one to apologize. When she answers I hear crying in the background, and she yells for her husband to take care of Oliver, their youngest.

"Do I have to do everything? Cassie's calling! Hi sweetie how's it going? I thought you'd banished me to No-Friend Land for sure."

"It's hard enough for me to admit defeat. Don't get smug."

"It's not being smug if I'm right, which I always am."

"Yeah yeah, you were right, and I should listen to your sage advice." She giggles and covers the phone speaker to block the sound. Alicia hates her laugh.

"So, it went well? Tell me everything!"

"Oh no. You get to wait for the journal just like Keeley and Lindsey."

"And Kevin. I told him he could follow the drama too."

"You're such a whore."

"And you're a shameless hussy. Kevin's a good critic. He'll tell you if the writing's crap."

We talk a little longer and decide to make plans for a girls-only supper summit at her place in mid-June. I want to see her kids and visit with Brian too, but that can wait until their annual Fourth of July party. I need to get as much Alicia-solo time as I can. Her family is and should be the most important thing in her life, but it feels lonely in the third-wheel corner. A girl needs her best friend.

"Are you going to call Keel and Linds and kowtow to them too?"

"Hell no," I say. "They can sweat a bit longer."

"You should call Keeley at least. She's afraid you disowned her. Who else is willing to listen to her boyfriend woe-is-me stories?"

"Point taken. Have a good night."

"You too, Cass. Isotoldyouso!" she says quickly before hanging up.

Email: Trulover888@yahoo.com to Shakespearelover@gmail.com

Date Two Information:

Anthony Schwartz, now you've seen him and know we won't set you up with someone gross. I don't know why you didn't trust us! Having so much fun! He enjoys reading mysteries and grilling out. Big Brewers fan. That's a yikes but nobody's perfect!

Your destination: Early dinner at WA Frost on Selby at 5:30 and a movie at 7:30. He picked the movie, so it will be a surprise! Have fun and behave yourself, woman!

Loves, Keeley Bear.

Getting ready for the second date is no easier than the first. Though less nervous, I now have to top the outfit I wore when we met. Is it possible that I gained five pounds last night? These capris are tight. I must be bloated from that Indian food and herbal tea I had for dinner. The first sandals I choose are too juvenile. My jewelry is a mess on the dresser. Do I smell something burning? It's just the curling iron heating up.

I'm excited for the second date and know that it will go well, and Tony and I will live happily ever after and when we're forty we'll joke about meeting online. Love at first instant message. Except I didn't meet him online. What kind of loser needs her friends to score dates for her? Plan suddenly seeming more ludicrous by the second. Go back to closet to change outfit one more time.

WA Frost is kind of fancy, and I'm not sure if the girls suggested it to Tony or if he chose it. Argh! Must tell girls that I need more info on these matters. What if he makes a reference to something they said online? It would be a scandal. Likely to make me a national laughingstock.

I don't need sanitary napkins under my armpits tonight, and I leave the apartment early. I should also let the girls know that an email in the morning does not leave enough time to mentally prepare for a date that evening.

This time I beat Tony to the restaurant and get us a table. The server is polite and inquires whether I'm waiting for another person. I order two waters with lemon and decide to wait to order a drink, since he was kind enough to wait for me at Bonfire. At my seat near the window I spy Tony marching toward the restaurant, cell phone glued to his ear and a disturbing expression on his face. His lips form an ugly snarl and he must be berating the person on the other line. His body language suggests anger and frustration, so it's most likely a work issue. I know how he feels. The book Kelly assigned me is less than ideal, but I'll tell you about that later.

Before he enters the restaurant, Tony slams his phone shut and jams it in his pocket. I hope it wasn't too serious. Perhaps something dreadful happened, and he'll cancel the date. At least he's doing it in person, not letting me sit here alone waiting. He shakes his arms out and walks in, ready to separate his phone business from date business.

"Hi again!" he says as I rise to greet him. We hug awkwardly but firmly and sit. "It's nice to see you so soon. I've been thinking about you for a week!"

"I was surprised too, when I had a good time," I say then realize this might be construed as insulting. "Not that I thought I wouldn't!

It's just that I don't date much." I blush at my lame response and imagine him running for the door.

"I get where you're coming from. How can you really get to know a person online?"

"Right! I was just saying that to my friend the other night."

"Because you can't see or hear each other talking—"

"No body language or vocal anomalies to decode."

"Now that you mention it, online dating might actually be easier than trying to talk to someone in person." God he's so easy to talk to! We fall into gleeful comradery over the elusiveness of finding a date, but a stern buzz comes from his pocket. Annoyed, he rolls his eyes and says, "Do you mind if I take this? It's my work phone. We're wooing a new client, and my team lead needs hand-holding every ten minutes."

"Sure. I know how work goes." He puts his napkin on the table and leaves, trotting outside before flipping the phone open. He must not be aware that I can watch him out the window, because he paces back and forth and gestures wildly with his free arm. I feel a rush of pride, because he's yelling at someone for interrupting our date. It means that much. Curse that colleague into the ground, Tony!

"Sorry, sorry," he says when he comes back and sits down. "They can't get along without me sometimes. It's like working at a daycare."

"Sounds like my job. When I have to get the interns moving, I feel like the only cowboy in the corral wrangling stubborn cattle."

The pocket whirs again, and he takes out the phone. But it's not ringing. He reaches for the other pocket and pulls out a second cell phone. I kid you not girls, this guy has TWO cell phones, and he carries them both around in his suit pockets. Who needs TWO cell phones? Even the President doesn't have TWO cell phones. Well, he might, but does Tony really need them? Feeling put out, I ask, "Do you need to take this call too?" Not seeing his obvious faux pas, Tony lays the phones side by side and says, "No I'm turning it off." Since he says "it" and not "them" I assume he'll leave one on. News to single men: Turn off the damn cell phone before going on a date! Enough with the passive aggressive bullshit!

The phone he leaves on rings twice before the appetizer is served, once during the main course, and once more when the server brings out Tony's strawberry cheesecake. By now I'm fuming. Listening to the phone buzz and watching it dance across the table and hit Tony's plate as he ignores it is infuriating. I want to reach over, grab the phone, and chuck it out the window. What could possibly be this important? And why won't he just answer it? If he needs to keep it on so badly, why doesn't he fucking answer it? I'm tempted to pick it up and greet the caller with my most acidic voice but restrain my urges.

By the dessert course, even the server is affronted by Tony's behavior. I glance up at him, my eyes pleading for the check, and he nods. Servers can pick out a bad date from miles away. They always know when to drop the tab and get the two people far away before an argument erupts.

I let Tony pay again. I was going to offer to pay, at least to chip in, but his behavior cements my indignation. He has no problem whipping out a credit card. When we leave, he says, "The movie should be good! It just came out last weekend and the reviews are positive." I don't think I can bear a two-hour movie plus commercials and previews if he's going to leave the phone on, but I agreed to give this a try, so I knuckle under.

"Sounds good."

His damn pocket jingles four times during the movie, a dismal gross-out comedy starring people I've never heard of. Whoever thought fart jokes were tantamount to comedic genius was huffing glue. Before the credits role I stalk from the theater, purse swinging on my arm like a pendulum. He runs after me and asks what's wrong.

"You left your phone on through the whole movie." He's affronted by my answer.

"So? It might have been important."

"But you didn't even *look* at it after it rang. How could you have *any* idea if it was important or not?"

"I can't turn my work phone off. The one for normal calls yes, but work comes first."

Is he serious? Even I know that work waits in the shadows during a social event, especially on a date. I let him answer it once, didn't I? Shame on me to believe he told them not to call again. I knew this online thing would never work! Why on earth did I agree to it?

"This isn't going to work. Thank you for dinner and the movie, but I need to go. Goodbye." I'm firm, which some singles aren't prepared to be. You have to be exact with your wording or the other person might get the wrong idea. I don't care if it makes me a bitch. I walk away, back to the parking lot, heels clicking on the pavement, and hoping that my posture says: "stay the hell away from me, muggers and bad dates alike."

I think of calling Alicia and lecturing her about poor choices in men, but it's after ten, and her kids are asleep. I'll have to wait until the summit at her house to criticize.

We lounge around Alicia's pool in summer shifts and jeweled sandals, sipping margaritas and listening to Kenny Chesney sing about warm, sandy beaches. We should be in Mexico on those warm, sandy beaches instead of languishing under umbrellas in the summer humidity. Sweat runs down my cleavage, and I consider pouring a margarita down my top.

Keeley looks fantastic as always: blond hair cascading down her shoulders and a hot-pink bikini that edges on scandalous. Her matching sarong lays unused on the ground next to her. She's the only one brave enough to sit in the sun. Alicia chose a more tasteful ensemble. The typical suburban mom, she has on a safari-printed one piece and long-sleeved gauzy tunic. Her oversized sunglasses bring old-fashioned screen goddesses to mind. Lindsey wears her sporty two-piece with an oversized men's denim shirt but makes it more feminine with a rope belt nipping in the waist. I'm not telling what I'm wearing.

I haven't told any of them how the second date went, but they know I'm pissed. I haven't said one word since we got to Alicia's. I printed out three copies of my journal for them to peruse and wait for their opinions. Keeley finishes last and sets down the pages, face gaunt and embarrassed. "He did what?"

"You read it," my first words of the afternoon. I sip my margarita and savor the tequila. Lindsey makes them strong, like a kick in the stomach.

"He seriously has two phones? Why do you need two phones?" she asks.

"That's what I said. In fact, I think I wrote it somewhere on page six."

"What an asshole," says Lindsey.

"He seemed so nice on the website. His profile didn't mention anything about being a workaholic," says Keeley, outraged that anyone would be less than transparent when writing down his or her personal pros and cons. I hope they didn't put "emotional cripple with horrible dating past" in *my* profile.

"Or an asshole," says Lindsey who drains her glass. "You'll need another." She goes into the house to fetch the blender.

"Damn, and he was our first pick," says Alicia, shaking her head. She reaches down into her straw beach-tote and pulls out the purple notebook and a matching pen. Opening it to page one, she slashes a line through Tony's name then tucks the notebook under her thigh. "Oh well, July looks pretty good too." Like she's commenting on the weather forecast instead of my love life.

"You need to consider dropping the whole idea," I say and gaze off over the pool, inspecting her flowerbeds. "If this is any indication of what I'll be going through, I want out."

"Oh no you can't!" says Keeley. "It's only the first month. And your journal's really good. You should keep going." Her enthusiasm makes me tired. Thank God Lindsey's back with more alcohol. She pours blended heaven to the glass's rim and grins down at me.

"I picked the next guy, so you have to do it," says Lindsey. "Besides, that raise won't earn itself."

"That's another thing, this job-based blackmail. I could write a strong-worded letter about that and get Kelly fired." I'm pouting and being a big baby in general, but after Tony Two-Phone I'm entitled to a little venom-spewing. "How'd you even get her to agree?"

Alicia smiles and sets her drink down on the little, green metal table beside her. "I went to your office and met with her. What a fabulous woman. She really likes you, can't get enough of your drive and work ethic. I believe her exact words were 'she reminds me of a young me.'"

"She did not say that."

"Something like it." She's being vague, a poor attempt at civility. Kelly told her all about my romance novel issues.

"She called me heartless."

"I'm sure she didn't. You're just being stubborn."

"We know you too well, Cass," says Keeley. "Please don't quit."

"You've made a career of quitting," pipes in Lindsey who dips her big toe in the pool and swirls the water around. "You stopped writing the second you got one rejection letter."

"That's not fair. It was a prestigious magazine."

"So, you sent your work to a place you knew would turn it down then gave up?" asks Alicia, eyes indiscernible through dark lenses.

"It's time to try on success, see if it goes with any of your shoes," says Lindsey.

"Since you mixed sage advice with fashion I'll have to oblige," I snarl.

"It's rule twelve anyway," says Keeley. "Twelve months, twelve men, twelve rules."

Confused, I stare at her, shielding my eyes from the sun's glare. Rules? They never mentioned any rules besides agreeing to the plan and writing the journal.

"There are rules now?"

"There always have been, you never asked," says Alicia and she reaches for the notebook again. She turns to the first page and recites, "'Rule One: You have to go on at least two dates per month with said month's guy.'"

"Unless the first one sucks, right?"

"Maybe," teases Alicia.

"And what's 'rule twelve'?"

"'Once Cassandra McTiernan agrees to the venture, it is a binding contract that cannot be broken on grounds that she will then be tormented mercilessly by her family, friends, and co-workers.'"

"Wonderful. Why isn't that rule one?"

"We saved it for last because it's the most important," says Keeley. "If you want to avoid horrible shame and relentless mocking, you'll trust us and stick with this."

I sigh and say, "What choice do I have? Who's the Man of July?"

"You'll find out soon enough," says Alicia, and Lindsey rubs her hands together, her eyes twinkling in the sunlight.

I hope her pale ass burns.

July

Tristan "Former Norman" and Rule Number Two: Don't laugh at your date's profession, it's rude.

July in Minnesota means three things: barbeques, humidity, and tornado warnings. Barbeques are fun, but if the humidity kicks in it becomes a game of who can stay outside next to the hot grill the longest before running inside for air conditioning. I've never actually seen a tornado, but I've seen a sky go from blue to green in minutes. Disquieting. The city tests the tornado warning sirens on the first Wednesday of each month, and it went off like clockwork the day I found out my new guy's identity.

Mom calls me as I leave for work, the sirens blaring in the background. Hysterical, she sobs into the phone and I can hardly understand one word in five.

"I—can—he—do—this—other—why—can't—meet—nice—no—left—me!"

"Mom slow down, what's the matter?" She hasn't cried to me in years. Always a flinty woman, my mother believes that negative outward emotion should be kept to a minimum. Happy faces are a must, even if someone's flinging excrement at you. Considering the time, she's at work, which makes the outburst more urgent. "Where are you?"

"In the bathroom, where else would I be?"

"*You* called *me!*" When she gets like this it's best to get everything out in the open right away, otherwise it takes too long to drag it out of her. Once she realizes she's talking to an actual person, her inner English Queen mode activates, and all is miraculously well again. Making her mad is one way to keep the emotion coming.

"It's your father!" She wails again, and I imagine snot bubbles forming in her nose. Honking comes from the speaker as she blows her nose.

"Is Dad okay? Did something happen?" Jesus he's dead, he's had a heart attack and he's dead. "Mom is he okay?"

"He's *fine*. Not a care in the world for other people's feelings." Her tone is acidic, usually reserved when discussing Dad, but today there's fire behind the resentment. "Not that I care about how he lives his life, but really, does he have to rub it in my face like we're in middle school?"

"What are you talking about? I thought he had an accident or something." I clutch my chest and my heart is thumping. Bile rises in my throat, but I push it back, gagging slightly.

"He's fine. Didn't I just say that? You're just like him. Never listen to anything I say. You two were always like that, ganging up on me. Joel's not here to take my side, you know."

"How did this become my fault?"

"It's not your fault, Cassie, it's this *woman*."

"You're making about as much sense as Aunt Josephine after one of her 'nights out.'"

"I'm not drunk. Your father, loathsome creature that he is, updated his website thingy this morning. His blog."

"Dad has a website?" Mystified at the prospect of my parents following current social-networking fads, I lose track of Mom's rant.

When did Dad have time to set up a website? Why didn't he tell me about it? And how did *Mom* find it?

"Oh yes and what a veritable laugh-fest it is. A friend of mine follows his blog and said I should read it. It has his elementary school picture on it. I thought, 'he's the most boring person on the planet. How does he have a website?'"

I didn't know Dad knew how to use the Internet much less set up web pages. I don't even know how to set up web pages. "Where does a woman fit into this?"

"He -" her voice quavers and I hear toilet tissue unravel. "He went on a date last night and just wrote how much fun he had." Upon finishing the sentence, she devolves into a crying wreck and drops the phone.

Dad went on a *date*? Has the whole world gone mad? Dad only dated two people his entire life. He's not adventurous, nor does he have time to meet anyone outside work. Maybe it's a co-worker.

Mom picks the phone up and continues, "Apparently he's been chatting with this harlot online for weeks. He's been anticipating their meeting for quite some time. But then why hasn't he mentioned it before?" More sobs. Mom has found out that Internet stalking is never a good idea, especially if the stalked is your ex-husband.

"Calm down Mom, just breathe for a minute."

"How can I breathe if he's out there having sex and I'm not?" Crap. Situation just got monumentally worse. There is a globally accepted doctrine that states: "No child, no matter their age, wants to hear about his or her parents having sex, even if they had to have sex in order to conceive him or her." I didn't think it would come to conversation about sex or lack thereof. Never want to imagine parents engaging in any kind of intimacy. Brain checks out for briefest moment, so I miss what she said after "sex and I'm not."

"Huh?"

"Don't say 'huh' Cassie it makes you sound uneducated."

"Wha?"

"I can see that you've no interest in comforting me," she says and blows her nose. It's back to automaton mode. "I better get back to my desk or Nancy will think something's up." Nancy is her nosy cubicle neighbor, the bane of Mom's job existence.

"Come on Mom, I'm sorry. I'm sure Dad's just—"

"Don't try to make me feel better, you never succeed. I just have to face the fact that your father is dating again. I never thought I'd see the day."

"He's not ugly, and he has a decent job and a car and a nice apartment. What woman wouldn't find that attractive?" I get defensive whenever Mom starts bashing my dad, mainly because he was always on my side during maternal arguments. And because he buys me snow cones at the State Fair every year.

"I *knew* you'd take his side."

"It's not about taking sides. You're attractive too."

"Too late. Now that I know where you stand, I feel better about wallowing in my own misery. Joel will understand." I've sent her spiraling further downhill. I never know how to talk to my mother without making her upset or dissatisfied with me.

"Call Joel. If he answers, say I'm pissed at him."

"What do I care if you're angry with him? I need some actual advice about what to do with this situation. Goodbye."

The line clicks, and she's gone. I hope she went back to work and didn't call my brother, because he's probably still in bed with some trollop or another. The last thing Mom needs to hear is that someone else besides her is having sex. Maybe that's why she called me first. She knows I haven't gotten laid in years.

I tell Kevin everything when I get to work about Tony, Alicia's insistence that I carry on with the dating, my dad's love life, and my mother's mental breakdown.

"It's so weird, thinking about them dating."

"What's weirder is them having sex. I mean they're old," he says, a terrified gleam in his eyes.

"You had to mention sex. I'll have nightmares for weeks." I start for my office, but Kevin follows me, always ready for more gossip. "Why are you following me? Don't you have some press statements to write?"

"You don't get away that easily. Where's my copy of your journal? I was promised vicarious romance."

I walk into my office and try to slam the door on him, but the sly devil slithers in and sits behind my desk. "No work until I get those scandalous pages."

"There's nothing scandalous about it. I had a good date then a bad date. The end. Get out." I put my briefcase on the desk, pull out his copy, and throw it across the desk at him. He catches it and leans back in my chair, preparing to read. "Please read it somewhere else."

"If you tell me to leave one more time, I'll loan this to Justin for editing."

"I don't care if Justin reads it. It's crap." He scans the first page then flips to the second and makes a face. "It certainly is. What were you thinking using a word like 'troglodyte?' So passé. And is that a spelling error?"

I lunge for him across the desk, but he leaps up and runs around me.

"I'm kidding. Just give me fifteen minutes and we'll discuss further."

"This is not a book club! We're not discussing anything!" But he's out the door.

Discussion Questions for "Cassandra's Journal" by Kevin Jones

1. *Considering the author's emotional state, how do you think the dates with Anthony really went? First person narratives are notoriously unreliable, as experienced with Holden Caulfield in The Catcher in the Rye. What parts of the narrative sound real? Which seem made up or embellished?*

2. *How do you view the narrator as a character in her own journal? Is she likeable, or do you find her personality cloying? Do you enjoy spending time in her head?*

3. *And what about the three friends? Do they seem arbitrary or cliché? Do you find the absence of a gay best friend character shocking and disappointing? Make up your own character and see if he or she fits into the narrative. (Make it a gay best friend character and you get extra points.)*

4. *Do you think Cassandra gets her point across? Why do you think she is so averse to dating? Is it that ex-boyfriend lurking in the shadows?*

Email: FellbeeotchLinds@hotmail.com to Shakespearelover@gmail.com

Date Three Information:

Tristan Howard, age 32, height 5'9," is an actor who also works as a bartender in the Cities. He enjoys comedies, musical theater, and playing his fiddle. (An actor and a musician! I know you'll like him.) He likes exotic food.

Destination: Calypso Café in Minneapolis at noon tomorrow for lunch, it's Greek, so be prepared for lots of fun! Don't make fun of him because he's an actor. I know you think people should have steady jobs, but everyone's not like you.

Linds

Before I go on phase two of the dating fiasco, I call my dad and plan on getting the scoop on his date. First, I look up his blog. It's a modest little page with a plain backsplash and Times New Roman font, nothing spectacular. He has a lot of followers, though, so I click on a random update. It's from a year ago! Dad's been Internet-literate for at least a year and has never mentioned it! I thought Mom had stumbled upon some new venture, but he's been working on this for a while. I go back to his first post, which is tentative but humorous. Dad's got the self-deprecation thing down. Must be the Irish coming out in him.

"I guess this is supposed to welcome you all into my life, which, to tell you the truth, isn't all that exciting. I am fifty-six years old, have had the same job since my thirties, and have been divorced for sixteen years. My ex-wife still berates me for my averageness, but that's something I can't help. Would I rather be a rock star or sports athlete? Not really. I have two great kids and a cabin up north if not much else. I shook hands with and said goodbye to my dignity long ago, so let's not dwell on that. All in all, this website is a chance to talk about the things people don't like to talk about: failed marriage, the fact that your kids might be screwed up, and how much you hate your job. They say you shouldn't talk about that stuff online, but my boss isn't much of a web-surfer. So here goes. The average joe's online journal. I hope somebody reads it besides my friend Carl."

The fact that my dad wrote "web-surfer" and "failed marriage" with such straight-faced honesty frightens me. Does he really think Joel and I are screwed up? If my dad doesn't believe in me who will for Christ's sake? Judging by the number of his followers, Dad is quite the popular guy. He's done what so many nerdy teenage boys have done: made themselves Internet gods, mini cartel bosses with braces and acne.

I breeze through his comments, and best friend Carl Landon contributes a lot, but most posts are from unrecognizable names. Many are from women throwing themselves at Dad. Jeez, he must get a lot more action than I know about. One comment invites an illicit act I have the decency not to mention here. Why do people find it so easy to be crass and inappropriate online as if it has no consequences?

The fact that my father has become more popular than many Twittering celebrities makes me feel nauseated. How in the hell did he pull off famous writing before me? My inner novelist swells with jealousy, and I forget that I'm thinking of my dad for a few seconds and plan the blogger's demise. Why can't I do what Dad did? Why can't I find my writing voice?

I open Microsoft Word and pull up my first journal. It's ten pages long, quite a feat for someone who has been afraid of her laptop for three years. I don't know if other writers get irrationally skittish around their computers, but the thought of so many blank white pages and a blinking curser still gives me nightmares. In the most recurring one, the blinking curser of doom chases me through the Weston's office, screaming that I'm a pretend writer:

"Rubbish! All garbage! Not one word makes sense! Whoever said you could write is a fool!" it scolds, and I race around in circles trying to outrun it. In dreams you can never outrun anything threatening, so as it closes in, I wake up, sweating and clutching my comforter. For me, there's no worse feeling than failure.

Dad answers on the third ring, "Hi pumpkin," he sighs, "I'm a bit backed up here. What's going on with you?" Even though he's busy, Dad always has time for my calls, so I ignore his comment and say, "I just read some of your blog."

"Really?" Now he sounds interested, giddy. "How'd you like it? I was nervous about telling you. Your editing talents are formidable. I don't know how people bear to send you their work." Did he just say formidable?

"When did all this start? Is it because Mom told all your old friends that you're dull? She didn't mean it. People say stupid things when they're mad."

"She was right. I am dull. It's just that some people like that sort of thing." I imagine him shrugging on the other line, a smile on his lips. His eyes crinkle when he smiles.

"So, I read."

"Don't pay attention to what people say online. Most of them are a bit bonkers."

"No kidding. Where did you meet this woman you're dating?" I'm praying she isn't one of the blog commentators, because God knows what she's really like. I now hope it's someone from his job, even though workplace romance leads to other problems. I don't think couples should be in close proximity to each other so often.

"Carl introduced us. He talked me into going out one night and bam! There she was! Sandy is such a nice woman. You'd like her."

"That's not important, Dad. I'm sure I would, but why didn't you tell me about this little project? You tell me everything."

"I didn't think you'd like it," he says, a little defiant. "Can't I have one thing for myself?"

"You sound like Mom."

He laughs—bellows practically—and says, "I suppose so, but she's right. I deserve something private."

"But it's not private! You have over four thousand followers!"

"Apparently that's not very many. And what's the matter with that? Most of them have never met me and never will."

I don't understand where his new bravado came from, but it irks me. Mom's going crazy. Dad's got a lady friend, and I'm being pushed around my life strapped to a gurney. Who decided to turn my snow globe upside down and shake it?

"Is it okay that I read it? I found it by accident." A little lie never hurt anyone, and Mom would not be pleased if I told Dad she tracked him online like an inept hunter. Hopefully he didn't know, otherwise things could get hairy.

"Sure. There's really nothing in there about you. It's mostly about work and my life in general." I sense an unsaid *yet* in there, and I'm not part of his life in general? What did he mean by saying he screwed us up? But I can't get up the courage to ask. Sometimes living in mystery is beneficial.

"You leave everything anonymous right? Besides the grade school picture." I've seen and heard about people getting fired or reprimanded for things they say online about their jobs. The last thing I want is for my dad to lose his job over some stupid Internet meltdown.

"Of course," he says, affronted, "I'm not stupid."

"I know. Well, I need to get back to work. Have a good day."

"You too, sweetie! I'll talk to you later! Say! How would you like to meet Sandy?"

I'd rather meet Fidel Castro in a dark, Cuban alley.

It's not that I mind if people don't have good jobs. I'm not judgmental or anything. But if a person is past thirty and still hasn't grown up, I feel weird interacting with them. I dreamt of writing professionally in college, but once I graduated, everything got real. Bills piled up and I needed a place to live that had a working refrigerator and air conditioning. Once "the facts of life," as my mom calls them, set in, I ditched writing and got the job at Weston's.

I reach Calypso Café at ten to noon and sit down outside. I've never been to this small restaurant, but I enjoy Greek food, so I intend to have a good time. Getting ready for this date was much easier than last time. I guess repetition really does make things simpler. Or my brain has finally gotten used to the dating idea and acquiesced to the torture.

It rained last night, so the sidewalk shone, and small tree branches shaken loose from their trunks litter the gutters. I like the smell of wet leaves drying in the sun: bittersweet and tangy with a slight moldy scent. It's the smell of age, a reminder that things move along faster than you'd like. It makes me think of our old house in fall when Dad raked massive leaf piles around the yard only to watch Joel and I decimate them with one leap. Leaves caught in my hair, Dad threw me in the air and caught me, laughing and scolding.

Two people leave the restaurant, and the fresh pastry smell wafts out. It's noon and no sight of my date. Not sure what to do, I wait a few more minutes then go in and sit at one of the red table-clothed booths. By twenty after I'm annoyed. Remember what I said about lateness.

He strolls in at half past and looks around the place, trying to spot me. It's easy to find me in a crowd, red hair glaringly obvious, and he waves and walks over, the host chasing after him.

"Hello!" his lilting voice carries, and people turn to stare, lunches interrupted. He nearly hits the host with a flying elbow, and she drops her menus. "Oh! Sorry!" He stoops to help with the menus, and I'm slightly less angry. At least he's polite to restaurant staff.

He's incredibly handsome, which probably gets him out of a lot of trouble, but his wiry frame moves in every direction like a marionette. Blond hair and pale eyebrows and lashes give him an almost invisible quality, but startling green eyes make you take a second look. He's quick to smile and look sheepish. The host can't help but beam at him as she sets the menus on the table. Definitely an actor, what charisma. I recall I'm perturbed with his tardiness. When he sits, he looks so abashed that I feel like a strict grade schoolteacher slapping his hand.

"Sorry I'm late. Couldn't find this place! I've never been here!"

"That's okay," I say with caution. His appearance is unnerving me, and he's almost too friendly.

"I mean, I'm usually never late, but I don't have my car today, so I had to take the bus, and the schedules mix me up." Despite poor English skills ("Usually never?" Which is it? Usually or never? Can't be both.) he is cute. Maybe I'll give him a shot.

"I don't like the bus either," I say. "I could never give up my car."

"I wish we had trains like in Europe. Not the expensive ones we have—costs more to take the train than fly—but the cheapo kind you jump on and go!" He's been out of the country. Interest growing.

"You've been to Europe?"

"I used to live in Brussels when I was a teenager. I traveled a bit, but I want to go back. Living in the States gets me down. Nobody has a sense of humor."

The conversation is dominated with talk of Europe and traveling: he wishes to go back and explore Eastern Europe, and I want to see Ireland, where he has been and highly recommends.

"You'd fit right in with the red hair. This one guy, little pub in Cork, called me a Viking and laughed his ass off at my accent. Couldn't pay for a drink all night!"

I barely taste my food as we continue chatting about which airline is better when traveling in Europe. He's keen on Ryanair, but I prefer using CheapOAir or easyJet to buy discount tickets.

"I never think that far ahead," he says and ruffles his longish hair. "It's better for me that Ryanair's just there to jump on."

He changes the subject to his fiddle-playing and praises his latest performance, "Had the whole theater out of their seats! I did a montage of *Fiddler on the Roof* and this new Sondheim riff."

Trying to make a joke, I ask, "If you ever go to Georgia watch out for a man dressed in black."

"Pardon?" He hasn't heard of the Charlie Daniel's Band.

"Never mind. So, Tristan's an interesting name. Did your parents get it from *Tristan and Isolde*?"

"I chose it because I liked Brad Pitt's name in *Legends of the Fall!*"

"It's not your real name?" I laugh, but it's strange. Why would he change his name?

My real name's Norman Jensen. Had to jazz it up, to stand out at auditions." The acting thing. It makes sense.

He's obviously not a very organized person. When he pulls out his wallet to pay, half its contents fall to the floor. We both bend to pick everything up, and there are euros and pound notes mixed in with American dollars.

"You must travel quite a bit to have these," I say and hand him the foreign money.

"Nope, just haven't cleaned this out in a while." For some reason I find this adorable and ignore the warning in my head: you're too neat and tidy to get along with a slob. Run! "What's the protocol for paying on a first date?"

Even this sounds charming when he flashes that grin.

"I'll pay half," I offer, but he counters, "Don't even think of it! I'm just kidding!"

There's a message from my little brother when I get home: "S'up slut? Call me!" What a kind, loving brother I have. I throw my purse down and call him back, hoping he's not in so I can avoid talking to him. I hate it when he's in a good mood and I'm feeling merely mediocre. Isn't it odd that two siblings can't be happy at the same time? Or sad for that matter? Always conflicting, I guess that's the way we're made.

He picks up, "Catering for Dummies! How can I help you?" His company's real name is McTiernan Meal. Dumbass.

"What's going on? I haven't heard from you since my birthday."

"Hey sis. I need to finish this order then I can talk." I hate it when he puts the phone down when I'm still on it, like I have all the time in the world to wait for him. Like his business is any more important than mine? Please. "I'm back! Did you hear about Dad? What a stud!"

"I heard all right. Mom called me sobbing the other day."

"She shouldn't be upset. Even Dad needs a shag once in a while." He says this in his best Monty Python voice, which doesn't resemble John Cleese even a little bit.

"You can't say 'shag,' Joel. You're not British."

"Are you the accent police?"

"Anyway, did you talk to Mom?" I'm curious what he thinks about my dating predicament but don't want to bring it up first. He'll rib me for ten minutes until I'm forced to hang up.

"She called me, hysterical of course. Said you're insensitive and don't understand her. And she's *really* pissed at Dad."

"I don't see why. She hasn't spoken to him in years. Not since Grandpa Jim's funeral."

"It's because Dad's getting *shagged*. Wouldn't you be going ape shit if you knew what Pete was doing?" The second he says it, Joel goes quiet. He hasn't mentioned Pete in a long time, but sometimes he forgets and slips. "And you're dating?"

"Nice save. I wouldn't call it dating."

"Does a guy take you someplace and pay for something?"

"Yes."

"Are you previously friends with these guys?"

"No."

"Then you're dating! Welcome back to the land of the living!"

"I wasn't dead, just retired." Even though he almost sent me into a depression vortex by talking about Pete, Joel can't help but make fun of me. "I've been on three dates since June."

"Whoa! Slow down! Hey, do you think Mom would be mad if I brought someone home for Thanksgiving?"

"Finally realize that Sergio's the one?" Sergio's his head chef and one of the most racist, homophobic people I've ever met.

"Hehe, no. Wouldn't that be a treat for his family back in the motherland? Her name's Gisele—"

"*Gisele*?" I ask.

"Shut up. And we've been seeing each other for four months. That's a new record!"

"Mom hates your girlfriends."

"She'll like Gisele. She's a ski instructor."

"In California?"

"She surfs too. But I think we might make it. I really like her."

So now Dad and Joel have a plus one for the holidays (though maybe not, because Joel's longest relationship was with our childhood dog Sparky) and I'm alone. Fun times will be had by all.

Joel seems to be thinking the same thing, "So have you gotten any lately or is it just the McTiernan men doing the happy dance?"

Curse him and his happy dance all the way to Hades.

Email: <u>FellbeeotchLinds@hotmail.com</u> to <u>Shakespearelover@gmail.com</u>

Date Four Information:

Tristan Howard: I hope you liked him, because he's still my favorite so far, though we have a long way to go and only three other guys picked out. Besides playing the fiddle and acting in a few local plays, Tristan is a regular at the Brave New Workshop improv comedy show on Sundays. You always say you want someone who's funny!

Destination: 8:00 Sunday night at the Brave New Workshop to watch his show! Surprise! It's off Hennepin, and there's a teashop nearby if you want drinks afterward.

Linds

I'm miffed about this "date." Not because I have to pay to watch the show, it's only a dollar, but because we're supposed to hang out and get to know each other. So far, I know he likes to travel cheaply, has an affinity for Brad Pitt, and no working knowledge of either classic country-rock or classic literature. How is he supposed to learn about me if he's performing to an entire crowd? Starting to feel selfish but don't care. I will cross my arms and sulk for a few minutes…

Finish sulking and am off for the theater. I get turned around because of construction and almost rear end a MNDOT truck. Life-threatening experience survived; I pull into a choice spot across from the theater. Its exterior is red and black, a bit revolutionary for my taste, and I realize I'm overdressed the second I walk in. Wearing black Bermuda shorts and a floaty pink silk top, I clash with the clientele. Most are younger than me or look younger because their attire screams street urchin. Grungy and dreadlocked, these twenty-somethings mill about the lobby and chatter like hungry birds.

There are a few polo shirts and plaid shorts, but they also stare at me like I'm the only red fish in a school of blue. Ugh. Where will I sit?

Tristan finds me at the ticket counter and says, "Glad you could make it! It's an awesome lineup tonight! I'm with Crucial Saboteurs. Grab a beer and have fun!" He is excited that I came, but he greets everyone else in line behind me in the same manner then races away, many young women and a few men leering after him. He's oblivious.

I get a Stella Artois from the surly bartender, who finally smiles when I drop a dollar in the decorated tip jar and go through the antechamber into the theater. Red and black splash the stage and walls, and I feel anticipation for the show. I do enjoy the theater but have never watched an improv show. Most comedians are too raunchy for me, except Eddie Murphy. He's hilariously dirty. I sit in the second row near the stage and sip my beer. The show starts, and the place goes dark. Everyone not holding a beer or coffee applauds, and the first group leaps on stage.

Tristan is not with this group, but they're kind of funny. Two girls who look seventeen but must be in their mid-twenties gallivant across the stage and taunt their male counterpart, mostly about his underwhelming bedroom performances. He's a good match for them, because he fires back incendiary comments about small breasts and an inability to stop nagging. I can't stop laughing and join the audience in clapping when they bow and run offstage. I can't wait for the next act.

Tristan marches onstage and introduces the next group, and he practically shines under the stage lights. He was made to act, to make people happy by performing songs, skits, or sonnets. He doesn't fumble or trip over words, and the two girls sitting next to me whisper and giggle as he speaks. As Tristan yells the next group's name, the girl next to me rises to high five him when he runs by. She leaps up and dumps her beer into my lap.

"Jesus!" I yell and jump up, running into Tristan, who bumps past me, not noticing who he hit. The girl doesn't notice that her glass is empty until she takes a sip and looks around. She sees me dripping and scowling and smirks.

"Sorry!" she says. "Bathroom's out there." How helpful. Embarrassed and soaked to my knees, I stalk through the aisles and out through the antechamber. The grinning old movie-style posters seem to point and laugh, "Look at that idiot! That'll teach her to wear silk to a comedy club!"

"Fuck off," I mutter and look for the bathrooms.

The sink basin fails to shield me, and water gushes onto my shirt and pants. I look like I went down the biggest slide at a water park.

I wait at one of the tables near the bar. The bartender feels sorry for me and hands me a towel. "Happens all the time."

Tristan finds me during the short intermission and gazes at my ruined shirt, ruffling his hair in consternation. "Here," he says and takes off his flannel shirt. It's huge on me but hides the beer stains. "Please come back in," he says. "I'm up last." He grabs my hand and I feel obligated to watch him.

"Okay. But I have to go home after. I smell like beer."

It's difficult to enjoy Tristan's part of the show, which is a "choose your own adventure" skit, when I'm soaked. I wince in my seat and move around trying to find a position where the fabric doesn't touch my skin. I hate wearing wet clothes, just ask my childhood friends. I would never go on The Wave ride at Valley Fair, because I couldn't bear being wet the rest of the day. They called me boring, but at least I was dry and not miserable.

Not at the comedy show. All I could think about was Mom's chief shopping rule: "If it says dry clean only on the tag, don't buy it." Stupid wet silk blouse. I despise dry cleaners, taking advantage of the human ability to stain everything the moment you take the tags off.

When the show ends and the lights come on, I find Tristan surrounded by admirers. The beer-spilling offender is chief among them, and she looks me up and down as I approach and snickers. Bitch.

Tristan sees me and breaks away from his flock. "Did you like it? I thought it was one of our best! Tim really had them going!" He looks so ecstatic I can't bear to tell him I didn't pay much attention.

"It was really good. The best improv I've ever seen." Though he knows it's the only improv I've ever seen, Tristan beams and grabs my hand. I feel like there should be fireworks when his fingers interlace with mine, but the only thing I notice is the way my soaked shorts ride up in the crotch. Not exactly a turn-on. I drop his hand and say, "I had a good time, but—"

"I know," he says. "There's just not…"

"Yeah." He's not upset, which is a relief. I think I like Tristan, but the sparks aren't flying. I couldn't deal with his annoying young fan base anyway. Just another guy whose work is more important than dating. "But I think we should get together sometime."

"That would be awesome! Maybe we can try that new Indian place next month!" We exchange phone numbers, and for once, I don't plan on deleting it the moment we part. Why is it so much easier to make male friends than finding a boyfriend? Is it because there's no commitment to worry about? Do we fall back into friendship to avoid intimacy? Whatever the reason, at least I have a new friend who enjoys interesting food.

August

Lolita Larry and Rule Number Three: A man's age is inconsequential, considering you're almost thirty and still have no boyfriend.

After Tristan and I part as friends, the girls decide it's time to take action. Being single now resembles being in a dog show: you have an owner, a trainer, and a groomer all ready to descend upon you if your hair is out of sorts. The judges examine you for any defect, checking eyes, teeth and undercarriage for irregularities. If one manicured fingernail is wrong, you're disqualified and forced to shamefully live out your days in a kennel with no grass.

Alicia, Lindsey, and Keeley arrive at my apartment, each carrying two bags. I'm unsure what's in any of them but prepare for the worst. Alicia brings out notebooks and planners and a few *Instyle* magazines prepared for who knows what. Lindsey has spaghetti Bolongese and salad for four and three wine bottles. Keeley is armed with makeup and hair products and fishes out some trendy clothes, looking at me then at the items. She makes contemplative noises and puts a few things aside but keeps some rather immodest skirts and one dodgy lace camisole.

"All right," says Lindsey. "I'm in the kitchen making dinner, Alicia's coordinating the next date, and Keeley's in charge of wardrobe." She takes her paper bags and disappears into my kitchen.

"Are we invading Canada?" I ask. Keeley and Alicia glare at me, as if the last two failed relationships are my fault.

"We thought you could use reinforcements, since it seems you're having such a *terrible* time dating attractive men," says Alicia, and Keeley nods in a rather condescending manner.

"Those two just didn't work out," I say and sip some wine, a nice pinot grigio. "I'm sure you three have other men hidden around the city."

"You've only got ten months left," says Keeley, making it sound like spinsterhood will be my only alternative come next May if I'm still single.

"You can say 'only' when I've reached April and had no luck."

Alicia sits next to me on the sofa while Keeley perches on the overstuffed chair and tries not to sink into it. Lindsey bangs pots and pans in the kitchen and whistles along with the radio. I keep a small radio in the kitchen for when I bake, and she's changed the station.

"Did I invite you guys over?"

"It's your turn to host dinner, so be quiet," says Alicia, and she opens two notebooks and sets them on the table. "Your next date will be next week."

"This is a business dinner? Should I put my work clothes back on?"

"His name," she continues, unabashed by my comment, "is Larry Wilkinson, and he's a lawyer."

"I thought you said no lawyers," I say and wrinkle my nose. The only people I fear more than lawyers are dentists and serial killers and not necessarily in that order. "You know I can't stand lawyers. They make me uncomfortable."

"I agree," says Keeley. "I dated this guy a few years ago who had just finished law school. He made me feel like an idiot when I didn't know what *modus operandi* meant."

Alicia nods and says, "I tested this guy thoroughly, and he's not a pretentious ass. He's in family law, deals with adoptions and child protection."

"And divorces," I add. Alicia rolls her eyes and says, "Don't get Lindsey started. She's mad enough that you chucked her guy."

"I didn't chuck him! We're having lunch next Friday!"

"You totally friendified him," says Keeley. The noise in the kitchen stops, so she whispers the rest: "That's when you're dating someone and say, 'I don't want to see you anymore romantically, but can we still be friends.'"

"I know what it means. You do that to guys all the time."

"But unlike you, I usually stay friends with them." She has a point. Keeley has more friends and long-distance pen pals than the Pope. "Speaking of friends, do you mind if I ask Justin to go dancing with us this weekend?"

"Justin *Conroy*?"

"Yeah. We've been chatting, and I think he's nice." Keeley flushes and Alicia makes herself busy fiddling with the notebooks, trying to appear disinterested. "You're just friends, aren't you? It won't be weird?" Can't think of a reason why it would be weird. Now that I think about it, Justin and Keeley make a lot of sense. She's a dreamy romantic and he likes poetry and dating beautiful women, though he doesn't make a habit of keeping them around for long. Maybe Keeley would keep his interest. Sinister thoughts of dating game reprisals float in my head, but I shake them off. Keeley's too innocent and sweet to sabotage.

"Of course, you can ask him. It's a great idea." She beams, and Alicia looks up and says, "Lindsey should be finished setting up dinner. We can discuss the fifth date when we're done."

"No sense ruining a fantastic night with dating talk," I say hopefully.

"Nice try," yells Lindsey from the kitchen. At least the spaghetti will be good.

I should have known something was up when Alicia didn't mention Larry Wilkinson's age at dinner. We talked about destination choices, and it felt nice to be involved. Alicia said it was necessary, because Larry stubbornly refused to choose a venue, and they wanted this date to stand a chance of impressing me (as if I'm some high maintenance super bitch). I chose drinks and appetizers at McGovern's in downtown St. Paul, hoping the outdoor seating might give me a lot of escape routes. Scaling a fence would be no problem for me if he started talking about lawyering, even if Keeley stuck me in her skin-tight clothing and stilettos.

I (meaning *we*) chose an outfit, jewelry, makeup and hairstyle, and though I resisted their attentions, I sort of enjoyed it. It's been a long time since my friends, and I got together and had a good conversation about relationships. Lindsey and Keeley are usually unwilling to discuss Alicia's marriage or children, possibly because they've never had either, and Alicia can't stand Keeley's whining about the awful men she dates or Lindsey's numerous conquests, be they real or imaginary. It was nice to be the center of attention for something positive, instead of being the relationship pariah.

Larry beats me to McGovern's by at least twenty minutes, because I get there with fifteen minutes to spare. Parking can be ghastly on the weekends, so I left my house with plenty of time for mulling about in traffic and waiting for people to parallel park poorly.

Keeley's clothes fit better than I thought: pale pink pencil skirt, nude lace camisole, and lilac lightweight cashmere sweater with short sleeves. Somehow the outfit makes me look tan, or it might have been that lotion Keeley gave me. I've never trusted self-tanner after the "orange ankles and elbows incident" of 2002.

The host leads me out onto the patio, which is crawling with the early bird happy hour crowd. It's mostly people over thirty who can't make it to late night happy hour anymore. Lacoste polos, pleated Brooks Brothers trousers, and stylish loafers abound, and there are nary a pair of plaid shorts in sight. Not quite comfortable in this setting, I manage to hold my head high, try not to fidget and hope I'm not sweating. I really should thank Keeley for the clothes again. I thought she was crazy when she showed me the options, but I'm a convert.

There is only one person sitting alone on the patio, but there's no way he can be my date. He looks at least fifteen years older than me, if not more. I wonder where the host is taking me. Oh shit. She's taking me right for that guy. He stands and clasps his hands, not quite looking at me but more to the side of me. I'm reminded of the movie *Rain Man* for a moment then feel terrible for the comparison. He's just nervous.

Cassandra?" He holds out his hand and finally meets my eyes. He's good-looking but nothing spectacular. Over six feet and broad-shouldered with a designer button-down shirt and linen pants. His footwear throws me off: open-toed leather sandals. I've never met a man this old who wore open-toed sandals. "Lovely to finally meet you." His voice is gentle, not what I expected either. My idea of a lawyer is booming and authoritative.

"You too." He pulls out my chair and pushes it in as I sit. *How gentlemanly.* He moves with care, graceful for a man his size, and I can see that he might be more suited to a courtroom full of people instead of with just one woman young enough to be his daughter. Or niece at least. His languid movements and soft voice might lull any jury or judge into submission.

"Have you ever been here?" I ask and wish our table had an umbrella. Even with sunglasses I shade my eyes. "The food's really good."

"I've never been. Just moved here about five months ago from Bismarck."

"North Dakota?" Another thing the girls failed to mention. I hope he doesn't catch the slip-up. Maybe he's never talked about it online.

"Yup. I joined that website when I moved here. It's easier to meet new people online these days." He pauses and looks for the server. "I thought I put that in my profile but maybe I forgot." Crap. "Once I write those things, I rarely proofread them. Do you find it difficult to write about yourself? You're writing, trying to think of all these great things you've done in your life, then you realize you haven't done all that much."

"I suppose so," I say, unable to identify with his comments. I had to write an essay about my accomplishments in my college applications but haven't navel-gazed since. "I try to be truthful. Some people make things up to seem appealing."

He nods frantically and says, "I know! And what about people who don't post pictures? I can't bring myself to talk to them, because what if they're lying? What if Amanda turns into Arthur on the first date?"

"That would be awkward," I say and smile despite my misgivings. I shouldn't count Larry out because he's a bit older than me, but I can't help feeling like Dolores Haze pursued by Humbert Humbert. I wonder if Larry's familiar with Russian literature and is thinking the same thing. Then I remember that men rarely pay attention to age unless the woman is older than them. She becomes a rabid, stalking cougar, waiting to sink her claws in his flesh. And men wonder why certain women are gay.

The server wanders over and seems incredulous about our pairing but doesn't make any comments like "what would your daughter like tonight, sir?" Too seasoned for that, the server takes our order then retreats, most likely to spread the news among the staff that there's a gold digger at table forty-one with hardly any clothes on. Suddenly feeling more self-conscious of my body than when in front of full-length mirror in department stores. I squirm and readjust my position.

"So," he says, "what do you think about the new social security bill?"

And he's lost me.

Too much wine at bar after date, had to call cab, get home, call Keeley, yell at answering machine, "why old guy terrible date who knows anything about new health care plan?" Going to sleep now, night night.

My phone rings on Saturday morning, and I'm on the couch. Why am I not in bed? Why isn't Prospero whining for food? I lift my face off the pillow, but it clings to my cheek and hurts a bit when I pull it off. I try to get up and pain shoots down my lower back. I crumple forward and tumble off the couch and into the coffee table, upsetting my books and coaster stack. They fall and crash so loudly on the floor that I moan and cover my ears.

"Shut up, phone!"

Meowing drones from behind me, and I pull myself up using the couch and look around. Everything looks fuzzy and spinny. Why can't my stupid body handle alcohol anymore? It never used to be this bad in the morning after drinking a bottle of wine. Or was it two? Counting the two glasses I had at McGovern's...no idea how much alcohol was consumed last night.

My bedroom door is closed, and the meowing becomes more agitated. Prospero can hear me moving. My phone finally quits it alarm. I stagger toward the bedroom and push the door open. Prospero speeds past me and right for his litter box in the hall closet. My poor baby! He's been in there all night! I hope he didn't poop in my closet. I trip over my strappy sandal from last night and sprawl on the floor, luckily stopping the fall with my hands instead of my face. Ugh. Must remember not to drink when relieving sorrows. But how else to relieve sorrows? Chocolate is out.

My phone beeps with a new voicemail. When I check it, Mom's voice bellows through the apartment, "Cassie? Are you there? Pick up it's your mother! Are we still on for lunch today? Cassie? Oh that girl—"

The phone cuts her off and I rub my forehead. It feels like someone's beating a drum in my brain. I lay on the floor until Prospero rubs his head against my butt. I have no clothes on, just underwear and bra. Wonder where top and skirt went. Should feed annoying feline before searching for clothing.

When I get up, I see the skirt laying on my bed, which is unmade. The sweater is on the floor next to my hamper, and the lacy camisole is draped over my bedside lamp. Prospero slept on the sweater; long silky cat hairs adorn the cashmere like fresh-mowed grass clippings. I put the sweater in the dry-cleaning pile along with my silk top from the ill-fated improv night.

Prospero scampers about and mews for breakfast.

"Enough, cat. Mommy's hungry too." My voice makes him race around faster, and I lurch into the kitchen with him at my heels. As I pour him some food, I ponder what happened last night. My laptop sits open on the kitchen counter. Maybe I wrote something in my journal. Sure enough, when I shift the mouse pad around, Microsoft Word pops up, and I read a lot of rubbish. I didn't know it was possible to slur in print. I delete the offending words (not really words but a gibberish language only intelligible by drunk people) so the girls won't get more ammunition.

I better call Mom back before she phones all my friends and co-workers to organize a search party. I also need to phone Alicia and suggest I receive accurate date information before agreeing to meet one of these suitors ever again.

I should call Keeley too and apologize for drunken ranting and ask if we're still on for dancing tonight even though I called her an irresponsible cow. Or at least I think that's what I called her, as the journal is unintelligible. Hope she forgives me long enough to let me complain about the date.

Keeley understands about the phone call. She expected it, in fact, and apologizes profusely for not telling me the whole truth about Larry.

"I thought he was a bit too old for you, but Lindsey made rule three just to include Larry in the running."

"I'm supposed to date my father's friends now? I'm not that desperate."

"He wasn't that much older than you."

"You know exactly how old he was. If I had to hear about the Rolling Stones concert in San Francisco one more time." She giggles and asks me if we're still on for dancing this weekend. I say yes and inquire if Justin will join us. When she says yes, I feel the same feelings any third wheel experiences: shame and loathing. I wish it were just us girls, but I suppose Keeley deserves a date now and again. I can't go hogging all the single men in the Twin Cities.

Dancing was great! I haven't had that much fun out with Keeley in a long time. Maybe it's because I wasn't feeling pre-date pressure and was happy not to worry about clothes and makeup. Keeley and Justin really hit it off. I think she likes him a lot, as she danced with only him all night.

Keeley found this great salsa club a few years back, and we frequent it at least once a month. The mood is low key, and the Spanish music gets everyone riled into a frenzy of spinning ladies and light-footed men. When you hear drums and horns it's hard not to tap your feet and move your hips with the rhythm.

When we go out, Keeley wears flowing skirts that twirl around her body and tight-fitting tank tops that wind up covered with sweat by evening's end. She's a popular partner, very able on the dance floor. Many men gave Justin death glares when Keeley kept choosing him for a partner. To my surprise, Justin wasn't too bad either. He spun, dipped, and danced Keeley about like a seasoned professional. They looked like a couple.

When we took a break and Justin went to grab beers, Keeley couldn't contain her glee. She grinned and kept talking about how wonderful the place looked and wasn't the music exceptionally good tonight, almost like they were playing just for us. By "us" I assumed she meant Justin and herself, but I nodded and smiled, encouraging her to keep dancing with Justin and have a good time.

Even I found some dance partners, though I'm nowhere near as good as Keeley. My favorite dancer, Dominic, was there, and we shimmied most of the night away. It felt nice having no obligation to talk to him, just dance.

Monday, after spending most of Sunday on the phone with Keeley hearing about how handsome Justin is and "isn't he a phenomenal dancer, Cassie," the man in question suggests we get lunch together. Kevin's on a short vacation, so it's just us, though Carly tries to wrestle the restaurant out of us.

"Going to lunch then?" she asks. "I always bring a lunch, but I forgot it today." She sighs and glances hopefully at Justin, knowing I'll never invite her.

"That's too bad," says Justin. "I'm sure the cafeteria downstairs is open." He grabs my arm and we head for the elevator, trying not to laugh. "She better not follow us," he whispers. "Kelly made me partner with her on this new manuscript, because it's pretty huge, a bitch to edit, and she's driving me crazy."

"I know what you mean. When she first started, Kelly assigned her to me. We got along so horribly that now Kelly never lets us near the same computer." Anyone who believes that a sentence can NEVER begin with "and" or "but" is clearly out of her mind. "The only time we see each other is in Kelly's office every morning." Which makes me wonder why she wanted to join us for lunch. Perhaps she's finally realized that no one likes her and her spurious opinions about Keats and Walden Pond.

We walk to the Asian market near our building and buy sushi, salad, and a liter bottle of sparkling water. He chooses a spot outside in the shade so we can people-watch. We sit and Justin opens two chopsticks packets and breaks them apart, handing me a set.

A woman saunters by with a well-coifed Alsatian at her heel, and Justin laughs.

"Once the State Fair starts, I'll really have some people to watch! But I guess people who dye their pet's fur to match their hair will do for now." But I'm not interested in the passersby.

"So," I say after swallowing a California roll, (God I love fresh ginger), "did you have fun with us at the club?" Mouth full, he nods, and then says, "It was really hot in there. I haven't been dancing in a long time, but I don't remember it being that hot."

"But you had fun?"

"Sure. It was nice to get out and have some beer. Let off some steam." He's not mentioning Keeley, not expounding, soliloquizing, or pontificating about her brilliance, her beauty, nor her dancing ability. Why is he not commenting on her perfect body? Her eyes? Usually that's all men can talk about when they see Keeley. Even Kevin thinks she's hot and he's not into perky breasts.

"You and Keeley looked good together. Every guy in the place was ready to take you out back and pummel you." He doesn't look at me but pours out the water in two paper cups. He's thinking about what to say, not sure how to begin. Oh crap.

"She's very sweet," is all he says before helping himself to salad. His sunglasses slip off his head and cover his eyes. "What kind of dressing did you get?"

"Sweet?" That's it? I'm so confused I don't notice the tuna sashimi fall from my chopsticks.

"And nice." I know exactly where this is going. It's what I've said about every guy Mom or Joel or my friends have tried to set me up with. They're good-looking, smart, funny, have a good job, drive a nice car, aren't bald or over forty, but they're *nice*. You never want to be labeled "nice" by someone you find irresistibly attractive. It's pre-relationship poison, like seeing "Have a nice summer" plastered all over your high school yearbook. If someone you like says you're "nice," you have no hope of sleeping with him or her, much less ever seeing him or her again. I get an image of Keeley bound up in bandages like a leper and am furious.

"She's way more than nice. She's every man's dream girl."

"Well sure," he says and shrugs. "She's beautiful. Has a great body. It's just…"

"Just?"

"I don't know how to say it," he scratches his head, looking for the right words. "Our minds don't mesh. I guess that's the right way to put it."

"You mean she's not smart? She has a bachelor's degree in psychology." Angry, savage thoughts race through my mind as the protective girlfriend gene kicks in. I'm ready to tear Justin apart if he even hints that she's not intelligent enough for him. Every woman can render a man testicle-less when her friends are threatened with slanderous words.

"She's very smart," he says, sensing danger, "just not my kind of smart." He looks bewildered, like a cornered rodent. I feel a small amount of guilt, but he needs to explain himself. "I didn't connect with her is all. No mental sparkage."

"I see," I say and focus on my food.

"Don't be like that. Haven't you said the same thing about the guys you've been dating?" I nearly choke on lettuce and pound my chest to dislodge it. His sunglasses are back on his head. Justin glances sidelong at me, a determined look in his eyes, like he's found my one weakness.

"Did Kevin let you read my journal?"

"What? No! It's just…you haven't talked about any of these guys except to say how terrible the dates went."

"So, you're *assuming* I dumped them because there was no…"

"Spark."

"Well, there wasn't." How dare he turn this bitter mental diatribe against me? I was having perfectly malevolent thoughts about him before he mentioned my dating record. He looks smug and says, "I'm sorry I didn't like her more, but I don't want to lead her on." Dammit, then he gets noble! Why can't he just let me be pissed at him?

"She likes you a lot," I murmur, and he's apologetic, saying he'll call her. "That's nice of you," I say, "but I can talk to her." We're quiet for a moment. Small birds cluster around the tables and pick at crumbs. They hope we leave behind some morsels. I wonder how the birds survived here before there was a city. How did they eat? I'm sure they had more natural foods like seeds and such. Are we making the wildlife around us unhealthy by feeding them our leftovers and garbage? Too deep of thoughts for Monday lunch.

"Why'd you agree to do this dating thing?" Justin asks, and the question surprises me. I didn't think he was interested in my love life. He hasn't inquired about the three men I've met so far, and he said Kevin didn't show him the journal.

"The girls can be very persuasive," I say and fail to mention the impending job offer dangling from Kelly's fingers.

"I didn't think you'd go along with it."

"Neither did I. It's kind of humiliating."

"How do you think the guys feel?"

"What do you mean?" I ask. Now that I think about it, I've never wondered about how the girls choose the men I'm supposed to meet. It's like ancient China where the mothers and the matchmakers joined forces and foisted arranged marriages on their children.

"It's kind of mean-spirited. Your friends talk to these guys, but they think they're talking to you. I'd be pissed if I found out the girl I was chatting with online turned out to be some female compendium fobbing me off on their friend who doesn't really want to meet me."

Well, now that he puts it that way.

"I suppose I could try harder." I thought I was giving this a solid effort but then recall constant pessimism and nicknaming of possible suitors. I should probably lay off.

He shrugs again and pours me the rest of the water before saying, "You could ask the girls to turn things over to you, so you actually 'meet' the guy before seeing him."

"I didn't think you could get to know someone just from emails. There's no way to tell what they really mean. No body language or facial expressions. Words are powerful, but most people couldn't put a coherent sentence together on paper if it would stop a nuclear cataclysm."

He reaches out and pats my shoulder, and I shake my head. This lunch has been more exhausting than I anticipated. Maybe we should have invited Carly along to relieve the tension. She would have been more fun.

"If they won't let you talk to your matches, then you should quit. At least you tried."

"I can't quit," I say, feeling miserable. "I think that's rule number twelve."

I get home to a message from Alicia: "Hey babe. No second date with Larry. He wrote the age difference might make things too difficult. Said he had no idea what you were talking about when you mentioned Rascal Flatts. Thought it was small town in New Mexico or something. Talk later. Bye."

Hurray, saved from agonizing second date. Now that I have the rest of August off, maybe I can go to the Renaissance Festival I've had to miss every year. I find whenever I have time off, I can never settle on anything and turn back to work. Fun huh?

I settle down at my desk and pull the romance manuscript toward me. I groan, knowing many "hot embraces" and "lusty feelings" await me. Reading these pages is like watching a horror movie. I keep screaming, "Don't go in there, you idiot! *He's* in there!" Only "he" is the main character's ex-boyfriend and not some deranged axe murderer. At this point I'm not sure which would be worse to run into.

I try to focus on the manuscript but am nagged by a tiny thought. I'm troubled by Justin's comments at lunch. How would I feel if I joined an online dating site, hoping to meet someone trustworthy and kind, only to be unknowingly coerced into a hostile date? How have I been behaving on these dates? Tony and Tristan both agreed to second outings, so I can't have been that awful. True, I did leave the date with Larry after one torturous hour, but that's because we had nothing to talk about except work, and I didn't get caught up in his lawyerly struggles, nor did he seem interested in what I do. I mentioned wanting to be an author when I was younger, and he nattered on about how he once wrote three hundred pages of a crime novel before laughing it off. He said, "a friend of mine offered to publish it if I could manage to finish, but who has the time for that kind of nonsense? I couldn't believe I wasted two months writing it!"

If there was a way to politely stick one's fist down another's throat and squeeze the larynx, I would have done it. It was not a good experience for either of us, and we parted with a firm handshake after I insisted on paying for my wine and quesadilla. I only became drunk and incoherent after he'd gone, and I switched bars and wines.

Maybe it's Justin's spurned male ego talking, or he's sticking up for his sex in general. Nothing like that could have happened to him…could it? Am suddenly feeling very rude and inconsiderate of opposite sex. Perhaps I can talk the girls out of this (what's the opposite of chauvinistic?) plot. I don't think I'll succeed, but I'll feel better if I try to dissuade them.

I have the feeling I'm in this for the long haul, no matter Justin's concerns. If a few egos are bruised in the process I can hardly be blamed. I'll point my finger at the girls and run.

That's a good plan, right?

Wishing I could curl up in bed or take a bath with a good book, I incline my head instead, turn to the page I left off in *Kiss and Tell* and delve back into Elizabeth Hanks's tale of love's woes and triumphs. In case you're wondering, I have yet to reach any triumphs and am wondering if finding love is all that important or integral for a full life.

Excerpt from *Kiss and Tell*, a novel by Elizabeth Hanks

Melinda knew the moment she walked through the door that someone was waiting for her. She resisted shaking the rainwater off her coat. Musky scents of men's aftershave filled the foyer, and a large black umbrella rested near the door. It had to be Jack. Who else would have a key? Melinda pondered why she had not changed the locks, because she should have known he would be back, if not for her than surely for his flat screen television. He could pry it off the wall if he wanted to, but she would be sure to send him the repair bill. How dare he come into her home?

She slipped off her kitten heels and tiptoed past the living room and dining area, hearing soft voices in the kitchen. It was a lilting opera Soprano. Jack detested classical music. She smelled bread baking and heard a pan sizzle with oil. But Jack was a terrible cook. Who could possibly be in her house cooking?

Fearing it was the gardener she fired for planting azaleas instead of rhododendrons, Melinda imagined sharpened hedge trimmers and the man's frightening laugh. Was that his voice in the kitchen or the opera's Tenor?

Melinda turned to run but then someone called from the kitchen,

"Melinda? Is that you? I hope you like Italian!"

It was Michael! Dear sweet Michael! Melinda recalled leaving the door unlocked before she went out in case Michael stopped by to set up her new shelves. She had not noticed them in the living room. But why was he still here making dinner?

The question bright in her mind, and a long smile on her lips, Melinda ambled into the kitchen and Michael stood wearing nothing but a blue paisley apron. His perfect backside rippled with muscles, and Melinda held a hand to her blushing cheek. He said, "I hope you're ready for heat tonight, because I made Linguine Arrabiata."

September

Go Green Greg and Rule Number Four: Don't sweat the small stuff.

"You did what?" I yell, and the entire bar turns to look.

"It's not that bad," stammers Keeley, shocked at my reaction.

"Not that bad?" I glare at her, and Alicia glances around at the gawkers, who quickly return to their pints and wine glasses. It's like a car accident: impossible to look away. "Not. That. Bad?"

We're having drinks at Ciao Bella in Bloomington, and despite misgivings of eating outside the Cities proper, I joined the girls for a pep talk and news of September's online model.

Fall has finally come and chased summer humidity away. The leaves are beginning to change from bright green to yellow, orange, and red, and it smells like bonfires and rain. Autumn in Minnesota is my favorite season, mainly because I can't stand intense heat or cold and get terrible allergies in the spring. It's time to wind down from a hectic summer outdoor schedule and get back to school or work, although I never stop working. Maybe I do have a problem taking time off.

I finished the first read-through of the Hanks romance and have yet to make one mark on the pages. I'll show Kelly that I can handle

Melinda and Michael's "pulsating pink sword." How that woman found so many synonyms for genitalia is beyond me.

"You'll have fun," says Lindsey. "You love Lake Harriet."

"I love sitting next to the lake with a picnic basket full of bread and cheese and wine. What am I supposed to do on a bike? I *fall off* bikes!" They all get a good snicker out of that, but I don't find it funny. The last time I rode a bike was in high school, and I fell into a ditch on the way to my boyfriend's house. "Why did you tell this guy I liked bike-riding?"

"Because it'll be good for you," says Alicia. "Trying new things never hurt anyone."

"Tell that to the Christians the Romans threw to the lions," I mutter and take a drink of pinot noir. Autumn means red wine. Yum.

"Over-dramatic as usual," says Keeley.

Aside: after my lunch with Justin where he crossed Keeley off his possible love connection list, I called her and explained that he wasn't in a good place to start a relationship. She cried and asked what was wrong with her, and why did all the good men throw her out with the garbage and the bad ones come along and fawn all over her. Was it her hips? Did he think she didn't dance well? Had she misquoted the poems she mentioned? (She mentioned poems?)

Mortified by Justin's disinterest and sure I had something to do with it, she hadn't called me until the end of August for this booze and gossip summit. She apologized for thinking I might have cautioned Justin against her and said she would never distrust me again. It was kind to let her know about Justin's feelings before she got truly attached. God, that girl can bounce back like a champ.

"What if I fall in the lake or run over a small child?"

"You won't run anyone over," says Lindsey, but she doesn't discount falling in the lake.

"If it looks like a collision's coming just stop and wait for the person to pass," says Alicia and Keeley titters in the corner of the booth.

"Does my imminent demise amuse you?"

"Only slightly."

"You guys suck," I say and cross my arms over my chest, lower lip protruding.

"It was a last second decision," says Lindsey, and Alicia and Keeley glare at her, as if this wasn't need-to-know information. I feel like a lowly private surrounded by generals deciding my fate on the battlefield. "What? She might as well know about the pre-date break-up. Could have happened to anyone."

"The what now?" Alicia shrugs and Keeley looks crestfallen. She does not look at me but says, "Pre-date break-up. It's so humiliating." She puts her face in her hands. "We had this great guy lined up for September, because we know you love fall and might be in a good mood."

"All of *this*," I say and motion around the table, "makes me crazy."

"And he seemed interested in you," Keeley goes on as though I did not speak. "And we had a really great idea for your date, but then he canceled. He said he thought it wouldn't work out between you two. He got really forceful about it actually." She finishes quickly and gulps her drink, a pink Cosmopolitan. The lemon twist almost shoots down her throat, but she chokes it back out. It plops into the glass and pink droplets fly.

"He broke up with you guys before I could even meet him?" Now that's funny. Although, if it had happened to me, I would be so mortified and pissed off that I might dive into a pint of ice cream and never surface.

They nod, Alicia and Keeley flustered and Lindsey unconcerned.

"Whatever," says Lindsey. "Forget him. Just another dickhead. Greg will be a nice change of pace. He's fit and likes the outdoors, just like you."

"My idea of "the outdoors" is probably a little different from his."

They tell me Greg Donaldson enjoys camping in the Boundary Waters and hiking through the Rocky Mountains. He's also climbed some of the most difficult summits in the world, including K2. He sounds intriguing, but if he thinks I'm trekking my ass up Mount Everest he has another think coming.

"It's just a bike ride," says Lindsey. "You're not signing up for the Tour de France."

"And how are we supposed to get to know each other while I'm screaming at innocent bystanders to get out of the way?"

"A picnic," says Alicia. "He's bringing food. You bring the blanket."

I should resign myself to this dating hell, because the girls are far more determined than I thought. I figured it might last two months, then they would give up, admit defeat. There is no sign of slowing down. I'm in for the long run, because they're not bored yet. My constant struggling has most likely made them a stronger unit, far better equipped to deal with my antagonism than I thought.

"And where am I going to get a bike?"

"From me, silly," says Lindsey, voice like poisoned honey. "Happy early Christmas." She swallows the rest of her wine. "So, don't expect anything come December."

Instead of dressing me like her life-size doll, Keeley writes a laundry list of outfits from my closet that will work for the biking extravaganza. Hoping that she chose cotton shorts, a t-shirt, and a sports bra, I shudder when I look it over:

That cute pumpkin-colored cap-sleeve top with dark wash denim capris and wedge sandals.

Rosy short-sleeve button down with brown Bermuda shorts and suede flip-flops.

Tan hippy tunic with denim skirt and espadrilles.

She wants me to wear a skirt on a bike. I have nothing more to add.

And heels. Sorry. That also had to be said.

Lake Harriet is beautiful. Part of the Minneapolis Chain of Lakes, it spans about 400 acres and three-mile bike and walking trails encircle it. Extremely popular once winter snow melts, sand volleyball courts as well as other sports fields dot the area, and beaches cater to sun bathers and swimmers. You can always see sailboats, canoes, and even yachts careening about in the water. There's a small collection of shops nearby described as "a small town in the City."

I like jogging here in the fall, because the foliage is grand, but usually wait until late September or October because of the crowds. Cyclists, runners, skaters, new moms pushing strollers, dog walkers, and high school sports teams frequent the area, making it too clogged for a relaxing run.

As I find a parking space near the Bandshell and pull my shiny new bike out of the trunk, I notice a group of Indian men and women playing cricket on a grassy area. An interesting occurrence outside Europe (or anywhere that's not the United States), I've never seen a live cricket match. I have no idea how the game is played or what the rules are, but the man in the middle throwing the ball is the bowler. Slender, with muscular arms and a steady gaze, the bowler runs at the batsman and hurls the ball. The speed, intensity, and grace of this small game are exciting, and I feel as though I'm in a foreign land instead of my city. I close my eyes, take a breath, and listen to the game's sounds. People cheer, and the teams laugh and slap hands after the batsman connects with the ball and makes his run.

"Are you Cassandra?" The voice pulls me from my reverie, and I spin around, almost losing my grip on the bike. It slides away from me, and I grab for the handlebars, but another firm hand grips the front tire and steadies it. I look up, but not very far up.

"Greg?" He stands only a little taller than me, and he might be thinner, all muscle under tight bike shorts and a fitted t-shirt. (I'm glad I chose jean shorts and a simple tank top.) His brown eyes are close-set and large, giving him a startled appearance, and his lips are thin and pale. An aquiline nose dominates his face, and I think of a yellow-eyed hawk. With those biceps and lithe body, he might be able to fly. A bike helmet hangs from one hand, and his other holds my hyperactive bicycle in place.

"That's me. Greg Donaldson." He drops the bike and reaches for my hand. A firm shake, one pump, and he's out. His hands are heavily calloused, I guess from climbing or doing some other manly thing, and he wears a thick woven bracelet on his right wrist.

Expecting someone different, damn girls and their lack of information, I fumble for words. "Cassandra McTiernan. Nice to meet you?" It comes out as a question, and I feel like an idiot. The bike makes another bid for freedom, but I grasp it in time. There is no car nearby, so he must have biked here. I wonder if he lives close by.

"Are you ready to ride? We should get moving before more people show up and take our space. There's nothing worse than trying to wade through crowds on a bike."

Ride? Already? But I wanted to practice more. Once around my block and standing on the pedals in my apartment has not prepared me for an actual ride. I must appear skittish, because he smiles and says, "You'll be fine. You said you haven't ridden in a while, so I'll go slow." I'm not sure if he's patronizing me, but I am grateful for the offer. I'm treating the bike like a bronco in the chute, and I think he can sense it.

"Do you have a helmet?" Not only do I have the most expensive and safe helmet out there, I also have shin and elbows guards. I pull them on and strap the helmet over my hair. That will be fun later. He grins at my appearance, which must be ridiculous, but at least I won't get too banged up if I crash.

"I'm ready." I straddle the bike, but it feels alien underneath me, like it might grow engines and hurl me into the atmosphere. Why did I agree to this? I find I'm saying that a lot lately.

"Let's go! It's only three miles so we can always go around a few times if you want." Off he goes, pedaling slowly and weaving across the sidewalk. He's waiting for me. Okay, hands tight on handlebars, feet strong on pedals, bike seat highly uncomfortable on butt, triple check. Whoever designed bicycle seats must have had a fat, cushioned ass, because without ample support, it's like sitting on golf cleats.

I push off and the bike breaks to the side. My feet shoot off the pedals and steady the rampaging vehicle, and I breathe heavier. Come on, Cassie. You can do this. It's just a bike. Once you learn how to do it, the knowledge never leaves. It's just latent and hiding at the moment. Hoping not to make a complete fool of myself, I set off once more, and this time nothing wobbles. It feels odd to ride a bike if you've given it up for ten years. The foreign feeling of not being encased in a car is perplexing, and I'm not sure how to describe it. Imagine forgetting how to read after years of neglect. That would be awful.

He waits for me up ahead and when I come flush with his bike, he matches my pace. The ride is leisurely, but he doesn't mind. He's looking around and taking in the scenery. A few people sit on the grass near the beach, picnic baskets open and blankets covered with cold lunches. The cricket game falls behind us, and the jubilant shouts dim to make way for kids splashing in the lake. The water's too cold for me, but us adults tire of swimming way before kids do. Birds fly back and forth across the bike path, some skimming our heads, and hated Canada geese group on either side of the path. Sometimes I think the geese are worse than pigeons, clogging up the roads in the suburbs and spreading to the Cities.

"You're doing great!" says Greg beside me, but I don't look at him. I'm afraid if I take my eyes off the road ahead, I might careen out of control.

"Can you tell I haven't ridden in a while?"

"Yeah," he laughs. "But you're fine. Riding a bike's easy. And if you fall off, that body armor's sure to protect you."

"The guy at the shop said I should get this stuff if I felt nervous about biking," I say, planning to sulk later. It's not my fault my friends have sick senses of humor. Honestly. Me on a bike? I'd rather be shopping. Why can't dates be more like buying shoes?

"I thought you liked cycling?"

"I do, it's just I haven't had much time to get out lately." I hope that covers my tracks, and Greg doesn't answer right away.

"Your bike's new too. Really nice." He sounds suspicious. Better head him off.

"Had a birthday in May. Present from a friend." Neither outright lies, but I feel terrible deceiving him. He didn't ask to go out with a head case whose cheerleading section's gone off its rocker. Better get off the subject. "You climb mountains?" I am so lame.

"Yes," he says, enthusiastic. I've hit a good subject. Maybe he'll talk through this date and we can get off the damn bikes. "I've climbed most of the big peaks in the States, a few in Central America, and K2 of course. That's the crown jewel in my collection. I'm tackling Annapurna next year, and that has the highest mortality rate of any mountain."

"Ah," I say. What would possess someone to climb something that might kill him? Avalanches, extreme cold, and no oxygen sound like tons of fun. "Do you enjoy it? The temperatures must be terrible. I'm not a heights fan."

"There's nothing like reaching a summit and staring out over the land you've covered. Just imagine an Amazon jungle or snow-covered peak. The adrenaline's unbelievable! It's mind-boggling that more people don't do it."

"Most people aren't as fit as you." He smiles at me as I look over for the first time. Maybe he's not so bad. Even if he is a bit short for my taste, he has a way with words. When I refocus on the trail my bike makes its move and I almost go down. As I struggle to right myself, something flies into my cheek and falls in my lap. I look down and hold back a shriek. It's a massive wasp. The bulging body skitters across my lap and flies up my billowing shirt, and the legs and wings tickle my stomach.

"Oh shit!" I yell and swerve around. Greg dodges me and hangs back, looking annoyed. He has no idea what happened. I'm allergic! "There's a wasp in my—"

It stings me, more than once but I only feel the first. I smack my stomach with my right fist and fail to hit it, so the damn thing sticks me again and again as I flail about trying to kill it. The bike can only take so much, and I lose my balance and fall to the side. I land on my shoulder and cry out as gravel digs into the skin and grass flies. I tear my shirt off and the wasp is gone, probably squashed but maybe royally peeved and flying away. Large angry welts cover my torso, and I realize I left my EpiPen, which is an epinephrine shot used to combat anaphylactic shock, on the bathroom sink. We're half a mile away from my car.

"That looks bad," says Greg, who stands over me, looking concerned. "Are you allergic?" Before I can answer I pass out.

I wake up to an unfamiliar ceiling and try to raise my head, but it feels like lead weights are holding it down. Ugh, what happened? Why do my lips feel puffy? Why does my entire body ache? The wasp! That bastard flew at me like a kamikaze pilot.

I hate hospitals. That's why I bought the EpiPen, so I would never have to come here after an allergic reaction. They tell you to go to the hospital even with the shot, but who wants to do that?

I'm wearing a revealing hospital gown and hope Greg didn't see me in it. How did he get me here anyway? He probably strapped my unconscious body to his back like a rucksack and biked here.

I sit up and grasp my head, but the thin plastic tube attached to my arm yanks me back in pain. Stupid IV. Stupid wasp. Stupid date. Where the hell is he? Why is no one in here with me? What if I died? And all for a blind date! Maybe the wasp is a sign that this needs to stop. My throbbing torso is evidence enough that things have gotten out of control. Even the sturdiest arguments are not going to win me over.

And I must look dreadful.

I smooth my hair down with one hand and look around. It's a standard hospital room, and I'm surprised it's private. They must have been afraid for me, because the lights are low, and the door closed. Yikes.

As I pull at the IV and wince, the door opens, and Greg pokes his head in. He glances around, sees I'm awake, and walks in, flowers in hand. How sweet! A small rose quiver, they smell wonderful and make me feel woozy again, but in a good way. There are many things a man can do to impress a woman, and flowers are on that list. Sure, they don't live long and my cat would eat them, but their simple beauty can win over even the surliest girl.

"Feeling better? It got scary for a bit."

"You didn't have to stay," I say. "I'll be okay."

"You look a little…"

"What?" Oh God I'm a monster. Why don't they give patients masks? The doctors get masks!

"Just tired. Your body's been trying to kill you for three hours."

"I've been out that long?" Crap. It was bad. A honeybee stung me in the foot on the grade school playground, and it swelled to the size of a melon. My teacher freaked out and called the paramedics. That was before the EpiPens, but the reaction was slow enough that the ambulance reached me in time. As I got older, the reaction got worse. My freshman year in college is often remembered by my family as "the year we almost lost Cassie," because I stepped on a hornet's nest when I stumbled back to my dorm, drunk off peppermint schnapps. Whoever said bees sleep during the night is nuts, because they attacked my stupid ass at one in the morning.

"The doctor said you'd be okay, but I had to wait. If I left, I'd feel terrible." He looks sheepish, holding the bouquet and swinging it back and forth like a child. "It was my idea to go for a bike ride."

"Don't feel bad," I say. "I should have brought my EpiPen thing."

"Maybe next time you will."

"Next time?" What's he talking about. If I were him, I'd get away from me as fast as I could cycle. This episode is bad juju if I ever saw it. They'll tell tales of my misfortune centuries from now: the girl who ruined perfectly good dates with her atrocious luck.

"You owe me one picnic."

My question is: if he didn't bring his car, where was the picnic basket? Because it certainly wasn't on his bike.

Mom comes and sits with me at my apartment. I'm taking it easy this weekend and even asked Kelly if I could stay home on Monday. Excited that I would take time off for myself, even if it is to heal from massive wasp stings, Kelly exuberantly said, "It's about time you did this for yourself without having to be coerced! How is the book coming?" Unsure if she means my date journal or the romance novel, I tell her, "fine." Her laughter tinkles in my ear, and she says goodbye before wishing me a swift recovery.

"Oh, pish posh, Cassie. Those don't look so bad," says Mom when I pull up my shirt to survey the damage.

"It looks like a medieval knight stabbed me repeatedly with a mace, Mom."

"Nothing a few band-aids and calamine lotion can't fix. Cheer up. You got a second date out of the damsel in distress act, didn't you?"

"This is not like having the chicken pox. And I didn't *make* that wasp fly up my shirt and try to kill me."

"Don't sulk. It's unattractive." She fluffs my pillow and goes into the kitchen to retrieve my hot tea. "Chamomile or Irish Breakfast?"

"No caffeine!"

"Really dear do you want to sleep the afternoon away? This isn't like you." Mom scrunches her nose and shakes her head when concerned or condescending. She thinks that everyone should be like her and go to work when they're sick, unless they're vomiting. Since I haven't puked in her presence it's time to get up, slap on make-up, and go to work. "You can't make money in bed," she often quotes Grandma Joyce, "unless you're a prostitute."

"I was in the hospital, and the doctor said to rest for the weekend."

"It's Monday. Fun times are over."

"He also said if I didn't feel better to take an extra day off. It won't kill me to miss one day." I can't believe I just said that. Maybe it's ire for my mother, or maybe the girls are rubbing off on me. Keeley and Lindsey think nothing of taking time away from their jobs, and Alicia was the call-in-sick queen in college. I rub my forehead and sip the scalding tea. Mom's opinion of tea mirrors my own: the hotter and stronger the better, but it burns my tongue, so I put the cup down to cool.

"You certainly wouldn't find me loafing about feeling sorry for myself," she says and sits on the over-stuffed chair across from me. She gives me the disapproving stare all mothers have in their arsenal and sighs. "What's that boy like?"

My mom has the aloof talent of calling my boyfriends "that boy" and avoiding first names. She didn't call Pete by his given name until we'd been dating six months.

"Do you mean Greg?"

"Who else would I mean?" she asks in the most obnoxious "you must not be very bright" voice.

"He's very athletic, likes to climb mountains when not rescuing me," I say and glare at her. "A bit taller than me and slim."

"Is he thinner than you?" Why do mothers have to bring up weight whenever they see their children? She tells Joel he's too thin when he comes for visits, and she swears that as I get older, I get thicker around the middle, even though my waist has been twenty-six inches around for over a year. She knows I run every morning, but she never brings that up, or how miraculous it is that I lost sixty pounds over the last three years. Why can't she talk about my accomplishments instead of recalling my downfalls?

"No. He's more in shape than I am, but not by that much. I run in the mornings, Mom. It's not like I'm overweight."

"You have a tendency to hold on to extra pounds. I'm just watching out for you, so you don't slip again."

"I won't slip. It's been two years since I was really overweight." I want desperately to change the subject, but she can't help herself. Once she's in the nitpicking mode it's difficult to stop.

"But you're still moping about Pete. All this time. You must be running away from *him* every morning when you go jogging."

"Have you been reading Dad's blog?" I ask, furious with her. She's the only one who talks boldly about Pete around me. When we dated, she couldn't stand him, but once he left she couldn't tell me enough that I let the best catch in the Twin Cities go. Bringing up Dad's love life will teach her a lesson.

"He's quite the lady's man," says Mom stiffly, rising from the chair. "He's still wound around his little tart, but now that I'm seeing someone too, I don't care who or what he does."

"Come again? You're dating someone?"

"His name is Gideon, and I met him through Connie at work," she says and primly smooths her blouse. "He's sweet and considerate and quite nimble in bed."

Mother!" Why she thinks I need to know anything about her sex life is beyond me.

"Don't be a prude. It's only sex." But she's a prude about everything else! God forbid Joel or I swore in the house or watched R-rated movies without her consent. Jesus, she never talked about her sex life with Dad, so why do I have to hear about...

"Gideon?"

"Yes. Beautiful name." I didn't think anyone would name their child Gideon outside of *Seven Brides for Seven Brothers,* but I could be mistaken. "From the Bible."

"How long have you been seeing him?"

"About two months." So right after her Dad's blog freak out. Interesting. Now they're in a dating competition? Can't I have normal parents? Don't I deserve something ordinary?

The welts on my body hurt and itch, but I fight the urge to scratch them. Is Mom making me itchier or is it just the stings? Is it possible that your family can discourage the healing process? Mom is the opposite of rest and relaxation. She wants to attack my illness and head it off at the pass. Unfortunately, she's too late to kill the damn wasp before it stung me.

"I want to take a nap now." I get up and fold the blanket on the couch. Prospero peeks from my bedroom and looks around. He doesn't like my mom. She always picks him up and messes with his ears, nose, and teeth as if she were his vet.

"Okay. Do you want me to bring you anything for lunch? I'll have a break around noon." She looks excited at the thought of catering to me, but I decline. I can only take so much of my mom when I'm ill.

"I'm not hungry right now, and I doubt I'll eat lunch."

"You should eat something. I'll pop back with some soup. Chicken noodle suit you?"

I love being part of the Fraternity of Runners. It's like a private club where only the brave may enter. Okay maybe not the brave, but at least the ones courageous enough to exercise through rain, snow, or sun. Running is almost like a religion. Not to sound blasphemous, but I'll bet more people belong to the running church than the actual church nowadays. Sorry Grandma, who's up in Heaven playing slots with Jesus, but at least I go to church at Easter and Christmas. I find more peace and serenity when racing down the sidewalk.

There is a strict sidewalk hierarchy in the city, probably on any walking trail, and being near the top is exhilarating. First come cyclists, who, as the biggest, get the right of way. Sure, they could be on the road with the cars, but I would choose life, so the sidewalk is a viable option. Next come skaters and runners. Both are faster than walkers yet slower than cyclists. Skaters often think they are above us hoofers, but they're sadly mistaken. Our sheer numbers would overwhelm them. Walkers of any sort be they with strollers, dogs, or just ambling along with earphones in, come last. Walkers are the lowest on the trail chain of importance because they're not putting out as much energy as the rest of us, nor do they have cyclist size. When a runner is coming at you, this means *you* walkers, please get out of the way. It takes focus and concentration to keep pace, and you make it difficult when we're forced to take cruise control off to get around you. I get out of cyclist's ways, so please clear the path for me. It's polite.

ou may be wondering what brought on that bitter tirade. I'll tell you why in a moment. Just one more thing about running.

It's my way of relaxing; getting the day's toxins out. I run the first three miles all out, no thoughts or troubles rolling around. The pavement feels right and true under my feet. It will never change nor judge me nor leave me alone. I may get hot or tired, but it will always be there. I like things that are constant. The last three miles are open for pleasant thoughts and daydreams. I try not to think about work, my family, or anything negative when running. It's cleansing to have one part of your day that nothing can touch.

But today my run was ruined. All I could think about was Greg and the things he said yesterday. If you can't tell, our second date did not go very well. Afterwards, I went to the drug store and bought the biggest Russell Stover's box of chocolates they had, went home, and ate every piece in an hour. Chocolate used to be my go-to depression snack, and after finishing the last truffle, not only did I feel sick, I felt like I did three years ago: sixty pounds heavier and without a fiancé.

Our picnic starts well. He brings a huge wicker basket brimming with healthy goodies: wheat bread, fresh cheese, organic fruit and veggies, and a bottle of organic wine, something I have never sampled.

We decide to avoid Lake Harriet and settle in Como Park, home of the free zoo and conservatory. I wonder if he'd like to walk around the conservatory when we finish. I love the flowers and calm atmosphere inside, and it's a school day so no loud kids and harried adults chasing them.

The sun is pleasant, about seventy degrees in the open, and a cool breeze plays with my hair. Bright leaves occasionally drop and the air smells fresh and peppery from fire-pits. It's a good day to be outdoors and away from work (I took another day off! Well, a half-day.)

He prepares everything: spreads the blanket, arranges the dishes and silverware, opens the wine and pours half glasses for us, so it doesn't get too warm.

"You have to try the wine with this Gouda," he says. "It's amazing." He places the cheese and knife in front of me, and I cut a small slice, ready to savor the flavor. It's wonderful by itself, creamy and not too salty, but the white wine shows it off perfectly.

"Mmm, this is great! I haven't had cheese and wine alfresco in a long time."

"That's a crime," he says and pulls another cheese wedge out of the basket. "I try to eat outdoors as often as I can. It feels free, I suppose." He slices the bread and inquires to my jam preferences: "There's no strawberry allergy I hope?"

"Nope. Only insects with stingers," I laugh and grab the jam jar. "You should see the pictures of me from freshman year when I trampled a hornet's nest."

"Was someone there to save you?"

"Kind of. My roommate dragged me to the infirmary, but no one was there, so she had to call an ambulance. I would have gotten into a lot of trouble for underage drinking if I hadn't almost died!" He gives me an odd look but doesn't say anything. "We had a laugh about it later, but she was freaked out for months. Wouldn't let me set foot outside without an escort."

"Do you like the wine?" he blurts, and I'm taken aback. Did I offend him?

"Yes, it's wonderful. I've never had organic wine. I suppose I should switch but it's expensive."

"If more people bought it, it wouldn't have to be so expensive," he says, almost chastising me. "The same goes for organic produce. It's only expensive because so few people are willing to throw out the processed junk and treat their bodies respectfully."

"You could look at it that way. Some people simply can't afford it."

"They could afford it if they avoided fast food chains and other restaurants." We're silent for a moment and I contemplate the bread. It tastes good but keeps sticking in my throat. The jam is very gooey.

"You don't like to go out to restaurants?" I ask, hoping it's an innocent question. You can't live in the city and not enjoy restaurants. There are so many to choose from with exquisite food. Not every place uses poor ingredients and high fat oils.

"Never. Restaurants need to make money, so they use cheap ingredients to get away with bad flavor. I have my own vegetable garden and have fruit delivered from growers all over the country. I don't trust most local produce."

"But we're a farming state," I counter, and he gives me an "oh please" look. "There has to be some good food here. There's a huge farmer's market in St. Paul and it has tons of organic stuff."

"I'd rather grow my own to be safe. You never know what those farmers are really using on the crops. If I found out even one apple had pesticide on it…" he mimes throwing up, and I'm shocked by his stubbornness. I get food from the market all the time and I'm fine.

"I eat out a lot but try to stay healthy."

"I'm surprised you're as fit as you are," he says and looks me over, unsure if I'm telling the truth. If I eat at restaurants I must be depraved.

"I run in the morning."

"That's it? No weight training or other cardio?"

"Nope."

"I find running dull. Especially in the gym. A treadmill doesn't take you anywhere."

"I only use the gym once the cold gets too bad in winter."

"But that's six months out of the year," he says, incredulous. "I don't know how you can stand it. Even running outside is so boring. My mind wanders. Now, cycling is more intense. You have to be focused to cycle at a competitive level." And running doesn't take focus?

"I find running therapeutic. Almost cathartic. What I can't understand is why people become gym rats. Exercise takes over their lives so nothing's left, but calories eaten, calories burned, and muscle tone."

"I suppose you belong to one of those open-all-night energy hog gyms too," he says, disdain dripping from his lips. What in the hell is he talking about? "And you waste energy by using air conditioning?"

"Do you leave your lights off all year long to conserve energy?"

"Of course not—"

"Then don't bash my air conditioning. We pale people don't like extreme heat." My argument is shoddy, but I'm getting angry. What right does he have to criticize me? About air conditioning? Maybe if I were a small third world country dictator hording all the AC then I could see his point.

"I don't either, but you don't see me polluting the planet just to keep cool. Wear shorts or something."

"Even with *shorts on* it's too hot in my place," I seethe, waiting for his reply. Obsessive people make me crazy. If it's not "we should all go back to being hunters and gatherers," it's "we're killing the planet by turning on a fluorescent light bulb."

"You should try harder. The more people turning off that unnecessary equipment the better."

Fed up, I say, "Where is all this coming from? I didn't do anything to you."

"You're an admitted criminal who probably dines at the *Olive Garden* once a week and uses air conditioning even though it's bad for the environment." He shudders, as if I'm a super villain bent on world domination. And the Olive Garden's not that bad, it's just not that good either.

"Criminal?"

"You said you stepped on the hornet's nest when you were drinking underage. You get fined for that and ticketed. Doesn't it go on your permanent record?" So that's what set him off. He's probably never committed any violation his entire life.

"And you've never made mistakes?"

"Never." That's foolish. No one's perfect. People make mistakes. I'll bet even Mother Theresa had closet skeletons.

"You've never smoked a cigarette or shoplifted? Never blew some girl off because she wasn't a vegetarian or something?"

"Aren't *you* a vegetarian?" he asks, arms crossed in a defensive posture.

"Hell no. Aside from a brief junior high delusion. I love steak."

"I knew it," he says triumphantly. "You lied on your profile." Uh oh.

"I never did. If you took something out of context it's not my fault." I stand and grab my purse, upsetting my wine glass. A dark stain spreads across the checked fabric. I hope it attracts ants. "I feel bad for any Sherpa who tried to get you up a mountain. Imagine trying to get your fat head up the Himalayas." I spin and walk away.

"You didn't seem this combative in your emails," he yells after me. Asshole.

"Maybe you should say you prefer submissive women in your profile," I say over my shoulder.

There must be a marathon or a fun run going on, because everyone in the Twin Cities is getting in my way this morning. I run at the same time every day, and it's never this congested. But today someone radio-trafficked all pedestrians to stand on the sidewalk and chat or walk on the wrong side of the sidewalk. It's like a road, people! This is not England! Move! Get in the correct lane!

My usual calm is replaced by a slow-burning rage that may explode onto whomever I meet next. I swerve around a pair of nannies pushing strollers along as if it were mid-afternoon. A hotel dog walker surrounded by labs, poodles, terriers, and mutts is dragged across my path, to and fro without apology. She glares at me when I become entangled in the leashes and almost fall. Extraction takes ten minutes, and when I finally start running again, I've lost my rhythm. What in the hell is up with people today? A meandering bicycle couple push me over the edge, and I race past them and cut back into my lane. They yell something after me about being more careful, and I feel like turning around and breathing fire at them. Fuck you.

All I ask for in the morning is some alone time, with maybe a few other runners here and there to greet as I run by. This early morning circus is completely uncalled for, especially after yesterday.

After eating the chocolate, I purchased last night, I went online and signed up for one of those free online dating sites. I wanted to see what the hell men want, because I ruined things with Greg, and I have no idea how I did it. Maybe he liked me because he saved me. I was vulnerable, and he could help me. The typical white knight syndrome? Is that what men are most attracted to? Someone who needed saving? Someone easily dominated? I had to find out.

The tacky website with its bold type and advertisements for other singles sites had hundreds of profiles. A single girl could find any type of guy she wanted, or so it claimed. I wondered if there are as many women signed up but don't have time to check the bisexual box and look. There were too many profiles to go through.

Most men had a long list of traits they wanted a prospective girlfriend to have: funny, out-going, athletic, slim, full-figured, blonde, good sense of humor, fun, truthful, trustworthy, caring, thoughtful, likes sports, watches hip TV shows, doesn't smoke, drinks occasionally, and intelligence. Pretty much every guy listed "intelligence" as one of his main attractors.

That last one threw me, because if that's what men want then why don't more intelligent women have boyfriends. You see career women divorced or alone because they became more successful than their husbands. Women like Keeley with college degrees and oodles of smarts don't appeal to the same type of guy: those college grads want nothing to do with her once they get past her looks and hear her thoughts. And I'm no genius, but whoever made me didn't leave out the brain. I see myself as a fairly smart person; at least I can keep up mentally with most people, except theoretical physicists and math majors. When I dated in college, guys told me how smart I was right before they dumped me. I was good for a bar trivia team but too daunting to go out with. Pete said the first thing that attracted him to me was my smile, then my brain, but he's gone too. Greg wasn't impressed with my independent thoughts and basically said he wanted someone who wouldn't challenge his opinions or beliefs. I'm up for a good debate, but people who won't see another's point of view bother me. Greg didn't like my brain. He wanted me to remain the wasp-stung, nervous-on-a-bike maiden, someone he could sweep off her feet and carry along with him.

I logged off the site, shut down my computer without writing in my journal about Greg, and went to bed early. Tomorrow's run would help ease my agitation.

Except it doesn't. The line outside Minnie's is so long it snakes out onto the sidewalk, and the customers block my path. Seriously, I think as I weave around them on the street, what are people thinking today? Is it a full moon?

An SUV jockeying for a close parking space nearly creams me and honks when I rush past, the passenger flips me off. I don't think it's going to be a very good day. My run is ruined, all I can think about is Greg and his outlandish complaints. I realize on the way home that I'm angry with myself for letting Greg get to me. I haven't been this irate since May when the girls sprang The Plan on me. Are the four failed dating attempts getting to me? Is there something wrong with me? I need to go somewhere I'm appreciated and talk with people who know me well and care about me.

Time to go to work, where at least some things still make sense.

"How is *Kiss and Tell* coming along?" asks Kelly. I stand next to Justin, Carly, and Joe in her office with portfolio and notes in hand. They glance at me, and Carly chortles under her breath. She's working with Justin on the enormous dramatic piece by Carlos Ruiz and is almost finished with the first edit. Joe has gone over his piece about whale watching off New England and is ready for another assignment. I feel uncomfortable with my manuscript and still haven't put a mark on it.

"Everything's going well," I say, trying to cover my embarrassment. I don't have anything to show Kelly besides a few handwritten notes. Carly whipped out a huge binder at the meeting's beginning and went into a twenty minutes monologue on how she and Justin have managed to condense one thousand pages down to eight hundred and still can cut more. Justin rolled his eyes and looked at me, begging for assistance, but I couldn't help him. Carly's his problem until they finish the manuscript. He didn't shave this morning and is looking rather rugged. I mimed choking and he suppressed a laugh.

I'm not laughing now.

"Do you have anything to share?" asks Carly, feigning sweetness, and Kelly clears her throat and says, "It is a difficult book to get through. A lot of work must go into it, and Cassandra is the perfect one for the job." Whew. At least Kelly stands up for me. Stupid Carly. I'm surprised she didn't have a PowerPoint presentation. "I expect to see your first revisions by Friday, Cassandra. Justin and Carly, you are both doing an excellent job. You three can go. Joe, I've got a new batch of essays for you."

We shuffle out and Justin mouths, "Lunch?" I nod and turn for my office. Kevin is back from vacation, so it's time for a "Three Publisheers" luncheon meeting. We fight for justice and protect Editing Queen Kelly from harm and slander.

I work on *Kiss and Tell* until noon, and Kevin peeks in. "You ready? Mountain Man over there wants to try the new sushi place down the street."

"Why didn't he shave today?" I ask and giggle. Kevin shrugs and says, "Maybe he lost his razor. Maybe he felt like channeling the Brawny guy. I have no idea. Ask him yourself."

"I will," I answer, a haughty lilt in my voice.

"So prim and proper, Miss Cassandra. The only editor who can handle rough sex and romance."

"Shhhh! What are you talking about?"

"*Kiss and Tell*. Isn't it racy and divine! What are *you* talking about?"

"How do you know it's racy? I'm the only one besides Kelly who's read it."

"I've read everything Elizabeth Hanks has written, so if there aren't some juicy scenes in the new one, call me straight and set me up with your sister."

"I don't have a sister," I grumble and grab my purse. "And the sex scenes aren't that good. I've read better."

"Bet you haven't *had* better." What a dick.

Justin looks shifty beside the elevators, and he keeps glancing left and right as if something is hunting him. "Hurry up," he says. "Carly's been hounding me about taking her to lunch since I got here this morning. Says we need to talk more about the Ruiz manuscript. She keeps cutting good stuff and I have to fight to put it back in."

The editor's dilemma, what to cut and what to keep. Some editors, like Carly, have no feeling for a work; they cut everything that seems superfluous and move on, like a glacier stripping a mountainside. I don't think she reads the manuscripts but combs them for errors then moves on. If a passage is in passive voice, for instance, she changes it automatically, where Justin or I might look at the sentence, tinker with it, then realize the author had a reason for writing the sentence that way, because there are no other passive voice sentences in the chapter. Editing is a difficult process, because we often cut the writer's favorite words or change things he or she desperately wants to keep, but we are necessary. If every writer got to keep all material in his or her work nothing would sell. Books would break shelves from excess adjectives and adverbs. But if Carly had her way, the most exciting and different parts of people's works would be cut away like spilt ends.

"Poor baby," says Kevin who grabs Justin by the tie and drags him into the elevator. "At least you don't have Cassie's problems. Too much sex," he whispers at the end.

"Not enough plot is more like it," I fire back, and Justin smiles.

"Romance novels don't need plot, hon," says Kevin. He ticks things off on his fingers: "The reader should laugh, cry, get horny and feel happy by the end."

It's certainly making me cry."

"About the narrator's misfortunes or run-on sentences?" asks Justin.

"I hate you both."

We walk to the sushi place and order an obscene amount of California rolls. Before digging in, Kevin asks, "How did the second date with Sir Gregory go?" I have yet to write about the second date, and the girls are getting antsy about lack of reading material. Kevin has been more patient, like a five-year-old who wants a sucker opposed to a two-year-old. "I don't have time to wait for your next tome, so spill."

Justin loads his plate with green wasabi and mixes it in his soy sauce, but he doesn't look at Kevin or me, disinterested. His inattention surprises me, since he was so keen to chastise me when we last had lunch.

"It didn't go as well as hoped," I say and grab a roll. The tiny crabmeat morsel pops out and lands next to my plate. I pick it up with chopsticks and stab it back into the roll, which makes the avocado and cucumber slide out. "Get in there!"

"I see," he says and glances at Justin. "It didn't go well."

"We got in a fight about organic food and energy conservation." Justin chokes on his food and Kevin roars and grabs his stomach. "It's not funny!"

"It so is!" says Kevin, and the server walks past with a raised eyebrow. Keep it down, he implies, this is not a feeding trough.

"It was stupid. I lost my temper. Although he was a huge pompous, arrogant ass whose penis is probably proportionate to his height."

"Did you know it saves more energy to keep your lights on at all times rather than turning them off when you leave the room?" asks Justin, and Kevin and I leer at him. Crestfallen, he looks down at his food and shrugs, "Just a thought."

"That can't be right," I say.

"I'm sure it is, even if it sounds weird," says Justin, who brightens at my reply. "There was a show on about it a while back—"

"Off topic," interjects Kevin. "We're discussing Cassie's love life."

"I'd rather discuss energy conservation with Greg again." I drop my chopsticks and one rolls onto the floor. Justin rises to get me a fresh set, and Kevin eyes him with suspicion.

"Have you noticed anything different about that boy?"

"No," I say. "Why?"

"It's nothing, maybe." A thought forms in Kevin's mind, and I watch it unfold in his facial tics. First, he narrows his eyes and stares off into space, his lips purse together and he licks them, then he nods slightly and looks back at me. "Do you think he's into Carly?"

"What? That's preposterous, and I mean that in a using-a-big-word kind of way. He can't stand her."

"Or is that what he wants us to think?" Kevin rubs his chin like a cartoon villain and says, "What if he slept with her and is trying to avoid her? Maybe that's why he looked panicked in the office." Kevin with an idea is not a good thing. If he's right, he'll act so superior you'd think he was the Queen of England. Even if he's wrong, he'll prance about the office and taunt you with his implied knowledge. It drives me crazy when he says he has a secret, because I never know if it's true or not. His hunches hit home occasionally, which makes him infuriating.

"You're nuts. He'd never touch Carly," I say and shudder.

"Just because you hate her doesn't mean everyone does. Bobby in marketing banged her two months ago, and remember Glenn who got fired last year? They hooked up all the time."

"Ewwww. Why?"

"Because she's hot *and* easy."

"She is not hot. And Justin's not into *easy*." Kevin laughs, and I feel like a naïve virgin who finds out that French kissing has nothing to do with traveling to Paris.

"Every guy is into easy," he says sagely and sips his green tea. "If I were straight, I'd take a whack at her."

"All men are pigs," I say and throw up my hands. "I might as well give up and become a spinster."

"If this were Victorian England, your tombstone would read: dead before thirty with no marriage prospects." I throw my napkin at him as Justin comes back.

"Now do you need a new napkin?" he asks, frustrated. He gives me the chopsticks packet.

"No, I'll be fine."

"What are you two talking about?" He sits and digs into the sushi, eyes intent on rice and pink ginger.

"Your beard," I say quickly before Kevin can bring up Carly.

"Thought I'd give it a try," he says and rubs the stubble. His hair grows fast! He must get a one o'clock shadow. "What do you think?"

Kevin says, "Did you know a man's facial hair growth is linked to his sex drive?" It's Justin's turn to stare, and Kevin says, "What? And your lights on all day theory wasn't bizarre?"

"I had a date last week, and she mentioned that men with facial hair are sexier." Justin had a date? When was this and why wasn't I informed? He used to ask Kevin and me for advice all the time. Not that we're experts, Kevin's a serial dater and I'm more of a terminal non-dater, but at least he shared with us. The thought of women finding Justin sexy is odd, and I rethink Carly's behavior. Maybe she's trying to get Justin's attention.

"It went well?" asks Kevin, but he looks at me.

"Better than Cassie's date apparently."

"And? Any fireworks?"

"We had a good time, and I'm seeing her again next week."

"Well," says Kevin, "at least one of us is getting laid." Justin's mortified face is enough for me to ask the server for our tab, who has it with him already.

"Any dessert?" he asks, knowing that if we say yes, he may go on a murderous rampage.

"Not today, thank you."

"So, Captain McBeardy Pants," says Kevin behind me in a singsong voice, "how exactly does one become a tuna boat captain?" Lift palm insert face.

October

Creepy Kenny and Rule Number Five: You will dress up this Halloween and you'll like it.

I gape in horror at my costume. There is no way in hell I'm wearing that monstrosity. Absolutely not. Even when I was sixteen, I wasn't tarty enough to put that on. Who do the girls think I am? Might as well ditch my job and join the Bunny Ranch, because that's where I'll be sent if I leave my apartment with that on.

The girls find it hilarious. Lindsey's costume is not much better: black latex cat suit with thigh high stiletto boots and black cat ears. Keeley is adorable as a sluttier version of Glinda the Good Witch, pink wand and crown glistening and strawberry blonde wig curled to perfection. Alicia can't come with us when we go out on Halloween. Kids tend to come first, Halloween parties far distant. She's wearing the same thing she's worn since her first son Mickey was born: a long white sheet with a hole for her head to go through and a white mask. I'm not sure if she's a ghost or the Lone Ranger if he joined a cult. She makes her kids' costumes every year, so it's impossible for her to focus on herself. Her husband attends his swanky office party and leaves Alicia to take the kids around their neighborhood. I've only mentioned Mickey so far (I'm a bit biased, since I'm his godmother) but the other two are okay. Mickey is six and can almost have conversations that last more than five seconds. His greatest accomplishment to date is the recitation of the alphabet. Her middle child, the only girl, is Beth, and she's three. She looks like her father but has her mother's attitude. She organizes her stuffed animals before bed each night and cannot stand if her room is messy. The boys drive her crazy. Adam is two and definitely in the "terrible" years, but he's been a terror since he was born. He's a hair-puller, and face puncher, and a screamer. Alicia ignores him whenever he makes a fuss, which worked with the older kids, but Adam couldn't care less who's listening to him. He just likes to hear himself screech like a demented barn owl.

Back to my ensemble. The girls bought it early this year, prepared to take me out somewhere "fun." My idea of Halloween hijinks involves a lowball glass, a bottle of scotch, and some sandalwood candles. Maybe I watch the *Charlie Brown Halloween Special*; who can resist The Great Pumpkin?

The lime green bodysuit covered with shiny, sequined leaves and branches sits on my bed, and I feel it staring at me, daring me to measure my thigh circumference to be sure they'll fit through the leg holes. Matching tights and bicep-length finger-less gloves lay next to the suit, and knee-high darker green boots are heaped near the bed. Keeley said she'll do my makeup, as I can't be trusted with glitter eye shadow. I'm Poison Ivy, or so Lindsey said. She wanted me to match her for some reason and was quite miffed when Keeley refused to be Harley Quinn. She wanted us to be the villainous trinity from Batman. I never even knew she liked comic books. Keeley will clash with us, though she insists Glinda is heinous in *Wicked*, and while I agree she was a manipulative bitch in that book, she doesn't measure up to the Joker's right-hand lady. But they're both relatively covered, albeit in skin-tight outfits. Mine looks like a one-piece swimsuit with accessories, afterthoughts when the person that designed it realized she looked like a greenhouse hooker. Lindsey says it will look smashing and shut up, it's rule five and you're going to have fun dammit.

If they give me a few shots before we go out, maybe I'll have a good time. Maybe they'll squeeze my suddenly massive body into that damn bathing suit. Why do thoughts of swimsuits and skimpy Halloween costumes send even the most toned women into hysterical suicidal thoughts? There's nothing worse than knowing you're fit then seeing saddlebags appear out of nowhere attached to your thighs like enormous leeches. I steer clear of dressing rooms during spring for this reason. The three bathing suits I felt were necessary for an impromptu spring break vacation two years ago linger in my lowest drawer under the lingerie I never use and the bandanas from my 5k races.

Halloween is not for two weeks, so I'll beef up my body a bit. Maybe I should go back to my old gym. It would be like greeting a friend thought lost at sea. I haven't set foot in a gym outside winter months since I lost the depression weight.

I fold the costume gingerly, wince, hold it at arm's length and toss it onto the dresser where Prospero can't lay on it. I may not like the costume, but Lindsey would be hurt if I told her it "accidentally" fell on the floor and Prospero "unintentionally" chewed the sequins off. She's shelled out a lot of money for me this year: the dating site, my ill-fated bike, and now this barely-there costume. How can something so tiny cost so much? The beadwork isn't even that great.

Email: Aliciasweetheart@sojourn.net to Shakespearelover@gmail.com

Date Eight Information:

Kenny Castlereigh, 28 years old, is a private business owner. He buys and sells rare antiques and has five stores in the Midwest. He hasn't attempted to sell us anything, so thumbs up! He likes comic books, especially illustrated classics like Treasure Island, which is also his favorite book. He reads! Hurray!

Destination: meet at his store downtown at noon and go for a walk through Nicollette Mall. Maybe stop for lunch in the area. It's a month for surprises and being open-minded. Kenny sounds unique but well-rounded in his emails. And here's your profile. We never told Greg you're a vegetarian, so I have no idea where he got that idea. Delusional? Possible deranged narcissist? It's definitely one or the other.

Love, Alicia

Username: CitiesOracle

I am a hardworking, spunky, stubborn redhead who's tired of trying to meet people in bars. I'm using this website to date casually, not necessarily to find a relationship, but you never know what can happen. If I find the right person, I'd be ready to settle down.

I drink occasionally and enjoy beer and wine in particular. Smokers need not email me; it's a major deal-breaker. Also, no lawyers.

I have a large extended family and one cat, Prospero.
I like running and staying healthy, reading, writing, dancing, dining out, baking, and traveling. I lived in Europe for a time, mostly around France and England.

My ideal first date includes dinner at an interesting restaurant. I'm pretty adventurous when it comes to food, and I expect my partner to share this interest. Ordering chicken fingers off the kid's menu at an Indian restaurant is a huge no-no.

I hope to meet some nice people and perhaps form some great friendships. I hope to hear from you soon!

The profile is good if a bit trite. I sound slightly like an aged Girl Scout, but guys like uniforms, right? The profile doesn't reveal too much, which I appreciate. I wish Alicia had slipped and revealed what website they signed me up for. I suppose I could go through each one and type in the username, hoping I picked the right password. That would take ages, so the thought leaves quickly. I also wonder why Greg thought I'm a vegetarian. Maybe he was trying to catch me lying. He seemed suspicious on our first date when I didn't take off on my bike like Lance Armstrong, but the girls would never embellish my accomplishments. Unless they really wanted to seal the deal with Greg. His profile must have been impressive, mountain climber and all-around douche bag aside. Sigh. I'd better choose my eighth date outfit. It's getting a lot easier now that I'm not expecting much. I don't think this is going to work. How can I possibly find my perfect match if I don't even know who I'm meeting?

I'm skeptical about October's match. When I picture someone who owns an antique store, I see a Max Von Sydow character: tall, gaunt, white hair, sly knowing smile. Old. The only people I've met that ran antique stores were ancient, able to appreciate their wares. How can someone my age enjoy collecting and admiring stuff from the 1900s?

But I'm one hundred percent wrong.

The "antique" shop is more of a vintage swap meet, but elegant. When I arrive to survey the sight, the large windows display mannequins wearing fashions from the 1960s, 70s, and 80s; a flash of Jackie-O sunglasses, neon colors, and bell-bottomed blue jeans.

Although the styles clash, the set-up meshes them together effortlessly, as if each decade is fusing into the next to make new statements. Whoever designed the displays has a keen eye for what was best about the last few decades' fashions. Each mannequin stands amidst items of interest from the last few decades. The A-line two toned mini-dress frolics with a 60s mod television, Beatles records on an old turntable, some tall white go-go boots, and vivid tulips. The head-scarfed, bluejeaned model sits next to sunflowers, pictures of Jimmy Hendrix and Janis Joplin, a pale pink guitar, and kitschy porcelain figurines. The flashy 80s ensemble (model complete with leg warmers) looks like Olivia Newton John's apartment exploded: the white backdrop sets off intense neon blue, pink, and yellow splatter paint as well as a puppet from the movie *Labyrinth*, Madonna-style beads and crosses, and an ancient eight track player and a BetaMax player whose slot pops open. We used to have one of those in our old house. I wonder where it went. Dad probably sold it long ago, but knowing his magpie tendencies, he might still have it.

Wow. I might get along with this guy, especially if he engineered these displays.

The inside is just as miraculous. It's filled with oddities such as metal movie posters, western novels with browning covers, and feather boas made with actual feathers. Most of the counters are glass-covered, so the merchandise must be expensive. There are a lot of browsers. People wander from corner to corner and caress the items with their eyes. One appreciative man stands in front of a gorgeous black and white piano with his chin in one hand and the other hand tapping his thigh. There are no price tags.

"Cassandra!" shouts a voice across the shop. The customers turn and stare, but when they see who is striding through them, they all return to the antiques. Kenny Castlereigh is enormous. My grandpa's phrase "built like a brick shithouse comes to mind." He stands well over six feet and reminds me of a Vikings linebacker. Did the girls say he played college football? He is muscular, not flabby, and has a pleasant, round face.

"Kenny?" He reaches out and grabs my hand, shaking it roughly.

"Ken Castlereigh at your service, ma'am. It's nice to finally meet you!" His voice booms through the store, but no one minds or looks at him after their initial glances. He must be this exuberant all the time. His two spectacled clerks go about their business chatting with customers, none of whom approach Kenny. His apparel is slightly off-putting as well: a tailored, double-breasted pinstriped suit with black wingtips and crisp silk tie. The tie has a scene from an X-Men comic on it. Wolverine's yellow head peeks out from the closed suit jacket.

"It's great to meet you too," I say. "Your store is extraordinary."

"Thank you!" He beams down at me, and I wish I had worn heels instead of flats. "It's taken me years to get it just the way I want it, and I rotate the window displays monthly. I was going to put up something for Halloween, but the set-up just didn't speak to me. I'm not into fake ghosts and witches."

"It looks great. Very creative."

"That's me to a T! Shall we walk a bit? Around lunch I always leave the store for a few hours to take in the city. I'm stuck inside so much; the boys say I need to get out more." He nods toward his clerks who glance in our direction and wave.

"Sounds good to me," I say and move toward the door.

We walk outside toward Nicollet Mall, which is a large indoor high-end shopping center. He talks constantly, about many different subjects from his store, to his family, and interests.

"Do you think I'd make a good super villain?" he asks when we stop for an iced coffee.

"A what?"

"A super villain! Like Lex Luthor or Magneto? I've always wondered what it would be like to be an evil mastermind!" He twitches his fingers together and tries to look sinister, but his toothy grin betrays him.

"I suppose," I offer, not sure what he wants to hear.

"My name's already alliterative, so I've got that going for me."

"Kenny Castlereigh doesn't sound too threatening," I laugh, and his face lights up.

"I would go by Kenneth Castlereigh until I found a decent pseudonym. And you could be my sidekick!" Sidekick? Right. Like I'd play second banana to anyone.

"I think I'd branch out and create my own evil empire." Kenny booms with mirth, and I'm reminded of Tree Beard from the *Lord of the Rings*. I wonder what makes people so jolly then remember when my uncle played Santa Claus at the Maplewood Mall years and years ago. He told my mom—(he didn't see me listening around the corner)—that he hated being nice to so many people, that it was really hard to keep up that kind of energy. His face hurt each night from smiling.

"A female super villain would be interesting! I suppose Poison Ivy is the most able in the DC universe. Cat Woman doesn't really count since she's a fence sitter." He raises his eyebrows up and down and few times and leers at me, as if he's imagining me as the botany-obsessed villainess. Weird, my costume has come back to haunt me, and I picture myself adorned in green sequins and leather.

"I think I'd be more of a power suit girl and run a corrupt corporation."

"Sure! That would be interesting! Say, would you like to meet this comic book artist I know? He could draw you in character!"

"Umm…"

"He's already done mine! It looks great! I don't have a costume either. It's more like what I wear now, a suit and tie." I'm not sure where he's coming from now. It's a bit strange. Not the usual first date talk.

"Maybe some other time," I say and pick up speed. "Where should we stop for lunch?"

"We can go back to the store. I sometimes go out, but I brought lunch today." He put his pointer finger in front of his lips. "Don't tell the clerks. They'll scold me!"

I thought we were going to lunch, or that's what I took from our conversation in the shop. Weren't we supposed to go to lunch after walking around?

"I suppose that would be fine."

"Good! We can eat in my office! I made couscous and homemade hummus!" I didn't know you could make hummus by yourself. I suppose it's possible; just get a bunch of chickpeas and go to town.

"Let's get back then. I have to meet my Mom later this afternoon." A lie, but Mom won't mind. She'll never know. I use her as an excuse to get out of a lot of things.

"Oh. I thought you were hanging out in the shop for a while." He sounds put out, but the email said nothing about "hanging out" at his work. What would I do if I stayed at the shop besides browse the aisles? I would never bring a date to my workplace. It would be really boring. I never understood bring-your-daughter-to-work days, because what kid wants to be stuck in an accountant's office or box factory all morning and afternoon? Sure, if your dad was a firefighter or a cop…but I doubt they let the kids see anything cool.

"I can't. I promised Mom I'd take her for coffee and chat." I shrug as if saying, "What can you do? It's my mom."

"Okay. But you will stay for lunch." It's not a question, but I treat it as such.

"Of course. It sounds good."

"Great!" he says and tries to put his arm around me. I angle away, but I don't think he noticed. "You're going to love it." He sounds so sure of himself.

Dad wants me to meet Sandy, his girlfriend, today. I'm not sure what to do or say. He's never been with anyone but Mom, or anyone I've met at least. What conversations could we have? Two grown women with nothing but my Dad in common. He's not the best talker either, especially when he's in an uncomfortable situation. My dad likes predictability. The easiest things for him to hang onto are traditions, nothing spontaneous. But he has the blog, and he's met this woman, so my perceptions of Dad are thrown.

He decides on our usual spot, which kind of pisses me off. That's our place. Even Mom understands the sanctity of Chelsea's Cafe. Dad has no idea this hurts my feelings, it's just his normal personality taking over: when we get together, we go there, so why wouldn't we go there now?

I arrive first and get a table outside. It's still nice out, for October, and the café has a few spots next to the building where they're shielded from the wind. I look over the menu and spy my favorite autumn treat: pumpkin pancakes. I cannot get enough pumpkin in October and November. I try to think of something clever to say to Dad about pumpkin and pancakes mixing together, because he usually finds such combinations preposterous.

I see Dad walking hand in hand with a short, thin blond. She's sprightly, dressed in trouser-cut jeans, a yellow three-quarter-length cardigan and fashionable sneakers. She's Mom's opposite in every way. Mom stands five eight and has broad shoulders, and she wouldn't be caught dead out in that casual outfit for brunch. Her brunette tresses would be swept into an elegant knot at her neck's base. Sandy's hair floats behind her like a cloud. She's very pretty, like a young Sally Field. Huge cheeks waiting to smile.

As they approach, Dad says, "I think I'd rather eat inside, sweetie. It's a tad too cold for me." But we always eat outside if the weather is reasonable.

"Are you sure?" I gesture at the primo spot. Sandy glances at it and moves to go inside.

"Very. It's just as good inside." She never drops his hand. Leading him away from me.

They sit next to eat other, and Dad puts his arm around her shoulder. Obnoxious. Next thing you know they'll be sharing the same malt with two straws. This isn't the 1950s. I don't want to be hostile, but they're making it difficult. I feel a sudden guilty pang for Mom's sake, and I picture Sandy with devil horns and a pitchfork. It's not difficult. The image just struts right to my mind's forefront.

"You're in publishing, Cassie?" she asks after we order. She ordered an egg white omelet with spinach and onions, no cheese. I got the pumpkin pancakes, but Dad never commented on the absurdity of putting a squash in breakfast food. Dad changed things up and got a Belgian waffle with blueberries instead of his usual. Who is this man?

"I prefer Cassandra. Yes, I'm an editor at Weston's." I sip my iced tea in what I hope is polite disinterest. Tennessee Williams' women do this to great aplomb, but I think it's coming across as rudeness.

"You're a writer too. Like your father?"

"I don't have a blog." Dad settles next to her and grins. He's just happy the two of us are in the same place. He hasn't picked up on our body language. Sandy leans forward, trying to show interest in my life, but her smile is strained, the lipstick smearing across her lips, and I sit back in the booth, arms crossed. He's oblivious.

"I love writing that," he interjects. "It's been the best thing for me. Gets all the negative thoughts out of my head and into the Internet."

"He has his own Wikipedia article," says Sandy. I'll bet she wrote it. They'll let anyone submit information to that site. Next thing you know the Revolutionary War started in the 1860s when some yahoo assassinated Archduke Ferdinand.

"That's nice."

"It's been a crazy time at work," laughs Dad. "My boss hasn't found out yet," he adds when he sees my wide eyes, "but my co-workers sure enjoy it."

"You don't name the company, do you?"

"No, dear. I don't even say what it is I do exactly. I say how I feel and stuff...I thought you were reading it." He looks crestfallen, and I feel terrible.

"I promise I will. It's been a long couple of months." I rub my forehead and recall Kenny's prepared lunch from the week before. I've never had couscous that crunchy.

"I suppose you *are* busy, with work and all," he says.

"She could look in on it every once and a while. Her mother reads it every day," says Sandy, and she shoots me a glare. "Young people aren't as busy as they let on."

What. A. Bitch. How dare she mention my mother? I don't care if she is a cyber stalker; Mom's just a smidge jealous, nothing harmful.

"I'm sorry, Sandy, but you have no idea what I do with my time. And I don't think my mother's Internet activity is any of your business." Luckily, the server delivers our food, and silence rushes in. Dad is excited to try something new, and he likes the golden waffle, but he's unsure about the gelatinous blueberry garnish.

"Shouldn't there be syrup?"

"Not on blueberry waffles, hun," says Sandy who pats his hand condescendingly. Dad shrugs and spreads the whipped cream and blueberries across the waffle. I pass the maple syrup across the table, but he doesn't notice. His ears belong to Sandy. Has she brainwashed him in some *Invasion of the Body Snatchers* fashion? I knew her sneakers were too cute for her to be nice.

"I used to work the same kind of job your Dad does, but it got too boring," she says. "I sell furniture out at the Hom store in Apple Valley."

"She's a natural saleswoman," says Dad through a mouth full of waffle. Sandy gives him a shove and smooths her hair.

"It's easy. I have the best sales record in the store."

"How many employees does a place like that have?" I ask. She runs her tongue across her teeth before saying, "Over fifty." I nod, showing minimum enthusiasm. "Your father tells me you're also the best in your office. How many editors do *you* work with again?" Dad beams at us.

"I knew you two would like each other! We should get together next week!"

I say four words I rarely string together, "You were right Mom."

"About what Cassie? I'm having a terrible day at work. Those girls from marketing went to lunch today and didn't even invite me."

"I thought you didn't like the marketing team."

"That's not the point. One should always be polite." Oh Mom. "But what was I right about?" She never tires of hearing that she's predicted something or had the correct opinion of something. She and Kevin should date; they'd be perfect for each other.

"You're right about that Sandy person Dad's seeing. I met her today."

"Horrible?"

"You could say that. Have you met her?" I don't see how that would be possible, since Mom never sees Dad. She has lambasted the woman over the phone for the past few months, so I thought she was jealous, but Mom's sixth sense must have kicked in.

"Not in person, but her comments on your father's blog screamed desperate floozy."

"Uh huh. She wasn't drunk and definitely not desperate. She's got Dad's balls on her faux-Prada key chain."

"A bit vulgar, but I agree. Your father's always been a pushover when it comes to strong-minded women. A girl like her could snag him like a champion bass fisherman."

"The thing is...he looks so happy." I trail off and Mom doesn't answer. There are so many things I'm implying: that Dad has not been happy for a long time, that Mom never made him happy, that he's finally gotten over Mom, and that he's moved on from our family. "Mom?"

"What your father does is none of our business. If he wants to spend time with that woman, more power to him."

"How is Gideon?" I ask before she starts ranting. Her tone warms as she answers, "Wonderful. He's so thoughtful. Just the other night, he brought over Chinese food, because I said I had a craving for it in the morning."

"In the morning?"

"Yes! When we woke up, I desperately wanted Kung Pao chicken, but he said breakfast was more in order in the morning."

More sex stories. I tune out my mom's deep tissue massage tale (seriously, did she make Gideon up or is he the greatest lover of all time?) and think about Dad. If he stays with Sandy, I don't know what I'll do. I don't want our limited time together marred by her presence, but I can't see how I can tell Dad I don't care for her without damaging out relationship. One way or the other, I'll end up hurting Dad's feelings, and he's one man I can't afford to lose. All the others can leave me alone right now.

"Do you like massages?"

"Excuse me?" I ask, fork full of pasta posed near my mouth. Marinara sauce drips onto the white tablecloth and spreads like red water.

"Massages. Aren't they fantastic?" asks Kenny, teeth bared across the table. Some parsley is wedged between his front teeth and it glares at me. Once you notice a fault in someone's appearance, it's difficult to forget. I try to look away from the green speck only to be more drawn to it when I look back.

"I suppose," I say. "I haven't gotten one in a long time, professionally. My friend Kevin fancies himself a masseuse."

"Kevin?" His voice is low, unusual for one so boisterous, and I sense danger. I forgot one of the key rules in dating: never mention the name of another person if they are the opposite sex, even if it is your gay best friend.

"He works with me. Though he's been using his talented hands on his new boyfriend Lyle for the past few months." Of course, there is no Lyle, but poor envious Kenny needn't know that. Best to establish Kevin's gayness *and* unavailability in the same go. It wouldn't hurt if I mentioned he is ugly or smells bad.

"He's gay!" Kenny practically shouts across the restaurant. He chuckles and gives me a look that says, if he were straight and single, I'd have to break a limb or two, and Kenny probably could.

"Yes," I say in a much lower register. "He has been for quite some time."

"You single girls all have gay friends, don't you? It's just like that TV show *Sex and the City*."

Why must men always bring up popular female media as if we're all part of some elite cult that subscribe to post-feminist ideals and models. Some of that stuff is fun and a bit accurate, but a lot of it's insulting. We're not all obsessed with sex, booze, and shoes. Okay I love shoes, but that's not the point. Just because I'm a woman doesn't mean I like chick-lit and *Cosmo*. I only do the quizzes.

"He is a good friend," I say and focus on the food. Kenny has taken me to a large Italian restaurant, which is more expensive than it's worth. The bread is either too crusty or spongy, and the marinara might have come from a can. The servers wander around in crisp black pants and long aprons with faux-superior facial expressions; perhaps the manager demands a haughty demeanor to accompany the derivative cuisine. I could barely read the menu for the dim "mood lighting." Why restaurants think it's a good idea that patrons can't see the food makes me wonder more about what I'm eating.

"I once hired a gay man to work at my store in Duluth!" Kenny says proudly and lifts his chin. What a champ.

"How kind of you."

"I really gave him a break. He was having such a hard time finding work."

"How's work going this week?" I ask, desperate to escape the conversation.

"Wonderful! I received a new shipment over the weekend and get to do inventory. I love sorting incoming merchandise. I can't expect anyone else to do it. Not thorough enough." He says this in a conspiratorial manner, like his employees might be at the next table listening.

"You're acting like the saltshaker's been bugged," I joke, but Kenny stares in horror at the silver shaker in the middle of the table. He regains his composure and laughs, "That wouldn't be possible! My clerks aren't that tech savvy. Now my competitors might be…" He glances around the dining room, eyes darting, and draws other customers' attention. One woman wipes her mouth and frowns while her husband shakes his head and the two teenagers next to us giggle and cover their smiles.

I feel ridiculous. "Why would anyone want to spy on you?" I regret this comment immediately, because Kenny spins back and launches into a bitter diatribe against the bank, who didn't want to give him his first loan, and other antique shop owners in the Cities who covet his merchandise and try to steal his customers.

"They're all jealous of me," he says. "Not one of them has the connections I have in the Midwest and New England, and that's where the most unique items come from."

"I see."

"There are some corsets in particular that I recently acquired that Mr. Rathbone at Modern Antiques would love to steal! I love corsets!"

"Corsets?" He acts like this is the most normal fascination in the world and says, "Yes! They're fantastic! My ex-girlfriend used to try on the new models for me, to get an idea of how to sell them." His ex-girlfriend modeled corsets for him? It's not the most disgusting fetish I've heard of, but Kenny's nonchalance about the subject is suspect. Why would you mention sexually charged wardrobe and an ex on a date? Especially a *second* date. I hardly know him and he's throwing this weirdness at me. People usually save that stuff for later, like years later!

"That sounds interesting." I search for the server and catch his eye. I raise my eyebrows in what I hope looks panicky, and he nods curtly before disappearing into the kitchen. I wasn't sure about Kenny after our first date, but he seemed kind, a bit loud and abrasive but a good guy. I was willing to try a second date, but this kind of talk is so off-putting.

"I don't have any in stock right now, but if I find something, I'll let you know!" What does that mean? Is he insinuating that I flounce about his store in negligee while he drools and jerks off in the corner? Not my deal. I save satin and silk for myself.

"Oh! The check's here!" The server, my new favorite person in the universe, swoops down and deposits the black checkbook in between us. I reach for it and pull it close. Damn it's expensive! I'm glad I turned down the second glass of wine, and not just because of the cost. A second glass might have left me too slow-witted to catch Kenny's odd behavior.

"I'll get it!"

"Don't even think about it," I say and slap my credit card inside before the server can leave. I give him a grateful look, and he smirks. "You made me a terrific lunch the other day, so it's my treat." Kenny grins and shakes his head. He seems fine with this and makes no other attempt to dissuade me. He must be used to people buying him dinner.

"Thanks! If I knew you were paying, I'd have ordered another round and some crème brulee." He pronounces the dessert "cream brool" and I try not to snicker, because he might think I find him

146

charming. I fight back the correction and bite my lip, waiting for the server's return.

When my new best friend arrives with the check I scribble in an enormous tip and grab my purse. "Well," I say, "I had a good time, but I have to get going."

Kenny doesn't stand when I do but stares at me, an incredulous look on his face.

"You're leaving already? We've only been here a couple hours."

"I know, but I have a busy day tomorrow," I lie and search for my car keys. Thank God I drove myself. Another word for you new daters out there: always bring your own car for a smooth getaway. "I'm stuck planning the Halloween excursion for my friends and I, and I still have to find a costume." A few lies never hurt anyone.

"What are you doing on Halloween?" he asks, and I can see visions of corseted me dancing around his eyes. In your dreams Kenny.

"I have to be honest with you. I don't think this is going to work out." I turn to leave and decide to let my inner villain fly. "Besides, I don't even like antiques."

"Are you sure it's okay with the girls if I tag along?"

"It's perfectly fine. Lindsey adores you and Keeley's been seeing someone. Just be sure your costume's up to snuff, because Lindsey's really competitive when it comes to the contest."

I'm getting ready to meet the girls at a suburban bar called Throwbacks, which I've never been to. It's about thirty minutes away from my place, but Lindsey says they're rocking on Halloween: they have great drink specials and a huge costume contest. Justin called ten minutes ago, frantic that he had nowhere to go, since Kevin decided to visit his brother in Chicago this weekend. I invited him along because nobody should stay home alone on a holiday, even

Halloween. The girls shouldn't mind. I'd better call them after Justin hangs up.

"You're absolutely, positively sure?"

"For the last time, yes!"

"Okay. I'll meet you at your place in half an hour."

"What? Wait!" But he's gone. I should ring him back and tell him to meet us at the bar, but I don't have time. It'll take me at least half an hour to get my costume on and makeup finished, and I have to call the girls and give them the male gatecrasher heads up.

"Hey Linds, it's me."

"Why are you calling me when you know it takes me almost two hours to get into this stupid costume?"

"You should have started prep earlier. Listen. Justin asked if he could come with us tonight and I said yes. Kevin's in Chicago, and he has nobody else to hang out with tonight."

She doesn't even pause before saying, "Fine with me just let Keeley know. She was hung up on him for a while. I've gotta go. The pleather's sticking to my thighs." She hangs up and I hear the rude dial tone. That was easy. I thought she'd have a thousand questions about what he's wearing and if he'd coordinate with us. Huh.

I dial Keeley and hope she's in a generous mood. She hasn't mentioned Justin for months, so I hope there's no ill will.

"Hey, girl," she answers after a few rings, "how's the costume coming? I left extra tights in case you ruined a pair."

"I haven't even gotten started on the costume. I was just calling to ask if it's okay if Justin comes with us tonight."

"Aren't he and Kevin going somewhere on Hennepin?" Her voice doesn't sound agitated, just curious. I sigh with relief. This is going to be much smoother than I anticipated. I might have time to get ready before he gets to my apartment.

"Kevin's in Chicago for a last-minute trip."

"How much does Weston's *pay* him?"

"His brother's rich. Are you sure you're okay with Justin coming?"

"I'm fine with it, but did you ask Lindsey? I thought she was going to murder me when I told her about my costume."

"I already called her. Maybe Justin will be dressed as Batman or something. That'll make her happy."

"Right. I'd better go take the curlers out of my wig. See you soon! Oh! How was your date last week?"

"About as much fun as a Mexican prison."

"I can't wait to read that chapter. Bye."

After talking to Keeley, I run into my room and survey the scene: the costume is laid out on my bed, reserve tights are on the nightstand, the curling iron is heating up in the bathroom, and I have my makeup selections ready. I talked Keeley out of helping with my look. Makeup and hair first, then the costume. Thank God my hair is already red, or I'd have to wear some stupid wig.

As I'm finishing my hair and spraying a lethal hairspray dose over the curls, the buzzer goes off. Shit, he's already here! There's no way that was half an hour! I look at the clock and see that he gave me an extra ten minutes, and even that wasn't enough. I guess men have a valid complaint that women take too long to get ready.

"Coming!" I run to the buzzer and press the button. "Hello?"

"It's Justin. Can I come up?"

"I'll leave the door open." I buzz him in and race back to my room to assemble the costume. I suddenly feel bashful having Justin in my place while I'm changing. It must be the unconventional clothes. No one's seen this much of my legs in a long time. I sit on the bed with the first pair of tights. They don't tear when I pull them on one leg at a time, thank you Jesus, and they fit over my stomach nicely. I was afraid they might create some kind of fat roll or that my legs would look like chunky asparagus stalks.

The top is really tight, but I can take small breaths, and at least my boobs don't fall out. Kenny would love this top: it's a corseted body suit. Some of the glitter cascades to the floor, but the leaves stay put. Dammit, I'll have to vacuum later.

The front door opens, and Justin calls a greeting. "I'm grabbing a beer! Take your time!"

"Almost done! Just give me a second!"

The boots are tall and barely fit over my calves. I've always had trouble finding boots that zip past my runner's muscles, but Lindsey found the perfect solution: vinyl. It's stretchy enough to encompass even my calves. The zipper winces under the pressure but goes all the way up. I can't find my headband and panic before remembering that I left it in the bathroom next to my nail polish. Or course my nails are a poisonous green. I throw the headband on and catch a sideways glimpse of myself in the mirror. Not too shabby. Lindsey did a great job picking all this stuff out. With my glittering yellow eye shadow and pink lips, I become a different person. I smile deviously, trying out my villainous persona. I choke back an evil laugh and step back into my room to check out the full-length mirror. I really could be Poison Ivy. They should have cast me in that terrible movie instead of Uma Thurman.

Feeling proud of myself, I strut into the living room to show Justin my costume. He sits on the couch with an open beer and stares when I enter. His mouth opens an inch or two, and his eyes appear foggy.

"Whoa."

"I know! I thought I'd look terrible, but Lindsey knows what she's doing!" I spin around slowly, and Justin's lost gaze turns into an embarrassed smile. He starts laughing and sips his beer.

"What?" I ask. Oh God I'm wrong. I look awful. My ass must look wider than Missouri. What was I thinking agreeing to this? I knew Lindsey would make me up like a vine-covered streetwalker. "Is it that bad?"

"NO!" he shouts and puts up his hands. "You look fantastic! It's just…"

"What?" I look down at my boots. Are they silly? Did I take it too far with the makeup?

"There's a pair of green stockings stuck to your butt."

Mortified, I run back into my room and look in the mirror. The green tights look like recently shed reptile skin, and they blend in with the costume, so it's no wonder I didn't see them. I peel the access tights off and fling them across the room.

When I step into the living room, I hope I look composed and not extremely flustered. Justin stands next to the sofa, grinning. I'm so annoyed with him that I barely register his outfit, but as my ire fades, I take him in: he brings to mind Mr. Darcy with well-fitting trousers, an immaculate dark brown coat, a cravat, and tall brown riding boots. It must have cost a fortune, and I had no idea Justin fancied Jane Austen. His hair is combed neatly, but his smile suggests rakishness. I've never seen him look so great.

"You look amazing!" I walk over to him to inspect every article of clothing. As I grab at the coat I ask, "How on earth did you come up with this? You're going to make us all look bad! Except maybe Keeley. She spends notorious amounts of money for Halloween."

"My sister thought of it. She said I'd look quite dapper as Mr. Darcy, though she thought I resembled somebody called Mr. Bingley 'in both looks and manner.'" He imitates his sister's lilting voice and shrugs. "I never got past page one in *Pride and Prejudice*, but these clothes are pretty comfortable. I just hope the bar's not too crowded."

He moves to pull at the tight neck scarf but holds back at the last moment. Despite the fact that he hasn't read up on his persona, I have to admit that Justin's laid-back attitude toward his costume is admirable. Most men wouldn't be caught dead in his attire. They'd have torn off the cravat and untucked the shirt in no time.

"It shouldn't be too bad. It's in some suburb."

"You don't think I look stupid, do you? I would have gone with something easier. Like scrubs and a stethoscope."

"Mr. Bingley fits you well. He's amiable and handsome." Justin's face brightens when I say this, and he blushes. Keeley will take one look at him and fall in love again. "I wish I could be Elizabeth Bennett instead of…" I gesture down my body, and Justin tries not to stare.

"Poison Ivy's one of the strongest female villains in comic book history, so I think she fits you too."

"Thanks, but I usually prefer more costume. Last year I wore my Ren Fest outfit. It shows cleavage but everything else is covered up." Sensing my embarrassment, Justin moves to take off his coat, possibly planning to hand it to me. "Don't be silly! The coat completes your ensemble."

"You're not cold or anything?"

"Ha, no, just not used to seeing so much of myself."

"What do you wear to bed? A potato sack?" he asks, bemused.

"None of your business. Now come on. We can't be late, or Lindsey will freak out."

He bows at the waist, one hand out in front. All he needs is a tall hat and the illusion would be complete. As we leave the apartment, he opens the door for me and picks up a gorgeous silk hat from the side table next to the entryway. There's no way Lindsey and I can win the contest with Justin in tow.

The bar is crazy busy. I've seen places in the Cities get a bit nuts over Halloween and the Zombie Pub Crawl, but Throwbacks has gone all out. Young and old alike belly up to the bar and yell out drink orders in a discordant yowl, but the bartenders don't seem too perturbed; they merely ignore everyone except the one person they're addressing. Bartenders have the best tunnel vision.

We didn't have to pay cover, because Lindsey knew the bouncer, and our costumes fit right in. Almost everyone is dressed to win this contest. One guy walked by in a fully functional Tin Man costume, and he bent his head slowly to Keeley, who is the Good Witch of the North. She looks sensational as always, and I'm jealous of her long hoop skirt, but it must be so uncomfortable. One guy passed by and practically knocked her over, but she whacked him with her sparkling wand. The bustier shows off her other ample gifts, and the guy stares before teetering away.

There are other creative costumes roaming about: a six-foot man dressed as a keg, a lot of naughty nurses and cops, some devils and angels, and two Princess Leias who should not have chosen the slave girl ensembles. But I think Justin has this is the bag. Every woman we pass stares at him and melts. Keeley has been pleasant toward him and shows no inclination to tumble into his arms. Lindsey looked him over jealously when we arrived, and she said, "Well, maybe I'll win next year." Her costume is skin-tight and shows everything I'd want to hide, not that I'm hiding much as Poison Ivy. I've gotten my fair share of gawkers, and one or two offers to buy my first drink. Justin turns them away with a haughty glare, and they seem intimidated by a guy who would wear a neck scarf into a crowded bar.

There's one guy who can't seem to take his eyes away from me: The Flash stands across the bar and won't look away. It takes a long time to get drinks, and I feel his gaze the entire time. Justin notices too, and he says, "Do you want me to drape an arm around you or something? Or make out?"

"He's probably just drunk." I grab my two beers and back away from the bar. Justin follows warily, keeping his eye on The Flash.

"Freak," he mutters.

"That would describe the whole bar. I didn't think it would be so busy."

"Me either. I'm sweating through my vest."

"Waistcoat. You hate to take anything off though. Maybe after the contest you can dump the great coat in the car."

"Which one's the great coat?"

We wander through the dance floor to find Lindsey and Keeley who scored a booth near the stage. It's loud over here, but at least we can sit down.

"Did you get lost?" yells Keeley. I'm surprised she can sit in that getup.

"It takes forever to get a bartender's attention."

"That explains the double fisting," says Lindsey, nodding at my beers. "See anyone you know?"

"How could I? I never come out here."

"You never know," says Keeley. "I've already seen a few guys I've dated." Not counting Justin? I ask in my head. Keeley has piled up a few exes. It's not shocking that some live out here. It's a nice neighborhood, but I wouldn't be caught this far from the city.

"It's really loud in here!" says Justin. "And the band's not even playing yet!"

"They're on break," says Lindsey. "They're great though!"

"Do you want to dance at all," he asks me, but I shake my head.

"I've got to finish these beers before you get me out there."

He doesn't get me to dance until four beers later, and by then his brown great coat sits on the booth behind him. It has to be at least one hundred degrees in here, and he's not even sweating! He swears he is, but I don't notice any armpit stains or back sweat. I feel like it's pouring down my face, but I've done a few make-up checks with Keeley, so I know the eye shadow has stayed in place. Once we start dancing it's hard to stop.

Keeley's skirt has a hidden feature: the top part comes off to reveal a shorter version, so she can dance. She swirls around the dance floor, looking marvelous, while Lindsey can barely move. She shimmies and sways and tries to do a sexy maneuver, but the costume holds her back. Justin takes turns dancing with all of us, but Lindsey has always made him nervous, and he and Keeley's history is too fresh, so he spends most time with me. I don't mind. I'd rather dance with my friend than the other weirdoes who dry-hump me. Justin disperses them with alacrity, and I thank him with my eyes. Unwanted dance partners are the worst. Listen up gentlemen: if the girl you're trying to grind on doesn't turn around or acknowledge your presence in any way, leave her alone and find a new quarry. It's not that she doesn't know you're there. She's not being coy or mysterious. She just doesn't want to dance with you.

At least I haven't seen The Flash since our first bar visit.

When we take a break from dancing, a guy dressed as a carnival barker walks toward us with tiny blue tickets. He hands one to each of us and says they're for the costume contest.

When the lead singer calls people up for best costume, we have to take the stage. Even with the beer I'm nervous. Standing on stage for the entire bar to see is quite different from mingling amongst the other hussies in short shorts and barely-there tank tops. At least Keeley, Lindsey, and Justin all go up too.

"Yes! One of us has got to win!" says Lindsey, her ticket raised in triumph. "If someone else takes that prize money I'll tackle them in the parking lot!"

"How much is it again?" I ask.

"Two hundred bucks! And momma needs a new pair of shoes!"

"Speaking of mommas," says Justin, "where's Alicia?"

"She takes her kids around their neighborhood, and by the time they get home she's too tired to come out with us," says Keeley, and Lindsey rolls her eyes. "But it's okay. We get it. She's just not able to hang out as much anymore."

"Couldn't she make her husband do it just once?" asks Lindsey, and she swigs her beer and crashes it on the table. "It's not like he has anything going on."

"We could fight about Brian all night and it wouldn't change anything," I say, because we've had this discussion too many times. "He goes to his work party on Halloween. He's been going forever, so he gets this day. You have to compromise in a marriage."

"No, you don't," says Lindsey. "I compromised my way right into a divorce. What if Alicia gets pissed enough about never getting to see us and freaks out on him?"

"I'm getting another beer," says Justin, eager to leave the conversation. "Anyone want another one?" Keeley and I nod but Lindsey ignores him.

"She can't keep kowtowing to Brian every time he wants to jerk off with his work buddies."

"I'm glad Justin left," mumbles Keeley. "It's embarrassing when she rants like this," she whispers to me.

"I know you're talking about me *Glinda*, and I don't give a shit. It's about time one of us said something to Alicia." I'm glad we agreed to leave our cell phones in the car, because Lindsey might drunk-dial poor Alicia, and it's after one o'clock. I hope she doesn't find the energy to run outside and call her.

"We totally agree with you Linds, but you have to see Alicia's side too. She likes spending Halloween with her kids, even if she says it drives her crazy," I say. "She'll miss making their costumes and taking them out soon enough."

"Then we'll get her back," says Keeley.

"Whatever. By then my ass will be too saggy to fit in any costume besides 'middle-aged woman.' How exciting."

We're silent until Justin returns with a pitcher of dark beer and four glasses.

"I thought we could all use something stronger."

"Here here," mutters Lindsey, and Keeley shakes her head. "I hope the contest starts soon so we can go home." This is the one thing I hate about Lindsey. Once she gets in a mood, there's no turning back, and she gets everyone down. She's sullen for the rest of the night. I understand why she's angry but harping on about it won't change the fact that Alicia has three children. She has to be there for her family before us. I don't like it either, but that's life. Lindsey should know by now that Alicia has made her decision. She needs to grow up.

Our pitcher's half gone when the band's lead singer taps the microphone and announces the contest starting. Keeley perks up and puts the top skirt back on. Justin shrugs into his coat and grimaces. He can't wait to leave either, but mostly because he's in a furnace. I don't think he'll wear that costume next year. Lindsey stirs her beer with her finger and mopes. I just don't want to go onstage.

The contest contains three categories: worst costume, sexiest costume, and best costume. I think we three girls should be up for sexiest, but I guess someone nominated us for best. We'd have had a better chance winning sexiest, because I think Justin's going to win.

Worst costume goes to a guy wearing nothing but tight, white underwear, and he whoops and hollers as the lead singer gives him an ancient trophy and a pair of sweat socks. A naughty cop gets sexiest, and I can see why: she's short but very busty, and she has muscular legs and a sultry swagger.

Then it's time for best costume. We all stand and take the stage with Keeley leaping forward and Justin sheepishly at the rear. Five other people come up behind us, and I'm annoyed to see the Flash. This time he doesn't look at me but stares into the crowd. It's even hotter on stage under the white lights, and I wonder how the band can stand it, but then again, they're not in heavy costumes. The other people's costumes seem shabby next to ours, except the Tin Man we met walking it, and the keg. I hope one of us wins.

The carnival barker takes turns standing beside one of us and asks the crowd to clap and yell for their favorite. Lindsey and I receive a lot of hoots and noise, but Keeley gets way more. The audience loves the keg and the Tin Man too, but they are barely audible for the Flash. Take that, weirdo. But the one who gets the loudest praise is Justin. People bang on the bar and women scream. He's Elvis up there. Even I start clapping when the host stands next to Justin, who blushes and smiles, which only energizes the noisy crowd. Someone throws a pair of lacy underwear onstage, and Justin hides his eyes in mock embarrassment. He loves it. He's playing the crowd brilliantly.

"You've made your choice ladies! The winner is Mr. Darcy!"

"I'm Mr. Bingley," says Justin into the microphone, and the entire female population would have left with him tonight. Keeley and Lindsey snicker off to my right as I stare at Justin in awe.

"Why don't you throw your panties at him?" asks Lindsey and I realize my mouth is hanging open like I just spotted a unicorn.

"Shut up! I just can't believe the women in here! This is insane!"

"Why?" she asks. "He's so hot you'd burn yourself just standing near him."

"He's just playing up his charm," I say with dignity. "He's a completely different person during the day."

"Yeah. *Completely* different," she says and smiles. Unsure of what she means, I ignore her and watch The Flash leave the stage. He doesn't look back, but for some reason I feel a pang of déjà vu. Who is that guy?

The host presents Justin with a giant check and an inflatable penis, and he couldn't look happier. He beams at me as we leave and won't talk about anything else in the car. He has to drive. There's no way I'm sober, and he only had three beers all night.

"I can't believe it," he says, his body shaking. "I thought one of you would win for sure! I mean come on. You three are so gorgeous! Why the hell did I win?"

"Because the women carried the vote, dumb ass."

"You're just jealous," he grins and tosses the blow-up phallus in the back.

"You better not leave that in my car," I warn. "What if I got pulled over or something?"

"I think you'd get out of the ticket."

"And into jail for being an enormous pervert. Take me home good sir! I need some sleep."

"As you wish madam." What a dork.

Justin pulls into my garage and I say goodnight. We plan on lunch for Monday, and Justin pretends that he left the penis in my backseat.

Then he pulls it out of his coat and laughs, saying it's a present for Kevin.

I walk upstairs and feel the blisters on my heels for the first time. The booze must be wearing off. I try to take off the boots without unzipping them but almost fall into the wall in the hallway. My keys seem to have buried themselves in my purse, and it takes forever to find them. Why don't I have a smaller purse? I stumble into my apartment and fling the boots in different directions. I hope I didn't hit Prospero. I start unzipping the corset when I notice a flashing voicemail notice on my phone. My mom must have called. Checking out my blistered heels, I push the play button on the machine and stand cold when I hear the voice.

"Hey Cassie. I knew you'd have the same phone number. I saw you at the bar tonight and thought I'd give you a call. You looked really good. Talk to you later maybe. It's The Flash, by the way."

The dial tone rings through my head and I feel instantly sober.

The man that kept staring at me at the bar…The Flash was Pete.

November

Four Cat Sam and Rule Number Six: Just because he has more cats than you, doesn't make him a loser.

When I need to cry and find that I can't, I chop and onion or two. Peeling the papery skin from the bulb feels like uncovering an old hurt; you know something's inside that will ruin your life but can't seem to stop peeling. After the skin is discarded, the white body sits on the cutting board, untouched. I cut it in half and set one piece aside, in case the first part doesn't produce tears. I learned in junior high science class that unstable chemicals in onions produce tears when you chop them. The sensation is impossible to fight, and it feels like you have no control over your eyes. Having tears run down your cheeks unasked is like a dentist giving you laughing gas when you know there's nothing funny about your root canal. But if you need to cry…

I usually keep a Kleenex box handy when slicing onions, but today I'm empty-handed. I want the tears flowing. I want them to slide down my face and onto the vegetable in front of me. I wish that crying would cleanse my mind of doubts and fears last night brought up. I want to take this knife and stab my phone, so his voice is not just deleted, but destroyed completely.

The onion's not working. I have a small pile of chopped bits, but the tears haven't come. I grab the second half and lean in closer as I slice, willing the fumes to wreak havoc on my tear ducts. This one finally does, and salty water races down my face and past my chin. It cascades into the chopped onions, flavoring them with my despair.

My mother would say I'm over-dramatic.

She never had an ex-fiancé call her after three years.

The phone brings me out of my teary haze and jolts my knife hand. I almost slice my thumb open, and onions sails across the kitchen, scattering. Great. I'll find onion chunks until Christmas.

I put down the knife—which I'd been holding so tightly my fingers turned white—and ran for my phone. Had it been ringing for long? Why did I have the volume set so high? Every sound was amplified in my mind, and Pete's voice shouted above the rest. God damn him.

"Hello?"

"Hey, it's me,"

"Alicia, do you have any idea what just happened?"

"How could I?" she sounds bored. "I haven't heard from you in a week." Crap. I thought I called her before we went to Throwbacks…maybe I forgot. I'll blame Lindsey for it later. "It's okay. You guys have fun last night?"

"It was great until I got home."

"Did Lindsey win the damn prize?"

"No, Justin did, but listen—"

"Justin went with you?" She is ruffled. "I couldn't go so you invited a replacement?"

"It's not like that," I say, exasperated. If she wanted to hang out with us so badly then she should have asked her husband to watch the kids. It wouldn't kill her to spend one Halloween with her friends. "Kevin ditched him. It was pure charity."

"Okay," she says. "Maybe next year I'll be able to come." Yeah right.

"So anyway, the thing that made the night horrible…"

"Someone spill cranberry juice on you? Did Lindsey make a fool of herself? Did Keeley make out with a chick?"

"No, and maybe just a little, and definitely no girl on girl, but nothing happened at the bar. It was really crowded but we had a good time. There was this creepy guy though."

"I love creepy guy stories."

"Stop interrupting!"

"Sorry."

"The creepy guy stared at me for half an hour, then called me. Left a message on my machine."

"How could some random guy call you? Keeley and Lindsey weren't playing bar-matchmaker, were they?"

"Nothing like that. They were too busy dancing and drinking. The guy was Pete." The air hangs dead in my ear, and Alicia breathes heavily on the other end but says nothing. Maybe she doesn't believe me. "I can play the voicemail for you." I must have sounded angry because she said,

"You don't have to. You shouldn't listen to it again." Too late. I listened to it about one hundred times last night. "You need to delete that message or burn your phone."

"Like a voicemail exorcism?"

"Exactly. Purge that dick from your phone. Do you think Holy Water would work?"

"Haven't tried that but begging him to take me back sure didn't work."

"What?" she practically screams. "You did *not* call him back!"

"Don't be stupid. I meant before…"

"Whew. I should hope you wouldn't be that desperate." What an asshole! I'm not desperate! I didn't even think about calling him back.

"Why would I call him?"

"Because you're you," Alicia sighs. "He's the only person you've ever forgiven for hurting you."

"That's ridiculous. I forgave you for getting married."

"Ha ha. That's not the same. What he did was awful, and you pined after him for so long—"

"I'm going to stop you and spare myself and your vocal chords the lecture. I know how you feel about him."

"I just wish you felt the same way."

"I can't hate him."

"Can't see why not, your friends and your family despise him."

"Because I loved him." I pause, and she doesn't answer. She's afraid I'll admit I still love him. He used to push my hair behind my ear before kissing me when he got home from work. "I don't think I can hate someone I used to love."

"Take a cue from Lindsey. She does just fine."

"Do you have a new guy for me?" I need to steer her away from Pete. I had to tell someone about his call, and Alicia is the best candidate, but she could harp on about him for hours.

"His name's Sam Eggleston and he lives in Minneapolis."

"Sounds great," I say and slump onto the couch. "Anything else? It would have been nice to know that Kenny was crazy before I met him."

"It's hard to tell exactly what people are like from these websites. I just read in *In Style* that it can take almost thirty dates before you find someone relationship-worthy."

"Fashion magazine experts can't be wrong. I knew I missed my calling. How many do you think it would take to make thirty dates?"

"In your case, only a few more."

"So, does this guy have metal hip joints or fangs or something?"

"Not that I know of, but you can ask him next week. You're going to the Mall of America."

"Why?" I love shopping, as most sane women do, but I've never taken a guy. Pete stayed away from malls when we were together. He mentioned something about my freaky mall radar and how much he hated Cinnabon. Who in the hell hates Cinnabon?

"He suggested it. There's a good restaurant on third floor, and we thought you'd like the food. It's sushi and American cooking, whatever that means."

It's a restaurant and not shopping. I don't think there's a man on this planet that could keep up with me in a mall that size. Too many shoe stores for one man. And if the date's a bust, I can always take laps around the mall and get a watch. I've needed a new one for months.

"For lunch?"

"Yes. He said to meet him outside Nordstrom on the second floor at noon. He seems really sweet."

"That's what you've said about the last five guys."

"You're too picky. Call me later, and we'll set our own lunch date. My *husband* owes me some girl time after this year's trick-or-treating fiasco." I love it when Alicia refers to Brian as "her husband," because it means she's shelled out at least forty bucks for good wine and chocolate for when I come over.

"What happened?"

"Let's just say that the kids and I returned home after Oliver rolled around in a smashed pumpkin to find Brian passed out on the floor *next* to the couch. He was still in his Frankenstein's monster costume, covered in beer." Oops. I kind of feel bad for the guy, but no one spills on Alicia's carpets.

Crave. It sounds more like a weird porno/art movie than a restaurant, but food and sensuality go together. Although there's nothing sexy about the couple trying to master chopsticks sitting on the terrace. Why a terrace in a mall restaurant? Bloomington's not that classy, and the Mall of America may be our nation's flagship shopping center, but why pretend to be a Parisian café if you're not? I shouldn't judge this place before I sit down. I fight the urge to giggle at the gaggle of older people wearing fanny packs perusing the menu that stands outside the entrance. Bad fashion and haute American cuisine. Awesome.

Alicia called early this morning because Sam changed the meeting place: work would keep him longer than he thought, and he would meet me at the restaurant. I despise when people are late and hate when plans change last minute, but Alicia said I'm picky, so I try to relax and give the guy a chance. I'm about to walk inside and look for Sam when someone taps me on the shoulder. I don't like being touched if I'm not expecting it, so I whirl around the almost hit the man standing behind me with my purse.

"Oh my god! I'm so sorry!" I reign in the bag and sling it back over my shoulder. Almost clocked my date. What a great start.

"Wow! You're really fast!" he says and retreats a step. "I thought you'd nail me for sure!" He looks perplexed to be standing near me. Slumped posture does nothing for his height, but he's taller than me with a thin, ropy body. He fidgets with his hair, longish like a twisting snake. "I'm Sam. It's great to finally meet you." He doesn't proffer his hand, so I stick mine out and he grasps it, a panicked, oh-shit-I-forgot-something look in his eyes. He looks pinched, as if an invisible hand presses down on his head, and his face reminds me of someone I knew in high school. The boy couldn't speak in front of girls and had to give his speeches for English class in private with the teacher.

"Nice to meet you too. I'm Cassie."

"You are so pretty!"

"Thank you?" I say, taken aback. I guess he has no problem talking to girls.

"I mean, your picture on the site is awesome, but in person…" He continues to twitch as if I terrify him. "Just wow!"

After his praise I narrow my eyes and examine him more closely. He wore what must be his "good" outfit: dark jeans, a long-sleeved black t-shirt, and Converse sneakers. By the way he's tugging on the sleeves I can tell he's not used to wearing it. I wonder where his coat is, because it's about forty degrees outside. Maybe he left it in his car.

"Should we eat?" I ask.

"Definitely! I wanted to try this place. I like to try different food. Makes life more interesting."

"I see."

The restaurant is large and moody, with dark wood and intriguing light fixtures. A soft golden glow comes from the lamps and overhead lights, illuminating several floor-to-ceiling glass wine cases. A long bar rests against the left wall where shoppers sit and sip cocktails or Diet Coke. The high ceilings were left open and show pipes and ductwork, and the shiny wood floors draw the eye. I haven't seen anything quite like it: a nouveau riche establishment, where women who prefer the Galleria might feel more at home in this huge mall. Even though Buffalo Wild Wings is right around the noisy corner, a woman might come to this place and feel she's having a fine dining experience.

"It's so nice in here!" Sam says and beams at the interior. He glances at his clothes and hesitates before approaching the host. I take the lead and say hello.

"Welcome to Crave," says the host, a well-groomed young man with a flawless uniform. "Will there be two this afternoon?"

"Yes. We'd prefer to sit in the dining area and not on the terrace please." He nods and scans his section map, searching for an open table.

"I never understood why it's so hard to be seated right away when there are open tables," says Sam, peering into the dining room. Embarrassed, I try not to look at the young host, hoping he didn't hear my date.

"I need to find just the right server for you, sir," he answers crisply. I feel awful. Why can't people let others do their jobs? Why can't they have a shred of patience? The only people I get down on are those whose performance lacks urgency, people who don't care about their work. This host probably hears meddlesome whispers from tired shoppers all day. He handled Sam well, and I'm sure it won't be the last customer he quells.

The host leads us to a booth near the sushi bar, and I smell fresh seafood and marvel at a chef chopping and rolling at an alarming rate. It's a wonder he's not missing fingers.

"I roll my own sushi," says Sam, standing tall for the first time. "I have a special roller at home, and I get the ingredients at Lund's down the street. I'll bet I roll faster than that guy. I don't even have to wear gloves when I do it."

"How nice." He slides into the booth before I take my coat off and grabs the menus from the host.

"We don't need to hear the specials. We can read just fine," he snaps and reads the four different menus. Who is this guy? He's shy around me, but rude to everyone else.

"Thank you," I say to the host, who flashes me an "I've seen them all" look. As he leaves me alone with my date, I realize that I'd rather be sitting in the booth with the underage host than with this guy. I take my menu (he won't relinquish the drink or specials menus) and look it over. The selection is excellent: sandwiches, entrées, salads, and pizzas, but I'm drawn to the sushi. Fresh food always sounds good when winter hits.

Sam picks his teeth with his pinky nail while reading the menus, and he pours meticulously over each one. When the server stops by for the drink order, Sam ignores her, and I'm forced to order him water and give another silent apology. I was going to have an iced tea but decided on wine. If I had to spend time with this guy, I needed something a little stronger than caffeine.

"Where'd she go?" he asks right after the server walks away. "I want an espresso!"

"You ignored her, so I got you water. She'll be back in a second."

He shakes his head and says, "It's so hard to find good waitresses today. They have no patience and always forget what you ordered. Is it so hard to let someone read the menu before coming over and staring them down? 'What you gonna have? Aren't you ready yet?' I can practically read their minds."

"I was a *waitress*. We prefer the term 'server.'" He doesn't look too concerned that he offended me and goes back to the menu, shy demeanor vanishing. The server returns with my wine and I take a huge gulp. She sets Sam's water down with a white napkin.

"Don't you have coasters?" he whines. "I hate when my glass sticks to these napkins."

"We might have some at the bar, sir."

"Then go to the bar and get me one please."

"Would you like to order something other than water?"

"I just want a coaster."

"Didn't you want an espresso?" I ask. He stares at me like I've ruined his game and slumps in the booth. I've seen this kind of thing before. A rude customer gets angry with the server for no reason then makes them run around the restaurant getting random things like coasters and never ordering what they actually want.

"And an espresso?" she asks.

"I guess," he answers and crossed his arms across his chest. "And I want it in an espresso cup. The last time I went to a restaurant they didn't have the proper cup."

"I'll make sure." As she walks toward the bar Sam glares after her and says, "So rude."

"What looks good?" I ask, desperate to change the subject.

"I suppose I'll get the sushi, see if it's as good as I make." Crap. Now he's ruined the sushi for me. New plan.

"I'm getting the butternut squash ravioli. It sounds really good."

"It does look interesting," he says and turns over the menu to read the description. "I'm not crazy about balsamic vinegar."

The server returns with espresso in a proper cup and a coaster, and we order. Sam displays more annoying habits by asking about every single sushi roll, whether she's sure the seafood is fresh, if the chef has any special qualifications, and if she prefers spider rolls to California rolls. He's testing our poor server. He catches her in an inaccurate description and hounds her about knowing the menu. She nods and smiles, bearing the verbal assault. I'm mortified but can't stop his ramblings. He lets her escape only to extol her many faults and incompetence. He finally decides to ask me a question that has nothing to do with the service industry's numerous problems.

"You have a cat, right?"

"Yes. Prospero is six years old."

"I love cats! They make such good companions. I have four: Milo, Gertie, Sunny, and Josie. They're great pets but even better friends." The girls failed to tell me that Sam was a male crazy cat lady. I didn't know those existed. Fascinating, also troubling. If he lived in the country I might understand, but he lives in the city and must have a small house or apartment. That's a lot of cat litter. "I don't mean they're my only friends," he says, as if brushing away that insane thought. "I play online games with my buddies on the weekends and sometimes we enter tournaments." He's an online gamer. I hate you ladies. No really. I hate you all. You must secretly want to destroy me.

"That's interesting."

"Really?" he beams. "No girl has ever found online gaming interesting. This is a perfect match!" Right. I thought people hid the crazy parts of themselves on first dates. Did I mention that I have severe commitment issues and was on a three-year dating hiatus until recently? No, I kept that to myself. Some things are not appropriate for first dates…like talking about how you taught three of your cats to use the toilet only to fail with the fourth.

I drink my wine and wait for the food. If I can get through lunch, I'll be fine. I'd leave now but I hate to hurt people's feelings, even if they're idiots. Maybe I can stop at DSW before I go home. Retail therapy is much cheaper than real therapy, and I get cute shoes. My mind wanders because Sam stops talking and waves a hand in front of my eyes. "What are you thinking about?"

"What?"

"You went somewhere else for a second. Thinking about something more fascinating than me?" He says this in a confident manner, as if there could be nothing more intriguing than him and his mythical battlefields and household feline antics.

"Something from work. I just finished editing a romance novel and found it so dull that I took ages to finish."

"Work can be hard. I run the IT desk for this company downtown. They sell software and computer parts to law firms and hospitals. It gets pretty hectic, but the hours are nice, and I get a hefty vacation pay."

The food arrives before he can describe his vacation extravaganzas, and his attention is diverted to the sushi. It looks beautiful, and as I look at the pile of odd-smelling gunk on my squash ravioli, I wish I'd chosen differently. I don't recall the menu featuring this little tidbit. The ravioli is very good, but I hate the mix of root vegetables and whatever else is on top. I smell balsamic vinegar, but the taste is lost in a sea of conflicting flavors. I usually enjoy peculiar food, but there's something off with the flavor profile, and the wine doesn't compliment it at all. Sam registers my distaste and asks, "Don't you like it?"

"It's fine," I lie and shove more in my mouth, grimacing.

"It looks terrible. Let me get the waitress over here."

"*Server.*"

Our server appears in an instant, noticing Sam peering over the booth's top like a prairie dog searching for predators. "How's everything tasting?"

"Awful," he says and shakes his finger at her. "Cassandra's ravioli looks like vomit, and my sushi is not well-prepared. The rolls fell apart the moment I touched them." He's not wrong about my dish, but his sushi looks fine. What the hell is he acting so belligerent for?

"I can order something else. May I see the sushi menu, please?"

"No, this is abysmal. The food and the service are lacking for sure." He glares at the server and says, "I'd like to see your manager." She doesn't attempt to reason with Sam, abruptly about-faces, and races for the kitchen. I hope she's seasoned enough not to let this douchebag get to her. I grab for my purse and fish out some money. Laying thirty dollars on the table, I stand and grab my coat. Enough is enough.

"It was very horrible to meet you. I can't believe you were so rude." He gapes at me like a freak show gawker, his mouth an endless black cave. As I pause to put my coat on, he stutters, "Where are you going? Don't you want something else?"

"Not with you. That poor girl doesn't deserve to be treated like that, but you certainly do." I shove my arms into the jacket sleeves and whirl away from him. "Maybe you should take some human being lessons before hoisting yourself on the innocent population." I turn back and grab the money. "You'd probably stiff the girl." I leave him stammering and search out our server. She emerges from the kitchen with her gargantuan manager in tow. I hand her the money, say it's her tip, and tell her that my "date" will cover the tab.

"Thank you," she says and smirks. "Please come back soon. Preferably not with that guy. He smells like old cheese."

"No problem."

Thanksgiving. The time when family gathers and celebrates the year's bounty. When mothers, fathers, and children come together and cook and bake pies and laugh and tell stories. That magical day when football and food rule all...at least if your parents aren't divorced and you have to split holidays, so they don't see each other and feel awkward. Welcome to the traditional American Thanksgiving, starring…my family!

"I can't believe they set me up with someone like that!" I grab the steaming bowl of potatoes from Joel's hands and mash the hell out of them. "And why does Mom insist on mashing her own potatoes? Instant are just fine."

It's a few hours before our annual Thanksgiving Day meal, and my brother Joel is tired from his late flight. His girlfriend Gisele was so exhausted that she's braving Mom's bed for a nap. She looks like a model, but Joel insists that she's a vet tech. Vet tech my ass. There's no way someone could afford real Gucci on that kind of salary. Easy, Cassie. Fashion envy will get you nowhere.

"Mom knows I like the whole experience," he says.

"Is that why we're having *three* kinds of potatoes?" I growl and mash faster. Seriously, who needs sweet, mashed, and scalloped potatoes for one meal? "Last year we got by with baked. Heaven forbid we only have one tuber for Thanksgiving."

"Last year I wasn't in charge of the menu. Mom emailed me and wanted to know what I preferred. Since I couldn't decide she got fixings for all three!" He goes to the oven to check the marshmallows on the sweet potatoes. "Dad would never do that."

"I wish you'd get off Dad's back for one second. He tries really hard to make Christmas nice for you."

"Yeah…I won't be coming for Christmas this year."

"What?" I spin around, and some mashed potatoes fall on the floor. "What do you mean you can't make Christmas?"

He doesn't even look contrite. Joel has this sheepish face most of the time, like you've recently caught him putting salt in the sugar bowl or noticed he's been wearing the same shirt for a week, but now he looks at ease.

"I have to work. It's no big deal. I'll call him or something."

"You're not serious?"

"Why shouldn't I be? I hate Christmas anyway." Now there's the surly, juvenile brother I know. "Dad won't miss me. He never calls me either." I hate that excuse. *The phone works both ways.* Well duh, but stop whining, pick up the damn phone, and call your father. If I call Mom every day, then he can make the effort to talk to Dad.

"You know Dad's not that proactive. Can't you just give him the benefit of the doubt?"

"It's easy for you, you live here."

"It's not my fault you moved to California."

"And it's not my fault you stayed here." He closes the oven door, and I slam the mashed potatoes on the counter, sending more flying.

"Those stupid potatoes are on broil!" I open the oven a fraction. "Otherwise the marshmallows will be ruined. Aren't you supposed to be a chef?" He throws his hands up and leaves the kitchen muttering about when Mom will get home and how I'm Genghis Khan. He pisses me off. It wasn't Dad's fault that he and Mom got divorced.

The apartment door bursts open and Mom yells, "Someone help me! The eggs!" She hauls five paper grocery bags, and a plastic one in her teeth. How did she enunciate with that in her mouth? I grab the bags in her left hand, and she takes the plastic one from her lips. A tiny piece of plastic rests on her tongue, and she tries to spit it out, gagging dramatically. "Those cashiers are trying to kill me! All the heavy things are in one bag!"

"What's the world coming too?"

"Don't get sassy with me. It's Thanksgiving." She drops the last two bags in the entryway and leans forward. "Where's your brother? Still sleeping, the poor angel?"

"He pitched a hissy fit about marshmallows and retreated to the bedroom."

She looks at me with concern and says, "He's had a long flight and a terrible week at work."

How is it that our parents can reduce us to toddlers in mere seconds? I feel bad for ridiculing Joel's numerous potatoes. "He'll be fine. What did you buy now?"

"Just cranberries, stuff for deviled eggs—you know that Gisele likes them?—and a few other odds and ends."

"Toilet paper?" I ask and pluck a small four pack from one bag.

"There's a man in the house, dear." As if that explains everything. Must we prep the place as if a king were gracing us? "Let him sleep awhile. We can take care of dinner."

"I cannot cook, Mom."

"I'm not asking you to," she snaps and marches into the kitchen. "All I ask is that you set the table and check how things are coming along. And get out the good plates. No not those! The other good plates!"

"Is there anything I can do?" comes a tiny voice from the hallway. Gisele stands awkwardly with her toothbrush in one hand and an old iPod in the other. She's even breath-taking after a nap! Short blond hair and a long neck make her look taller than she is, and her tan legs stand out like crazy against white cotton shorts. Doesn't she know it's winter here?

"Oh no, my dear!" says Mom. "Just make yourself comfortable. Cassie and I will take care of everything. Do you need something warmer to wear?"

"I brought some sweaters," she admits and peers down at her ensemble in fear. "I've never been somewhere this cold in the winter." It's an innate Minnesotan ability to simultaneously despise and envy the warm-weather people. I want to chide her about being a big wuss but secretly wish *I* were somewhere warmer for winter. Still, what a crybaby. I'll bet she's never had goose bumps before either.

"You'd better change, dear," says Mom. "It's supposed to be a cold one." Mom could keep the apartment a bit warmer. It's sixty degrees in here, and with the wind it feels colder, whether you're inside or not. One of the other reasons to love the Midwest: in winter you'll never be warm, just accept it and move on with your life.

"I'll bet you're wondering how people can stand to live here," I say, fighting the shivers that want to jolt through my body. Must not show weakness to the outsider.

"It seems okay," she answers, blushing. She blushes a lot. The pretty, shy types are what my little brother goes for. He hasn't changed since junior high. Do all men secretly prefer the silent librarian-esque girls? I hope not, because there is no way I'd wear those chunky glasses. "I was hoping to see snow, though..." she trails off and looks out the living room window.

"It will snow soon enough," says Mom as she bustles around in the fridge. "Cassie! Get over here and help your mother!"

I smile at Gisele, hoping it appears genuine, and turn to assist Mom with a gargantuan bag of brussels sprouts. "What the hell are these for?"

"Language!" She tips the bag into my hands and pulls more ingredients from the chilled compartments. "I thought we could have a nice, new dinner this year. Try some recipes."

"Besides the three kinds of potatoes?"

"Don't be snippy. Your brother doesn't make it home very often." She has a large package of ground beef in her hands, and I can't help but notice it's not turkey.

"That doesn't look very traditional."

"You're so closed-minded."

"No, I'm not."

"Sometimes I can't believe you're my daughter. Where's your sense of adventure?"

"Mom," I say, looking at the odd food assortment on the counter, "I don't think Magellan would have considered spaghetti and meatballs adventurous."

"What does Magellan have to do with Thanksgiving?"

"Never mind. What else are you making?"

"Cranberries done Norwegian style—"

"Which is?"

But she ignores me and continues, "Couscous with mushrooms and sun-dried tomatoes, a strawberry frisee salad with a citrus vinaigrette, and for dessert—"

"Please say pumpkin pie."

"This thing your old babysitter told me about…flan!"

"Flan?" I sigh. What about pumpkin pie? That's my favorite Thanksgiving food. Joel gets three potatoes and I get flan?

"Yes! It's a custard from *Mexico*." She says Mexico as if it were some magical far off place we could only dream of visiting. I probably shouldn't tell her that my high school Spanish teacher made flan for our entire class junior year. I didn't care for it then, and I doubt I'll like it now. "And there's a caramel sauce to go with it!" Oh Mom. What could have possessed you to become a gourmand so late in life? This must be her boyfriend's doing. At least he won't be joining us for dinner. His other family takes precedence. I was looking forward to a traditional Thanksgiving dinner. Maybe I should have gone to Alicia's house instead. I can smell her stuffing wafting through the vents.

"Did you at least make Grandpa's stuffing?"

"It's called dressing, Cassie, and no, I'm making these other wonderful things. We won't need the dressing."

"What's dressing?" asks Gisele. I'm surprised she's still listening to us.

Before I spit the acidic comeback on my lips, Joel saunters from the bedroom and drapes an arm across Gisele's narrow shoulders. "It's the stuffing that comes out of the turkey, babe."

"Oh," she says, confused as a cat on a bicycle. "We never have turkey on Thanksgiving."

"What do you have, pray tell?" I ask, and Joel gives me a look.

"We usually order takeout," she says, a reminiscing gleam in her eyes. "I love Indian and Chinese."

"Right," I say and smirk at Joel. What a catch, little brother. I wonder at male dating expertise and reconsider why I'm single.

It doesn't take long for spaghetti to cook, so we're ready to sit down by late afternoon. I set the table then Mom rearranges everything in a more elegant fashion. Gone are my festive orange and brown napkins with leaf designs, replaced by linen napkins. She also takes the centerpiece I made in fifth grade (a cornucopia filled with seasonal plastic fruit) and brings out her own creation: an elaborate combination of candles, fake leaves and flowers that smell like cinnamon. Admittedly, hers is very beautiful, but we've always used my centerpiece. What warrants such flagrant psychological child abuse? Is no tradition sacred anymore? What's next, no presents at Christmas?

She seats us around the large rectangular table: herself at the head, Joel next to her, me at the foot, and Gisele on her other side. We could have sat next to each other, but apparently that's too much like how we used to sit. Heaven forbid Joel holds hands with his girlfriend under the table.

"We should begin our dinner by saying grace," says Mom, beaming at the assembled goodies on the table. It all smells fine, but I miss turkey and green bean casserole. "Cassie?"

"What?" I ask, startled. I was remembering fresh whipped cream. I might have been drooling. "Oh, right. Grace." Gisele looks as confused as me, but I grab her hand and Joel's and begin. "Bless us oh Lord for these thy gifts which we are about to receive from thy bounty through Christ our Lord, amen." I say it bullet fast, and Joel grumbles along with me. Mom seems perturbed at my speed but releases our hands and reaches for the spaghetti bowl.

"I almost forgot!" she gasps, and I pause, mid-reach for the sweet potatoes. Joel nibbles a crescent roll, and Gisele piles cranberries a la Oslo on her plate. "We need to go around the table and say one thing we're thankful for. I am so thankful to be having this meal with all of you, especially Joel and his friend." And I will be playing the part of chopped liver today, on the side of stinky onions. "Joel? Gisele? Who would like to go next?"

"I'm thankful for my job in sunny California," says Joel around a mouthful of roll. "And for Gisele, of course." They make gooey eyes across the table, and I almost say I'm thankful for my gag-reflex.

"And I'm thankful for Joel! And this fantastic meal. Thank you, Beatrice. Everything looks lovely." Suck up.

"And Cassie? Don't forget about Cassie," says Joel, grinning. I should slug him and dump the mashed potatoes in his lap. See him get over those second-degree burns.

I try to think of anything I'm thankful for this year and come up with squat. What should I be thankful for? I've gone out with five guys so far this year and none of them remotely registered a feeling.

My friends ganged up on me and coerced me into their tawdry machinations, and they included my boss. I'm forced to edit romance novels until Kelly thinks I've mastered them, and Carly gets Justin all to herself. He was *my* editing partner, dammit! Let's see, my father is a better writer than me and is dating the reincarnation of Imelda Marcos. My brother has decided to break Dad's heart and stay in California for Christmas. Anything else I can be thankful for? In the end I can only think of one thing.

"I'm thankful for Prospero."

Silence cascades around the apartment like a flood. Gisele smiles, not knowing who Prospero is, Joel frowns, and Mom looks perplexed, her fists clenched.

"You're thankful for your cat?" she asks.

"That's so sweet!" gushes Gisele.

"Yes. I'm thankful for my cat." I reach for the one thing on the table I actually want to eat, and slice through the marshmallow layer to reach the gooey orange insides.

"What about this fine meal I've prepared for you? Or for your brother being home? Isn't there anything else you're thankful for?" Her pleading does nothing to my resolve, and I stare at the sweet potatoes. Sure, this is immature, but I've had it this month. All I wanted to do was have Thanksgiving and maybe chat with my brother while watching a movie. Now, I have to share him with *Gisele*, and the meal is pretty much a bust. And if I mention either of these things my mother will explode, her ears most likely landing in the flan on the counter.

Joel clears his throat and gets Mom's attention. "This tastes awesome, Mom."

"Thank you, sweetheart! I worked so hard."

I sweep my bangs out of my face, tossing my head, and Mom glares. "I don't understand why you even bother with that haircut,

Cassie. You have to push those silly half-bangs out of your eyes every five seconds. If you want bangs, get bangs, or put in a hair clip. You're driving me crazy." Since Gisele has the same hairstyle, she blushes and tucks her hair behind one ear. Mom doesn't notice her discomfort and keeps berating me. "You've been a nuisance all day. I don't ask for much. A peaceful Thanksgiving, wouldn't that be nice, I thought, but I guess it's not worth planning if you're going to mope all day long."

"Mom," Joel starts but she cuts him off.

"And your poor brother took a late flight to be here and all you do is fight and make him want to leave early."

"I have work, it's not Cassie's fault."

"Stop, Joel. I know you feel unwelcome here, and I know it's not me driving you away. Who else can it be?" Her eyes bore into me like drills, and I stand, wipe my mouth, and leave the table. "See! There she goes. Stomping off instead of telling us what's wrong."

"She's had a rough few months…" I don't hear what else Joel tells Mom. I take my coat from the hall closet and exit quickly. Maybe there is an open store where I can find some counterfeit stuffing and a piece of pumpkin pie. I might not cook well, but it would be better than stupid brussels sprouts and runny flan.

I'm at home when Joel calls me to apologize for Mom's outburst. Prospero lies by my feet on the couch, purring. At least someone's happy to see me.

"I can't believe she said those things, sis. It's not like her to explode like that."

"Yes, it is. Remember, you don't live here. You get Good Mom. I get Yelling, Shitty Advice Mom." He hears the venom in my voice and changes the subject.

"I know you've had it rough this year, so I'll forgive you for making fun of Gisele."

"I only made fun of her in my head."

"Even so."

Damn Joel. He can always tell what I'm thinking. "I should have gone somewhere else for Thanksgiving or bought all the groceries myself."

"I don't think that would have won you any points either."

"No kidding. She would have said that I was usurping her day to shine. It's been really hard with her. She's so jealous of Dad."

"Why would she be jealous of Dad? Like he has anything going for him."

"Please, I don't want to fight."

"Fine," he sighs, "so how's the love life?"

"Horrible." Joel laughs, and I chuckle too. It reminds me of when we were kids and Jean Foster liked him. She was a skinny little thing with braces and knobby knees. I teased him mercilessly that summer. He only punched me once, but since he was nine it didn't hurt that much. We still laugh about it.

"I could give you some pointers. I'm a gold medal dater."

"I know. I've seen some of them."

"Seriously! I know a lot about dating."

"You know about dating women. What could you possibly tell me about dating men? Did you have a weird college experience I don't know about?"

"Nothing like that. Didn't I warn you about Pete when you first started seeing him? I have this innate ability to pick out assholes." He says it so proudly that I don't chide him for bringing up Pete.

"It's your superpower: douche vision."

"Exactly. That's how I met Gisele. She was dating this prick movie producer who told her she's fat all the time."

"If Gisele's fat then I'm morbidly obese."

"Neither of you are fat! If I were a chick, I'd kick a guy in the nuts if he called me fat."

"That's assault, little bro."

"Confess to a girl cop. She'd let you off the hook." We're giggling like mad again, both imagining me running to a cute policewoman and bearing my heart and felonies. When I catch my breath, I ask Joel what he thinks of Pete calling me on Halloween.

"That dickhead *called* you? I'm going to fucking kill him!" That's a bit extreme.

"Slow down. I didn't answer or anything."

"Good! That guy was nothing but bad news for you! Don't you remember how mean he was? I wanted to kick his sorry ass every time you made us hang out. I kept my cool out of brotherly love, but he's not your fiancé anymore. After he dumped you—"

"I'm going to stop you right there."

"I don't care. Do not call him! I would forbid it, but that'd just make you dial faster."

"I hate Pete," I lie, hoping Joel believes me. The last thing I need is to help pay for Joel's lawyer fees. Pete would be a messy red puddle on the pavement if Joel found him. "I won't call him."

"No matter how lonely you get this Christmas?"

"I promise."

"I don't believe you, but I guess it's your life." He sounds so sullen I almost laugh again.

"I would never go back to him. He ruined my life."

"Sis, you let him ruin your life." This stuns me, and I find I can't breathe. Is that what everyone thinks? That I let Pete walk all over me, dump me, and find a new life?

"Is that what you really feel?"

"I'm sorry. I hate that guy." He didn't deny it. He believes I let Pete bring me down…maybe he's right. Maybe I was cavalier about my feelings. Maybe I let things slide with Pete. "You there?" he asks.

"Yeah. I gotta go. Prospero's hungry."

"I fly out tomorrow. The sun's calling me, and Gisele's afraid her tan's fading."

"Did I tell you how charming I find her?"

"Shut up." Sure, he can tell me how he feels about Pete, but the second I mention Gisele. Sheesh.

December

Dark Tan Dan and Rule Number Seven: Orange is a perfectly natural skin color.

Minnesota winters are harsh. It takes a special person to survive. I trick-or-treated in a Cinderella costume during a blizzard, I drove two hundred miles in sleet just to visit my cousin in Des Moines a few Januarys ago, and I run outside, until the snow gets too deep.

October doesn't see much snowfall, and November can be more windy than snowy, but December is when Mr. Frost kicks things in gear. The first morning after a snowy night is exquisite. The trees are spray-painted sparkly white, the ground covered in pristine crystals, unless an early dog walker sullies it. The clear sky is stuck in time, the clouds barely moving or not present at all. We'll be sick of the snow by January, but that one miraculous morning glows in our memories until Christmas.

Once New Years is past, the snow should be gone. Holiday festivities scream for snow, and a Christmastime without the white blanket seems alien, but after the presents are opened and the Auld Land Synes sung, there shouldn't be more snow. The snow angel's novelty has passed. The snowmen droop and lose their shapes. The icicles dangle precariously overhead like Damocles' sword, waiting to impale those caught unawares. Don't laugh. I've seen it.

But now it's December, and that first bedazzling snowfall has graced the Cities. I thank God that I have underground parking. The plow drivers don't mess around. If you're parked on the wrong side of the street, they'll tow your ass. The magic of the holidays.

Keeley calls me before I go to work, knowing that I get a new assignment today. She wants to spring the next guy on me before I get bad news from Kelly—another romance novel.

"Hey babe! How was your Thanksgiving?"

"Uncomfortable and belligerent. Yours?"

"Fine. My mom made nothing, thank baby Jesus. She let the cook handle things this year." Keeley's mother is a famously terrible cook. The last time I ate her food I couldn't get off the toilet for three hours. I feel jealous that her mother can relinquish control.

"So, what's the bad news? I know you've got the next guy lined up and ready for slaughter."

"Don't worry. He's not like the last one. And for the record, I was against setting you up with Sam. Alicia thought he was charmingly aloof, but every picture on the site showed his cats. I'm all for cats," she adds, hoping not to offend me, "but one is enough."

"Hear, hear," I say and ruffle Prospero's ears. He flips over and tries to bite my fingers. "Try for someone normal this time."

"I picked this one! His name is Dan something, an architect!"

"That sounds promising." People who build stuff can't be that nuts right? They wouldn't let crazies design skyscrapers, would they? "Any other info? Or do I have to research I.M. Pei?"

"He's sooooo interesting! He sailed across the Atlantic, went zip-lining in the rainforest, and drove on the wrong side of the road in England!"

"He's well-traveled."

"Yup. He mostly likes to talk about his business trips."

"He's gone a lot? Why does he live in Minnesota?" I thought architects liked to live in bustling cities like New York and Los Angeles, not in Dullsville, Midwest. Sorry St. Paul. "Is he a snowbird?"

"He has a place in Florida, some condo, but he likes to stay in Minnesota until January." Just like me! What wouldn't I do for a place in Cabo during those horrid months known as January, February, and March? Even April's iffy most years.

"How would you like to go skiing?"

"Not really. Not even a little bit." Is she serious? I'm about as good a skier as I am a cyclist. Plus, I don't have the thighs for ski pants. "How ridiculous would I look skiing?"

"Shut up, you can totally ski. We go all the time."

"When exactly."

"You know. That time in Ludson. All us girls went. We had a blast!"

"You mean that one time five years ago when I sat in the chalet drinking Bailey's and hot chocolate? And Lindsey fractured her tailbone and Alicia left early because Mickey was sick? *That* one time?" I hear her breathing on the other end, trying to think of other fabulous skiing expeditions we've been on, but she's got nothing.

"Oh hell, just go fucking skiing with the guy. He's totally hot and has money."

"Those are the only reasons to date a guy?" She giggles and tries to come up with some other reasons, like she tried to think of ski trips.

"There have got to be other reasons!"

"Lindsey might know some," I say.

"The only reason Lindsey *dates* is to get laid."

I agree to skiing and regret it the moment I set foot in Afton Alps. I remember coming here in grade school and junior high, dragged along with the elated kids who have their own skis and numerous lift badges attached to their coats like medals of honor. I fell a lot, got multiple bruises, and pulled muscles I did not know I had. I cannot stop very well and inevitably cease my descent by falling over. The last time I was here I almost hit the fence at the bunny hill's bottom. I do not enjoy outdoor winter sports.

Today I wear my puffiest winter coat, a turquoise Columbia, along with a knit hat, gloves, and boots. I don't own skiwear, so I'll have to rent. The long, slim skis feel strange on my feet. I'd rather be strapped above a pit of hot coals. My breath freezes in midair and I cough, hating the sudden iciness in my throat. Who enjoys this? Is it even really a sport? My hair flies around my face with the wind, and I wish I'd put it in a ponytail.

As I trudge to the chalet to meet Dan, a sleek black BMW rushes past and careens into a parking space near the doors, throwing up snow cascades as it goes. He almost hit me! The nerve of some people! These affluent assholes are always the same.

Of course, the driver is my date. He steps out of the car and surveys the scene, a handsome face and dark black hair slicked back from a prominent forehead. His features are perfectly shaped, and I understand why Keeley found him attractive. His broad shoulders say: muscular, fit. His clothing is expensive, sleek, and black. There's only one problem: he's orange. Ten thousand times in the spray tan booth too orange. Oompa Loompa orange. Not tan. Not burnt sienna. Not even sun kissed. Freaking orange.

Now gentlemen, let me tell you about fake tans and the women who are not attracted to them. I'm one of them, but I'm sure I speak for many more in our great nation: put away the fake tanner and just let your skin be itself! I'm alabaster pale in winter, but do I spend obnoxious amounts of cash on something that makes me look like a pumpkin? Never, nope, non. The black clothing is not helping him at all. Mortified, I try to keep from laughing as I walk toward him. When he sees me, a blinding fluorescent smile greets me. So, he colors lots of body parts. There's no way those choppers aren't bleached. Is no part of this guy real?

"Cassandra?" His voice is thick and pleasant, self-assured. It reminds me of an old soap opera star, the guy in his late forties who still gets twenty-year-old girls.

"Hi Dan. Or do you prefer Daniel?" Yikes. First meetings are so awkward. I wish there was a way to traverse this part of the date, and I'll bet men do too.

"Dan's fine. The weather's perfect for the first run of the year!" He must mean skiing, because I run year-round.

"It's a bit windy," I say and clutch my arms around my body.

"That's okay. It makes things more interesting." He looks me up and down.

"What?" I ask, annoyed. My attire isn't designer ski, but it should do.

"You don't have skis or boots."

"You got me there. To tell you the truth, I don't ski very often." He is obviously shocked at my confession, as his mouth gapes open. I hope the girls didn't regale him with my dizzying skiing endeavors. Crap.

"But you live in Minnesota! It's almost as good as Colorado!" I highly doubt that, but I suppose he would know. "Afton Alps might not be the best, but it's not bad. Didn't your parents take you when you were younger?" I shrug and shake my head. My mother likes winter sports about as much as she likes pets, and my dad never had time to take us. He used to ski in his youth; there's an odd picture of someone doing a ski jump at his apartment. I've never asked about it, because my father doing anything that thrilling is impossible.

"Wow. That sucks. I was four the first time I put on skis." He rubs his hair back into position and gives me a nervous glance. "Are you sure you want to ski today?" He sounds like a pro flinching at his rookie pupil. He must have wanted to show off his prowess on the tougher slopes. I doubt I'd be able to get down those hills in one piece.

"I was hoping we could maybe cross-country ski for a bit then get some lunch at the chalet. I could try some hills, but I usually end up sliding down on my butt."

"That's fine. I have cross-country skis too." I have no idea how he fit the skis into his tiny car, but he popped the trunk and they slid out like clothing in a vacuum-packed bag. They are very nice, new I'm sure. The downhill skis show more wear and tear. They look much older, as do his boots, but they must be top quality. He handles them like bags of diamonds.

"Don't you need different boots for cross-country?"

"Not with these! They work on both skis. Specially made for my feet."

"Interesting." When a lady says "interesting" she usually means "weird." It's strange that he has custom-fit ski boots, right? I can't conceive of a reason he would need them unless he lived in Aspen.

"I have a small cottage in Vail, so these babies come in handy." Okay, so not Aspen. Three residences? He must move around a lot for work.

"You have places in Florida, Vail, and in the Cities?"

"I have a small flat in London too. That's where I spend most of my time in spring. I do a lot of business there." He designs buildings in England? This guy is pretty impressive, not counting the skin tone. Maybe I should give him a chance.

He walks beside me to the chalet, where he places his skis in the rack near the door. He straps his boots on after going in and this alters his gate, though his long legs easily keep pace with me. He shows me where to rent boots and skis and asks the employee where to go for the cross-country trails.

Once we start skiing, I loosen up. It's a nice aerobic alternative to running, and the motion is much the same, but more elongated and flowing. We get into a groove and cruise around. The trail has a few small hills, nothing to upset my footing, and the crisp air smells wonderful in the evergreens. When the trail is wide enough, we ski side by side and he asks if I want to lead when it narrows. He's so damn courteous I'm not sure what to do or say, and I find myself flushing, and not just from the chilly air. He's loose with information about himself: how he came from a middle-class background in northern Minnesota, went to a New York college on scholarship and excelled at graphic design and architecture, and eventually found clients in England who admired his simplistic designs. He doesn't mention siblings, so I tell him about Joel. He has two sisters, but they're much older and still live up north. One of them married a Canadian!

"That's not so strange. If he were from Zanzibar…"

"But this guy's a Mounty."

"Okay, that's weird."

When we near the trail's end Dan asks if he could see me again. I peer past the tan and pearly teeth and find that he's a nice, handsome man who is interested in me. Maybe he's embarrassed by the orange and didn't want to mention it. He probably just got too dark a treatment by mistake. Lots of people whiten their teeth.

My breath steaming out in long puffs, I say, "Yes."

"You actually looked past someone's flaws and saw the angel underneath?"

"He's not a leper, Lindsey," says Keeley, hurt that I made fun of Dan, albeit in a good-natured way. "He wasn't that tan in his pictures."

"I know he's your favorite out of the bunch, Keel," says Alicia, sipping her Chardonnay, "but it might not work out."

"Or it might," I add and glower across the table at my best friend. She's been snappish all night, and I can't figure out why. Whenever the conversation turns to her, she changes the subject or picks at Keeley, the easiest target. Alicia shrugs and Keeley lifts her eyebrows at me. She's excited that I liked Dan, despite his citrus-hued skin. I even spoke with him on the phone a few days after our date to set up another rendezvous.

"What are you two love doves doing for the, dare I say it, second date?" asks Lindsey. She's not drinking tonight, which adds to the evening's thorny mood. She told me she needs to cut back on the booze, and while I support that decision, it sure has made her cranky. Alicia snorts at the comment, and I glare at her again. What's the damn problem? I would ask, but she will never say anything with Lindsey and Keeley around. I'll have to wait until later.

"For your information, we're going to dinner and a movie. The best Oscar bait always comes out around Christmas."

"You're not exchanging gifts, are you?" asks Lindsey.

"God no! We haven't even been on a second date."

"Does he know you're not getting him anything?" she adds, mischievously.

"He didn't mention it," I sniff and look at the ceiling.

"Right. Better make sure he's not buying you some lavish gift only to come away empty-handed."

"He won't be empty-handed!" says Keeley. "He'll be on a date with Cassie!"

"I love you too, Keel. What do you bitches want for Christmas?"

"World peace, you know, the usual," says Lindsey.

"Something sparkly or shiny," says Keeley.

Alicia doesn't answer. Instead, she checks her phone for the ninetieth time.

"It's five minutes since the last time you checked." She throws her phone in her purse, not looking the least bit apologetic. "What's going on? Are you late for something? Or are we just not entertaining enough?"

"I'm not feeling well," she says and pushes her wine glass away. "I have to go girls. Sorry to cut it short tonight."

"We haven't even been here half an hour!" shouts Lindsey, and a few Brits patrons glance over. "At least finish the wine. That's alcohol abuse!"

"I really have to go."

"I'll call you later," I say, but she either doesn't hear me or doesn't care. She grabs her purse and is out the door in seconds. The falling snow whirls around her when she leaves, her boots crunching salt on the sidewalk.

"What crawled up her ass and died?" asks Lindsey. She takes the wine glass and hands it to Keeley. "Please finish this or I will."

"What crawled up both your asses?" I ask, and she smiles. "Seriously, do either of you know what's up with her?" They both shake their heads and look puzzled. "It must be Brian. Or the kids. She didn't want to talk about Christmas."

"Maybe money's a bit tight right now," says Keeley, sipping wine.

"Maybe she's finally getting that divorce I've been suggesting," adds Lindsey.

"Something's wrong."

"Holy shit is something wrong. Don't look, Cassie."

"What?" I ask and look around.

"Why the hell do people insist on looking when you tell them not to?" asks Lindsey. "Pete just walked in."

"What?" Keeley and I shout in unison and turn toward the door. Pete enters, snow heavy on his shoulders like dandruff. "You got Brits in the divorce, didn't you?" asks Keeley, shocked.

"No shit. He agreed to stay away. This is our place," growls Lindsey, ready to pounce and tear his eyebrows off. I have no idea how to react. When we split up, Pete and I named places neither of us could go, because the other might be there. He chose some bars close to his apartment, and I picked Brits. It's my favorite place besides home; my refuge with my girls after a rough week, my Cheers, my Central Perk. He hates Brits! I want to shout, scream at him to get out, but I think Keeley and Lindsey will beat me to it.

He spots us as he heads to the bar and pauses mid step. He looks at each of us: Keeley red and reeling, Lindsey feral and snarling, and me whiter than even I thought I could get. Shit, Lindsey's going to ruin her manicure. He doesn't seem surprised to see us and sidles past without a second glance. Mortified, I hang my head and sip my drink.

"Don't you dare look embarrassed! He should *not* be here! This is *not* right!" Lindsey stands up, but I grasp her arm and hold tight.

"Don't start something. He came here to see me sweat."

"Of course, he did! Give me my purse!"

"You don't have a gun, do you?" squeaks Keeley, shocked at Lindsey's fury.

"No, I'm just going to beat him senseless with it!"

He saves her the problem by coming up beside the table and saying, "Hi girls." Lindsey's eyes bulge cartoonishly, and as I picture her striking Pete with a giant hammer, Keeley grabs her and runs. "We should go to the ladies, Lindsey." My support system flees, and I'm left with my ex, the great and terrible. I hope they don't take too long in the bathroom. Maybe they're lurking nearby, ready to expedite him from the area should I signal.

"What are you doing here Pete?" He looks good, too good, fabulous. Shit, I thought I could try and hate him. It's not working! Joel was right. I'd let him kiss me if he wanted. Must hate Pete, I say over and over in my head. My panic must have registered on my face, because he answers, "You didn't call me back after Halloween."

"Stalking me in my own territory now?"

"It's the only place I knew you'd be. I've been coming here for weeks waiting to see if you'd show up. The bartender is starting to get suspicious." His smile is like summer. No! Stop looking at him! That was always your problem!

"I thought we agreed you would never come here." I'm trying to be like steel, but I feel like butter in a microwave. "This is my place."

"Don't be like that—"

"Like what? Pissed?" He did this so often. He made me feel bad for being angry with him. How many arguments did he defer by pulling the same tactics over and over? It won't work tonight. "You shouldn't be here. Lindsey's ready to shank you."

"I saw," he laughs, as if that's the most absurd thing in the world. Lindsey may be small, but she's scrappy, and always goes for the crotch. "You wouldn't let her kick my ass, would you?"

"I'm considering it."

"Come on, Cass. It's me." The man I loved who left me for someone else. Keep saying that. The man I loved who left me...

"I don't want to talk to you."

"I'll leave if you promise to see me."

"I don't want to see you." All I had to do was wait for the girls to come back. They would rescue me. Please rescue me.

He smiles his most infectious grin and touches my hand on the table with gentle fingers. I remember those fingers and nearly faint. Why is it that only Pete can make me feel this way? Is he magical? It's a dark, dangerous magic; impossible to resist.

Where are those bitches?

"Say you'll call me." I tried to call you so many times after we broke up, like when we were a couple and you never answered unless you wanted something from me. I called you once two years ago so drunk that I almost forgot I called you, except the evidence was on my phone, and Alicia cursed me for months. You never once tried calling me until Halloween, now that I've lost the weight you helped me gain and wore a costume that made me look like a comic book hooker. Never once.

Despite every alarm clanging in my brain I say yes. Lindsey will strangle me when she gets back from the bathroom.

"Where the hell were you?" I yell into the phone, ignoring the traffic light. A horn honks behind me, but I push the thought of angry drivers away and focus on Alicia. She answers right away, so I know she's not busy. She probably didn't have to leave the bar so soon either. "If my best friend had been there, I might have been able to resist him!"

"You're an adult. You can think for yourself." She sounds annoyed, but I care about that as much as that last stop sign. At least there aren't many drivers out tonight. Too much snow.

"Obviously, I can't. Lindsey and Keeley left me alone with him for two seconds, and I agreed to call him! What am I supposed to do now?"

"You don't *have* to call him. Just pretend you don't remember his number."

"I tried that, you asshole. He wrote it on a stupid coaster. That brown ale does sound good though..."

"Don't drift off. Throw the stupid thing away. 'Oops! I lost it and now I never have to speak to him again.' It's a winning situation."

"I can't believe you. First you act all condescending and weird on the one night a month we get you alone, and now you're acting like this isn't serious. You know Pete. He won't stop until I call him. He'll stalk me from Duluth to fucking Tanzania!"

"Let's not drag the good Tanzanians into this," she says. "You let Pete follow you and coerce you. It's not some mystical power. You just don't know when to say no."

"I don't know how to say no, you mean."

"That too. Just ignore him—"

"And he'll go away? I'm not one of your kids." When I say that she starts bawling, and I'm startled. Alicia doesn't cry easily. Oh crap! I've hurt her feelings! What did I say?

"I'm sorry! I didn't mean it! I—"

"I'm pregnant," she sobs, and I imagine snot bubbles blowing in her nose. That used to happen when she drank too much and blubbered all over our apartment.

"Isn't that good news?" She has three children, but Alicia always dreamed of a huge family, ever since we were little. She had a Barbie Dream House that she filled with her brother's tiny Army men, saying they were Barbie's and Ken's kids. There had to be at least twenty green fatigued guys in that Dream House. Imagine the laundry.

"NO, IT'S NOT GOOD NEWS!" she shouts back and cries some more. She'll drown if she doesn't get a grip.

"But you said last year you might want one more," I say, trying a gentle delivery. I never know how to handle hysterical Alicia. She's the caretaker. The role-reversal is not a good thing. "Have you told Brian?"

"No! I can't get the words out! You're the first person I've told!"

"Where are you?" She's not home, because her husband and kids would wonder what was wrong. I hear no concerned voices in the background.

"My mother's house."

"You drove all the way to Shakopee?"

"Don't lecture me! You're driving around too!"

"You could have stayed at my place. I have a spare bedroom."

She sniffles and doesn't answer for a moment. Faded music plays in the background, maybe a late-night game show. Her mom is nuts for *Wheel of Fortune*.

"I didn't think of that," she finally says. "I need more Kleenex."

"I can't help you there. I'm pretty far away."

"I was talking to my mother, but I think she fell asleep. She didn't even budge when I started yelling at you."

"Tell me exactly what's up. You need to talk to someone who's not comatose."

"It's been a hard year. Brian's not getting as many jobs, and I thought about going back to work at the realtors, but if I'm pregnant I can't work. Money's so tight I can barely afford a month's groceries. I shouldn't have gone out tonight. And the other kids are too young to help with a baby! I suppose Mickey could babysit a bit, but don't older siblings resent that?"

"I did. One summer I had to drive Joel to driver's ed, even though the year before I had to ride my bike or walk, and you know how I am on a bike. One day it poured, but Mom wouldn't let me skip. Then stupid Joel gets a freaking chauffer."

"Thanks for that colorful anecdote. It made me feel so much better."

"You're welcome, sarcastic pants."

"And Oliver's barely three. What am I going to do?"

"Wait a minute! You were drinking wine!"

"Is that all you're worried about? It wasn't wine it was white grape juice. I told the server to switch it for me, so you guys wouldn't suspect." Clever girl, I think in my finest British accent. Very clever. We definitely would have known something was up. "I have bigger problems than faux wine."

"You need to tell Brian, that's the first thing."

"What if he's mad? He loves the kids, but they tire him out."

"He hasn't been working as much, maybe he needs this time with the kids. You've shouldered the parental burden for nine years! Don't you think it's time he put in some hours?"

"You make it sound like community service."

"And I can watch them sometime, or Keeley. Not Lindsey. She's a terrible influence."

"Jesus, they'd be drunk or found outside Tijuana selling tortillas or something."

"There's the jokester I know! Brian is a great dad. He needs to help you out. It's time he took Mickey fishing with him in the spring and taught Sonja how to throw a softball. My mom and dad traded weekends with Joel and I, to teach us something useful or fun. Mom useful, Dad fun. Sure, they ended up divorced and I'm a helpless cause and Joel's dating a supermodel moron, but it was fun back then."

"You're right. I don't know why I didn't say anything. I'm sorry."

"It's fine. You're obviously stressed out to the max."

"You have no idea. I didn't even ask you about Dan or how skiing went. I'm so sorry."

I chuckle, thinking of Dan picking me up out of a snowbank. It happened when we first started on the trail. Did I tell you how gracefully I tripped on my left ski and toppled into a drift?

"That's okay. It was fun. He's really nice and very considerate."

"Not at all like fake Sam?" We both snicker and I think her tears are drying up.

"Who picked that guy?"

"Quiet! He seemed great online. A bit shy but not pushy or rude at all. A few cats but nothing too shocking. People are so secretive." Sweet, trusting Alicia. We should all know that too many cats mean trouble.

"You only learned that from fake online dating?"

"Shut your face."

"Never."

"Don't worry about Pete either. If you don't call him or give him the time of day, he'll eventually give up. You need to be strong. Don't let him pester you. Call Lindsey and she'll break his kneecaps."

Great. Now my best friend, the kindest soul, is suggesting bodily harm. There might be something there.

My dad is subdued this Christmas Eve. Joel's presents sit stacked near the sliding glass window that leads to the small deck, three packages neatly wrapped in blue snowman paper. He stares at the boxes and says, "I'll just send them to him."

"Daddy," I start but have no idea what to say. Nothing will calm the sadness on his face, his eyes downcast and brows drooping. I've rarely seen my dad so distraught. He looks forward to Christmas like every sane person, but it's extra special for him: this is the one time a year all three of us are together. Joel is so cruel for doing this. I can't stand Mom most days, but I attended most of Thanksgiving. It's about keeping the family intact. Joel doesn't seem to care about that. May those three lonely gifts stab him three times in the chest.

"It's okay. He was busy with work." I can't tell him that all non-Scrooge enterprises are closed for Christmas, but he already knows. He's trying to keep a happy face for me. It is not working. "And flights are so expensive this time of year." He could have purchased a ticket months ago. God damn you, Joel.

"At least we're together," I say and pat his shoulder. He's wearing the same thing he wears every Christmas: a reindeer sweater Joel and I gave him when we were in grade school. I'm amazed he kept it so long. Mom never wore the stuff we gave her. We finally got old enough to realize the gifts were ugly.

"I'm happy you're here, sweetie. I wish Joel could have made it, but I made us a great dinner." I'm skeptical, because I inherited my take-out ordering skills from my father. We can dial like crazy but should never be trusted with ovens and stovetops. "I saw that face.

I've been practicing. Sandy is a great chef." Of course. Sandy taught him how to cook.

"What's her specialty?" I ask, faking polite conversation. She probably knows how to mask brimstone and spite in anything. Just like Julia Child.

"She's great at everything, to tell the truth," beams Dad, brightening for the first time this afternoon. Once again, I'm annoyed. Why can't he be happy with just me? "She's a deft hand at the stove but knows how to bake too. And she introduced me to wedge salads, balsamic vinegar and these little cake things, sounds French…"

"Petites fours?" She knows classic French recipes? This woman is good.

"That's the ticket! I can't make those yet," he chuckles and shakes his head. "Not too savvy with baking, but I did make us a chocolate cream pie! The crust is store-bought, but it looks good." My dad is the only man in the world to be embarrassed by store-bought piecrust. "And I did champagne chicken breasts, they're really tender, and I tried green bean casserole, since you missed it at Thanksgiving, and there are mashed potatoes with gravy of course."

"It smells great, Dad." He goes into the kitchen to check the chicken. I'm so proud of him, even if he's been taken over by a harpy. Dad 5.1 is effervescent and confident. He's no longer the defeated soul Mom left in her wake. "And your place looks awesome." He went all out on decorations this year: tinsel on the tall (fake) Christmas tree, our old ornaments strewn about the boughs, meticulously wrapped presents in two different papers, sweet-smelling cherry blossom and pine candles, and a porcelain Christmas village I've never seen.

"Sandy bought the village for me. She said I needed something spectacular to fill the space where my old chair was." That's what's different! His comfy puffy Lazy Boy is missing.

"She threw away your chair?"

"Oh, heavens no," he shouts from the kitchen. "It's at Sandy's apartment. She wanted me to feel welcome there."

"How nice." I grit my teeth. Stay calm, Cassie. Don't storm out of here and set fire to that woman's apartment building. Retain your sanity.

"And wasn't it nice that she let us have Christmas together? She thought it would be hard on you to share me during the holidays."

"What a saint."

"I'm not an idiot. You don't like her." I look up from my hot cocoa and he smiles down at me, a bowl of rolls in his hand. He offers me one, and I take it. They're not homemade, but they look wonderful.

"These remind me of Grandma."

"She loved to make bread but hated doing it at Christmas." He grins and looks at the Christmas tree, shiny in its finery.

"'Too much to do! Too much to do! How can you expect me to make bread when there's so much to do around this place! And your grandpa! He's no help!' Yeah. I remember that." I nibble the bread and Dad tousles my hair.

"Everything will be all right. We'll all be together next year."

"I hope so." I tuck my feet up under my legs. "I miss getting together with the whole family." He sits next to me and sighs.

"It'll be like this for a long time. Even though those times are long gone…it's hard for me too."

"I know. I'm glad I could be here, though. Joel's missing out." He hugs me to him, and my hot coca sloshes, a few drops falling on my jeans. I don't mind.

"Yes, he is." We sit for a moment and ponder the tree, recalling past meals and family gatherings. The first Christmas I remember features a six-year-old Joel refusing to eat dinner because he wants to open presents, a day long running of *A Christmas Story* on television, my mother yelling at Grandpa that dinner is ready and getting cold while he tinkers in the garage, and me getting my first writing journal. I was eight. The cover was bright purple. I wonder where that old thing went.

"Say, Dad?"

"Hmm?" He is caught in memory's hazy embrace.

"Want to watch *A Christmas Story*? After dinner I mean."

"Whatever you want."

The timer goes off in the kitchen, but we stay seated for a while longer. I cannot recall a more peaceful Christmas. Nor a sadder one.

New Year's Eve approaches rapidly after Christmas Day, the year anxious to begin. Lindsey wanted to have a party but decided against it in favor of one last night of debauchery before she actually starts giving up alcohol. She did well for about one week but caved after a horrible incident involving a Volvo and an eighteen-year-old claiming to be twenty-five. That was a spectacular evening.

I despise the time following Christmas. People become their old, indifferent selves. Gone is good will toward men. Away has flown the notion of caring and sharing. Even the Salvation Army's red pails retire for another year. Christmas is the best time of year, a month when people are pleasant and jovial. It smells better, food tastes better (and not just because Starbucks releases the fabulous gingerbread latte), and bells ring loudly in the streets. Even bad eggs like Lindsey are polite. She went to Christmas mass this year! And she swore she'd never go back.

Lindsey chose Brits for our get together, perhaps hoping that Pete won't dare show his face again. He tried calling me twice, but I never answered. Yay me! She thinks if I see him, it's all over and I'll sleep with him. I've brought an insurance policy: Dan. His fake tan is fading, but he remains a bit carroty. He wears a fitted suit and colorful tie. Keeley goggles when he appears by my side at ten o'clock, and Lindsey approves.

"Linds, Keel, this is Dan. We met online."

"We know!" says Lindsey, exasperated. "She talks about you *nonstop*." I blush, because I've only mentioned him a few times, but he's pleased and replies, "That's good to know. I was hoping I made a good impression that day." He grins at me and stoops to kiss my cheek. Even this chaste moment makes me nervous, so I raise my glass and clink it against his and change the subject.

"Lindsey was just telling us about her last date." Her eyes narrow, and Keeley giggles. "Do you need another drink, Keeley?"

"I'll wait for a while. This place is pretty crowded!"

"I know!" shouts Lindsey. "It's almost like it's New Year's Eve or something."

"To a New Year!" says Dan.

"And a new month?" asks Lindsey, raising an eyebrow. I feel like kicking her shin but resist. Dan might not find abusing my friends amusing.

"A new month?" asks Dan. "I suppose we can celebrate that too. But I hate January. That's usually when I leave town and head to Florida."

"Usually?" asks Keeley. God, these two are terrible. How did I survive so long with such horrible friends?

"Well," he pauses and looks at me, "I might have a reason to hang out for a few months."

"Very interesting," chirps Lindsey. "In that case, *I* need another drink." She downs her whiskey soda and threads through the crowd toward the bar.

"What are you drinking, Dan?" I ask. He holds a tumbler half-full of brown liquor.

"Scotch. Being an English pub, you'd think their selection might be limited, but they've got quite the shelf. This is Glenlivet. Fairly old, too."

"I enjoy scotch but don't drink it often," I say. "I think the bottle I have at home is five years old. It's Glen-something."

"Any of the 'glens' are fine," he laughs, and I feel Keeley watching our interaction with keen interest. I wonder why she doesn't have a date tonight. If there's one thing Keeley's good at finding, it's a date. "Are you flying solo tonight, Keel?" Dan asks.

"It's Keeley, Dan. Sorry, I use their nicknames all the time."

"That's okay," says Keeley. "You can call me Keel. Not everyone gets to though, so don't go spreading it around."

Once again, we are Alicia-less. She and her husband are going out tonight for a much-needed date. They found a babysitter and didn't tell us their destination. I hope they have a great time. Alicia deserves a night out. I didn't tell the girls about the pregnancy either. They should know, but Alicia wants to surprise them. Knowing her, it will be in some sweet, jarring way, and the girls will be so shocked they'll forget to be angry. It's okay. I can last one New Year's without her, even if I have an incredible date, I want her to meet.

Lindsey returns from the bar, face ashen. She doesn't have a drink.

"What's wrong?" asks Keeley. "You look terrible! Did you do some shots at the bar?"

She shakes her head and glances at Dan and me. Oh shit. Please not tonight. She looks over my shoulder and I turn, knowing exactly what I'll see, because he needs to make some kind of romance-movie statement. I thought only teenage girls were drama queens.

Pete moves through the crowd, heading straight for us like a great white shark after blood. He looks fabulous, a bit rumpled yet sexy. I look at Dan's coiffed good looks and see no comparison. Pete is compelled to ruin my life repeatedly.

"Hi everybody," he says with a jubilant grin. "Lindsey left me behind at the bar." He smirks at her and I imagine steam and other noxious substances seething through her pores. "Happy New Year!"

"Uh…" Keeley can't find the words, and Dan looks puzzled but holds out his hand. "Happy New Year to you as well," he says. "Are you Lindsey's boyfriend?" She pretends to choke on her nonexistent drink and Keeley scrunches her nose in disgust.

"No," Pete laughs and extends a hand to me. "I know Cassie from a long time ago."

"Not long enough," mutters Lindsey and Keeley pokes her.

"I see," says Dan, uncertain how to respond. "Old college friend?"

"You could say that," answers Pete. "We had a lot of English classes together." He pauses and gives Dan the once-over. "Trouble with the tanning bed, man?"

I don't know what to do. Dan flushes through his fake tan and grips his glass tight, he could fracture it. Lindsey and Keeley stare, unable to repel Pete from the circle. I feel like a lawn ornament, useless and still. I'm a bird hypnotized by a venomous cobra, merely waiting for the strike. I have to say something. I'm standing in this dense crowd with my date, my old fiancé, and two friends who are no help. The air seems filled with smoke, though they banned cigarettes long ago. I can't breathe. I can't think. Is this what love is supposed to be like? A strangler's grip on your throat? A shock waiting to sting when you least expect it? Is this the only man I'm destined to feel this strongly for? It can't be. I need to stop this right now. He can't be the only one for me.

"I need to talk to you for a second," I say and point to a dark corner. He follows, practically prancing behind me. If he thinks he's in for a New Year's kiss he's out of his fucking mind. Who does he think he is, attacking a stranger? Making fun of him just because he's with me? What makes him think he can treat me like this? Oh, that's right: because I let him walk all over my rigid corpse for all those years.

We reach the corner; I spin and almost smack him across the cheek. I fight the urge and say, "That was totally inappropriate. I'm here with Dan tonight." I'm dimly aware that it's almost midnight and hope I can be rid of Pete before the countdown begins. "You need to leave me alone."

"I can't stop thinking about you, Cass," he whines, trying to touch my arm. I push his hand away, and he looks crushed. "We were always supposed to be together. Why do you think I tried so hard to get a hold of you since Halloween? I need you."

"It's always about *you*, Pete. Our entire relationship was about what you wanted and when you wanted to do things. You said you only proposed to me because you thought I might leave." He ruffles his hair and flashes an apologetic frown. This face worked on me years ago when he wanted me to do something he knew I'd hate.

"I was wrong to leave you. I've been miserable for three years."

"That floozy you ran off with didn't stick?"

"She was just a distraction."

"And there's your problem. So easily distracted by the next pretty thing that walks by, or in her case, drunkenly staggered by." I hear the bartender yell that we only have thirty seconds until midnight and ignore Pete and search for Dan in the crowd. I want to kiss him at midnight. I've been planning all week! One of the worst things in a single person's life is having no one to kiss on New Year's Eve. "I have to go." I look once more at Pete, and he looks astonished, perplexed that I rejected him. "Go home." As I try to leave, he grabs my arm and twists.

"Why are you doing this? I'm trying to apologize!"

"Let go! You're hurting my arm!" I pull free and he gapes. Everyone in the bar is yelling, but I can't make out the words.

"You'll never change, Cassie. Still the same pitch perfect bitch." The bar patrons' words become clearer, "Five!"

"I don't care what you think. I moved on, and so should you."

"Four!"

"No one leaves me! Why don't you understand that I can't live without you?"

"Three!"

"I need you like I need fucking cancer!"

"Two!"

"You're a horrible person!" I scream over the crowd. "And I never needed you!"

"One!"

He reaches for me and pulls me in, his lips scraping against mine like sand rubbed in a wound. His kiss is cold and calculated, but full of rage, and I can't break his grip. He holds the back of my head in place and tries to part my lips with his tongue. I hit his back with ineffectual fists and attempt to bite him. Luckily, Lindsey reaches her cracking point.

She knocks Pete in the head with a beer bottle, saloon-fight style, and he releases me and curses. Blood seeps from a cut on his scalp, and he pushes me away into Lindsey. We fall as I crash into her, and Pete disappears.

People gather around us, including Keeley. They whisper and peer down like they're watching *Wild Kingdom*. Keeley takes my hand and pulls me up, then we grasp Lindsey's arms and get her back on her feet. We picked a bad night to wear heels.

"Are you okay?" asks a drunken guy in a red polo. I blink and recall Pete kissing me then falling backward. "That was righteous! You totally took that guy out! I bet my friends that you're lesbians! Was that guy in your territory?"

"Beat it jack hole or you'll get my other bottle!" threatens Lindsey, and Keeley grimaces. Another man fleeing in the face of Lindsey's wrath. "Drunk mother fuckers. I'm so glad I quit drinking."

"What were you thinking?" Keeley asks Lindsay, brushing the dust off my dress. I didn't notice I was dirty. I check my butt. Nothing there. Oh yeah. I fell on Lindsey. "He could have kicked your ass."

"No way! That guy's always been a giant pussy."

"I don't feel well," I mumble. Then I remember Dan. "Where's Dan? What happened?"

They exchange worried glances and clear their throats.

"He left," says Keeley. "He saw you two kissing and booked it."

"Faster than the Roadrunner, babe," interjects Lindsey, rubbing her butt. "You don't look it, but you're really heavy."

"Shut up! Why did you let him leave? It's not like I invited Pete to lip-rape me!"

"I couldn't stop him," says Keeley, ashamed. "And Lindsey was already running over to help you. She said there was no way that dirt bag would get away with what he did."

"Repayment for all those times I had to listen to her bitch about him," she says.

"Shit. Shit, shit, shit!" I stomp my foot and feel tears forming. He ruins everything! Absolutely everything!

"Let's get you another drink," Lindsey suggests.

"Okay," I mumble, and pass through the dissipating crowd to reach the bar. If I can't have Dan for New Year's, I can get good and wasted.

The cab pulls over and I forget to pay. The cabbie jumps out after me, and I apologize, giving him a huge tip. Though his fists are full of money, the driver eyes me with suspicion as he gets back in. He pulls away quickly, and I can't find my apartment building. Where did that idiot take me? My shoes droop in my left hand, my clutch purse in my right. Do I even have my keys?

It's not my street. But I recognize it. Did I give the wrong address? Then I notice the graffitied telephone booth on the corner. I'm at Justin's apartment! How did that happen? There's no way I can get another cab on New Year's Eve. Shit and hell and dammit! And I'm so sloshed I can barely walk two feet ahead of me. Maybe Justin's home. What time is it? I search my bag for my phone. It's a little after three in the morning. It's January. Happy New Year to me.

I search my contact list. Please be home, Justin. Please be sober enough to drive me to my place, or at least have some pajamas and a comfortable couch. He answers after a few rings, "Hello?" he sounds tired, but not slurred. Great! He's not drunk!

"It's Cassie."

"Your name comes up when you call."

"Oh. Well, I really need your help."

"Can't it wait until tomorrow? I'm exhausted."

"Um," I bite my lip and hope he'll let me in. He doesn't live too far from my apartment, but it's freezing, and my feet can't handle these shoes for one more second. It's odd that my feet aren't cold on his steps. "I'm kind of outside your place."

"What?"

"I took a cab from the bar, but I must have said the wrong address, because he dropped me off here. There's no way another cab will come by."

"No kidding. It's after three." He sounds exasperated, a bit annoyed. I would be too if someone drunkenly called me at three in the morning outside my door. "I'll buzz you in and I can take you home."

"Thank you so much! I owe you big time!"

"You owe me enormous time," he grumbles and hangs up. When the door buzzes I rush inside and take two flights of stairs up to his apartment. I've been here a few times, usually hanging out or for small work parties. It's weird to be here alone, though.

"Hi," I say when I turn the corner. He's at his door, rubbing his eyes. His adorable flannel pajama pants sag on his hips, and he wears an old t-shirt with Led Zepplin splayed across the front. His feet are bare like mine.

"Hi," he sighs. "Come on in. I need to wake up a bit first."

"That's okay." I walk in and sit on his couch. I like his Spartan apartment. His furniture is simple and classic, not what you might expect from a man in his late twenties. The paintings hanging on the walls are modern; a nice contrast to the furniture, and soft light plays in the corners from architectural lamps. It reminds me of something a writer would want in his apartment. So silly of me, Justin is a writer. A few poetry books scatter the coffee table: Shakespeare, Auden, and Burroughs. Quite the selection. There's a small volume open to a Sharon Olds poem, and I recall my senior poetry seminar in college. Dr. Parsons *loved* Sharon Olds. "Did you go out tonight?"

"Yeah," he says, leaving his bedroom and coming to sit beside me. "Some guys from my basketball team wanted to hit the clubs." He rubs his eyelids. "Not the best idea. We're not teenagers anymore."

"You're *so* old."

"Doesn't look like partying was the best decision for you either."

"I didn't start wasted. It progressed."

"It usually does. Where were you?"

"At Brits with Lindsey, Keeley, and…" He hates when I talk about the online dating thing, so I don't want to mention Dan.

"You were there with Mr. December."

"For a little while." My shoulders slump and I lose focus for a moment. Pete destroyed any hope of seeing Dan again. "He was nice."

"So why so maudlin? You look like someone skinned and ate Prospero."

"You don't want to hear about it. It's too depressing."

He tilts his head to the side and frowns, concerned. "Sure, I do, if you need to talk about it."

"It's just so unfair," I say.

"What is?"

"Everything. Dating, men, my friends not getting the Power of Courage until it's too late."

"I hear you."

"I don't understand why things can't work out, just once, for me," I say and lay my head back on the couch and stare at the ceiling. He puts his hand on my shoulder and I look over.

"Life isn't fair," he says. "It's old and corny, and everyone says it, but they never believe it. Love isn't some magic equation."

"You mean A plus B doesn't make C?"

"C being love? Nope. That's why I don't believe in Internet dating. There's no way a computer can calculate love. Attraction maybe, but not that."

"I thought Dan might be more…but then stupid Pete was there."

"Your ex-boyfriend?"

"My ex-*fiancé*. The bastard scared Dan away. He kissed me at midnight and ruined my whole evening."

"You kissed your ex-fiancé? The one who left you at the alter?"

"He didn't leave me at the alter!" I say, words flared in anger. "He dumped me right before the wedding and left me for a trampy blond girl named Amber."

"But you kissed him, and you were on a date with this other guy?"

"No. He forced me to kiss him. I yelled at him and told him to leave me alone. Forever! I wanted to kiss Dan! But he left too. Right after Lindsey hit him on the head with a beer bottle."

"Lindsey assaulted your date?"

"No! You're getting it all wrong! Lindsey hit Pete, but it was too late. Dan flew away." I wave my arms in the air to mimic flight, and Justin smiles but tries to hide it. "Why are you laughing? This isn't funny!"

"It so is."

"No, it's not! Stop laughing!" He laughs harder and covers his mouth but won't stop. I pounce on him and punch his chest. "Stop it! Pete ruins everything! The New Year started and as usual, I have nothing!" When I start to cry, Justin stops giggling. "Nothing."

"That's a strong assumption. And inaccurate."

"Oh yeah," I sniff and wipe my nose with a fist. "What *exactly* do I have now that I didn't have last year?" His hand moves toward my face and wipes a tear away. I become keenly aware that I'm straddling him. His chest feels strong under my hands, and his heart beats frantically. I look in his eyes and see fear and tenderness. It's a weird combination, but also fresh and gratifying. Holy crap. Someone wants me. I never thought it was Justin.

I bend my face to his and he rises to meet mine. Our first kiss is awkward but passionate, lips parting and meeting with delicate force. I pull his shirt over his head and fling it over the couch and out of sight. He works more patiently on my blouse's buttons. He doesn't break one. I slip free from the blouse and it flies to meet his shirt. He runs his fingers through my hair and sighs. "I love your hair," he whispers.

I smile and reach for his pajama bottoms. I haven't had sex in three years. I hope I remember where everything goes. He helps me slip off his pants and then...there's nothing.

January

Steven Shaved Legs and Rule Number Eight: Never sleep with a guy and leave in the morning without breakfast.

Oh no. Oh God. Shit, shit. I run from Justin's apartment, shoes in one hand, and my purse in the other. I have no idea where my coat is. I hope I left it at the bar, because I love that coat. But that's not what I'm upset about.

This morning, I had a *When Harry Met Sally* moment, and not the good part at the end where they get together and make that cute video about why they're great for each other. I mean the part in the middle where Sally is distraught because her boyfriend broke up with her and she's getting older. She and Harry make out and end up in bed together. Harry is wide-awake the next morning, terrified by Sally's closeness and her happiness that he's lying beside her. That same thing happened this morning, only I'm Harry, and I feel awful.

Justin smiled in his sleep, naked, and I was naked too! Bits and pieces of the night before come back to my headachy brain: crying, talking about Pete, Justin laughing, then…nudity. I don't recall how many times we did it or how we came to be in his bed. The last thing I recall took place on the couch. You can imagine my dismay. There

I was, in bed with one of my good friends, in a very compromising position. The clock read six, so I slipped out of bed and looked for my clothes. Not in his room.

It's extremely awkward wandering around naked in someone else's home, especially if you're trying to be quiet and sneaky. Objects come out of nowhere and impede your progress, like trying to escape the masked killer in a corny horror movie. I ran into his coffee table, one lamp, and the couch, and luckily nothing fell over. I wanted to scream when I stubbed my toe on that damn table, but I held it in. The last thing I needed was for Justin to wake up and offer me coffee or tea or more sex. It was so awkward. I keep using that word, but no other describes the situation. I felt like a damn teenager again, and not in a happy-go-lucky way.

I finally discovered my skirt under the couch, my blouse behind it, and my bra on the coffee table amidst his poetry books. My shoes sit by the door near my purse, and I couldn't find my coat. When I tried to put on the shoes, my feet shouted outrage. Mega blisters covered my ankles, the soles raw. How did I not notice that? Does sheer panic mask pain? Once I felt it, the pain wouldn't go away. I couldn't wear those shoes.

I opened the door, snuck outside, and crept to the stairs.

Now I'm in a cab. They're numerous after New Year's Eve, and I know what each driver is thinking: it's easy to get fares this morning. Walk of shamers need rides home. I'm doing the limp of shame today.

The morning is crisp and cold, and I miss my coat. Since Brits won't be open, I'll have to get it on my lunch break tomorrow. Oh no. Work. Justin will be there. What do I do? What can I possibly say after fleeing the scene this morning? He'll either be really mad or understanding. Or he might be hurt. I cannot bear listening to myself explain why I left. I can't call in sick, because Kelly is giving me a new assignment. I went through the last romance novel quickly, another book by Elizabeth Hanks just as ridiculous as the last. Kelly nodded approval at my work but said I still needed one more to get the message through. I'm praying for a new author. But I can't face Justin. He'll be so pissed. I can't hold Kelly off forever.

After the driver smirks as I exit the vehicle and I hobble to the elevator, I decide to go in tomorrow. I need to check in with Kelly, and it would be immature to avoid Justin. What we did is perfectly normal. Friends have sex all the time, and they seem fine afterward. Don't they? Can men and women who sleep together ever really be friends? Keeley would say no, and Lindsey would ask why you wanted to be friends with men who weren't gay. Alicia and Brian started out as friends with benefits, but I don't want to marry Justin. I want to change last night. Whatever triggered our encounter needs to be erased.

Even on sturdy shoes I shamble into the office the next day like a geriatric hurdler. I'm later than usual and Amy, the receptionist, gives me a surprised look. It feels like everyone is staring at me, though I know they're nursing their own hangovers. Shame makes echoes.

Kevin is the only person watching me, and when I don't greet him but go straight to my office, he follows and slams the door. Startled, I toss my briefcase in the air and it lands behind my desk.

"What the hell, Kevin?"

"You had sex." He crosses his arms and glares me down, daring me to contradict him. Damn, his radar is well honed. He's like a sex bloodhound.

"Shhhhhh!" I say loudly and look around. Then I remember that we don't work at the CIA and my office is most likely not bugged. "No, I didn't. Go away."

"I knew it. Your defensive stance and denials won't work on me. Kevin knows all when it comes to doing the nasty."

"Don't call it that."

"Fine. The beast with two backs."

"That either. I'm in no mood today for Shakespeare." Which makes me think of Justin…and his butt. I move behind my desk and pick up the briefcase. "Thanks for scaring the shit out of me."

"You can cancel your morning bathroom break."

"I said leave. I don't want to talk about it."

"Did you do someone you shouldn't have done?"

"No."

"Did you make out with another woman?"

"NO!"

"Girl on girl is so hot right now. Let's see…an old boyfriend?"

I get up and frog march him out of my office. He doesn't need to know every little detail about my love life. He can read about it in my journal.

"I'll find out sooner or later." I shut the door in his fox-eyed face and spin around, bracing myself against the door. I need to stay calm. Kelly and that idiot Carly will know something's wrong if I don't get a grip. Should I talk to Justin before our monthly meeting? I don't think so. Save that mess for lunch. Shit! I'm supposed to have lunch with Justin and Kevin today. Kevin will know what happened with his weird-vibe ESP.

I attempt to think of an excuse to miss lunch, and someone knocks and says, "Meeting!"

"I'll be right there!"

Okay, Cassie. You are a powerful, resourceful woman who knows what she wants and is really good at her job. You will not be unmanned by Kevin's sly innuendos, Kelly's lack of taste in books, nor Justin's pained expressions. Take a deep breath and go to the meeting. You can totally do this!

"Good morning, Cassie," says Kelly. "Thank you for joining us." I crowd in Kelly's office beside Carly and Joe Carlson and mumble an apology. Justin stands next to her desk and smiles at me. Thank God, I don't have to deal with weepiness. He looks fine. Carly smirks at me, and I want to punch her. Joe ignores me and taps his pen against his notebook, impatient to begin. "Right," says Kelly. "Justin is assigned Mark Lawson's new mystery. That boy keeps pumping these things out like crazy. Keep an eye out for run-ons and a tendency toward hyperbole." Justin nods and takes the manuscript. "Carly can do the poetry collection from up north. Joe, I want you on a new author, Shirley Mason. She's got real grit. And Cassie, I have a new author for you as well." Awesome! No more romances. I think I've had enough for a long time. "Joe and Cassie, I need to go over a few things with you about these new acquisitions. Justin and Carly, you can go."

Justin doesn't acknowledge me when he leaves, but Carly pushes me out of her way with her shoulder. Joe notices but doesn't say anything. Typical Monday.

"Joe. Mrs. Mason is a prickly old girl. We need to handle her with utmost care and precision. She demands quick work but expects perfection. Her work is edited, but it needs polishing. Don't be afraid to kill some of her babies. I've circled a few in the first three chapters that need cutting. We all know writers have their favorite passages, but some of these must go."

"Take an axe to her trees. Got it," says Joe, and he leaves. I feel a tongue-lashing coming. I'm wrong.

"You did well on the last book," she says and tilts back in her chair. "You're getting better at leaving in some good scenes. I think you cut half of *Kiss and Tell* but left plenty for *Sign of the Monarch*." That's because I couldn't stand reading it anymore and merely corrected the grammar in the second half. "I have a completely different writer for you."

"And a new genre?"

"My dear, your lesson has yet to be learned. No new genre. An emerging author who needs your expertise." She hands me a thin manuscript, maybe two hundred and fifty pages. I'm used to handling three to four hundred pagers, so the paper stack feels light.

"So short?"

"But well written. I find that the shortest work often yields the best results."

"She's edited the entire thing herself already?"

"She swears no, but I am not so sure. The prose is tight."

"If she's such an accomplished editor, why does she need us?"

"Why, indeed?" Kelly smiles her elfish smile and gestures to the door.

I have to admit, I'm curious.

With no reason to cancel lunch, Kevin, Justin, and I go down to the cafeteria. It's too cold outside to brave the streets, and we don't want to lose our good parking spaces, so moderate-to-crappy food it is. I feel like my face might melt off from the heat, I'm blushing so hard.

Kevin chatters in the elevator and all the way to the cafe, going on about his New Year's and the guy he met. "Bjorn is tall, muscular, and so sweet. He's not very bright, but I can forgive him. It's not like

I'm going to marry the guy." He laughs and Justin snorts. I try to be mirthful but sound fake. Kevin doesn't say anything, but I know he's fishing for information. He reads my body language, gauges my vocal tone, and watches every facial tick, all while nattering on about Bjorn. Who names their kid Bjorn?

We sit in the semi-crowded room and stare at our trays. The cafeteria has little to offer on the best days, and this afternoon is no exception. My wheat roll is a tad stale, but the tomato soup is hot if bland. The coffee is okay, but it needs help. I wish they had honey. Justin and Kevin pick at their food as well, and Kevin dominates the conversation.

"I didn't take Bjorn home, though. He needs a few more dates to determine eligibility. Then there's Bobby. I'm not sure about him either. He's super intelligent but not the best bod. That new intern from the fifth floor seems interesting, but my gay-dar's not flashing on him. He probably bats both sides. So, Cassie who'd you sleep with last night?" He slips it in like a master manipulator, and I almost say "Justin." Instead, I choke on my soup and spray roll bits on the table. Justin reaches over and pats my back, and I cringe away from him. Not much, but the motion is enough. Kevin's eyes go wide, and Justin looks away.

"That good an evening huh?" asks Kevin, looking from me to Justin. "You must have had a dry night with that reaction. Oh well. Maybe I'll call Keeley or Lindsey later. They probably had some fun."

I leave work early, unable to look Justin in the eye or talk to Kevin. I'll go home and start reading the new book. Maybe some light frivolity will distract me. As I push the garage button in the elevator, Justin slides in. The door closes, and I'm trapped. I feel like a woodchuck willing to gnaw its leg off to escape an iron trap's jaws.

"Hi," he says.

"Hi."

"So, you were gone when I woke up."

"Uh huh." Come on elevator, go faster. The sooner this ends the better for both of us.

"It surprised me is all. I thought you might stay and chat before you left."

"Um."

"It's all right. I totally understand. It was weird, right?"

"A bit."

"But good too right?"

When I don't answer his smile fades. "Oh."

"I'm sorry, Justin. I didn't mean for that to happen. I don't even remember everything." He draws away from me. "What I do remember was nice," I add, but it must be the wrong thing to say, because he turns toward me, his expression unreadable.

"Nice?"

"Um." I suck at this. "I'm really bad at this."

"You could have given me the brush off to my face instead of cowering all day."

"Wha?"

"You've been acting weird all day. Kevin knows something's up. He's been bugging me, hinting since lunch."

"I didn't mean—"

"Of course, you didn't." He looks really mad, and I'm not sure how to quell him. "You know I've liked you forever, why would you sleep with me and sneak out when I'm passed out? It's not like I was dead sober either. I felt terrible when I woke up and you were gone. I thought I did something wrong."

"You didn't...I didn't know you had feelings for me."

"Everyone knows I like you! Kevin's been teasing me about it for three fucking years!"

"I didn't know—"

"Don't lie to me!"

"I'm not. It's just—"

"Then why did you come over last night? Why the hell did you tell your cab to come to my apartment?"

"I don't know. I was drunk."

"And you were crying about Pete and some Dan guy." He shakes his head. "I should have known this would happen. I should never have kissed you back."

"I made a mistake."

"It was a mistake?" Crap. I cannot say the right thing to save my life. When will this elevator to hell let me off? "That's not the way I meant it. I don't want this to ruin what we have."

"And what do we have? It doesn't seem like much."

"You're one of my best friends—"

"I don't want to be your friend. Not anymore." The elevator air turns chilly, and he stands before the door, ready to bolt when it opens. It's amazing that no one else attempted to get on, otherwise our argument might have ended differently.

"Please, Justin."

"Just…just leave me alone for a while."

The doors open, and I realize I made a huge mistake. Justin is one of my lifelines, a good listener and so fun to hang out with. I can't let him go like this, so angry.

"Can't we talk more about this?"

I leap from the elevator as the door closes on me, ouch! He is heading for his car, keys in hand but no coat. Just like me this morning. He doesn't want to go back to the office and get it. Afraid of Kevin's knowing glances and comments. He looks at me with more scorn than I could have imagined. I feel like disappearing on the spot. I never knew I could elicit this much rage in someone. Is this what Pete did to me? Red blotches cover his freckly cheeks, and his lips are a thin white line.

"No. You broke my heart."

"That's melodramatic," says Alicia, and she brings me a hot mug of chamomile tea.

"It's not," I say, tired and demolished. "It's pretty accurate from what he told me."

"He's acting like a high school girl." She's trying to be supportive, do the good girlfriend thing and put down a bad boyfriend. I know she's hiding her true opinion, because she wears her I-want-to-give-you-a-lecture expression.

"If there's one person I need to hear the truth from, it's you. Cut the bullshit and say what you want to say." Her face scrunches and her nostrils flare. She's fighting her word vomit. "Did you know Justin had snuggly feelings for me?"

"Of course, I did!" she yells then covers her mouth. I nod, telling her to go on. "We all knew. Lindsey picked up on it first, that time you introduced him to us at Fantastic Fern's?"

"That was the first time you met him!"

"I know. Lindsey's that good. That's why she gets laid so often. She picks up the unconscious I-want-to-do-you vibes." I slump back on the couch and kick my feet. Why didn't they tell me?

"You could have let me in on it."

"And ruin everything?" she laughs. "He seemed so perfect for you; we didn't want to tip you off."

"What does that mean?"

"You exclude every guy who shows attraction to you. You toss them out like last night's dirty bath water."

"That's not fair."

"But true. I've known you forever, and you've always been like that. Even Pete had to woo you for four years."

"And look how that turned out," I say, grumpy. It never feels good when your friends are right. I wish Alicia had her information wrong, but this is one of the reasons she and the girls concocted The Plan, to catch me off guard and force me to date strangers. I have the tendency to push men aside the moment they decide to ask me out. It's a talent.

"Don't be such a sour puss."

"I'm not one of your kids, you can use grown-up words with me."

"Don't be such a bitch, then."

"That's a bit strong."

"No, it's accurate."

"I meant the tea." She looks down on me, hands on her hips, then she smiles. I push out my bottom lip and pout. "It's too hot."

"Drink it and shut up. Let Justin come around in his own time. It won't do any good to chase after him. He doesn't want your attention right now. Don't go through Kevin either. Justin will see that as manipulation and never speak to you again. He'll come back when he's ready, and not a second before."

"You sound like a self-help manual. 'Don't speak to one of your best friends, even though that's the most logical thing to do. Communication is never effective.'"

"Don't make fun of the relationship guru. In your case, Justin would push away any apology you threw at him and might quit his job or move away. Men can be such babies when they're rejected."

"I didn't reject him."

"Yeah, you did. He needs time to move on and get his feelings in order. Be courteous but don't seek him out unless he tells you to. He might even tell Kevin when he's ready, so keep that boy close."

"I always do."

"Not in a naughty way. That's why you're in trouble."

"Does everyone want to crawl up my ass and lecture me?"

"Only your best friend."

Kevin's Top 10 Reasons Why You Should Date Justin

10. *He has a really hot body.*

9. *He's sensitive. The guy reads poetry for fuck's sake.*

8. *He's straight, so he's got that going for him. And you. You like straight guys, right?*

7. *He hates the people you hate. (Carly, Hitler, Joseph Stalin, Nora Roberts)*

6. *He hates the things that you hate. (Pecan pie, mustard, real mayonnaise, romance novels)*

5. *He brings you coffee for no reason and remembers stuff you like.*

4. *Look at that face! It's like when I first read The Iliad! He's basically Achilles.*

3. *He can't use tanning booths, because he's pale like you.*

2. *He doesn't play video games, unlike me, but that might be a reason not to date him.*

1. *HE LIKES YOU! NOT MANY PEOPLE DO! Just kidding about the second part.*

Oh, and here's the info for your next date. Keeley and Lindsey are still afraid to talk to you, and Alicia asked nicely.

It's the middle of January, so I'm concerned for my date. He's wearing shorts. It's a few degrees below zero. You might have heard of a little thing called frostbite. Down south it may be a scary myth, but in the Frozen North, it's a reality. I've seen people missing toes and fingers from unfortunate ice fishing and hunting accidents. Okay, I've never seen them personally, but I saw the pictures. Who wants their limbs to turn black and fall off? This guy apparently.

We arrive at the bowling alley at the same time, which is odd, because the road conditions are hellish. I thought one of us would be late. His legs are the first things I notice: not just because he's wearing shorts, because they're shaved. He has dark hair all over his head and arms, so it's not blond or hard to see. It's gone. Is he a swimmer or something? My mother always told me it was rude to stare and also rude to bring up people's shortcomings. Would you want someone to tell you your nose was huge, or your ass was nonexistent?

"Hi, Cassie! I'm Steve!" He holds out a hand and encompasses my fingers in a firm handshake. "I hope you like bowling!" He's tall and muscular; the calf muscles ripple nicely when not blocked by hair. Does he not like wind resistance on his legs?

"Hi. I'm not the best bowler, but I hold my own. My dad was in a league."

"Awesome! Me too. But I quit last year. Team politics." I wonder what kind of falling out could be catastrophic to a bowling team. Did some chick Yoko Ono their best player? Did the anchor lose his edge? "I guess we should get our shoes!" He is excited about this date. Nearly every sentence ends in an exclamation point. And he smiles way too much. Oh God. I'm one of those people who hate others for being too happy.

"I hate bowling shoes. I should have brought my old ones." Yes. I own bowling shoes. Leave me alone.

"I thought about bringing mine, and my ball too, but I walked here. Too much to carry in the snow." He walked here? Did shaving his legs kill his brain cells? "And since I lost a bet to this guy at work, I have to wear shorts through January. It's fricken cold out!" No shit, Sherlock. A lost bet explains the shorts, but he failed to mention the conspicuous absence of hair. I nod and move to the shoe rental counter.

We get oddly scented shoes and make our way to our lane. A rowdy group of teenage boys is to our right, and a tall, angular gentleman is to the left, no one else on his team. He moves like a spastic spider down the lane to throw his ball, but his follow through is perfect, and he gets a strike. Steve admires him, and the guys to the right hoot as one of them gets a gutter ball. They remind me of high school trips to the bowling alley. It was fun to get a bunch of people together and goof off at the local place, especially for moonlight bowling on the weekends. I can almost see the details of the backdrop in black light, neon colors shining.

"Ready?" Instead of silly nicknames, Steve wrote our actual names for the scorecard, which you have to figure out manually. Great. My math skills are not exemplary. I'm about as good at this kind of thing as I am taking advice about relationships. If I get a strike or a spare I'm screwed.

"I hope you can do the scorecard. I'm not the best at it."

"Oh sure. The first league I was in used old scorecards. I like the automatic ones better, mainly so you can have a few beers and not worry that someone's messing up the totals."

"No, you wouldn't want that to happen."

"It's a very serious sport." About as serious as backgammon or checkers. I smile, trying not to laugh. I have to remember not to be judgmental on the first date. Dan turned out awesome, even though he was more orange than a traffic cone. It's too bad Pete had to ruin things on New Year's. I might not be going on stupid first dates anymore.

He wins the first game decisively, getting over two hundred. I barely make one hundred and vow to do better in the second match. I'm having fun, to be honest. I recall bowling being entertaining, but it's even better playing with someone who's really good. He doesn't get angry if he misses a spare and is jubilant over my successes. The only problem is that he keeps ordering more beer. After our first pitcher, I switch to soda water. One of the first rules of the blind date is not to drink too much, because once those inhibitions are gone, so is your first impression. He's not a mean drunk, but he becomes sloppier the second game. His score suffers as he gets halfway through the second pitcher, and I almost beat him. I wonder if his team fractured because of this problem. Who wants a guy that can bowl over two hundred until he gets some alcohol?

He grins brightly at the finished tenth frame and scrawls our final scores in the last spot on the sheet. He stares at his score and shrugs. "Oh well. I'll do better next game."

I pause. It's near midnight, and I should really get home to feed Prospero. Listen up ladies: if you're thinking more about your cat's welfare then about your date, it's time to leave. The sparks are not flying.

"I'm sorry, Steve, but I have to go. It's getting late, and I have a big project to work on tomorrow for the office."

"That's too bad!" He frowns, trying to find a way to make me stay. "Do you really need to work on it tomorrow? Can't it wait for Sunday?"

"Afraid not. I have plans on Sunday." No, I don't. I just need to leave. I'm not proud of lying, but I barely know Steve, and I don't think I want to know him better. I check my watch to show my concern for the time. Steve nods sadly.

"All right. I hope you had fun! I sure did!"

"It was really fun. I just have to go."

"See you again sometime?" Is he not leaving with me?

"You're not leaving?"

"Nah. I think I'll finish the set. Never leave a set unfinished!" I think he's doing the same figuring in his head: if the game is more important than your date, cut your losses and finish the game. Guys and girls aren't that different after all.

February

Lovelorn Logan and Rule Number Nine: Just because you do not have a boyfriend on Valentine's Day does not make you a leper.

Mom calls a summit meeting three days before the most dreaded day of the year. Single people, you know what day that is, and all assholes in relationships, suck it. She wants me to meet Gideon, her boy-toy. I haven't spoken much with her since Thanksgiving, and whenever I talk to Joel, he has no idea what Mom's opinions are. Brothers are useless. Why couldn't I have a sister?

I'm sure she has something up her sleeve. Maybe Gideon has a good-looking son or a nephew desperate for a Doomsday date. Or maybe she just wants me to meet her beau. That's a weird word: *beau.* I have a difficult time calling someone a boyfriend or girlfriend when either party is in their fifties. It sounds wrong.

I agree to meet with her for Sunday brunch in St. Paul, the Chatterbox Café. They have enormous mimosas and cinnamon French toast you would kill for.

It's not too cold today; the wind subsided around eight this morning, right after my run. My run felt like trudging up a mountain, and I was on flat ground. I'm wrapped in a scarf, mittens, a winter cap, and my puffy Columbia jacket. They aren't very figure flattering but staying alive and warm is my chief concern.

I arrive at the restaurant first and get us a booth by the window. The server is interesting: a longish brown beard, very thick, covers his round face, and his vitality glows from within. There are those few people that can light up any room with the force of their personality, and this guy is one of them. His voice is loud and sonorous, and his bearing is laid back but confident. He inquires about the people I'm waiting for, and from my answer ("my mother and her new boyfriend") he understands that I need a giant cocktail.

"One mimosa coming up!"

Unusually, my mom is running behind. She hates lateness, something she drummed into Joel and me long ago. I feel better arriving at a destination at least fifteen minutes early. Tardiness gives me a rash.

Where the hell are they?

Twenty minutes late, my mom struts past the window, a tall man on her arm. She laughs merrily at something he says and tilts her head back, teeth showing. My mother obscures the man, so I don't get a good look at him. He must be why they're running behind schedule.

As they approach the table, I glare at Mom and tap my watch.

"Sorry we're late," she gushes and pulls me from the booth by my arm with enough force to launch me into the kitchen. She stands me before Gideon and beams. "This is Gideon Foster. Gideon, my daughter Cassandra."

He is incredibly handsome. My mother always said she would never get involved with someone as ugly as Dad ever again. Dad's not ugly! He's just plain! Gideon's clothing suggests wealth: a silk red scarf, full-length Burberry trench, sleek black shoes, and strong, masculine cologne. It might be Armani. He reminds me of an old school movie star, Errol Flynn or Kirk Douglas, but far more good-looking. Where did Mom find this guy?

"It's a pleasure to meet you," he says, voice crisp and honeyed. "Your mother speaks of you constantly." I'll bet she does. Gideon makes me want to break out my best Katherine Hepburn impression, but I better not. Mom wouldn't appreciate my humor.

"I've heard a lot about you too, but never how much you look like George Clooney." Mom glowers at me but Gideon laughs heartily.

"You're too kind. Your mother is too modest." He looks at her and his eyes twinkle, and Mom looks equally happy. Damn them. I was planning on avoiding all happy couples this month. "It's my fault we're late. I wanted to stop by this fascinating antique shop and your mother acquiesced." Wow. He just said "acquiesced." I cannot help but be impressed, then I feel suspicious. Who is this guy and what is he trying to steal from my mother?

"Find anything interesting?"

"Not this time, but I enjoy random shops of that nature. You never know what you'll find." He nuzzles Mom, and I fight the vomit reflex. I sit down and sip my mimosa. The server appears from nowhere and ushers Mom and Gideon into the booth and gets their drink order.

"Are we all doing the brunch buffet?" he asks.

"I believe so," I say and look at Mom and her man, who are not paying the least attention. I turn back to the server and nod, trying not to scream. How is it that my mom and dad have found love for a second time and I've yet to find an actual good relationship. It doesn't seem fair. Maybe I should ask out our server and have done with the whole thing.

After a few trips to the awesome buffet, I'm stuffed with enough French toast to lessen my annoyance at their canoodling. I watch them more intently. He is attentive to Mom's every need. He carries her plate and lets her sit first in the booth. He reminds her about her napkin before it falls on the ground and wipes the corner of her mouth when whipped cream rests there. Ugh. They're romantic and mushy and into every kind of icky public affection. I never felt comfortable with these displays. Maybe that's why Pete called me cold and unfeeling. I remember one time when we went to brunch with Pete's parents. I had gained weight since our engagement, a lot of weight. Pete knew how stressed I was at work and with planning the wedding. I told him every night how things were falling apart, and that I needed him to help me out a little. His idea of helping me out was to ask me if I really wanted to eat pancakes at brunch, since I was so nervous about fitting into my wedding dress. He said it loud enough for his parents to hear, and they had both blushed at my expense and tried not to laugh. Mortified, I ordered the fruit plate instead and miserably picked at overripe cantaloupe while they enjoyed their breakfast. I can still remember the café smells: burning oil, overdone eggs, and too-sweet maple syrup.

"How is work, Cassie?" asks my mom, pulling me back from the memory.

"Fine. I've got a new project."

"Your mother mentioned that you work in publishing," says Gideon, wiping his mouth with his napkin. "What do you do exactly?"

"I'm an editor, so I get manuscripts and go through them thoroughly. I look for grammatical and language issues and decide whether the book is in the right order or if the story needs more work."

"But aren't you a writer? I thought maybe you wrote for the company or something?" He looks confused, and Mom picks at her food, unsure what to say.

"I was never a writer," I admit. "But you can't make rent on that, so I joined Weston's." When I was younger, I thought that an editing job would let me work on my own stuff. Numerous unfinished short stories litter my desktop. I squirreled away one hundred pages of a novel before succumbing to the overwhelming workload Kelly put on me as an intern. The only writing I'm working on now is this stupid journal and whatever I'm assigned to edit.

"You shouldn't give up if it's your dream," Gideon says in a kind tone. "I wanted to be the state's best investment banker, and now I am." Mom nods, a proud gleam in her eyes. "It's not very glamorous, but I've always enjoyed numbers and I was dreadful at chemistry, so here I am, not an engineer or a doctor, but I still help people." And got rich doing it. No wonder Mom likes him. He's way more successful than Dad could ever be. At least at investment banking.

"People always need money," I say.

"Yes, they do," says Mom in a warning tone. She can tell when I'm making make fun of someone. She once called me pretentious and I called her self-righteous. We did not speak for three weeks after that incident. "You should be very proud, Gideon."

"You must think me boring," he says to me.

I shrug and say, "No, not boring. My math skills are atrocious. Just ask my friends. The only percentages I ever worried about were whether a table gave me twenty percent or not."

"That makes sense," he says and laughs. "I used to tend bar in college. My family had practically no money, and scholarships only get you so far." Finally intrigued by Gideon, I lean forward as he continues. "I couldn't stand the rich kids who came in and spilled beer all over the place. The bar was my second home."

"Mom and my dad helped me out as much as they could," I say, and Mom smiles, happy we found something in common. I can tell that she worried whether I liked Gideon but would be perfectly fine telling me to mind my own business if I said he wasn't good for her. "But I still have a ton of debt. That's mainly why I stayed with Weston's after my internship."

"Did they pay you?"

"Unusually, yes. I got the coveted paid internship. The company only had one spot they could afford to pay, and the resumes were competitive. Luckily, I edited my high school paper almost single-handed. That impressed Kelly, my boss, so she pushed for me to get the position."

"Do you think it was a good idea to stay there? Now, I mean. Don't you want to get back to writing?"

"Of course. Someday. But it's complicated. I have no time for myself that doesn't involve running, cooking, or sleeping."

"The first thing I learned about work is not to be its slave," he says. "Remember what you really want to do with your life, and don't let work get in the way."

That's easy for you to say, Gideon. You've already surpassed your rough years. I feel age thirty pressing on my neck, and no publications under my belt. I had planned on being published by twenty-five, and to have a book deal by thirty. What happened to me? What happened to my plan?

"Don't get so down, Cassie," says Mom, and she takes my hand, something she hasn't done in a long time. "I know you'll write the great American novel someday."

I never knew Mom had that much faith in me. Is she just putting on a show for her boyfriend? Or is this what has been missing over the years? Someone's belief that I could do what I wanted? Be what I wanted? Dad says he's proud of me no matter what, and Joel reads all my work and gives encouragement. But I always knew their good opinions were a given. They would never criticize my work or me. Maybe what I really needed was my greatest critic to acknowledge me. Are we all slaves to the critics? Or is it just me?

I meet Logan Hilton (no, not that Hilton) at a small café in Minneapolis. The girls made me choose a name out of a hat when we went to the bar last weekend, because they were arguing over what guy should be next. Lindsey mentioned scraping a barrel bottom and Alicia punched her in the arm. I do not have high expectations for this date, not because the girls couldn't focus on the perfect February man, mainly because I'm still upset over the Justin incident. Alicia's advice is difficult to take. I used to spend most lunches with Justin and Kevin, but it's too hard. Justin brings his own lunch or leaves the building without saying his destination, and Kevin tries to cheer me up, but it's no good. He wants to talk about what went wrong and why Justin and I can't be together. He believes we're meant to be or some crap like that, but he backs off when I give him my acerbic stare. Work has been miserable, and I'm behind on the new manuscript. I've barely gotten past the title page. It's about a couple having trouble communicating about their relationship. That's all I've figured out so far about the plot.

It's freezing outside, so I'm wearing my usual winter attire. I get to the coffee shop early so I can see what the new guy looks like. I don't need any surprises today. The shop is decked out in red and pink hearts, and lacy doilies adorn each small table. Next to the register sits a glass Cupid figurine with a bow and arrow. This month makes me feel like barfing. It's so fake, like we're all looking into a diorama of a relationship. The man is bullied into buying overpriced cards and flowers when he could get them half off the next day, and the woman is expected to fawn over these gifts and made to believe that if her boyfriend does not comply with her wishes he should be shunned for a least a month. I may sound like your everyday cynic, but I've had a long time to build up this snarky attitude, and believe me, there are a lot of people out in the world who do not celebrate February fourteenth. They survive, even those in relationships. If a couple can't get past that day unscathed, I think they're in danger.

I order a cappuccino and survey the passersby, which are not many. A group of businessman rush past, hands thrust in coat pockets, breath steaming from overactive mouths. A teenage girl in pink earmuffs glides by the window, impervious to windblown hair.

My date is right on time, which is awesome. He looks exactly how Kevin described him: middle height, slim, and good-looking in a bookish way. He has two deep dimples in his cheeks and they're a bit distracting, like twin dark caves. His hands are enormous, clad in black leather gloves, not proportionate to the rest of him. I wonder if he plays the piano. I get the impression that he has been on a lot of dates. He seems at ease and comfortable in this first date setting, and he obviously knows the staff. The barista brings him a huge coffee covered in whipped cream.

"My one vice," he says when I eye the mound of white frosting, and thanks his friend. "I can't fight the craving, so I might as well give in."

"If whipped cream is your one vice, I think you're too good for this world."

"Well, I might have other idiosyncrasies, but I hide those pretty well." We laugh, and he sips his drink, careful not to receive a white mustache from the cream. "For instance, I'll bet you had no idea that I like Keanu Reeves movies."

"I would never have guessed."

"His fans are usually covered with acne and talk about Kung Fu."

"And overuse surfer lingo like 'rad' and 'gnarly.'"

Feeling slightly like a dork, I can't help but enjoy Logan's company. He reminds me a little of Dan. He's older than me, but that doesn't bother him. He's interested in books, many movies that don't include Keanu Reeves, and snowboarding.

"I'm terrible with winter sports," I say, recalling my date with Dan. "Give me beach volleyball over ice skating any day."

"It's pretty hard to play beach volleyball right now."

"I don't enjoy sports throughout the seasons. It's not like food."

"How so?"

"Well, I like squash and Honey Crisp apples in the fall, because that's when they're in season, and I wouldn't touch a tomato until summer or late spring. The winter ones taste like cardboard. Sports are like that too; they come in seasons. Would you like skiing in the summer?"

"You're a foodie?"

"Not so much. I'm a mediocre cook, some say 'bad.' I like foods that don't take much coaxing to become meals."

"TV dinner fan myself, at least all through college. I lived on instant macaroni and cheese."

"Who didn't?"

We don't mention that V-Day is approaching but make plans for a second date. Tomorrow marks the fourth year I've been alone on that day. We cynics may hate stupid St. whatever day, but it's still hard to admit that you feel lonely and terrible when you have no one to buy you a flower or send you a crappy card. We're a sorry lot, aren't we?

The fourteenth comes and goes like always, and I try not to remember what Pete and I used to do. Even though I hated the day, Pete made reservations at some restaurant, and we had a good time. He made a big show of giving me presents, and I wonder now why he didn't give me gifts on random days of the year. That would have been more special. Pete never listened to me about Valentine's Day. He wanted to "celebrate our love." I was happy to celebrate it alone in our apartment, but Pete was a showman. If he couldn't be the ringmaster in the V-Day circus then he didn't have any fun.

He also made a show and proposed in front of a billion people. He didn't put the ring in dessert or anything lame like that. He didn't have a violin-toting amateur musician serenade us. He didn't tie it to a champagne flute and toast our love. He simply got down on one knee and asked me if I would make him the happiest man on earth. Corny, but how could I refuse? We were surrounded! And I desperately wanted to make him happy. What a fool.

Note to all you men out there: do not propose to your girlfriend on any significant date. Not on Christmas, Easter, your first date anniversary, your parent's birthday, her birthday especially, nor any other bank holiday. You want that day to be special on its own, not to be overshadowed every year by something else like the birth of Christ. You can't compete with Jesus.

The day after that horrible atrocity of a holiday, my mother calls and invites me over for tea. Since she hates tea but enjoys pretension, I accept. I immediately wonder if Gideon will be there and hope he's not. I liked him in general, but once was enough. Although I have a feeling he'll be hanging around for some time.

When I get to my mom's place it's a bit past two in the afternoon, and soft music sails out her door when I knock.

"Gideon suggested this CD. He says it will calm my nerves," says Mom when she ushers me inside.

"It's nice." It sounds like beach noises, whales and whatnot. Very soothing. Not very suitable for tea, however. Mom's not one to break protocol on social visits. Interesting. Maybe Gideon is loosening her up.

"It reminds me of that trip we took to the coast when you and Joel were very young."

"I don't remember," I lie. Who can forget playing in saltwater for the first time or almost flaying their foot on a sharp shell? Joel stepped on a jellyfish, and Dad peed on his foot behind a clump of tall beach grass. It was hilarious.

"I do. It was a lovely time. July at Redondo Beach. The water was so warm and beautiful."

"Um hum."

"Come in and get comfortable. Tea's almost ready."

I walk into the dining room and am surprised to find the table bare. She usually brings out a mismatched collection of tea wares; tiny spoons twinkling in the lamplight, and china cups with chipped rims and saucers that are too small or too large. Today, there's only the usual placemats and a large bowl in the center containing pinecones. They smell like cinnamon.

She comes in with the teapot and two coffee mugs clutched in her hands, a small smile dances across her face. She looks frightened, like I might yell at her. I've rarely seen my mother look fragile. She's about as dainty as a garden gnome, no matter how many cashmere cardigans she has. I'm used to her forbidding posture and powerful voice. This new mother scares me about as much as my dad with confidence.

"Are you feeling okay, Mom? Did you get the flu that's been going around?"

"No, I'm fine. I get headaches in the morning but nothing to worry about." She sets down the cups and pours hot water into each. Two teabags sit in the cups, ready to steep. A light woodsy perfume floats out of the cups and engulfs us. I'll never know why Mom insists on drinking tea when she doesn't like it. Maybe it's the scent she craves. Tea always smells better than it tastes. Unless it's chai tea.

"So," I begin, unsure what to say. "Gideon was nice."

"Yes. He's helped me a lot."

"I see." I have absolutely no desire to hear what he's helped her with. No new renovations, so it's got to be in the bedroom department or something equally appalling. We both sip and I know she wants to say something but can't seem to spit it out. "He was kind to mention my writing," I say, too bitterly. She looks up and her eyes flash. There's the old Mom.

"He only talked about it because he was nervous. You have no idea how you make people feel."

"Like what?"

"You make them feel stupid. Like everything they say is utter rubbish."

"I was perfectly cordial at brunch."

"You were snobby and aloof. Gideon had to pry words out of you. I felt a little embarrassed. I talk about you all the time, and he was excited to meet you. Now he feels like he made an ass of himself."

"I didn't know I was making him uncomfortable," I mumble. I did know. That's another talent, distressing perfectly normal people with my words.

"You never mean to make people feel inferior. Usually."

"Do I make you feel inferior?"

"Sometimes." Now there's a revelation. I have no comeback. My mom is the strongest, most opinionated person that I know. I didn't think anyone could make her feel inadequate. "I try to ignore it, but it makes me feel bad. I don't read masterpieces. I don't know as many big words—"

"For God's sake."

"Let me finish! Don't roll your eyes at me either. I hate that." I try to control my eyes, but they have minds of their own. I think I first rolled my eyes at my mother when I was two.

"My eyes just do that sometimes."

"Alarmingly often. They should have fallen out of your head years ago. I never realized how someone so pigheaded could have ended up with someone so manipulative."

"If you're talking about Pete…"

"Who else?"

"You adored him! You said I should have tried harder to save our relationship!"

"That was when you were engaged. You made a commitment, and I didn't want to see you break it and be disappointed in yourself. You hate to fail."

"Why are you bringing this up now?" My mom and I are not known for our heart-to-heart confessionals. She saves her ears for my little brother.

"Gideon's afraid that you hate me." Her face falls, and I notice her age. She usually wears a smidge too much eye makeup, and her lipstick is too bright. My mom fights aging like Muhammad Ali, standing over it like a triumphant Olympian. Today her face is unadorned. Every wrinkle comes out in the light and shadow, and I think of Grandma. My mom is becoming Grandma. Does that mean I'm becoming more like my mother?

"I don't hate you, Mom," I sigh and put my cup aside. Tears begin to form in her eyes, and I know she doubts me. Why wouldn't she? We were never as close as she and Joel or my father and me. I stormed out of Thanksgiving dinner, and she thinks I acted awful with her boyfriend. Parents are so complicated.

"Do you know what it's like to feel left out?" she asks. Of course, I do. I sucked at sports in school and was always chosen near last. I was an A-student surrounded by others whose scores never matched mine, and in college I missed out on a lot of dates and nights out because I was too busy studying and writing.

"Yes."

"To be left out of a family?" I'm not sure where she's going with this. Left out of what family?

"What are you talking about?"

"You and your father, always doing things without me. Having your secret grown-ups-only club. You never included me in anything."

"But you hated baseball games and the State Fair."

"That doesn't mean I didn't want to spend time with you! I would have gone to anything if it made you happy."

"You came fishing with us one year and made us go home early! You despised it! You said you never wanted to go again!"

"That's because it was ninety degrees, you and Joel were burnt to a crisp, and your father had too many beers. It was dangerous to stay out on the lake. I actually love fishing. I just didn't want another outing like that." I don't remember it that way, but I was young. Dad hid his drinking well. There's almost no way to tell if he's drunk. Maybe that's why he doesn't drink as often now.

"And what about my school plays? Dad was the one who went to those."

"I didn't go to the first one because Joel was sick with the stomach flu, and in junior high you told me not to come."

"I did not!"

"You did, though not to my face. I overheard you on the phone with some friend, and you said your parents were lame and that you'd be mortified if we showed up. I think the show was *The Wizard of Oz*, and you played the Tin Man." Her memory exceeds mine. I was the Tin Man, and I did tell my friend that I didn't want anyone to see my performance, but that's because I was nervous. I only called them lame to seem cool. I totally wanted their support, but what teenager admits that?

"What about you and Joel? He's obviously your favorite." She scoffs and throws her hands in the air.

"Your brother is dear to me, but he doesn't give as well as he receives."

"He's male."

"I don't expect as much of him as I do of you. It's different with boys."

"Is that why you don't care whom he dates?"

"I care! He's my son! I don't want him to end up with some bimbo. And don't say a word about Gisele. She's a nice girl, just a bit dim."

"I wasn't going to say anything." Yes, I was.

"Your brother knows what's good for him. That's why he moved to California. He knew this place would hold him back. Maybe he'll become famous and be able to buy me a new house," she jokes. Mom loved our old house, even though it was nothing special. It was a two-story brown building built in the 1980s with a little park right behind it and a huge shade tree in the backyard. We had barbeques on the deck in the summer, and it never got warm enough in the winter. Joel and I buried three goldfish, one lizard, and two parakeets in Mom's flowerbeds by the garage. She swore we were crazy when we held funeral services for our pets. Some roof shingles fell off in the end, blown away by wind, and one of the kitchen windows wouldn't open after my idiot uncle painted it shut, but it was home. She cried when she put the "FOR SALE" sign up by our mailbox.

When they got divorced, neither could afford the mortgage, so they had to sell it. When they caught a buyer, Mom went to her garden and tore up the flowers, saying the new owner might want to plant something different. The realtor told her the young couple was allergic to pollen, but she didn't want to admit that to us.

"Maybe I'll get you a new house," I say. The silence between us is immense, and I feel like a swimmer attempting the English Channel. "I might get promoted soon."

"That's lovely, honey, but what you really should be doing is writing. I know it's what you want. It's what you always talked about in college."

"It's an impossible dream. I need to be more practical."

"There's time to be practical when you're my age. You're too young to give up on a dream."

"And what was your great dream that you gave up?"

"I lived mine. All I ever wanted was to be a mother. I married your father because I was getting older and thought my time might pass me by."

"You regret marrying him?"

"Not once. I know I rag on him to you and your brother, but he gave me you two, and he's a nice man, just not for me." So that's it. My mother didn't marry for love. She only said yes to my dad because her womb needed a resident. Is that what will happen to me? I want to find someone to love, someone to be with until we're old. Did she think she would stay with Dad through anything?

"Why did you get divorced? If you were so determined to have a family? It seems a bit redundant to me."

"We made each other miserable." I look up and she's gazing out the living room window. Steam wafts from her cup, tea not drunk. She's been a mystery to me my entire life, and I realize that she didn't want it that way. I chose Dad over her every time. He wanted to do fun things like go to sports games and travel an hour to see the world's largest ball of twine. To a kid, those side trips meant everything. That a parent wanted to do something crazy was awesome. Mom preferred to stay home and cook or bake, and I wasn't interested in domestic activities. I wish I had been, because I would make my dinners edible.

"I know," I say. Joel and I knew that our parents weren't happy together. I don't know if I ever saw them happy together. They had moments with my brother and me, but never as a couple. "Was Dad not romantic enough?"

"He is the epitome of wasted effort. He bought me gifts I had no use for, never asked what I wanted." She finally pulls back to me from her window gazing. "He's kind and generous but he didn't take the time to find out my interests. I love to have adventures and do things. I used to love going out. I was quite the drinker."

"Yeah right."

"No really. My roommate in college placed bets with the biggest men in a bar and challenged them to chugging contests, which I always won."

"You had an agent?" I laugh. Picturing my mom drunk is never fun but imagining her defeating hulking college boys is hilarious.

"We had a lot of fun. I met your father through my roommate. He was her boyfriend's high school classmate. They thought we'd hit it off. He adored me, but I didn't feel much. Like I said, a nice guy, just not my type." But she married him. "Life takes us in interesting directions. Not usually the ones you plan to take." That's for sure. "I want you to know that whatever you do with your life, I'm proud of you. And please don't hate Gideon. He makes me very happy."

"If it makes you feel better, I hate Dad's girlfriend way more than Gideon."

"That makes me ecstatic."

Rejuvenated after my talk with Mom, I'm excited for my second date with Logan. He seemed down to earth and funny on our first outing, so my hopes are set back to "high." I wish I could win beer-swigging contests like my mom then I might have an entertaining story to share with Logan. I get home, plop on the couch and pet Prospero's ears. He is the only man that truly understands me. That's a frightening thought. I grab a yellow legal pad from the coffee table and rip off the half-filled page of notes on *Spade a Spade* and write out a few anecdote ideas. I could tell Logan about my experiences in theater, but I doubt he'd be interested in my small acting talent. Maybe my run as editor of the school paper would intrigue him.

I visited Europe in junior year of college. There was an incident involving a giant spider, my girly scream, and a cute Australian guy. I almost forgot cardinal rule number one of dating: never mention the exes, no matter how insignificant. Those are intimate tales meant for serious settings. A drunken fling with a Parisian mud expert might not be as enthralling as you think.

Giving up for the moment, I grab the Pia Brown manuscript and give it another try.

From Spade a Spade by Pia Brown

She knew Barry was not right for her, and still she walked slowly down the white silk runner, lily bouquet in hand, lace veil covering her eyes. At the beginning of "Here Comes the Bride" she hesitated, but her father did not notice. He pulled her along like a seeing-eye dog intent on crossing the street. Maya could use a cane. Her high heels threatened to topple her, but her father's grip kept her in place. The music flooded in one ear and stuck in her brain, thrumming. Did anyone else notice how annoying the song was? She might as well have picked "Why Do Birds Suddenly Appear."

Her flowers smelled rancid.

When her father dropped her arm, Maya turned to him, a look of pity on her face, which he could not see. She whispered, "I'm sorry," but her father merely smiled and patted her hand. She faced the church alter and focused on Barry. He looked great, but he always did. His blond hair slicked back reminded Maya of their first date. Beach sounds and scents wafted through the chapel, and Maya imagined seagulls in the parking lot and tide pools forming around the limo waiting for her and her new husband.

Her one and only true love.

But there was that little problem of him not being her true love. Maya heard stories about brides who backed out on their wedding days, and nothing too terrible happened to them, except karma coming back and whacking them in the face or pushing them in front of a moving van. She wanted the pianist to stop playing. Jesus Christ, did she know any other songs?

She marched toward Barry as if hugging a cactus, and he frowned slightly. Her posture failed, and she slunk up the steps to stand beside him. Once there, he clasped her hand and nodded encouragement. Don't worry, his smile said, we're almost done.

In more ways than one, thought Maya

The priest, whom her mother had insisted on presiding over the service, emerged from the background and stood before them, open book in hand. Maya stared at him; eyes wide. Now was her chance. It was time to go. Just go, she thought, but she did not move. What would people say? Barry would be devastated. And his proposal had been perfect: rose petals, champagne, the beach where they met, sunset, a giant diamond ring. What was wrong? They had been together for two years. She never felt like running before today.

Barry was perfect, a canny businessman who wanted children and a Standard Poodle. What other man would get a huge fluffy dog for her?

Maya's chest lifted and stuck, and she forgot to breathe. Her breath escaped in a rasp, and she coughed loudly at the altar. Barry looked at her, concerned. She waved him off and laughed, patting her chest. The priest raised a disapproving eyebrow, and she nodded for him to continue. She flashed a thumbs-up for the guests and titters flew around the chapel. At least the crowd believed her ruse. But Barry would know something was wrong when he raised her veil to say the vows. She could not look at him and say the lies she thought were truths three months ago.

Maya hated those girls in movies who married the wrong man because they believed they couldn't do better, but she felt a kinship with them now. Shit. Her life had become a romantic comedy. Soon Ryan Reynolds would appear and caper down the aisle toward her, flourishing a ring of his own.

I laugh and set down the manuscript. This writer might have something going for her. An anti-romantic comedy person writing a romantic comedy? Maybe Kelly had given her a gem after all.

I pick the venue for the second date, an indoor miniature golf course. I'm not adept at sports, but mini golf is a world all its own. Let's get down to it: I'm awesome. No one wields a mini golf club like me. I wear khakis and a polo shirt, to make fun of traditional golf, and am impressed that Logan chose the same ensemble.

"We're matchy-matchy golfers!" I say, and he laughs. "You aren't a serious golfer, are you?"

"No way. I suck at real golf," he says, and twirls his putter. "But this game is super easy."

We walk to the first hole, the easiest of the course and I ask how his week has been. He putts it in for a hole in one and shrugs. "Regular week. Work and the usual stuff. Watched *Top Chef* on DVR when I got home."

"Now I'll expect a home-cooked meal."

"I'm a watcher, not a doer. If I tried to make fois gras, I would completely fail."

"Who wants goose liver anyway?"

He lets me lead the way to the second hole, which consists of a silly plaster parrot that talks in your back swing. Jerk. Logan moves to cover the bird's mouth, but I shoo him away. The manager might get mad if we disfigure his course. I make my first shot through the Astroturf maze and miss the hole by inches.

"Looked good to me," he says and lines up his shot. His goes the same direction, and the ball rests near mine. "I think we're pretty even. So, what did you do this week?"

"Not much. I felt like getting tipsy on the Dreaded Day but decided against it."

"The Dreaded Day? Valentine's Day?" he asks.

"But of course. What else do single people call it?"

"Satan's Dance, Yearly Hell Day…how about Trail of Tears Day?"

"That's already a recognized holiday." His demeanor changes after this exchange; I think I touched a nerve. His shoulders slump, and his hair appears less magnificent. Maybe he had a bad V-Day too. I hope I didn't make him feel uncomfortable. Crap. Great job, Cassie. No wonder my friends had to set me up with men. I certifiably suck at dating. It makes me wonder if there's a vaccine for bad dating skills.

"Everything okay?" I ask, hoping to get the standard response.

"Not really." Damn. When someone who's not a close friend asks if everything's okay, you're supposed to say, "Oh yeah, everything's kosher!" Otherwise things get awkward. Do you really want to know that your dentist has an STD or that your neighbor who has never spoken to you from apartment 2B is having boyfriend issues?

"I'm sorry," I say lamely. What am I supposed to say? I'm not Oprah.

"It's fine," he says, swinging his putter around in a circle in one hand, "I had a shitty Valentine's Day."

"Didn't most of us?" I ask, trying to bring the mood back around to fun.

"My ex called and wanted to move back in." Oh no. He did not just bring up the ex. "My ex-roommate that is. He was hell to live with, never cleaned, had the most obnoxious friends, smoked pot all day long. Not an overachiever." Whew! Not ex-girlfriend.

"Ah, that would be a difficult decision to make."

"That's not the half of it. After I hung up with him, my ex-girlfriend called." Dammit. All hope is lost. The "do not enter" door of exes has been breached. Mayday! Mayday! He's going down! "We haven't spoken in half a year and she calls on Valentine's Day. Who does that?" he asks, looking at the Eiffel Tower shaped obstacle looming ahead.

"My ex did the same—"

"It's not like the bitch tore my heart out and ran it down the garbage disposal then poked it with a stick just to make sure it was dead. Oh wait, yes she did!" His voice rises and the five teenagers behind us snicker and point their clubs our way. I'm the poor sap stuck with the loud crazy person at the indoor mini-golf course. "It's not like she took out a twelve gauge and shot me down like a baby harp seal! That's exactly what she fucking did!" With his last exclamation he hurls his putter like an Olympic javelin, and it sails through the air and impales the Eiffel Tower. French enthusiasts will not be happy. I thought we'd at least get to the twelfth hole before the manager asked us to leave. A pudgy man who resembles Winston Churchill races toward us, and the cackling teenagers roll around on the Astroturf behind him.

"What in the hell is going on?" he yells and skids to a stop next to me while Logan rages through the course like a man-shaped Godzilla, knocking down fake pine trees and terrorizing the mother and toddler who are in front of us. The poor kid clings to his mother's leg and wails, while she tries to pry him off and flails her club at the approaching Logan.

"I think my date is over," I mumble.

"You're goddamn right it is! Get him out of here!" Watching the overweight manager huff and puff drives me to action. I can't be held responsible for Logan's tirade. Christ we're only on a second date!

"He's all yours," I say before spinning and marching into the clubhouse to get my coat and running outside as fast as I can.

"He opened the ex-box?" asks Lindsey. "There's nothing but trouble in there."

"Cardinal sin," adds Keeley, and Alicia and Lindsey nod. "Can't that stuff be saved for deathbed confessions?"

We gather at the Caribou Coffee near Alicia's house. She called an emergency summit, mainly because she wants to tell the other girls about her pregnancy, but she also plans to discuss strategy for my next date. It seems I'm not doing such a great job enticing men to a third date. Maybe they need to screen for insanity before sending me on these outings.

"At first, I was relieved, because he talked about an ex-roommate before the other ex. I thought, Halleluiah! Here's a guy who knows his dating etiquette. Even a novice like me knows the simple rules."

"Don' get drunk," says Keeley sweetly.

"Don't show your true self," laughs Lindsey.

"And never talk about your exes," finishes Alicia as she downs her latte.

"Thirsty?" asks Lindsey, eyebrow raised.

"Why can't you show your true self?" asks Keeley. "I'm always honest with people."

"You can be," answers Lindsey. "You're gorgeous. Men don't care if you're a bit nuts so long as they can imagine your legs wrapped around their heads."

"Lindsey!" scolds Alicia. "Little ears can hear you." She rubs her stomach and the girls stare at her, uncomprehending. "I'm pregnant."

The table erupts with comment lava: Lindsey wants to know how long she's known about her newest bundle of medical bills, Keeley asks what Brian thinks, and I try to quiet them down. "Shut up! I don't want to get kicked out of two places in one week!"

"Brian and I are happy," says Alicia. "We know it will take a lot of patience to deal with another baby, but we have the other kids to help out—"

"You're making your kids get jobs? Isn't the youngest three?" asks Lindsey.

"They can help baby-sit and watch each other. Brian agreed to take fewer jobs so I don't go crazy by myself. The realtors offered me a part-time position if I want back in, but I might pass."

"You can come work with me!" says Keeley.

"No thanks, sweetie. I don't think I'd be a very good pharmaceutical girl."

"Why haven't you married a doctor yet?" asks Lindsey, staring at Keeley, who blushes.

"Aren't we still on Alicia?" I ask.

"Nope," she says. "I've dropped my bomb, now it's time to address more important concerns. Your dates have been atrocious for the most part, and the nice ones are chased away or made into friends."

"Friendification is easier than *boy*friendication," snaps Lindsey. "Look at the idiots I've been seeing."

"You never talk about them," says Keeley, suspicious, and Lindsey peruses her nail beds.

"Ladies," says Alicia and pounds her coffee cup on the table. "This is important! We only have a few months left! We're running out of men!"

"Famous last words of the Amazonians," I mutter, and Alicia doesn't look amused. Thunderclouds form on her brow and lightening emanates from her eyes.

"Never fear, Lindsey is here!" she shouts and throws down two sheets of paper. I pick them up and see a profile from some website. I don't recognize it. Lindsey probably copied and pasted it, so I couldn't sniff out the source. Crafty like a cobbler, she is.

"Mateo," I say and keep reading, "enjoys hockey, Indian food, and rock climbing. He has a dog and a cat named Ink and Claw and lives in Minneapolis, the nice part."

"Did he really write that?" asks Keeley.

I go on, "He has traveled to Africa and Asia but prefers Minnesota because of the seasonal changes."

"Sounds perfect," admits Alicia.

"I know," says Lindsey who crosses her arms across her chest. "I saved him for last."

"How come you never showed us this guy?" asks Keeley, peering over my shoulder. "What does he look like?"

"None of your nevermind. He's for me to see and Cassie to discover."

"I'll bet he's ugly," laughs Alicia.

"I promise he's not. Look at his name!"

"It's just Spanish for Matthew," says Alicia, and Keeley giggles. "Just because you say it in a sexy way doesn't make him more attractive."

"Sure, it does," I say. "I would never go to an *Anthony* Banderas movie. He sounds nice, Lindsey."

"You're way too okay about this," she says and narrows her eyes, trying to find the crack in my armor and worm out how I really feel. "Last year you practically skinned us alive and sold the skins."

"Wouldn't have fetched much profit," I say. The girls laugh, but Lindsey keeps her eye on me. "I'm excited that it's almost over and we can get back to man-bashing."

"Isn't that what we've been doing?" asks Keeley, sweeping her hair from her shoulders as two well-dressed men walk past. They turn and ogle her, but a sneer from Lindsey sends them packing.

"I have no idea how you attract such douche-bags," says Lindsey, retching. "Are you giving off some scent we can't pick up?"

"'Asshole,' the newest fragrance by Calvin Klein," says Alicia.

"'Pretension,' not just for the wealthy anymore, by Gucci," I add.

"What are you talking about?" asks Keeley, and she cranes her head around. "What douche-bags?"

"The best part is that she doesn't even notice," says Lindsey, shaking her head.

"Notice what? You guys suck."

March

Full Moon Mateo and Rule Number Ten: You are not alone. There are tons of other single women out there who couldn't care less about dating! (That's not even a rule! Pipe down it's the best we could do!)

"You only have a few months left?" asks Kelly, reclined in her chair, my corrected manuscript in hand. She's referring to my dating scheme, but I hope she's also alluding to my promotion.

"There are three guys left, but I'm crossing my fingers that March is the lucky month."

"I've found that you don't find happiness until the end of the story," she says, a tad mysterious. She's been reading too many romance novels.

"Then I guess May will be it." She nods and waves the manuscript. "This is good work, Cassie. Did you enjoy it?"

"I actually did. It reminded me of the one romantic novel I like, *Bridget Jones's Diary*."

"I don't believe there has ever been such a quirky heroine. Perhaps that's why you like her."

"She's real, or as real as a fictional character can be."

"Characters are only as real as we make them. The reason Bridget Jones resonates with women is because she *is* them, flaws and all. Perfect heroines make for an awfully dull read."

"Agreed. Are there any more by this author you might want me to look at?" I cannot get over how much I liked *Spade a Spade*. At first, I didn't want Maya, the main character, to stay with Barry, her fiancé and husband by chapter two. Unhappy with her decision, she made the reader despise Barry, though he was perfectly nice. When Maya left him in the middle of the book, I cheered, but then I also cheered when she got back together with him in the end, finding that the men she dated were cruel, immature, or greedy despite being devastatingly handsome. Do I need to move to Florida to find these gorgeous men? Because that's where it seems they all came from in the novel. Despite the simple premise, I enjoyed her writing style and the way she made each of Maya's decisions seem logical, all the while implying that she was a little batty.

"Alas, she hasn't sent us another novel. She's waiting for our editing job before she decides to go with us."

"Is another publishing house wooing her?"

"If they could throw male prostitutes through her window they would, but no one can find her. She's elusive."

"I had no idea she was so popular."

"But she knows. She's one of those authors who realize their particular talent and utilize it to their benefit." She gazes at me as if trying to convey a message, but I'm not getting it. Kelly knows I used to write. Perhaps she's goading me into continuing that turbulent path. As fledgling authors come to know, the road to publication is both infuriating and exhausting, and it rarely ends in a pot of gold.

"What do you have for me?"

"I need you and Mr. Conroy to team up on a big textbook project that has come our way. We don't usually do textbooks, as you know, but the offer was more than convincing. These people are changing publishers, and they heard great things about us, so I need to send in my best."

Things with Justin are still on the sour side. We haven't said more than "good morning" and "good evening" to each other in two months. Kevin mediates paperwork that passes between us, hoping us two crazy kids will get together. Even though we don't usually handle these huge projects, maybe it could help us.

"That sounds good to me."

"Wonderful. I have already spoken with Mr. Conroy. He seemed less that pleased with the project, but I suppose that has to do with the subject matter. Perhaps I'll be able to bend his will toward inane elementary school knowledge as I bent you to romances."

Don't be so sure, I thought, and smiled as if I couldn't wait to see the material. How was Kevin supposed to arbitrate such a large undertaking? Justin and I would spend hours together on this. Maybe by the end he'll forgive me.

I realize forgiveness is not likely when I pass his office and he glares me away. Head down, I proceed to my office, unaware that Kevin is watching.

I have more to worry about than Justin's problem with me. My date is thirty minutes late, and I'm about ready to leave. We were set to meet in Nicolett Mall by eight and get a table at Ichiban, an interesting Japanese teppanyaki dining experience. He must be richer than me, because it's not the cheapest.

I sit at the bar and sip a plum wine, the sticky sweetness distracting me from his lack of punctuality. I'll stay for the date, if he gets here in about two minutes. When the wine is gone, so am I.

As I down the rest of the wine, the hostess taps me on the shoulder and announces that my party is finally here and ready to be seated. I pay for the wine and march for the entrance, not caring how good-looking this guy might be. I'm still going to make him feel like shit for making me wait so long.

He stands by the host desk, a small bouquet of violets in hand, and I'm stunned into silence. He is no Antonio Banderas; he's ten times hotter. Alarm bells go off instantly in my brain: how is this guy still single, and why the hell does he need to get dates online? He must have desperate women lining up at his apartment complex, waiting to catch a glimpse. He's a little over six feet tall with black hair and dark, unsettling eyes. The dark purple flowers he holds set off his gorgeous tanned skin, and I hope he makes an effort to wear the color every day. I'm not sure how else to describe him. Imagine the most beautiful man you've ever met, fantasized about, or seen in the movies, then imagine he's standing right in front of you.

"Mateo?" I hold out my hand, and he reaches for it, bowing and planting a kiss on my knuckle. How corny! And yet, because I'm lost in his eyes, I don't mind.

"Cassandra?" His voice is perfect, not too low, not too high, with an ethnic lilt in the vowels. I nearly orgasm when he says my name. Seriously! Why so single? I would join his harem in a heartbeat, and as an independent, confident woman, I never thought I'd say those words in that order, ever. "I hope you haven't been waiting long?"

That's right! He made me wait for over thirty minutes! What kind of gentleman makes a girl think she's been forgotten or forsaken?

"I've been in the bar for a while. Didn't we agree on eight?"

"I apologize. I was having trouble choosing the flowers." He looks abashed, and I can't help but smile. He was only late because of flowers! Then I remember that I'm supposed to give him my honest opinion of his behavior.

"Next time could you try to be on time?"

"But of course! First dates always make me nervous, and now I've gone and ruined ours."

"You did catch that 'next time' thing, didn't you?"

"I never presume to know what a woman means, for you are all as mysterious as the Barcelona fog." He makes me sound misty. He holds out the flowers, and I take them, inhaling the heavenly scent. Who knew flowers could smell so good? I suppose the giver can make the aroma more intoxicating. "Shall we have dinner?"

We're escorted upstairs and seated at one of the large tables, where the chef prepares food on the silvery flattop surface, basically a giant sauté pan. I can't wait to watch the show. I hope we get one of the older Japanese chefs, because they're more entertaining.

Mateo pulls out the chair for me and places our drink order, inquiring what I want.

"I'll stick to wine, white please." He peruses the wine list and makes a good selection, the most expensive bottle on the menu. If he asks me to split the check at the end, I'm not sure I'll be able to cover my end.

When the drinks come and the server takes our order, Mateo is pleasant and curious. He asks about ingredients and how the food is prepared, and the server is delighted to share how they prepare the seafood, sushi, and other fine dishes they feature. He's also attentive to my needs, asking whether I like my salad or if we should get an appetizer. When the chef appears and does his tricks, lighting an onion on fire and flipping it into his hat, Mateo is ecstatic and yells,

"Bravo! Bravo! Good show!" His delight is infectious, and I find the routine more dynamic than I recall from a previous visit.

We share our entrées and talk about Minnesota and why he prefers it to traveling overseas.

"My job takes me many places, and I was lucky to have understanding parents who allowed me to travel as a young man. But I love Minnesota. I was born here, and I've never believed that old saying, 'You can't go home again.'" I wonder vaguely about his accent then push the thought aside. Maybe his parents have accents.

"I love traveling. I wish I could afford to do more, because there are a lot of places I want to visit. I've never been to South America, or Africa, or Australia…"

"All wondrous places filled with interesting people."

"That's just it. I want to see new things and new people. Things get dull around here when winter really hits. None of those wimpy November snowfalls, but the blizzards in mid-March. It sucks to be cooped up for four months."

"I enjoy the snow, but I agree, it must be taken in small doses, otherwise, you lose your appreciation for its beauty."

"There's nothing beautiful about my car turning into a snow-bank overnight."

"Especially if it is surrounded by other snow-banks which may be cars but might be big piles of snow."

"I once dug into a huge pile, thinking I parked my car there, but there was nothing underneath but more snow."

We laugh our way through the sorbet and I wish the evening could go on longer, but he has an early morning meeting. I can't tell if it's a made-up meeting, so he can get out of the restaurant and out of my company, but he asks to see me again. I say yes, eying his designer suit and mirror-shined shoes. This is a man I could get used to in my bed, hell, even in my life. He's charming, funny, and did I mention handsome? I silently thank Lindsey for this setup as Mateo walks away from the restaurant. He looks back at me; waves, and I clutch the flowers and quietly damn myself for acting like such a little girl. Should grown women get this excited about men? Do we actually believe that things will end happily ever after? Are we all this optimistic inside, or is the pessimist merely taking a much-needed breather before showing her ugly face again? I wish the optimist and pessimist could get along, but as Mateo disappears into the night, I feel Negative Nancy fighting for my brain's driver's seat. Why can't I let the sunshiney part take over for more than a few hours? Why can't I let that bitchy nag go?

As fantastic as my date with Mateo was, the first meeting between Justin and I to discuss the textbooks is disastrous. We decide (he decided) to meet in public. I suggest the coffee shop midway between our apartments. Kevin offers to accompany me, but I can't bring myself to give up on Justin. We could make it as friends, I know we could.

Snow lines the sidewalk, but it's a balmy thirty-six degrees, and the sun plays hide and seek in the clouds. I put on my more stylish cashmere-wool blend coat and brave the new weather. Minnesotans are suspicious of nice weather in March. It's an enigma, not to be trusted, a lot like that hunky guy at the gym who stares at you and gives you compliments, only to repeat the line on the next woman who walks past his bench press machine. We prefer the cold to continue until it's ready to be over for good. Anything above freezing is merely a cruel tease. When will Mother Nature have mercy on us Northlanders?

I arrive at the shop first and get us the biggest table. We'll need to set out the material. The elementary school textbook group sent Kelly a plethora of choices: they've had multiple pitches for style and chapter placement, and they sent copies of every publishing company's ideas. I doubt the companies would like us looking at their hard work, and I wonder how the textbook people got away with it, but I also know that these are the ideas that didn't work, a nice starting off point. This way, Justin and I won't have to worry about sending off something the company will hate.

I get a nonfat latte and wait for Justin to arrive. He's right on time, the picture of Midwest chic in a thick flannel shirt and tan puffy vest. I always thought men looked so cute in puffy vests but seeing Justin outside the office for the first time makes me want to throw up a little. How can we possibly do this without him killing me?

"Hi," I say as he sets down his briefcase, overflowing with notes and images. He must have been sketching all night. I don't have drawings. I feel incompetent.

"Hey. I need coffee. Are you ready to go over the first chapters?"

"I think so." He nods and strides to the counter, where the teenage barista gives him a once-over while taking his order. When he walks over to the pick-up counter, she leans over the partition and looks at his ass, an appreciative look on her face. Something flares in my stomach, and I cough, wondering why I feel nauseous.

I set up four piles, one for each chapter. We're going over the history text first, which is in both our wheelhouses. Justin minored in history at college, and I've been obsessed with American history since I first heard of Franklin Delano Roosevelt. Sixth graders don't go over anything too strenuous like the World Wars; it's an overview of how the United States came into being, some Revolutionary War stuff, and geography. They gloss over a few things here and there. I suppose the slaughter of American troops and native peoples doesn't make good dinner conversation when discussing homework. I recall my mother's reaction when I first asked her why Hitler wanted to kill all the Jewish people in the world. I don't think she was prepared for that conversation. Mom is a math and science person; she told me to ask my father.

Justin sits down across from me and glances at the paper piles before pulling some things out of his briefcase. I chuckle, because seeing a man dressed like an Eddie Bauer ad holding a briefcase is slightly amusing.

"What?" he asks.

"It's nothing. How about this heat wave?" He doesn't answer. Fine. If that's the way he wants to do this. "I looked everything over, and I think the book should go over geography first then move into history. It will be easier if the kids know where everything is before adding the dramatis personae." He nods and pulls out a drawing of North America. He color-coded it and added little caricatures of people who live in certain parts of the United States, Mexico, and Canada. It's been done in other schoolbooks, but I didn't say anything. It's pretty cute.

"I agree," he says. "Did you remember to bring the stuff for the science book too?"

"No, I thought we were focusing on history today." I wanted to stay on one task at a time. If we each took a book and went over it, the project would go faster, but it wouldn't be as good. Our strength comes from pooling our collective thoughts and resources. Justin and I could make some pretty kick ass textbooks if we work together.

"I wanted to do science today."

"Well, you didn't tell me," I say, miffed. Didn't we settle on history at work the other day? "We agreed to work on the history text today then tackle the science and math next week. Those will be the hardest."

"Maybe for you," he mutters, and I ignore him.

"I just want get this done."

"Believe me, so do I."

"Listen, I'm not Carly. It's not like you're strapped to the rack."

"Maybe Carly would've been a better choice." We sit in silence for a moment, and he sighs. "The history book seems pretty straightforward. There's nothing too challenging in there."

"I agree, but remember those kids that hate history?"

"I didn't pay them much attention. I always got extra credit on tests for doing the extra essay questions."

"Me too. But I had this friend, Nancy Shaw, and she sucked at history. She asked to cheat off my papers all the time."

"You didn't let her, did you?" he asks, bemused. The idea of me letting anyone cheat off my work is so off the wall it would have to be stored in Ripley's Believe It or Not.

"Only once when she begged me. I regretted it, because the teacher caught her. I fessed up to letting her peek, but he wasn't mad at me. Luckily he didn't fail her."

Justin pulls the first chapter over and takes a look, nodding every few pages. He makes notations next to my comments and writes an entire paragraph about the Midwest and why it's important to modern times. The company must have asked Kelly to focus on our area of the country. Justin is very learned in local lore, so I let him write those blurbs.

"So," he says, finished with chapter one. I don't look up from the map I'm checking.

"Yeah?"

"It's March."

"Uh huh, Ides and what not."

"So, you only have two more months of terror left."

I check his features from the corner of my eye, hoping he doesn't look angry. He appears at ease, his features a bit pinched, but he's smirking.

"Yup. Not too much to hope for." I have no intention of discussing my phenomenal date with Mateo. That would be more awkward than Pinocchio in high school wood shop.

"I don't want to say I told you so…"

"Are you kidding? Everyone likes saying that."

"Only if it makes them feel better."

"When has it not? I love telling my brother 'I told you so' when his model girlfriends turn out to have less personality than turnips."

We lay off the personal talk for the rest of the meeting, and we don't devolve into a fistfight. The girls would be proud. I don't think Justin and I are back to normal, we certainly won't be having any friendly lunches soon, but it's a start in the right direction. Maybe he'll find a way to forgive me. If he can't, I'm going to have to find another attractive straight man for Kevin to eyeball over coffee; he says he's going into withdrawal.

Forget about me, ladies. We need to find Kevin a man instead.

I let Mateo choose our next rendezvous, because my last pick didn't turn out as well as one would hope. I wonder if the mini-golf manager wound up with a putter up his ass.

Mateo elects for a quiet drink at a small wine bar. I've never heard of the place, and it must be chic, because Mateo tells me to dress up. Since I can't find any miraculous Dolce in my closet, I decide on a knee-length emerald dress, which is flowy and elegant. Black pumps and jewelry complete the outfit, and I grab my Spanish-inspired black lace shawl before leaving. It's chilly out again but still not below zero. I hop in my car and blast the heat, deluding myself that some of the hot air will remain inside while we have drinks.

I've become so accustomed to these dates that I don't sweat anymore, and I recall with fond remembrance the incident with the pads under my armpits. That was embarrassing. Have I become so old hat with dating that I've become numb? I felt so blasé about meeting Mateo. Now I can't recall the spark from our first date without measuring it against the other men I've met this year. Is this what Keeley and Lindsey feel like when a guy takes them out? Do they calculate in their heads whether the man stands up next to the other guys they've dated, and if so, is there a moment when they say, "this isn't going to work," and write off an entire evening? I don't want that to happen to me. I want my meeting with Mateo to feel fresh, not bogged down by preconceived notions and prejudices from past bad dates.

I pull into a ritzy St. Paul neighborhood and try to find a parking space, which is impossible. I don't want to pay for a ramp, so I drive around until I find a spot. It's far from the wine bar, but at least it's free. I trot down the sidewalk, afraid to be late. I know it's okay for the woman to be a few minutes late, but I couldn't stand it if it happened. I gave myself a lot of time but did not account for parking, so I pick up speed. As I near the corner where the bar sits, I fail to notice the large crack in the sidewalk. Triumphant that I'm on time, I take the fateful step and my heel slides into the crevasse but not back out. It sticks, and I fly forward as if a bowling ball is stuck to my hand. My foot leaves the shoe and I sprawl on the concrete. Mortified, I lie on my stomach and don't notice the pain until my embarrassment-haze passes. Someone runs up to my prone form and asks if I'm okay. I hear laughter in the voice and my cheeks flush.

"You're bleeding!" yells the voice. A sympathetic murmur floats over me, and I feel an aching flash in my knee, palms, and chin. I touch my chin and my fingers come away scarlet. My hands and right knee are a wreck; blood pools and dribbles down my wrists and toward my expensive shoe. I wrench it off and see that I lost the other to the sidewalk canyon. It's huge! How did I not notice that?

"Somebody go inside and get some ice!" shouts the helpful voice, and I look up. It's a gorgeous woman dressed in a Burberry trench and silky trousers. "Are you feeling well? What happened?"

"I fell," I mumble, and I swear I feel a loose tooth. I clutch my mouth and try to stand, but my knee gives, and I stumble down again, wincing.

"We saw you fall. Manny went inside to fetch ice and bandages."

"My date," I say, knowing I'm definitely late.

"Is he in the bar?"

"The wine bar."

"I'll have Manny go get him when he comes back. What's his name?"

"Mateo," I say and sit down on the dirty ground. I hope I didn't sprain anything, because as the adrenaline wears off, I'm feeling sorer. There's something about an intense accident that befuddles the brain. Your body knows it can't deal with the combined pain and humiliation, so it shuts down for a while, waiting for you to get a grip.

My body doesn't give me much time.

The full moon stares at me from the cloudy night sky, and I wish I had a gun, because I'd shoot it, I'm so pissed at myself. If I paid for a parking garage, this would not have happened. The woman presses a napkin with ice against my knee and takes my hand to hold it in place. She must be concerned for her coat's welfare. No need to get a stranger's blood on it.

I don't follow her conversation with Manny but recognize Mateo's voice, nervous and concerned, hovering above me.

"Hello," I say, and I must look atrocious, because he recoils and covers his eyes. "Do I look that bad?"

"I don' like blood," he says, and moves away. "I'm sorry." He practically races down the sidewalk in the opposite direction. I shrug and look up at the woman and her date, Manny, a robust older man. He shakes his head and watches Mateo's hasty progress down the block.

"I hope that's not your boyfriend, miss. He's a bloody coward." Manny's British accent tickles my ears and I smile. "No. Just a promising second date."

"My dear," Manny says, and pulls me to my feet, the stylish woman holding my shoes beside him, "I can't believe you even went on a first date with that man."

"Blame my evil friends."

"At least your shoe isn't irreparable," says the woman.

Email: Alicasweetheart@sojourn.net, Trulover888@yahoo.com, FellbeeotchLinds@hotmail.com from Shakespearelover@gmail.com

Ladies, I have come to the conclusion that this experiment is flawed. I don't think my worst enemy could have found me more horrible men. I'm writing because I don't feel like talking to any of you, and because I'm taking painkillers for my mangled knee. The shoes are fine, but my dress was ruined. Even my fabulous dry cleaner said it was a lost cause. You owe me ninety dollars for the dress and five million for my lost dignity.

Your former friend,

Cassie

April

Horror Movie Howard and Rule Number Eleven: Didn't you understand the rules? No back-outsies.

Email: <u>Aliciasweetheart@sojourn.net</u> to <u>Shakespearelover@gmail.com</u>

We've given you a week to cool down and heal, but now it's back to business. You only have two months to go, and I won't let you quit without a fight. Most guys are jerks. There. I said it. It's not easy finding a good guy out there, but I know you won't find one moping in your apartment or hiding behind Kevin. He told me you threatened to hand out his number to the ugly drag queens at the Gay Nineties if he made you call us. And Justin won't return Keeley's calls. Apparently, he doesn't believe in what we're doing.

It's April, and the snow is melting. It's time for renewal and hope springs eternal and all that literary crap you like. We worked really hard on this project, and we did it for you. It's time for you to get back in gear and finish what you started.

Was that motivational enough for you?

When I eventually answer Alicia, she sends another smug email about how well she knows me and the information for the next guy. It feels like I've been on a speed-dating session. No one else could've had this many dates in less than a year. Except maybe Keeley.

Despite Kevin's betrayal, I forgive him and invite him to the next textbook session. Justin and I have been getting along, so Kevin figured it was time to accompany us on a lunch date.

They don't lie about April showers, which, in Minnesota, can easily morph into April blizzards. Today, the rain falls with a cold wind from the west, and our umbrellas attempt escape. When my umbrella gives in to the gusts and buckles, Justin offers his, and we run for the coffee shop. Kevin holds the door.

"Damn," I say. "That was my favorite umbrella."

"You have more than one?" asks Justin, and Kevin and I stare at him.

"Didn't anyone tell you? Women love accessories almost as much as me."

We order very hot drinks and squeeze access water from our clothes over the garbage cans. My hair must look amazing. I flatten it.

We sit, and Kevin takes the seat next to me, Justin across from us. "It's nice to see you two working together," Kevin says and sets down his hot tea.

Justin gets out the material for the math book. This will be arduous. We both hate math more than the recently arrived Canadian geese. Besides freezing rain, there's nothing more horrible than the returning feathered hordes. The bastards shit all over everything. It's not like we meant to pave over your old migration grounds! Don't chase me and hiss at me! I'm not stalking you! I wish a competent hunter would come and clear the sidewalks, because the geese are more meddlesome than my girlfriends. And Kevin. Combined.

"So, how did Carly fare on the last project?" I ask.

"Not well, from what she said," answers Kevin. He'll talk to anyone in the office so long as gossip is involved. "And she absolutely hates that you two got the textbook deal."

"We're better than she is," Justin says.

"When will it be finished?" Kevin asks.

"Probably by May," I say. "We have four books to cover."

"It would have gone faster if we split the workload," says Justin, winking.

"But then we wouldn't have come up with the clever English book table of contents."

Kevin reaches for the first math book chapter and Justin slaps his hand. He rubs it and scowls. "What the fuck?"

"You'll mess it up. Chapter one was a bitch."

"So are you."

"Any idea on who's getting the promotion next month?" I inquire, knowing Kevin might have some insight. He knows the office secrets better than anyone.

"That info's off limits. But guess what's not?"

"I give up," I say.

"I hate guessing," says Justin. Kevin isn't bothered by our lack of fun. He kneads his hands together and grins, sure his news will derail any thoughts of promotions and arithmetic.

"I've got a boyfriend." Justin's and my mouths drop. Sir Perpetually Single is no longer singular?

"What?" asks Justin who pushes aside the next chapter we're covering.

"Yes, Boy and Girl, this dazzling gent is no longer on the market."

"Since when?" Kevin said he would never settle down because there were too many great gay men in the Cities to meet and possibly have sex with. What the hell happened?

"Since March. His name is Philip, and he's from Portugal."

"It figures you'd meet someone foreign," I say.

"I can't picture you sitting for a family portrait, buddy," says Justin. The coffee shop air glitters from the rain outside, and it reflects in Kevin's eyes, making them sparkle. No one has made his eyes sparkle before.

"He's not really foreign. He was born in New York."

"Then why did you say he's from Portugal?"

"He was working there for his law firm before transferring here."

"Why in God's name would you move to Minnesota after living in Europe?" I ask. I know if moved I would never come back unless it was for Christmas and I might even make my family fly to my European paradise. Some of my dates are trans-global too, yet they keep coming back to Minnesota.

"He's retiring."

"How old is he?" asks Justin, and I lean closer to Kevin. A world traveler and he's older! Kevin only dates younger men!

"Fifty-four. He's made a lot of money, so after a few cases here that need tidying up, he's finished with lawyering."

"That's not a word, babe," I say and look at Justin, who grins.

"It is now. He wants me to move in with him, but I'm not sure. I've been independent my whole life. I made my dog make appointments for affection."

"That poor thing," I say.

"Do you think it's a good idea?"

"You've only known him for a month!" I say, but Justin shakes his head and says, "Time doesn't matter, sometimes. If it's right, you'll know."

Kevin nods but looks skeptical. "I think it's right, and we've had such a great time. But do you think it makes me cheap?"

"Like a trophy boyfriend?"

"Yeah."

"Not at all," I say. "Not if you have feelings for him and treat each other with respect."

"Respect and I haven't been speaking," he says, and I know what he means. Kevin isn't known for his long-lasting relationships. Maybe he's afraid that he'll get bored and want to move on, only to find that his fabulous apartment has already been reoccupied.

"It'll be worth it if you love him," says Justin. Where did Justin come up with all this lovey-dovey crap? He's good at it. Maybe Kelly should let him handle the romance novels from now on.

"That settles it. I'm telling him yes."

"Can I call him King Philip of Portugal?" I ask, rubbing my hands together and raising my eyebrows.

"No."

We have a miniature celebration, and I wonder how someone like Kevin can meet someone and agree to live with him in only a month, and it's taken me many failed dates and one cataclysmic break-up to end up here. I'm still alone, only now I feel worse than when I started the dating journey. I don't think this is what the girls had in mind when they sat around concocting the plan.

I'm only a little jealous of Kevin. Maybe ten percent jealous.

"Jealousy is healthy," says Lindsey as we walk into the gym, ready to do some weight training. She's on a dumbbell kick and asked me to come along. I have the feeling she's been obsessing over some buff bodybuilder and that's what keeps her coming back. I hope I'm not left doing bicep curls while she flirts with a spandex Adonis.

"I feel terrible. I should be happy for him."

"Why? That fucker's taken another eligible man off the market."

"Philip of Portugal is gay, Linds. He was never on our market."

"I have a theory that all gay men are waiting for the right woman to turn them straight."

"I hope you're joking. And have you met Kevin? Breasts scare him. He actually covers his eyes at movies when they come onscreen."

"Imagine what *Showgirls* must have been like for him."

Lindsey leads me into the weight room, and I was right: there are at least a dozen hot guys in here, and they're all in various degrees of sweatiness. Why would Lindsey want to meet guys here? I don't feel particularly stunning after a workout, and she perspires more than I do.

"Who's the guy?" I ask and drape my towel around my neck.

"What guy? Do you see a guy?"

"They're everywhere."

"Honey, these are *gym* guys. They're only here to work out. It's nearly impossible to hit on one."

"They're skittish?"

"Young colts that need to be broken," she says and sighs. "But they resist the process. I've been coming here all winter and have yet to get laid by one of *these* men."

She's right. When two relatively good-looking women enter a room full of men, you'd think one or two of them would look up appreciatively. Nada. Nothing. Zip. They're all glued to their machines and weights, oblivious to Lindsey's abs and my incredulity.

We prepare to do Lindsey's prepared set list, and I notice no other women are in the weight room. "Where are all the women?"

"Not many in here," she says. "They stick to the track mostly."

"So why do you come here?"

"Lifting weights is almost like yoga. It's relaxing once you get into it."

We do three sets of every exercise, and Lindsey is considerably stronger than me. She uses twenties and I'm stuck with tens, and I have to switch to eights near the end. She powers through every exercise fluidly, and I admire her arms.

Glistening, we head for the showers and then to the sauna. We're the only people inside, and it's nice to hang with Lindsey without the other two girls. We rarely get time together.

"How does it feel to know you only have two months of dating left?" she asks.

"I wish everyone would change the subject. It's almost over, so that's a plus."

"Alicia warned me you'd be difficult."

"You guys are lucky I'm even finishing. Alicia's guilt trip email saw to that."

"It's not like we made you do this, you know." I gape at her, and she covers her face with a towel. "Hot in here."

"You blackmailed me! What do you mean you didn't make me? Kelly hinted that I wouldn't get promoted if I didn't do it."

"You'll get the promotion no matter what."

"How do you know?" I huff and hiss and throw my extra towel at her. "You don't work there. You weren't there when she sat me down and humiliated me."

"We sat down with Kelly and explained your little predicament."

"Which predicament would that be? The one where I'm about to lose my job or the fact that I can't find a boyfriend?"

"Don't get sassy." She takes the towel off her face. "We told her our plan, and she fell in love with the idea, said it should be a movie. She was going to promote you no matter what, but she was going to put you through the ringer about the romance novels too, so we had nothing to do with her plans. She paired her efforts with ours and the rest is history."

"You've been playing me? I didn't need to agree to the dating thing because Kelly would have given me the job anyway?"

"Yup."

"You tricked me." I can't believe what I'm hearing. I could've forgone the dating and only had to deal with the stupid romance novels? "I wish I had something else to throw at you."

"The towel around your boobs comes off too you know."

"Shut up. I cannot believe this. I have no words."

"Apparently you have a lot of words."

"Why did you make me do this? Nothing good has come from it. I'm still single, I alienated Justin, I've been torturing myself for almost a year—"

"Dating isn't torture. You just treat it like it is. Some of those guys were great. Aren't you still friends with number two?"

"Tristan? The actor? I suppose. I went to see another one of his comedy shows a few months ago. But that's not the point. All I've discovered is that dating is just as horrible as I remember. And let's not forget my run-ins with Pete, where you and Keeley abandoned me. More than once."

This time, Lindsey hurls her towel at me. I catch it and watch the furious storm cloud descend her face. She points a finger at me and says, "That was her idea! She wanted you to face Pete alone, because if we took care of it, you'd lose strength of spirit or some stupid shit. I wanted to kick his ass back to junior college, but part of me agreed with Keeley. Pete stole your strength a long time ago. It was nice to see you get it back."

"And why didn't you write me a letter at the beginning of all this?" That question has been nagging me for a while. Why didn't Lindsey put in her two cents like Alicia and Keeley? I thought it was because her heart wasn't really in the extravaganza, but now she's talking so passionately.

"What?"

"Keeley and Alicia both wrote down their reasons for pushing me into this farce, but there was nothing from you. I figured you'd let me bail out halfway through if things weren't working out, but then you let me down again! You were supposed to let this thing drop."

"You don't know me very well then." She watches me pout for a moment, and I'm glad no one else has wandered in on our spat. Two grown women wrapped in towels, otherwise naked, yelling at each other. "Cassie, I didn't write a stupid letter because I knew you could do this. You didn't need encouragement. I'd rather use the whip than the carrot anyway. I'm not the softest person in the world, but I do know a little about love."

"So, you think."

"I was married a long time. I know the ins and outs of a relationship better than any of you. Alicia's never divorced, and Keeley's never been married. You and I are the closest, because we've both had our hearts crushed by the men we loved and tied ourselves to. I admired how well you did after Pete left you: you got back in shape and worked even harder at your job, but along the way you forgot one important thing."

"How to love somebody?"

"How to love yourself. You run away from your problems, literally. You work yourself so much that you've forgotten your writing. And you can't let anyone in because you're too afraid of losing yourself in someone again."

"Aren't you?" I feel tears forming and let them trickle out like water from a blocked faucet. She moves over beside me and rubs the tears from my cheeks. I try to push away, but she puts an arm around me. "Of course, I'm afraid. Why do you think I sleep around so much?" We laugh, and the door swings open. Three older women march in, strip their towels away, and parade by us, naked glory swinging. That's our cue to leave.

"Seriously," says Lindsey as we leave the steam room and shut the door firmly. "Those old bags should warn a girl before they do that."

"It's natural and beautiful."

"My ass is natural and beautiful. That was just frightening."

As we're leaving, she takes my hand and spins me around. "You're almost done, Cass. Just two more guys to get through. I wish this had worked, but I don't know if these last two will crash and burn or be The One."

"Come on Linds. You and I don't believe in that crap."

"A girl can dream," she says, and we head for our cars, the air warming as the sun peeks out from under its cloudy blanket. Maybe spring is finally here. Time to tan up this pasty pale skin a bit.

Just so we're clear, tanning up entails rubbing odd-smelling tanning lotion all over my body and hoping that it works. Being pale is the redhead's curse, but we rarely get skin cancer if we take precautions. Like not using tanning beds or an SPF under fifty.

I run to the drugstore near my apartment and stock up on a few different lotions and bronzers. Just because I can't crisp in the sun doesn't mean I can't fake it. The clerk eyes my purchases, her brown skin clashing with peroxided hair. She either has no idea that she's doing irreparable harm to her hair and skin, or she can't be bothered. She looks like Paris Hilton after a bender. "Does this stuff even work?" she asks, gum bobbing on her tongue.

"You'd be surprised," I say and beat a hasty retreat.

I have a date tomorrow with Howard Hansen, and I'm not sure how it will go, especially after Mateo showed his true colors and fled like a little girl from my bloody chin last month. I thought the full moon brought out the animalistic fearless side of people. Guessed wrong. Howard suggested seeing a movie, which I find odd for a first date. At least I won't have to talk to him if he's boring. The movie will take care of that. Maybe he picked a movie for the same reason. Women can be just as tedious as men.

I reach my apartment and fling the plastic drugstore bag near the sofa. I'll need it later. Walking around naked in one's apartment is perfectly acceptable, as any self-tanner applier knows. The trick is to watch out for the ankles and the elbows, and the feet rarely take on as much color for some reason. My stomach is the worst, a milky white expanse. It can blind onlookers if I'm not diligent with the tanning lotion. And don't put it on your face. It never comes out the way you planned, and sometimes it burns.

Before applying, I open my laptop and type up the conversation I had with Lindsey at the gym and consider why men don't pick up women there. It's a place where you can almost see the body for what it is. I suppose they're too focused to notice the hotties with okay bodies that saunter around the track in sports-bras and shorts. I prefer to stay covered, at least a t-shirt and yoga pants. Maybe the lack of variety has stunted their sex drives. They're tired of cute girls running around in spandex. Right.

I call my mom and get her voicemail, and it's the same with Dad. We need to plan my birthday, as both expressed desire to throw me a thirtieth party. Can I get both to commit to one party? Perhaps now that they both have significant others I can force them together for one day. I'll get Alicia on that.

I can't believe that thirty came so quickly. It snuck up on me like a cheetah hidden in tall grass, and age is just as speedy. My poor little antelope body can't outrun it forever. I remember to ask Lindsey how turning thirty felt and smile. She'll hate me for acknowledging her own impending birthday. Thinking of Lindsey at forty makes me feel much better about turning thirty. Much, much better.

A theater downtown shows grainy classics like *Casablanca* and *Gone with the Wind*. I'm expecting one of those kinds of films when I walk up to the steps and look at the marquee. I nearly lose my fabulous Indian dinner. *Texas Chainsaw Massacre*. Is it at least the old one? Of course not. Can you have an anniversary screening for a movie that only came out a few years ago? Maybe it's older than I think. Why would this awesome theater show something like that? **Horror Movie Marathon!** screams a sign near the entrance. Dammit ladies, I said no more surprises! I suppose I could have looked up the information online, but I had no idea this theater showed shit like this. I enjoy horror movies, but only in the comfort of my apartment, where I have a cat to cuddle and don't mind if I spill popcorn and where the floor isn't sticky.

"Hi!" says an excited voice in my ear. I jump a few feet and cover my ear. "I didn't mean to scare you!" He giggles and does a small jig. What the hell? Who is this character? He resembles a former classmate of mine: about five-seven, brown hair, freckles but not pale, shining eyes looking for trouble. Hey…is he the guy from my sophomore year? Jumping around like that he might as well be a happy little elf.

"That's okay. I was checking out the movie poster."

"Scary right? I haven't seen this one in a long time. It was awesome back then, so no reason it should suck now, right?" Why did he add "right" after every statement?

"Sure. Do you want to go in?"

"Yeah! The movie starts in five minutes. I like to cut it close. I hate the commercials that come on before the movie. It's like a conspiracy or something."

"The theaters have to show commercials to get funding. People don't go to as many movies anymore." Cowed by my information, he nods and loses some pep. He gets it right back when we go inside. The foyer is filled with plastic movie monsters and cardboard cutouts. Maybe the horror movie marathon could have been held in October? Just a suggestion.

He races to the ticket counter and says, "*Texas Chainsaw Massacre* for one!" One? Is he not going to buy my ticket? All right men, listen up. Women may believe in equal treatment of males and females, but this belief does not include the first date. At least for me; call me old-fashioned. Some good-natured bickering over the check is fun, but I'm not one to argue when a guy reaches for the tab. The parties involved thereafter can determine the second date, but the first date is the man's chance to show courtesy. By not buying my ticket, Howard condemns himself permanently. I almost turn around, but the girls would want me to try, so I buy my ticket as well.

"Are you two together?" asks the ticket seller. He lifts an eyebrow, and the stupid red velvet cap rises on his forehead. I make a "thanks for reminding me" face and turn to follow Howard.

"Where should we sit?" he asks, frantic. He procured a box of popcorn from nowhere and is munching on it. It doesn't look like the kind they sell here, so where was he hiding it? "I like the middle, smack dab in the middle. How about you?"

"The middle is fine—"

"Great! I'll go save the seats!" He runs ahead of me and into the dim theater, almost knocking over two teenagers. Why are there always teenagers around on my bad dates? They're everywhere, waiting to mock my misfortune.

"I don't think we'll have trouble finding spots," I say, but he doesn't hear me. He ploughs forward and gets the two seats directly in the theater's center.

"These look good," he says and plops down, some popcorn flying. "Want some?"

"Where did you get that?"

"I snuck it in," he whispers and grins, ecstatic that he got away with it. I doubt the guy at the front cares enough to stop him from eating his own food. I wave the popcorn away and wrinkle my nose. I don't like to eat mysteriously acquired food. "Suit yourself."

He doesn't say much before the curtains part and show the huge screen, but he whoops and hollers when the lights go out. "This is so awesome!"

"How old are you?" I ask, but he doesn't hear.

The previews fly by with his added commentary: "OOOO I want to see that so much!" "Oh my God that looks so freaking wicked! Spielberg is a genius!" "That looks like crap, why would anyone want to see a movie like that?" "How did that get greenlit?" And so on, ad nauseum.

I can't enjoy the movie, even though it's pretty terrible, because he won't stop whispering. I try to tune him out, but if he thinks I'm not listening he pokes my shoulder and asks if I heard him.

"I'm watching the movie," I say, and shush him. This doesn't work. After a few moments, he's back to nattering on about whatever. The teenagers behind us say, "Shut up!" That's the final insult: when a teenager has to tell a grown up how to behave in public.

"I have to use the restroom," I whisper. He nods and refocuses on the screen, amazed that a movie's playing.

I go out the doors and march past the ticket counter, where the clerk smirks and tips his hat to me. I scowl and run outside. There's no way Howard's getting a second date.

"And now Alicia says he won't stop emailing my account, saying that I hurt his feelings by leaving. She doesn't answer him, but the emails are escalating. Apparently, he threatened to turn me in to the website's managers. What the hell could he say?"

"Can't you get kicked off the site?" asks Mom, sipping her coffee.

"Who the hell cares? Maybe it would be for the best," I sigh, faking concern.

We sit outside Minnie's, the café from my morning runs. Mom skipped the latte and went right for a red eye, a shot of espresso and dark roast coffee. She drank half of it quickly, and now sits nursing it, teasing out the last drops.

"Long night?" I ask.

"Why yes, but we were talking about your problem."

"Don't worry. All Alicia has to do is send copies of his emails to the administrator. Howard will be the one kicked off for harassment."

"What a shame. All he wants is to find love."

"With his manners, I'm surprised he hasn't been booted yet."

The café owner comes outside and checks her flowers. Even while digging in the potted soil, she wears a light cashmere sweater, fitted khaki capri pants, and adorable ballet flats. She nods at us, and we smile, toasting her with our ceramic cups. She smiles and winks then goes back inside.

"I suppose Attention Deficit Disorder doesn't show in writing."

"In handwriting it would," I mutter, gloomy that we're still discussing my date.

"Don't be so maudlin. Isn't that a fabulous word? I heard it on Oprah the other day."

"It's a great word. I'm not being *maudlin*. Yesterday was a long day. I got all fake-tan-lotioned up and it didn't matter. He wasn't interested in me at all. He just wanted a human wall to throw words at. He must get that a lot."

"Don't be mean. Were you this judgmental about the other men you've been seeing?"

"Mother…"

"You know what I mean. Didn't we agree that you needed to work on that?"

"Sometimes snap judgments are correct, and you should go with your gut."

"Yes, but you do it so often. Do me a favor, the last man, be kind to him. See where that tactic gets you."

"Fine. Any thoughts on my party?"

"Tons! I have loads of ideas! Your father and I were conferring on a venue."

"Dad? And you? Conferring?"

"Don't be like that. We get along like adults when we need to." Since when? "We thought the party might be held at his new place." New place? "He moved to Sandy's apartment and her building has a lovely outdoor area, perfect for parties. In late May, the weather should be divine!"

"Dad moved? He didn't tell me!" Mom looks flustered, and she moves her cup back and forth in her hands. I glare at her until she looks me in the eye. "When did this happen?"

"Two weeks ago. Don't be angry. He didn't want to burden you."

"He's not a burden!"

"You are so busy with your work project and dating, he didn't want to pester you."

"This is *her* doing, I know it. What a bitch!" I stand and turn to go, furious at both my parents but mostly with Sandy. "I'm going over there."

"Do you know where she lives?"

"No, but you must, since you're all cozy planning *my* party."

"Cassie, stop it. This is unbecoming of a lady."

"I'm not a lady, and neither are you, Mother!"

She clinks her cup down gently and stands up. "That was uncalled for."

"Mom, I'm sorry—"

"No, you're not. I try with you Cassie, but I never succeed. Can't you be happy that your father and I can be in the same room again? I'm happy for him and Sandy, and he's overjoyed that I found Gideon. We've moved past our bitterness. It's time for you to move on as well."

She leaves, heels clicking on the concrete sidewalk. A busser comes outside and clears our dishes as I stand with my mouth open. Did Dad not tell me about moving because he thought I was busy, or did he know I detest Sandy and wouldn't agree with his decision? I'm guessing the latter. I made my own dad set me aside. Wait, he didn't set me aside. He made a choice. He knew Sandy and I couldn't get along, so he separated those parts of his life. I don't want him to have to do that! He's my dad! I've been so selfish.

I can fix this!

I run after Mom, my purse flying behind me, flip-flops slapping the pavement. She didn't make it far, and I spot her ambling down the street with her hips swinging. She's pissed. I can tell by the swagger.

"Mom!" I yell, and she turns. She sees me but keeps going. "Mom, wait!" She doesn't pick up speed, so I catch her, but she ignores me when I close to her side. "I'm sorry."

"I'm not leading you to her house. She's done a lot for your father, and she doesn't deserve to have you belittle her in her own home."

"That's not it. I want to make things right. She annoys the hell out of me, but I haven't spent enough time with her. Maybe I can grow to like her."

"Your father is in love with her."

We both stop. I'm breathing hard and Mom's eyes are glassy.

"In love?"

"Yes. And I'm in love with Gideon, and we both love you. That should be enough love to hold this ramshackle family together."

I reach out and pull her into a hug. She resists for a moment before folding into me. I pat her back and tell her it's okay. I can handle Sandy if I have to, for Dad.

"He needs you, Cassie. You're his daughter. But parents need other kinds of affection too."

"I totally get it. No more lecture! I'll call Dad and let him know that I'm happy for him, and whatever party you want to plan, go for it. I'd hate anything anyway, considering."

"Thirty is a difficult age to celebrate." We laugh and pull apart, not caring about the staring passersby.

"You're right. There's just one more thing."

"What's that?"

"You're right about Dad and Sandy, but you're dead wrong about Howard. He didn't even buy my ticket."

"On a first date?" I nod, and Mom looks shocked, as though I'd thrown cold water down her silk blouse. "Let us never speak of him again."

294

May

Pirate Paul and Rule Number Twelve: All's well that ends well, even dating.

Finally, the time has come. It's the first of May and that means I have one more man to meet and possibly toss or keep. You might think I'm callous, but after the year I've had, this last guy is more like the last roadblock before my exit than the restaurant at the top of the exit.

The girls are sad, Keeley especially. They were hoping that I would find someone to be with, or at least go on more than two dates. They abandoned their you-have-to-go-on-at-least- two-dates-with-each-guy rule a while back. This was wise, considering the cannon fodder they set me up with. Each man taught me something, and each one exhibited a habit I know to watch for. In short, I learned some things. Alicia will be so proud. In truth, I enjoyed the process, at least a little. I'm friends with Tristan and have fond memories of lost Dan and had a lot of good food along the way. The scar is finally fading from my chin, and although my knees will never feel the same, I'm glad I fell that cold night in March, otherwise Mateo might have kept me fooled for a long time. I know how I must have appeared to my friends and family after Pete left me when I watched helplessly as Logan trampled a mini-golf course. I apologized to them all, but they forgave me. After all, my heart was broken. I guess I knew better than Logan how long it takes to get over someone.

I'm most happy about how the Pete situation panned out. He got a head full of beer bottle, and I got a heart full of closure. Most men fear the word "closure," and I'm not a big advocate of it either, unless the relationship you had was long and intense. It's necessary to move on. Otherwise, we get stuck back where we were, no matter how many miles you run or how much back-breaking work you do.

How's that for an ending, ladies? Because this is the end of the dating journal. I won't write about the last date, because it doesn't really matter. What matters is the journey…

Yeah right. Fooled you. No more what I learned nonsense. Of course, I have to tell about Pirate Paul and my birthday party and all that followed. You guys know most of it, but I think there are still some surprises up my sleeve for the ending. Watch that last step, it's a killer.

Keeley emails me the last information I get in this little game. She'll miss picking out men for me and says she might give the online thing a try, since she can't seem to connect with anyone through normal dating. I tell her that she's being ridiculous, but she says, "It's not as easy as you'd think. I get asked out a lot, but there's never any deep connection. All they do is look at my boobs and talk about how beautiful I am and lie about having a yacht." If those are the worst things men have done to her, I'd like to set her up with some of the distinguished bachelors she unleashed on me.

She offers to come along on my last date, not as a chaperone, but to hide out at the bar armed with a cell phone plan. It's simple. If the date looks like it's going badly, your friend, who is either watching at the bar or poised at home waiting ten minutes in to call, dials you up and says there's an emergency. If the date itself is cause for an ambulance, you bail, saying someone's in the hospital or that your friend's goldfish died. The perfect getaway. Many people use the "back-up plan," so don't be offended if your date's phone happens to ring once. If he or she stays, you know you're doing well, if they leave, better luck next time, and remember not to wear the Dr. Seuss necktie.

I say "sure," as I know she's dying to watch me in action. What the hell.

We get to the bar early so Keeley can get positioned. She sits at the bar and orders a glass of chardonnay. "Ready?" she asks. She wears a black sheath dress, dark glasses, and a trench coat.

"What's with the spy getup?"

"I'm being inconspicuous."

"You're anything but. Take off the coat and the glasses. You look like the world's worst CIA agent."

"Damn, I was going for Audrey Hepburn meets FBI." I shake my head and return to the host station.

"Hi," I say to the well-dressed hostess. She smiles and welcomes me to the bar, exactly as she did when Keeley and I walked in. "There will be two of us. A man named Paul will be joining me."

"Wonderful. And your name?"

"Cassandra.

"That's pretty! I wish my name was pretty like that."

"Thank you..." I think. "Can I sit anywhere?"

"I'll show you in." She grabs the drink menu and walks into the seating area. High-top tables and booths sit in semi-darkness, the better not to see your date. "Is this fine?" She puts me at a booth where Keeley can see in the mirror behind the bar. Keeley gives me a blatant thumbs-up, and I giggle. "Oh, it's wonderful. Thank you."

She's about as covert as a unicorn.

I'm apprehensive about this date, mainly because it's the last, or second to last if this one works. I have worse luck on second dates, or maybe it just feels unfortunate because those guys fooled me on the first date only to show a true color on the second. It's because people can't be themselves on first dates. They're job interviews: you dress nicely, prepare questions and answers for the other person, and hide the deep-rooted neuroses waiting to spring. I've never been this unnerved by an interview. I'm good at those. It's these personalized meetings I can't seem to master.

Keeley grins in the mirror above the bar and looks at her watch. She puts up five fingers. He has five minutes to be on time. If he's late, maybe I can have a get out of jail free card. I don't think the girls would let me get away with it. They'd have one more surprise in the wings if Paul doesn't work out.

I wonder about Paul, more than I've pondered the previous men. Keeley told me that he's tall, likes surfing, and acts in children's theater productions. He likes the beach and kids. Not much to go on. And most men consider themselves tall, except maybe Danny Devito.

The server brings me water with lemon while I wait and makes a few wine suggestions. I'm thinking pinot grigio if there's a good one, but I can't bring myself to look at the wine list. I think I need to size Paul up before I consider ordering.

Right at nine o'clock, the door opens and lets a nice May night breeze into the bar. The potted plants rustle in the wind, and I smell fresh grass. What a pleasant scent. I look over to the door and know that the man who walked in has to be my date. With my luck, who else could he be?

Paul stands at the host station, very tall, so Keeley wasn't lying there. He is handsome, like a young Denzel Washington with gorgeous skin and a big smile. I can't see anything wrong with him…beside the fact that he's dressed head to toe in a pirate costume. That's right. A pirate. Knee high leather boots, a ruffled white shirt, tight leather pants, a bandana, and a fake sword strapped at his waist. All he needs is a parrot and an eye patch and the illusion will be complete. The hostess beams as he asks if Cassandra is in the bar. She sniggers and leads him over. Despite the getup, Paul appears at ease, almost confident in his historically inaccurate exterior. He looks like he just stepped off a *Treasure Island* cover. Or off the Pirates of the Caribbean ride at Disneyland.

I catch Keeley's eye in the mirror, and her expression is unreadable. Paul has rendered her unconscious. I'm glad Lindsey didn't want to come. She would have fallen off her barstool laughing and blew our cover. I mouth, "I'm going to kill you," before Paul reaches the table.

When he strides over, I stand and hold out my hand, trying not to stare.

"You must be Cassandra," he says, voice deep and musical. "I've been waiting a long time to meet you. Your profile is very popular."

Flushing, I say, "I've had quite a year." I don't know what else to say without asking about the costume. Maybe if I ask about surfing. "It must be difficult surfing in Minnesota." Jeez. What an idiot.

"Nigh impossible," he says and smiles. His smile is compelling, if only it could distract from the fake sword. "I would rather attempt it in California or Australia." We sit down, he pulls the chair out for me.

"I've always wanted to go to Australia," I say, hoping this might get him started on a nice long monologue. Where did the server go? I need a big drink. I wonder if they have those bottle-size wine glasses.

"Before we get into that, I'd like to explain my clothing." Oh no. He wants to explain. It's none of my business how he gets his kicks or how he developed this style. "I'm in a production of *The Swiss Family Robinson* for the children's theater. Rehearsal went way over, and I didn't want to be late. I apologize. This isn't the look I was going for when I thought about our date." Whew! He's not weird! It's for his job.

"I was wondering."

"I know. So was the cab driver." I laugh and find that it's not fake. Perfect! I kind of like him. I just wish the ruffles on his shirt weren't so ostentatious.

"It does look a bit odd."

"You think so? I thought the pirate look was making a comeback."

"According to whom? *Pirate Monthly*?" I smile.

"Guess I haven't caught up on the back issues."

We have a lovely evening. The server suggests a great pinot grigio for me, and Paul sips cabernet while we chat about traveling, where he dreams of surfing, and where I want to live eventually. He's surprised when I say Venice and mentions that it's sinking.

"I know," I say. "That's why I need to move there sooner than later then move back when the water inches toward my first-floor window."

I lose track of Keeley while we talk, and I'm not shocked when I notice she's no longer sitting at the bar when I hazard a gaze. She must have caught on that Paul and I are having a fine time. Three hours pass, and I'm more tired than I realized. I've never talked this long to a man who wasn't a friend or ex-fiancé.

"It's getting pretty late," I say. "I really should go."

"We have been sitting here awhile. I'm sure our waiter would like it if we left."

"Nah. It's not busy. I'm sure he's been taking bets with the kitchen staff about how long the date would last."

"Because I look ridiculous?"

"Yup," I say. "I don't think any other pirate has had such good fortune."

"Before we go, I have one thing to ask you."

I look at the black book and see the astronomical check. The wine was more expensive than I remembered from a few hours ago. "What is it?"

"Did your friend at the bar approve?" Shit.

"Friend?" How can I explain Keeley? Is he guessing, or did he spot her right away.

"The blonde. She left two hours ago."

"Um. Uh…"

"It's fine," he says and grabs my hand. I look into his eyes, and they're gleaming with repressed laughter. "I'm pretty observant. And she is an absolute failure as a spy."

"How did you know?"

"She couldn't keep her eyes off us for an hour, and when she left, she stared me down. Not the best coconspirator I've ever seen, but not the worst."

"I'm so sorry."

"Like I said, it's fine. My cell phone went off in my pocket and I didn't have to answer it."

Well, at least if I got caught, it's nice to know he had the same back-up plan.

"He invited himself on our next girls' night," I say, and Alicia holds back a chuckle. "It's not funny! He totally knew Keeley was watching us. I'm surprised she didn't have binoculars to match her trench coat."

"She wore a trench coat?" asks Alicia who rubs her belly.

"Oh yeah. The government recruitment squad will be knocking on her door anytime soon."

Alicia's house is quiet, serene. Not what I'm used to. Brian took the kids out for lunch, knowing Alicia needed some time off her feet. She's getting bigger, but Alicia isn't one to gain a lot of weight when she's pregnant. She's had three dry-runs, so she knows what to eat. We sit in her living room, decaffeinated iced teas in hand. He husband made it for us! What men do for their pregnant wives.

"You getting enough exercise?"

"Chasing three kids does wonders for stamina."

"Three kids and one husband."

"Actually," she says and rubs her nose making it pink, "Brian has been so attentive. He knew how worried I was about this baby, so he's picked up the slack. Much better than with the last one."

"The last one has a name."

"I know, but there's too many to remember all the names." We laugh, and she starts coughing. "Sorry. This one's giving me seasonal allergies. Never had problems before, but the doctor said the pollen count is ridiculously high this spring."

"You can get allergies from being pregnant?"

"Sure. I'm glad it wasn't something worse, like gestational diabetes. A friend from work had that, and she was miserable for nine months. I can handle a few sneezes and a runny nose."

"I was wondering how my secret party plans are going?"

"You're terrible. And it's impossible to keep a secret from you."

"It's hard to keep it a secret when my mom and dad call constantly asking what food I would prefer and if I'm still fighting with Justin. How they knew Justin and I were on the outs I'll never know."

She sips her tea and lets her eyes wander before answering, "It's going to be phenomenal, the party of the year!"

"That's what everyone's friends say about thirtieth birthdays."

"And mine better be just as good, missy."

"Your birthday isn't for another seven months! Give me some time to plan."

"Fine. Anyway, we're inviting everyone: your boss, colleagues, some author Kelly wants you to meet—"

"What!?"

"Oh crap. Now *that* was a secret. Kelly's going to kill me." She gets up, struggling for a moment. "Damn balance is shot! They never tell you that you become less coordinated with every pregnancy."

"Don't change the subject! What author?" I race after her retreating form. She ducks into the kitchen and hums a little tune, ignoring me. "Don't be coy with me! I can read you like a book and edit you after I'm done!"

"Forget what I said. It's nothing to worry about."

"No more bombshells! I can't take it!"

"You'll have to wait and see." I pout and fold my arms across my chest. "Don't be so immature. It wouldn't be a great party unless we put something over on you."

"The next thing I know you'll have invited Pete to my party."

"You're being dramatic." She dumps the rest of her tea into the sink. "We only invited the guys you dated this year."

"If you weren't pregnant, I'd strangle you."

"I made a mistake," says Keeley. We sit outside her apartment on the deck, the sun hitting our skin. I've layered on the SPF fifty, but Keeley's trying to tan. She laughs when I rub lotion everywhere. "What?" I ask, "I don't want to look like I bathed in ketchup before my party." We lay on rubbery plastic lawn chairs, a pail of summer shandys in between. I mention my upcoming date with Paul, and she doesn't answer. After a few minutes of me talking about the date and how he caught her, she said, "I made a mistake."

"With what?" I wonder if it's about her job. I hope she didn't get fired or something. The economy isn't the greatest. "Do you need help?"

"It's nothing like that." She raises her chair's back and looks at me, a serious expression on her face. She looks guilty.

"What's wrong?" She's worrying me. Please don't let it be her family. They live so far away. I'd hate for her to leave. The last time there was a family emergency, she was gone for a month. .

"It's terrible, and I never thought I'd be the kind of person to do something like this." I pull my chair up and face her. She's near crying, which happens often but is never pleasant. "You know how I was talking about going online like we did for you?"

"Yeah, vaguely."

"Well, I've been on the same website for about three months. I'm sorry I didn't tell you. I didn't want to steal your thunder."

"Is that all? I thought someone died or something."

"It's worse."

"What could be worse? Lindsey told me about Kelly and how I had the promotion all along, if that's what this is about."

"Alicia picked Paul for you, last month."

"Okay." She keeps pausing. I have no idea where this is going.

"I hadn't seen his profile, I just got the details from Alicia. The problem is, I went out on a date with him. Before you did. That's why I bolted so fast."

"You knew who I was meeting that night?" I'm very confused. What does she mean?

"No! And I didn't think he noticed me until you mentioned he caught me staring."

"How could he not? When did you go on this date?"

"The week before."

"And you didn't think a guy you met named Paul, who works at the children's theater, could possibly be the same man meeting me?"

"That isn't on his profile, and we didn't talk about it. Alicia must have gotten it out of him when she set up your date." She starts crying, and she puts her face in her hand. She shakes and sobs and I'm not sure what to say.

"It's okay, honey. You didn't do it maliciously."

"No, but that didn't stop me from agreeing to a second date!"

"What?" A second date? But didn't Paul set *us* up for a second date? I recall our last conversation at the bar, and he mentioned coming to our next girls' night, but was that because he knew Keeley would be there? Thinking on it, I can't remember if he said it was a second date or just a fun get-together. He picked her. He chose Keeley.

"I know! But I really like him, and I was so shocked to see him, especially in a pirate outfit. I didn't recognize him at first. He said he was seeing other people but that he thought we might have something. I've been emailing him for as long as I've been on the website. I was afraid to meet him at first, so we've been talking online."

I don't know how to react. Keeley didn't steal my boyfriend; she didn't even steal my date. I stole hers. And she feels bad. But I'm pissed too. Why didn't she tell me about her date? Why didn't she stop my date? I would have understood. Now I feel like I had a connection only to find he was interested in the hot blonde at the bar. I fight the urge to yell and curse my friend. She can't help what she looks like.

"I guess it's over then," I say.

"What?" she sniffs.

"He's yours. I don't want to make a fuss over one date. You obviously like him a lot. And if he asked you on a second date, I don't want to stand in the way."

"Really?" No. Not really. I want to rip her hair out like they do in tacky girl-fight movie scenes. I never thought I'd feel this way about Keeley. I've never been more jealous of her or more furious with myself for being jealous. "You're a good friend Cass. I was so worried. I didn't even tell Alicia or Lindsey when I found out. I hope you can forgive me."

"No problem." But there is a problem. I've been feeling down on myself for a long time now. I never thought one of my closest friends could bring me lower.

I don't talk to her for a week.

My party approaches, and I don't feel like celebrating. I haven't spoken to Keeley, and Alicia is making me feel terrible about it. Lindsey shrugs when she hears about the dating debacle and tells me to get over it. Paul obviously wasn't the man for me. Alicia says that Keeley has been moping around, not getting excited about her second date, which went very well. She tells me to let Keeley be happy for once, and I realize that I've never known Keeley to date anyone for very long or talk about anyone in particular. Is her life a series of endless dates? How can someone so beautiful and smart not be able to find someone? If she can't, then how the hell can I? I tell them both that I need time to digest the information. Don't I deserve a little time?

I'm on the phone with Dad constantly as he gets the party details in order. He's discovered it's better that I know about the party, so he can ask my opinion about the set-up. Instead of Sandy's place, he booked the roof space at Brit's, a lovely outdoor area with grass and a huge wall where they show movies during the summer and early fall. There are about fifty people coming: people from work, friends, family. I specified no children except Alicia's, but she promised to get a babysitter. I don't think she wants to be watching her kids when she could be having fun. Her husband Brian is bringing a cake; that detail remains a mystery.

As does my enigmatic author guest. I tried to pry the information from Kelly, but the sly thing pretended she didn't know what I was talking about. She offers me the promotion, and I'm so ecstatic I don't badger her about the author. Maybe that's why she shifted the focus of our meeting. Who could she possibly have joining us for my silly thirtieth birthday party?

Mom is so excited that Gideon gets to come. Apparently, he might not have made it; something with work, but he finished and will be joining us. Dad is bringing Sandy, which is fine. I talked with him about the move and how upset I was that he didn't tell me. He apologized and reminded me that I hadn't warmed to his girlfriend. I said she seemed like a lovely person and maybe I jumped the gun a bit. I invited her to the party, and I could feel Dad's smile across the line.

Joel is flying from California, but Gisele can't make it. She has about a million interviews and auditions, to quote my brother. That's fine. I don't know how many significant others I can handle at one party.

As the day draws closer, I get nervous. What will turning thirty be like? I should ask my mom, but then again, she doesn't like to be reminded that I'm younger than she is.

I'm meeting Alicia and Lindsey for one last twenty-nine-year-old coffee the day before my birthday. They've been sending me harassing emails and cards. Alicia says I have thirty birthday cards coming in the mail, and so far, I've gotten about twenty.

The sun is out in full force, hardly any clouds block it. A soft breeze blows from the west, ruffling my hair, which is hanging loose, something I don't do often. I feel my scalp relax, unconstrained by a hair band.

Alicia parked near the curb. I walk in, desperately needing an iced chai. The tiny bell jingles as I enter. They sit near the window. Keeley is with them. Shit. I hadn't planned on seeing her. Damn those girls! Who doesn't love a forced friendship intervention?

"Hi," they all say when I sit down. I stare at my hands and tilt my cup back and forth.

"Hey." We sit quietly for a few moments, and I can feel the taut energy flowing between us. This is ludicrous. Lindsey must think so too, because she clears her throat and says,

"You both need to grow up and get on with it. I'm sick and tired of the stalemate."

"Here here," chimes in Alicia. She raises her glass and glances at me. Why do I have to make the first move?

I sigh, and Keeley looks up, frail as a baby bird. "I heard your date with Paul went well."

They all inhale quickly, and Alicia and Lindsey wait for Keeley to answer.

"It was wonderful, but I wish you'd called me." Now it's my turn to feel guilty.

"I'm sorry, Keel. I was slightly jealous."

"Slightly?" cuts in Lindsey.

"*Slightly* envious of your good fortune. I liked Paul, and I guess things got kind of messed up. You have every right to date him."

"Well now that's settled—"

"Shut up Lindsey," says Alicia. "These two need to clear the air."

"I wish I didn't like him so much," Keeley whispers.

"Oh honey, it's okay." I say, realizing how much she's hurting. I thought she was angry with me about the whole situation, but it turns out she is more worried about our relationship than hers and Paul's. Now this is what girlfriends are for. "You can totally keep seeing him. I don't mind. The fact that you're so concerned for me makes me love you even more!"

"Do you mean it this time? You really don't mind?"

"Not a bit. And to prove it, you can invite him to my party."

Alicia and Lindsey laugh into their hands and Keeley grins.

"So, Miss Alicia," says Lindsey, "the air clear enough for you? Can we talk about something else?"

"Sure. My boobs hurt," she says.

"That's what you get when you don't use protection." Lindsey shrugs and nods, a not-so concerned look in her eyes.

"So," I say before they get into the joys-of-having-children argument, "do I have to go on any more dates?"

"Not a one," sighs Keeley. "There are no more men."

"Are you making a joke?" asks Lindsey.

"Aren't I allowed to make a joke every once and a while?"

"Not if it makes me almost faint."

"Ladies!" says Alicia. "We need to raise our plastic coffee cups and toast Cassie. She made it through twelve months in the dating trenches, experiencing what most normal single people experience. She came out more savvy, more gorgeous, and more confident."

"I did?" She shoves my arm with her cup and keeps going, "She may not have found the perfect man for her, but maybe she learned what to look for."

"New friends?" I ask and chuckle.

"Shut it, we're trying to be nice to you," says Lindsey.

"And so, the Great Dating Extravaganza comes to a close," says Alicia. "You've got a promotion, a sunnier look on romance novels, and most importantly, us!"

"What would I do without you?" I ask sarcastically.

"For one, your vagina might have closed up for good," says Lindsey.

"Ewwww!" cringes Keeley. She wrinkles her nose and sets down her cup. "I've lost my coffee appetite."

"Lighten up youngster! At least you're not turning thirty tomorrow."

Really. What would I do without them?

May

My Birthday

It rains lightly on my birthday morning, and I pray that it stops before this afternoon, when my party starts. There's nothing worse than unfortunate weather on your birthday. One year, a tornado ripped through the Twin Cities, uprooting trees, destroying my neighbor's car, and sending a traffic sign through our lobby's window.

At least the weatherman predicted clear skies for later.

I go for a morning run in my bad-weather shoes, and they squish with each step. Today's run is more difficult; it must be my age showing. My legs are sore when I get home, and the hot shower feels great. Prospero rubs against my calves when I exit the shower, spreading cat hair over my freshly shaved legs. Damn cat. I should brush him later.

I picked out my ensemble last night to avoid the I-have-no-clothes panic dance. It looks like the I-have-to-pee dance only more urgent and hysterical. My navy and white floaty short skirt lies next to a lacy, chocolate camisole and my jean jacket, in case it gets chilly. Strappy but sturdy woven rope wedges sit by the bed. I stow a pair of flip-flops in my roomy tote, just in case. A girl can't be too prepared.

My hair won't cooperate with the curling iron, so I straighten it instead and smooth my bangs over one side, just the way my mom hates it. I secure the strands with a bobby pin and move on to makeup. My *Instyle* is open on the counter where I've marked a few choices. There's an awesome purple eye shadow option with cat-eye liner, but it might be too severe. The natural look with beiges and browns isn't special enough. The rose shadow and deep burgundy liner should be perfect. I thought about fake eyelashes then remembered the last time I attempted them. I throw the box under the sink. Three mascara coats will have to do. After lip-gloss I'm all set. I wait for Dad to pick me up, and we'll be on our way. Though I turned thirty around midnight last night, at this moment, I finally feel older.

At half past, I hear my buzzer and run to let my dad in.

"Come on up! I'm almost ready!" He doesn't answer, so I race into the bedroom to grab my jacket. I recheck my makeup and hair, slip on my watch and swap my plain studs for some dangling earrings. They look better with my long hair. I really need a trim.

Dad knocks on the door, and I leap over Prospero, who knows I'm leaving and wants to impede my progress as much as possible. I shout at him to get out of the way and pull the door open. "Hi Da—"

It's not my dad. Justin came to pick me up.

"Was there a change in itinerary no one told me about?"

"Your dad asked if I could get you. There were a few things he needed to take care of at the restaurant."

"Well, that's fine. Let me grab my bag."

"Wait one second. There's something I need to say before we go." He's not going to chastise me on my birthday, is he? I thought we were past this. How could my dad do this? I have no escape route, so I put my bag down and wait for the reprimand. I cross my arms across my chest.

"First, happy birthday."

"Thank you. I feel pretty ancient today."

"You look great."

"Thanks. New shoes." We stand for a moment and I shift my weight from foot to foot. "Anything else?"

"Yes," he says. He takes my hand gently and holds it. "You're one of my best friends, and I feel awful for how I treated you when…you know." By his bent posture, I can tell he's been wanting to say this for some time. His eyebrows furrow and he brushes a hand through his hair.

"You don't have to apologize."

"I do. I was mean and spiteful, and we were both drunk when it happened. I shouldn't have pressured you."

"From what I recall, I jumped on you." He laughs and looks me in the eyes. I realize how much I've missed Justin. We made up but still haven't been talking much. Work is bearable, but we lost whatever friendly spark we had. "Let's just say that we're both morons and leave it at that."

He's wearing the cologne Kevin gave him for Christmas, a woodsy, rich scent. It brings to mind our long textbook proofreading sessions. I inhale deeply and recall his lips on mine. The image stops my breath, and my knees feel weak. Whoa. That came out of nowhere.

His hair flops to one side, giving him an inquisitive air, and his smile is easy, not forced. I take in his face, every freckle darkened by the May sun. It dawns on me that every woman in our office has a crush on him, and I remember Lindsey calling him a fox. I laughed off these women before, because he was just my good friend. He's been there for me through the entire year, pushing me to make decisions that are good for me. He always asks how I'm doing and inquires about my projects. He puts up with Kevin and me making fun of his outdoorsy clothing and love of old poetry. Even when he was furious with me, he never made me feel less than, I did that all by myself. He never puts me down.

I squeeze his hand, and he squeezes back. If he lets go, this is nothing. He's done with the idea that we could be together. Do I want him to let go?

"Agreed. And for the record, I'm glad you're finished with the dating torture chamber. You didn't deserve that. I felt like strangling your friends, or at least sending them nasty letters."

You know that moment in the movies where the dumb heroine finally figures out that her best friend/old lover/hated nemesis is the one for her? There's an "OH" moment, and you can read it plain on the actress's face. What was she thinking? The audience knew all along that man was meant for her, so why was it so difficult for her to figure out? What the hell was she waiting for?

His hand doesn't drop mine.

I hold my breath. Here goes nothing. I reach up, grab his head, and pull it down toward me. His eyes widen, and he stops me.

"What are you doing?" His fingers have twined around mine, but his eyes say, please don't stomp on my heart again, because I can't take it. I can feel him holding his breath.

I take my time thinking of an answer. He deserves my utmost attention. He needs to understand what I've realized.

"I've never seen you clearly until now. And I love what I see." I try to tell him with my eyes that I've let the last year go, that no man I've met this year has measured up to him. He was kind to me on New Year's, and respectful. He didn't take advantage of me. If anything, I took advantage of the situation, let my sorrow wash over good sense. But maybe it was my brain telling me something else.

So many thoughts! He needs to know that I've been waiting for someone like him, the absolute antithesis of Pete. What took him so long to show up? Oh yeah, I'm an idiot and never noticed him. I want to say all this to him but can't spit it out. I attempt a stammer.

Before I can say anything else, Justin puts his arms around my waist and sweeps me around, kissing me all the while. My feet leave the floor and one crashes into the lamp on my end table. It soars across the room and clunks against the wall, but we don't notice.

It feels like forever and not long enough when he sets me down. The room is spinning, and I can't help but check my hair. He pats a loose piece back in place and shakes with laughter.

"Is this for real? Or is it the script I came up with in my head and I'm dreaming?"

"It's real," I say. "Come on. We'll be late for my party."

The rooftop bustles with people when we arrive, and everyone yells "Surprise!" as we bound up the steps, hand in hand. The staff claps and grins; I know most of them from frequent patronage. Friends, family, and lots of people from work stand on the grassy roof and around small tables. They hoot and holler and put fists in the air, and I spy the girls nestled in a group at the front. Each is laughing, and they hold each other up. Alicia smiles as though she knows something has happened, and Keeley is practically crying. Lindsey gives me a thumbs-up and winks. I drop Justin's hand—he knows I have to greet the girls—and run toward them. They wrap themselves around me and pat my back.

"I knew this would happen eventually," cries Keeley, and Lindsey rolls her eyes.

"You didn't know anything."

"I picked Justin out for her all along."

"Shush, you two," says Alicia. She arches her eyebrow. "As usual, Cassie was the last to know."

"As usual," I agree and roll my eyes. I turn and beckon Justin forward. He's standing with Kevin and they make their way over. Kevin looks self-satisfied, as though licking expensive wine from his lips. He grabs my hand and presses it but doesn't do the I-told-you-so foxtrot. Justin shines from someplace deep within, his eyes and skin glowing.

"Kevin told me he's been secretly trying to get us together for years. I told him I was all for it when I met you, but he warned me it would take to a while for you to wake up from your, how did you put it Kevin, 'no-sex-induced stupor.'"

I shove Kevin and say, "He would tell you that."

"At least I didn't point him toward Carly," says Kevin.

"She isn't here is she?"

"Of course not. I wrote the guest list."

My parents swoop in, one on each side, their own significant others in tow. Sandy and Gideon congratulate me, and I start to like Sandy when she doesn't even glance at the handsome Gideon. She only has attention for my dad. I say thank you and pull Mom and Dad closer.

"This is great, guys. I didn't think you two had it in you."

Mom says, "We've been known to cooperate from time to time."

"Since when? 1983?"

"Give us a little credit, squirt," says Dad. "We collaborated long enough to get the two best kids in the world."

"Here here!" Joel steps in and picks me up in a bear hug. He nearly drops me, and I slap his arm when he releases his grip. "Not so rough!" he cries in fake anguish.

"These shoes are expensive!"

"Only you would spend a ton of money on shoes you'll wear once."

"I don't know," I say and gaze at Justin, who is deep in conversation with my parents. My mom breaks down and hugs him, and Justin's startled expression is hilarious. "I've already got some good memories attached to these babies. I might wear them a few more times."

"You finally found out that he likes you."

"How the hell did *you* know? You've only met him like what, twice?"

"That's all the time I needed." He waggles his brows and I hit him again, a smidge lighter this time. "Ow!"

"That didn't hurt."

"I find you abusing your poor brother." Kelly melts through the crowd of well- wishers—my cousins are already doing shots in my honor across the way, and Joe Carlson from work chugs a huge beer next to them as they cheer—and glides beside me. She looks fabulous: thick pearl ropes dangle from her neck, and her dress must be Chanel; she would settle for no less. And while some people have taken their shoes off in the grass, Kelly floats above the ground on killer heels.

"Are those Manolos?"

"Of course."

"And my brother deserves whatever he gets. He's the favorite after all," I say loud enough for my mom to hear. She turns and laughs, flipping a hand at me as though what I said was usually true, but not today. Joel does an awkward sideways shuffle away to join our cousins and leaves me with my boss.

Kelly would never stoop to hugging, so she presents her fingers for a firm handshake. I nearly scrape my palm on the enormous rock on her middle finger.

"The party is wonderful. Your parents did a lovely job."

"Thank you. I've been dreading today, but it seems like everything is going smoothly."

"Quite. I want to introduce you to someone. This person has been desperate to meet her editor." A tall, slim woman drifts to her side, and I can't place her from author photos we have at the office. This is the mysterious author, but who is she? Her hair is cut in a short, brunette bob, and she dresses stylishly in a quirky floral print maxi dress and metallic gladiator sandals.

"Thank you for coming to the party."

"I had to meet you, and I wanted to do it in a more social setting. I don't enjoy going to publishing offices. Too many odd people."

"I agree. Sometimes I think Kelly and I are the only normal ones there." I'm not sure what else to say. Her voice is smooth and low, like listening to a string quartet where the bass has center stage.

"My name is Pia Brown. I wrote—"

"*Spade a Spade!*" I yell and cover my mouth. Not too many people notice, but my mom looks over as if to chide me for being too loud. "I adored that book!"

"That's what Kelly said. I was very impressed with how you edited the work. I especially liked what you did with the structure. I never would have thought of moving that scene to the beginning of the book."

"You mean the one where she thinks she's met the new love of her life?"

"Exactly. I'm not a very romantic person, so writing these kinds of books allows me to be freer with my thinking. I'm afraid I'm rather cynical when it comes to love."

"Aren't we all, after a certain age?" asks Kelly, sipping champagne. A server walks by with a try of champagne flutes, and I grab two.

"Thank you," says Pia when I hand her a glass. "I've never been to this restaurant. It reminds me of the pubs I used to frequent in London."

"You lived in London?" I yell again.

Pia, Kelly, and I talk for almost half an hour. She's such an intriguing person. She invites me to visit Europe with her when she goes next year, and I tell her I couldn't possibly intrude. She insists, and Kelly nods imperceptibly. She also tells me that she wishes me to be her exclusive editor, and I gladly accept. Apparently she has a bunch of novels squirreled away, waiting to be published, and she plans on writing more.

"Cassie has been promoted," says Kelly, "so she'll be totally available to you whenever you need her."

"I won't be that invasive. I try to write two books a year, and they're not too much trouble. I'm no Dostyevsky."

"Thank God," says Kelly. "I can barely get through the Russians without dying of boredom."

"It's settled, then," she says. "Pia Brown is sticking with Cassandra McTiernan."

Unable to contain myself, I reach out and hug her, and unlike the smiling Kelly, Pia is only too glad to return the grasp.

The servers come out with platters of food: shepherd's pie, curry sauce with thick-cut pub fries, and tons of other grand-smelling delicacies. They maneuver us to tables, so we can enjoy the meal. I sit by the girls, Kevin, and Justin who gratefully takes my hand again and swings it back and forth.

"How you doing?"

"Great! I met Pia Brown!"

"I know. I saw you get all fan girl on her."

"Shut up, I couldn't help it. She wants me to be her exclusive editor, and Kelly said yes!"

"That's awesome!"

"I can't believe you all kept this a secret for so long. Especially Keeley." She blushes and puts her hair behind her ears. Paul and Brian are mingling with my brother and some other guys from work. They both appear happy and confident, something I've never seen in Brian at these functions. And Paul is deliriously handsome in gray linen pants and a white button-down shirt. He looks across his table at Keeley and grins. Keeley waves back and turns crimson. Kevin's boyfriend is away on business, and while I'm disappointed that I didn't meet him, Kevin came bearing a huge gift box from the two of them, so I don't mind. He promises to introduce us soon and hints at double-dating strategies. When Justin catches on to the conversation, Kevin pipes down and shovels mashed potatoes into his mouth.

We talk and laugh through dinner. Lindsey regales us with her latest conquest, Alicia talks about the baby and how her arches are killing her, and Keeley boasts about work. Kevin and Justin are at ease with the girls, which is wonderful. I don't say much, just watch them chat and laugh and clink glasses over numerous topics. Justin's hand rarely leaves mine, and I find that I don't mind the P.D.A. I guess I needed to find the right guy with the right hand.

After dinner, Dad stands up and taps his wine glass with his knife. Everyone stops talking and looks his way, prepared for a speech. My dad isn't known for his oratory skills, so a few family members cringe and take long pulls from their drinks. I'm happy Dad is speaking. He tells the best elaborate stories. I don't care what the rest of the family thinks.

"Speech!" yells Joel, and everyone chortles and applauds. Dad waves us down and puts on his reading glasses. He pulls a square of paper from his pocket and unfolds it.

"Good afternoon everyone. Welcome to my lovely daughter Cassie's thirtieth birthday party."

"She's old!" shouts Joel again. Dad glares at him and makes the lock-and-key motion in front of his mouth. Joel imitates him and sits back in his chair with folded arms. My cousin pats Joel's arm. What a comedian.

"If I might continue. Thank you. Being Cassie's father, I've known her all her life. I remember the night she was born; it was raining so hard the sewer grates overflowed, and our neighbor's car was carried away down the street. Obviously, there was a serious new presence in the world." He shuffles his feet and puts the paper down. "I don't need that anymore.

"She grew up like many little girls: wishing she was a boy so she didn't have to wear dresses on Easter, learning to ride a bike and not hitting parked cars like her brother." He stares down his glasses at Joel who shrugs. "And trying to cook with her mother, though never mastering many recipes.

"Cassie's life has been full of ups and downs. We used to go fishing together, even in high school, and she told me about school troubles, boy worries (though there weren't many of those thank goodness), and her future. You see, she wanted to be a writer but was concerned it wouldn't make much money. She was right, but that shouldn't have stopped her from writing. She found the best job in the world, working with authors and words. I know she's loved each minute as an editor, and I was proud to hear she was recently promoted." He pauses so the group can applaud, and I turn red. I had no idea he had such a speech prepared.

"This year in particular has been trying for my girl." Where is he going with this? "For those of you who don't know, Cassie has been caught up in the most entertaining and educational dating experience anyone could have. With the aid of her friends," he points to our table, and the girls and Kevin clap and nod, "she has weathered twelve months of obstacles and setbacks. She bravely took the challenge and ran with it, much to my pleasure." He stops and rubs his eyes. "I have a confession to make, and no one except Cassie's friends know about this little wrinkle in the plan. It was me who called Alicia, Cassie's best friend, and convinced her to conceive a plot, a way for Cassie to meet someone." He stops again, my mouth agape as I listen. What the hell is he saying?

Dad shifts his gaze to me and smiles.

"You don't have to blame your friends any longer. It was me all along."

I cannot believe what I'm hearing. My friends, family, and colleagues are gleaming with pleasure. Those who knew about the dating game nod and bow their heads, trying to wrap the information around their minds.

"I'm so proud that she didn't quit. There are no words for how proud I am. I knew she could get through the whole mess, and she did. I hope her mind and heart are more open now, that she can leave behind whatever past disrupted her." He's talking about Pete, saying he knew how sad and heartbroken I was. This revelation is astonishing. Even Justin looks perplexed. I glare at the girls, but they only flash conspiratorial grins. This is even bigger than keeping the author a secret.

"To her future, my daughter, my Cassie, let's all raise a glass and toast. Happy birthday sweetheart."

"Cheers!" everyone yells, and I can't drown out the applause and merriment of the guests. My mouth still hangs open, and Dad strides toward me. He pulls up a chair as everyone else begins talking again. Our table is silent and listening. Justin leans forward and asks, "Is that why you asked me to pick her up today?"

"I had a little spy inform me that you two needed to make up before the party. I had no idea you'd come out a couple." He slaps his knee, looking immensely pleased with himself.

"A little spy?" I glare around the table, but no one meets my eyes.

"It all turned out, honey," says Dad. He puts a hand on my shoulder.

"You're responsible for a year's worth of torture and humiliation?"

"Don't look at it like that. It was time for you to stop being depressed. You had your mother and I worried for too long. Your mother said it was giving her wrinkles."

"I can't believe this. Why would you do that?" I pull my shoulder away.

"You have to understand. After the Pete situation I didn't hear one word from you for a month. You slept for days and wouldn't eat. Even your brother couldn't bring you out of your trance. When you started running and eating better, I knew something in you had clicked, but it wasn't enough."

"It was enough. I was doing fine."

"No, you weren't Cass," says Justin. The girls nod.

"We had this conversation last year, babe," says Lindsey. "You were pissed off then too."

"I had every right to be! You messed with my life, made me think I could get fired or miss my promotion. Made me go on all those nonsensical dates. I have felt like the world's biggest idiot for an entire year." I won't cry. I won't cry. I cannot cry on my birthday. People will think I'm depressed about getting older.

After a moment Justin turns me to face him. I look into his eyes and see concern. He wants to help me, but I feel so betrayed. I expected this behavior from my friends but not my dad. He's the one person I knew I could trust.

"Listen to me," says Justin. "If you hadn't gone through this whole process, we might never have gotten to this place. We might have missed our chance. I was too intimidated to ask you out, and you had a thick, protective bubble around you. This year was good for you."

"You told me it was a mistake. That we were playing with men's hearts."

"I was jealous. Why should they get to date you when I'd been waiting for years to get up the balls to make a move? I couldn't stand that you might end up with one of those assholes."

"Some of them weren't assholes."

"That's what I was worried about. Thank God Keeley snapped up Paul, because have you seen that guy?"

We all glance at the boys' table and watch Paul reluctantly arm-wrestling one of my cousins. He defeats Robbie in about one second then looks sheepishly around, hoping no one is watching.

"He is so awesome," sighs Keeley, and Lindsey smacks her.

"We're talking about Cassie's mental breakdown not your perfect lover!"

"So, what if it took a million guys to make you see me?" asks Justin, and he squeezes my hand.

He's right. I never would have guessed that Justin liked me. We would have gone on our delusional, miserable ways, working with each other but never fully realizing what could be. If I hadn't cast the other guys away and gave Paul up to Keeley, Justin might not have had his chance. I regret what happened between us in January, and Justin registers the hurt in my eyes.

"Forget about everything that came before, like your dad said. We've got all the time we need."

"Plus, there's a massive cake coming, and you wouldn't want to cry on it and ruin the frosting," says Lindsey.

I smile thinly at Justin and tighten my grip on his hand. I turn to Dad and take a long look. He seems apologetic but firm in his decision. He's sorry that the past year was hard for me, and he wishes that it could have happened some other way, but he's too happy with the outcome to be truly remorseful.

"Thank you, Dad." We stand and hug, and our table claps, Lindsey giving a few fist pumps.

My cake is wheeled in for the grand finale. The girls did a fabulous job; layers of red velvet cake and cream cheese frosting, my favorite. On the top it reads: "Happy Birthday Cassie! May the Next Year Be Full of Surprises!" Like I really need more surprises. The thing is covered in candles. There is no way I'll be able to blow them all out. I turn to the girls, Kevin, and Justin and summon them forward. Finally, obedient, they all gather around me.

"There are way more than thirty candles on this thing," says Alicia, eyes wide.

"This blaze might set the whole damn restaurant on fire," says Kevin.

"Just help me blow the stupid things out before they bring out the fire extinguisher."

Everyone counts to three and the six of us lean over and blow as hard as we can. Even with the extra help, one candle remains stubbornly lit in the center. I pick it up and give it to Justin.

"Will you be my boyfriend?"

He touches my finger, leans in, and blows the flame away.

"Sure." His blithe answer is all I need. No mushy shit for us!

"I knew she'd find someone eventually!" howls my mother who then bursts into tears. Gideon takes hold of her and grimaces. He mouths, "I'm sorry," but I have to laugh.

Leave it to my mother to have the last word.

After

I know what you're thinking: isn't this chick's story done yet? Isn't it time for the celebratory girl power song to play over the credits? Almost. Just bear with me for a few more pages.

Tons of things happened after my birthday. June came, July came, and then August roared into view, and all my latent fears about starting a relationship with Justin disappeared with summer's ebb. He's so attentive but knows I need space. He doesn't get angry when I need to be alone or with the girls, and when I ask him to come with us for the new Boys and Girls night, he happily accepts. After all, he has Brian and Paul to hang out with now. Sometimes Kevin infiltrates our get-togethers.

He is still hopelessly in love with King Philip of Portugal (which I totally call him to his face and which Kevin hates) and they live together in Minneapolis at Philip's chic apartment. A more blissful couple I've never seen, apart from Keeley and Paul, Alicia and Brian, and Justin and me.

Lindsey continues on her search for the perfect man, and she finds him quite often. But they never stay around long enough to bring to our festivities. She says that they'll ruin her fun, and Lindsey appreciates her fun.

Alicia is not due for a while, but she's showing big time. Her husband and kids have been great, supportive. This new baby has lit a fire under Brian's ass. Either that, or Alicia finally took our advice and had the necessary conversation about sharing parental obligations. All I know is that he's seeing less of the boys at the bar and more of his wife and children, and he couldn't be happier. They're waiting to find out the baby's sex, but Alicia confided to me that Lindsey would be the godmother no matter what. That should be interesting.

Keeley and Paul are going strong and thinking of moving in together. Cohabitation is new for both of them, so I hope all goes well. She's always sitting on his lap and saying really schmaltzy things to him, touching noses with him, and generally making a romantic ass of herself. He reciprocates fully, something I haven't seen in a man in a long, long time. And I couldn't be happier for them. They're a good fit.

As for my family, Dad and Sandy are still together. We often go to brunch and I even went shopping with her a few times. She has good taste and I admire her affection for my father. She is truly genuine, and she wants to make my dad happy. I gave up my dream of Dad and Mom reuniting.

Dad's blog is still online, and he writes it religiously. He hasn't been fired, and when I asked about the escalating work references in the blog, he said that he knows way too many company secrets to get canned. After discovering he was the mastermind behind the date-a-thon, I don't doubt that he's kept his ears open a long time and gathered sufficient evidence to say whatever he wants about his job online. Props to Dad.

Mom and Gideon also moved in together, into a small house in Apple Valley. She's sad that we don't live as close but making the slog out to the 'burbs isn't so bad, except for the stoplights. Gideon plans on having Thanksgiving and Christmas at their place, and Dad agreed. He's getting exhausted planning family events. I can't wait for all of us to be in the same place for the holidays again. Come to think of it, my mom and dad did get back together in the end.

Joel and Gisele broke up, surprising no one, but he's seeing someone new, a normal girl, he says, not a model or an actress. For a *normal girl* she sure is statuesque and beautiful. Leave it to Joel to nab the only gorgeous nonmodel/nonactress in L.A. He wants to come out for both holidays this winter, and Dad almost cried when he heard. It was too much for Mom to take, and her nerves are nearly shot, or so she says whenever I call her, which is every day. Justin laughs at my complicated family dynamic, and I tell him to be quiet, because his family is no picnic either.

Pia Brown and I continue to work together, and Kelly calls us her power couple. Pia turned out two books over the summer, so I've got my hands full dealing with her work and a few other projects Kelly sent my way. She often has Justin collaborate with me, and now that Kevin has my old job, he can join us as well on the big assignments. Luckily, Carly decided editing was no longer for her, and she quit. This was right after she found out that Justin and I were dating. Joe Carlson was the last to wish her well in her next endeavor, practically shoving her out of the office and into the elevator. He wiped his hands when the doors closed and shook his head. A few people heard him mutter, "Good riddance," when he marched past.

A new development has also emerged that might interest you. Without my permission, devilish Kevin absconded with my dating journals, put them together in a binder, and gave them to Kelly. She read the entire thing in one day and called me to her office. Kevin looked so damn smug when I walked past his office, I could have slugged him. He steepled his fingers together and grinned wickedly.

I sat in Kelly's office for an hour, and she mostly spoke. She offered to publish my journal if I could turn it into a book. At first, I didn't understand. What was she talking about? There's no way my wayward natterings could be a book.

"You have good material here," she said and tapped the binder. "Kevin was right to give it to me. He'll make a great book bloodhound."

"But how do you expect me to do this while juggling Pia and the other manuscripts?"

"Because I know you can do it. You have however long you need. I don't expect you'll need an advance as you've already gotten a substantial raise. We can talk advances with your next book."

"Next book?"

"If the first goes well, I'll have to put you in the author stable. I hope you can figure out a way to write *and* edit. Because I would hate to lose you as an editor." With her small smile, she waved me out, and my next mission began.

Justin doubled over when he heard and gave Kevin a high-five. I didn't know where to begin.

"How can I do this?"

"Just think of it as a conversation with me over martinis," suggested Kevin. "That should be easy."

"I can't write drunk!"

"Why not? Hemingway did."

"I hate Hemingway."

We went to my office and I collapsed in my chair, no longer fawning over its comfy-ness. Justin and Kevin sat down across from me and gave me reassuring looks.

"We know you can do it, Cass," said the best boyfriend in the world. "You used to write all the time."

"That was before. What if I don't have it in me anymore?"

"That's bullshit," says Kevin. "A writer never loses her mojo. Sometimes it just gets neglected. You need to take it out for a spin, fill the gas tank, and run rampant down some country road."

"Right."

"Exactly," says Kevin. "Write."

And so here I go. I'm about to write my first serious novel. Well, not serious serious. I reread my journal, and there's some funny stuff in there. Justin bought me a stack of yellow legal pads to take notes, and my laptop sits at the new desk in the corner, waiting. It stares ominously at me, and at first, I'm scared. What if I can't make it into something workable? What if it fails?

Then I remember that's what I thought about the dating game and look how that turned out. Justin is at the grocery store buying supplies for dinner. He's going to cook while I write.

What a man.

That's when it hits me. I have this in the bag. All I have to do is imagine myself at Brits, with a beer, surrounded by my girls and the boys and chat with them. After all, isn't a book really a conversation you're trying to have with other people?

I sit at the desk, open my laptop, and make my way to Microsoft Word.

Thirty minutes later, Justin comes through the door. He doesn't say a word, because he hears the most miraculous sound coming from the corner: energetic typing.

The first thing I wrote was the title page, with no title yet, and the dedication.

Untitled
A Biographical Novel by Cassandra McTiernan
For the girls, you know who you are.
For K and J, who gave me the pep talk.
And for my parents, without whom I wouldn't be here to write.

Acknowledgements

It took an army of cheerleaders to write this book: family, friends, teachers, colleagues. Thank you to my mom and dad, who told me I could be whatever I wanted. Kind of backfired: they'd rather I'd chosen accounting. Without their support and readership of second-grade ramblings, this book would not exist.

To my brother, thank you for listening to me talk about characters, how they were doing things I hadn't expected or planned, and how I was languishing at the halfway point. You were always there with a pat on the back and a "why don't you just move on to the next chapter and worry about that later?"

To my Olive Garden and Beyond friends, whose names are in this book: Alicia, Lindsey, and Keeley. My cadre of foul-mouthed, enthusiastic fans who kept me full of new material.

Thank you as well to Dr. Jennifer Brantley, who ushered my college-age writing onto a new level. She kept telling me to push, and that successful writers weren't necessarily the best ones, but they *were* the ones who just kept writing.

And to everyone who reads this book and sees a bit of themselves in it. Thank you for reading, and I hope to see you again!

Colleen McMillan is a Minnesota native who currently lives in the Twin Cities with her cantankerous cat, Duncan. She also likes to call Paris her second home, but don't tell the Parisians. She was educated at the University of Wisconsin, River Falls and received her master's degree in Creative Writing at the University of Kent, Canterbury in England.

Twitter: @Colleen40303158
Facebook: @ColleenMcMillanAuthor